cyberscribes.1

THE NEW JOURNALISTS

SN98

Anne Hart

Library of Congress Catalog Card Number: 96-61862

First Edition: 10 9 8 7 6 5 4 3 2 1
Printed in the United States of America
Trade Paper: ISBN: 1-880663-65-1

Ellipsys International Publications, Inc.
4679 Vista Street
San Diego, CA 92116

Tele: (619) 280-8711 Fax: (619) 280-8713
E-mail: scribes@ellipsys.com
Web: http://www.ellipsys.com

Development Editor, Designer, and Illustrator: Claire Condra Arias
Copy Editor: Stacy L. Marquardt

I dedicate this book to
all who write, package, publish,
broadcast, netcast, and market information
for the latest digital media.

To those writers who send their endless good-byes
and other articles by e-mail to their
publishers and who plug and play
into the highest density
journal brimming with resources
for the new, newer, and
newest media.

— ANNE HART

Spell for Requesting
a Water-Pot and a Palette

O you great one who see your father,
Keeper of the book of Thoth, see,
I have come spiritualized, besouled,
Mighty and equipped with
The writings of Thoth.

Bring me the messenger of the earth-god
Who is with Seth,
Bring me a water-pot and palette
From the writing-kit of Thoth
And the mysteries which are in them.

See, I am a scribe;
Bring me the corruption of Osiris
That I may write with it
And that I may do what the great and good
God says every day,
Being the good which you have decreed for me,
O Horakhty. I will do what is right
And I will send to Re daily.

— The Ancient Egyptian Book of the Dead

Contents

Figures and Illustrations

The Ancient Egyptian Book of the Dead

Illustrations

Screenshot Internet Addresses (URLs)

Fishbone

Foreword

cyberscribes.1 explores the convergence of print and broadcast journalism on the Web and the emerging markets for those who find the art in technology. What began as a study of the trends, strategic alliances, and the technologies that are shaping the industry soon grew into a celebration of the people who are launching new careers in uncharted territory. The project eventually became so broad in scope that we split it into two volumes: *The New Journalists* and *The Storytellers*. You might say we separated fact from fiction.

The New Journalists examines how professional writers of nonfiction material can use the newest media to advance their careers and also as an outlet for creative expression. Writers of interactive content wear many hats and often the lines of distinction between fields become blurred. We hope the purists will forgive our broad view of the indus-

try because traditional journalism and reporting the news are only part of the story, as rules and roles once clearly defined are rewritten. The news in this field is that creativity is highly valued and collaboration is the key to success and survival.

The experiences and opinions that many people have shared throughout this book will give you valuable insight into the lives and careers of those who have found diverse and interesting employment in many facets of the new media. However, not all are success stories and you may not agree with every point of view that is shared. These varied opinions and experiences help shed light on windows of opportunity so you can see who's doing what and why—and most importantly, where you might fit in. Our goal is to present a range of ideas from which you may draw your own conclusions and to provide an accurate snapshot of the state of the art and industry.

Crucial issues will be addressed along the way—issues related to the hybrid mix of news, entertainment and commercial content, electronic vs. print publishing, computer security, age discrimination, and electronic rights. While some believe the changes in the publishing industry brought about by the new media are a threat to the nation's literacy, others view them as a kaleidoscope of opportunity.

We would like to thank all who shared their experiences and valuable insight as these "Voices from the Industry." Their contribution has helped us capture the excitement, controversy, pitfalls, and opportunities ahead for writers on this frontier of the "second" Web.

We would also like to thank the Jacques-Edouard Berger Foundation for providing the cover illustration from their collection of World Art Treasures. The relief depicts a net weaver from an Egyptian tomb at Saqqarah–Mastaba de Kagemni. Also, to the British Museum Press for allowing us to reproduce the spells translated from *The Ancient Egyptian Book of the Dead.* My favorite, "Spell for Escaping from the Catcher of Fish" is an ode to Net users that transcends time.

We hope this book will help you identify the key players in the industry so you can take advantage of the tremendous opportunities in this rewarding field where "content is king." During the year it took to develop this material, we followed new technologies along several fronts—sometimes even before there was an industry-accepted term to describe what they were doing. It wasn't always clear how these pieces would fit together or which technologies would ultimately be embraced by the market. Today, the direction is clear—with broad industry support for the "push technology" model combined with the release of an open platform for synchronized, streaming media, we have the birth of a viable new broadcasting medium.

These newest technologies and the underlying market philosophy make everyone a player—carving out a fertile plateau in an ideal climate where writers, designers, publishers, broadcasters, producers, and advertisers can unleash their creativity. Let the show begin!

— CLAIRE CONDRA ARIAS
PUBLISHER

Introduction

This book is about recreating new careers from the old and the trends that are shaping new media writers. It's all about the power of connecting and how writers, editors, and journalists who have been downsized from dailies, book publishers, movie studios, production houses, magazines, and the information industry can retrain, gain new skills, transfer familiar knowledge, aptitudes, and abilities, and find new careers as content writers, designers, or producers in the new media.

The bridge from the old to the new must span from a physical to a virtual place to create new opportunities in **your chosen career.** You may work in front of a live audience of viewers, readers, and users. You're going to learn how to share a robust multimedia experience with your audience and track your audience for feedback. Your new career as a writer or in the related information industry will focus on a way to help your audience learn better through interactive learning and entertainment.

The new media writer creates interactive linkable hypertext programs that link their creative writing or journalistic news reporting to Web researchers around the world. Multi-cast closed-captioned content broadcast live from the Web gives writers a global audience.

Everything you write online becomes part of a collaborative whole. Writers will be needed to develop content for Internet-based television around the globe. Your **byline has a global address.**

My specialty is to discover how technology changes lives. The lives of full-time freelance writers now are divided into the technological haves and have nots. **Writers who want** to earn maximum opportunities to break into professional writing as a full-time occupation need to embrace the new media and then decide which parts of it they need.

Each writer becomes a Web researcher finding articles written on a variety of subjects and using important parts of what they find—like the latest trends—**to create** a patchwork of information for other writers, editors and publishers. New media writing is interactive, searchable, and linkable to anyone, anywhere. That's what the power of connection is all about. Writing content for interactive television programs for the Internet creates **a worldwide bridge**.

Internet broadcasts offer writers a powerhouse from where they can focus on any place in cyberspace. Writers **can combine the best of broadcast television with** the interactivity of the Web to create a new insight and a new entity.

The first step a writer can take is to bring together local chambers of commerce, radio and television stations, and other associations involved with **interactive communications.** Within these groups you'll find Web czars and caesars, mistresses and masters, media jockeys and techno-scribes, digital artists and interactive storytellers. When you bring all this talent together, you have content that is worth the connection.

Remember when Marshall McLuhan wrote, "the medium is the message?"

When I was a freshman at NYU in 1959, we hung out in a dark, black-painted coffeehouse in Greenwich Village where beatniks read poetry to **the beat of** bongo drums. It was enchanting and tantalizing to sit there with my friends, Aphrodite the Greek, Virginia the Armenian, Carol the Swede, Arlene the Czech, Sandra from a Polish Village, the violinist, and Patty from Dublin.

Eventually, I left the **poetry and music** to go to the bathroom. On the wall of the tiny john, in big, bold, scrawling letters, someone had scribbled, "Who's Afraid of Virginia Woolf?" I looked at the graffiti for a long time, mulling it over in my mind and remembering the real Virginia Woolf who was F. Scott Fitzgerald's wife. She went mad in the twenties trying to write in "a room of her own." I thought that perhaps, another English major, like myself, had scribbled the message in protest of yet another reading assignment of F. Scott Fitzgerald's works. Later, I incorporated "who's afraid" into one of my stories,

"**And** I Must Rise to Fear," but never gave another thought to the question.

However, another young writer who frequented the same coffeehouse pondered **the** question as he sat on the throne. Edward Albee didn't ignore the medium of this message, or the deeper, big-picture, intuitive, feeling meaning of the question. He went on to write the play, *Who's Afraid of Virginia Woolf?* which eventually became a movie starring Elizabeth Taylor and Richard Burton. The Pulitzer Prize winning author made a fortune from a play inspired by a **line of graffiti** scribbled on the bathroom wall inside a dark and dingy poetry-spouting coffeehouse.

The moral of the story is to pay attention to graffiti scribbled on the bathroom wall —or **scribbled on the Web**, for that matter. You never know where you will find the theme of your next great novel, play, or movie script.

Is the medium still the message when you have five hundred television channels broadcasting nothing that interests you? **The issue** may not be about content, but timing.

Viewers, more than readers, want immediate gratification—whether from the Internet or from TV. What if the viewer **is** given many more choices? What if the viewer is allowed to participate in the programming? What if the viewer becomes a user? Then the message becomes not the medium, but **the choice.** With so many choices, how will we make up our minds? The convergence of broadcast media with information technology is combining the wisdom and knowledge of the Internet and its developers to enable everyone in the world, theoretically, to have his own show. *You* **are the message.** *You* are the big picture.

If you're looking for a wider grid, tap into technology and move with the shakers. Join organizations like the International Interactive Communications Society or the Digital Multimedia Association and learn from those who are using the technology to build the Web and create interactive media products. By combining two different fields, you'll discover whole new subjects about which to write.

Writers and infomaniacs, you alone will **change** the way information is provided. The Web is moving from a slide show to a broadcast network with hyperlinks to any other multimedia site. It's an international media. **Look to** Internet television. Seek out university extended studies programs that connect businesses with **creative and intuitive people.** Join your local software industry councils. If there are hundreds of software companies in your locality and fifty of them are working with the Internet, think how many might want to connect with your writing services.

Become the leading edge and form regional technology alliances. The Internet and the new media are there for your use. Profit from it. If Internet TV is big, how much bigger will be the need for digital creative writers?

This book does more than merely point you in the right direction. It shows you how to fit like **a puzzle piece** into the changing, new electronic media that combines print publishing with online updates of timely information. How should you buy, sell, hold, or transfer your skills to the new media? The answer is to buy into the Web. Sell your creative skills. Become a producer and hold onto your updated links. A global reach is worth the stretch. It brings empowerment. But before you can profit from giving people more choices, you first have to connect.

New trends for writers are shaping the publishing, video, and audio markets with an increased demand for better content. Creative writers of both fiction and nonfiction literature, journalists, technical writers, and screenwriters are entering powerful contracts with a new breed of publisher to create content for the new media. The convergence of high technology with humanities, arts, sciences, politics, public relations, psychology, sociology, and current events means more collaboration **between teams** at a time when journalists are finding keener competition for the available jobs.

The writing life is a study in contrasts. Impressive monuments and edifices of technology are shadowed by oppressive poverty and crime. A writer can investigate a story **online** and then send it through the pipeline.

Do new trends reveal that writer's profession become broken, neglected, and mismanaged? Is it **capable of** providing basic survival wages for good journalists? Are the print newspaper, magazine and book publishing industries on their way out?

Examine the trends that are overtaking the rusted gurneys of these industries. Thousands of new journalism and creative writing graduates with masters degrees in hand are finding a grand demand for their new media skills. The Internet is **generating** new jobs for writers, new communications businesses, and **a revolution in creativity** that awaits the verbally proficient and expressive.

Innovation and intuition in writing increase the demand for new genres and outlets for a variety of versatile and timely information. Besides entertainment and learning, writers are needed to supply content for every facet of business endeavor. In a field so new that few people have longtime experience, writing for the new media means writing for more media that is emerging from less.

The rules have changed and a new patchwork is **emerging from the old** network. This new patchwork for writers shows up in anecdotal evidence on the Internet. Look at the quality of the writing today and imagine what it will be when seasoned writers hit the 'Net running.

Twenty years ago, I used the term "new **media**" when writing about an online document retrieval system for a documentary TV show. That system, called ERIC, was an early component of what we call "the Internet" today. In this book, the term "new media" really refers to the *newest* media in the ongoing evolution of technology and the arts.

Writers for the newest media have crossed the line of no return. The trends, **like the truth,** are in the wind. We are only at the beginning of the Internet revolution of collaboration, convergence, and cooperation. Writers, publishers, and producers are standing on the threshold of an urban frontier.

As you are reading this skill-building book of methods and examples, the virtual communities of writers, publishers, and producers are growing. New trends have **to be studied** and acted upon with new books, hooks, films, videos, and software.

The bottom line for new media teams of writers and publishers is to create more content for the information industry. Convergence and collaboration, and the death of competition, played out on the Internet mean there's a new wish list for out-of-work journalists, technical writers **in search of creative expression**, market-hungry novelists, and screenwriters.

Writers, the trend is on the upswing. It's time to get your new media act in high gear for fighting crime, chasing rhyme, and making time.

About Anne Hart

Anne Hart is the author of fifty-one books, numerous scripts, and more than three hundred articles, as well as several novels, plays and screenplays—writing fulltime since 1963 as her sole profession.

With a Master's degree in Creative Writing and post-graduate coursework in Television, Film Production and Screen Writing, Anne enjoys writing about new ways people use the Internet, specializing in how-to books about creative expression in the newest media and in the emerging technologies.

She also writes about business startups and contemporary issues, careers, and the relationship of personality development to computer communications and telecommuting on the cyber frontier of the Internet.

Anne has a Lifetime California Community College teaching credential for Writing, Journalism, Language and Literature, a Lifetime Adult Education teaching credential for Psychology and Data Processing, and is authorized to administer the Myers Briggs Type Indicator (MBTI™) personality indicator.

She has been a member of the National Association of Science Writers, Society for Professional Journalists, Computer Press Association, Association for Psychological Type, National Writers Union, American Medical Writers Association, Graduate Women in Science, and Mensa.

Her hobbies include the study of ancient DNA, genetics, new media art, music as therapy, ethno-musicology, and paleoarchaeology-paleoanthropology.

Spell for Escaping

from the Catcher of Fish

O you net-users, trappers, and fishermen,

O you children of your fathers,

Do you know that I know

The name of that great and mighty net?

'The All-Embracing' is its name.

— The Ancient Egyptian Book of the Dead

CHAPTER ONE

A Digital Renaissance
Where Art Meets Technology

We live in a time when information can be transformed into any shape one may wish it to take. It has been said that this is an historic time in which the design of information has overtaken the design of objects. For writers, the boundaries among film script writing, production, art, product and package design, copywriting, advertising, storytelling, and business services have merged in an unprecedented way to create new markets in cyberspace. This cross-pollination of new ideas that brings art and technology together is finding fertile ground in the infotainment/entertainment industry and in the information/news/courseware design and scriptwriting industries.

Art has been commercialized and digitized. Digital artists command wide-ranging salaries and opportunities. Digital writers are needed to team up with the artists. For the person who can acquire both skills, the opportunities and possibilities are boundless.

Writers and artists join to create special effects in text and graphics, sound and light. The new media allow people to cross careers. Set decorators now design 3-D virtual interiors for businesses. Special effects film technicians design CD-ROM games—and vice versa. Architects design film studios and virtual places in cyberspace. And writers design Web sites with digital graphics. Non-entertainment businesses are selling entertainment and software companies are selling news.

The goal of artists and writers today is to deliver high-quality content to the home, place of work, and school. As more bandwidth is piped into the Internet, the digital infrastructure is fast becoming a lucrative business opportunity for creative people to make money selling imagination—an imagination which, when channeled, will reshape the economy.

Writers, your new medium is here. . . You can be among the first to branch out into interactive intuitive writing on the Web.

How are businesses using the newest media?

Now is the time to start writing for the newest media, whether it's news, education, entertainment, or a hybrid mixture of all of the above. Today's Web provides news and entertainment in cyberspace, as well as education, job training, and college degrees.

The technological world is unfolding in ways that are great for writers. Time Warner, for example, has launched a high-speed Internet service called Road Runner that supports broadband multimedia broadcasts on the Web. The fiber optic cable connection is one-hundred times faster than a residential telephone line and create a new writer's market for online content. The venture combines the technological expertise of Time Warner Cable with the journalistic resources of Time Inc., and the creative talent of Warner Brothers. Other companies—including Hewlett Packard, Motorola, MCI, and Microsoft—have provided supporting technologies and services to help build the new infrastructure for online data transmission.

http://www.pointcast.com

The *PointCast Network* broadcasts news and information directly to a viewer's computer screen. Information can be customized according to each individual's interest and displayed as a SmartScreen™. The service is being expanded to provide news for local areas.

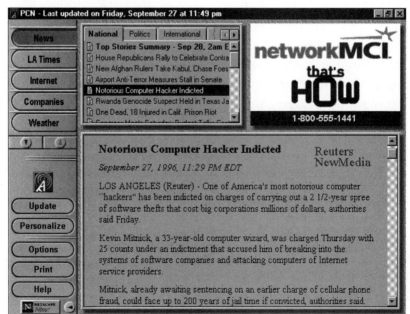

It's an opportunity for writers to reach a broader market, making money in creative expression, such as writing innovative programming and content development, or designing illustration, video, and other arts. Companies such as Discovery Communications, Inc., a purveyor of cable TV and Web-based entertainment and information, are developing Web video technology that works within the confines of the Internet. Much of the technology originally developed for interactive TV has been repositioned for digital TV. The popular Web programming language *Java* was originally developed by Sun Microsystems, Inc. for the interactive TV market.

Publisher, Knight-Ridder, Inc., is expanding its newspapers into Web sites—a great boon to journalism majors and seasoned writers. Sybase Corporation, a software firm in Mountain View, CA, has revised its multimedia software first developed for interactive TV so that now it can target Web content writing and programming.

According to the *Los Angeles Times* and CNBC TV, employment in movie production and entertainment has surpassed that of aerospace in Los Angeles and Orange Counties. In other areas, more jobs are opening. In a single year, movie production and amusements accounted for 208,900 jobs in the Los Angeles and Orange County areas alone, compared to 121,400 in aerospace. The same year, film and entertainment added 18,800 jobs.

Digital Domain and Mattel Inc. have developed a joint venture using the vast pool of digital artists and entrepreneurs who grew up in the film industry. Today, moving beyond the film industry, digital arts products, services, scripts, and companies combine to form a whole new industry that merges art with technology.

Cinnabar started in 1982 as a scenic design firm and special effects house for film and television. They are also independent consultants for businesses that want entertainment effects in public spaces for retail environments, restaurants, and other non-entertainment places. It is creative energy that shapes new worlds, animated billboards, displays, and business environments. Writers, artists, and technologists now work together to conceive images and design for businesses ranging from fast-food places to playgrounds.

Art has overtaken commerce, and writers are being recruited by the design-based industries and manufacturers of the digital era.

Cultural-products industries are where the money and jobs are today for writers and artists. Creative expressionists can be found working in fields such as entertainment, apparel, architecture, advertising, public relations, furniture design, and movie production as content developers for CD-ROM and Web-based applications. Cultural industries such as video production are growing fastest because of cutting-edge computer technologies and software development.

Industrial artists and writers are creating a newest media industry, a digital renaissance where content and design share center stage. Special effects in writing, art, film, commercials, music videos, games, theme park attractions, short 3D films, and cable are bringing the Internet and the new media into the home.

Partnerships with news networks, software developers, and cable TV companies are where writers and artists can look for a place to cash in on a future and a fortune. The digital infrastructure has created a future in which the arts and technology will work as a unit and be channeled directly into people's homes.

http://www.nytimes.com/yr/mo/day/front

The online version of the *New York Times*, published by the NYT Electronic Media Company, is available on the Web at no charge. Each issue is the online equivalent of the daily printed edition, with additional links, forums, and features. Don't miss the crossword puzzle!

2 What is a "content creator"?

Using the current authoring tools, most interactive writing and programming, called content development, can be transferred to the Internet with little or no modification. Writing Web content is a new market for writers as well as software engineers, artists, and other entertainment, educational, and technological people.

The Web has created a new field for all types of writers and reviewers called *new media marketing*. Bell Atlantic, Nynex Corporation, and Pacific Telesis Group will focus on the Web with an elaborate site for TV fans who can check out reviews of shows and chat. Reviewers of books, movies, and shows can now reach a broader audience by posting their commentaries online.

Instead of focusing totally on interactive programming for CD-ROM or Digital Video Disks (DVD), the Web is now the center of attention for creative writers, artists, courseware designers, reviewers, and writers of technical and business related material.

Specialized writers for science and medicine have their Web niche, too. What brings all of them together is that they are helping to build the body of information we call the Web.

You may develop an interactive version of your article or book as a promotion to build name recognition and help sell the printed version. Web sites are customer bases in the making. As the site develops, more links may be added to form a mega-Web site linked to industry giants.

Research has shown that the use of interactive multimedia increases learning retention dramatically. On the average, people retain 20% of what they see, 40% of what they see and hear, and 70% of what they see, hear, and do.

Those who have been trained to write for TV, radio, or print can easily shift to writing for the Web. The mediums differ, but the required professional writing skills are similar.

Who are the new journalists?

Those who majored in communications, journalism, creative writing, English, professional and technical writing, scriptwriting, or related subjects will find an abundance of opportunities in online journalism. A new electronic journalist may be a news reporter by day and a webmaster by night—combining photojournalism with digital photography online.

Job descriptions and titles are becoming electric and eclectic. Webmasters, webmistresses, cyberhosts, and media jockeys are new occupations that simply did not exist before. Some tasks of these new occupations are to manage Web sites, track information and traffic on the local network server, as well as to establish links to other sites.

Most authoring jobs in the new media require the writer to use HTML (Hypertext Mark-Up Language) or a newer, higher octave now in design. Programmable extensions in *Java* or CGI script may be used to add programmable features to a basic HTML page. The new journalist is a multimedia producer who combines words with hypertext links, formatting each page to interact with other documents, images, and Web sites.

Online journalists are frequently asked to write their pieces in HTML. There are hundreds of sites on the Web to download tutorials. To find them, simply do a search with any search engine. You'll find over 5,000 references to hypertext or HTML tutorials such as "*HTML is Easy as Hell!*" and "*Composing Good HTML.*" You'll find page design and graphics assistance listing recommended file and multimedia formats for Web documents and lists of books about the Internet.

If you search under 'writers' you'll find long lists of information of interest to writers seeking assignments. You'll find information of pertaining to special interest groups, projects, associations, job services and supplies for writers— as well as publishers' guidelines. To find companies that hire writers who can format in HTML, query your search engine on 'freelance', employers', or 'jobs'. I found many job offers for freelance writers who know how to translate their feature articles into HTML and create Web sites with text, graphics, and animation. Online journalists are usually required to have a working knowledge of Web editing tools and multimedia authoring software.

Journalists must now train in more than the "Big Five" computer applications: telecommunications, word processing, graphics, spreadsheets, and databases. According to Jerry L. Sloan, Professor of Public Relations at E.W. Scripps School of Journalism, "Students today must have a complete command of the computer, Internet and Web to make it in today's world. It is nearly as much of a requirement as the ability to write well. We are at a dividing line—those who came before didn't have to have it, although it was a plus. Those coming from behind are quickly catching up, and will be completely computer literate, totally comfortable on the Internet and virtually Webmasters on their own."

Computer applications relevant to the field of journalism should be considered a core subject by colleges, universities and writing schools seeking to prepare students for the writer's market of today and tomorrow. The skill level required for general assignment has been raised to a higher octave.

http://www.sfsu.edu/~beca/info/592-1.html

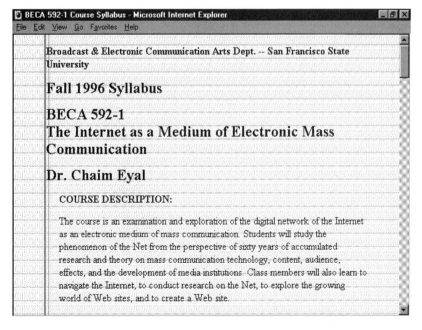

The BECA Department at San Francisco State University offers a program in radio and television broadcasting augmented with courses in digital audio production, desktop video production, new communication technologies, and writing for the newest media.

4 Is the Web ready for professional writers?

Take note of the strategic alliances developing between telephone, TV, cable, publishing, and software companies. It's collaboration between companies on a level never seen before. For example, Time Warner Entertainment recently became an equity partner in Interactive Digital Solutions, a joint venture with Silicon Graphics, Inc. and AT&T Network Systems. The mission of the company is to provide integrated, multimedia software environments for interactive services. What does that mean?

It means that if you're a writer, it's time to ask your local cable companies about their strategy for the Web. Find out which companies are offering high-speed or satellite Internet services. Whether the connection is by fiber optic cable or digital modem, these new ISPs (Internet Service Providers) will be in need of compelling content to differentiate themselves from the competition.

Tele-Communications, a cable operator, helped start the interactive TV movement several years ago. The company has invested in an online venture called

17.2 million personal computers with CD-ROM drives are currently in U.S. homes; by 1997, that number is expected to grow to 46.2 million.

—Robertson Stephens

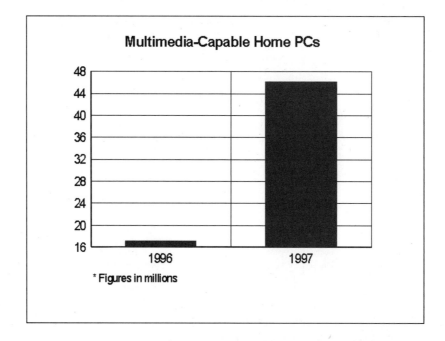

Multimedia-Capable Home PCs

* Figures in millions

This Englewood, Colorado firm wants to spread the news about high-speed Internet delivery.

In 1996, approximately one third of American homeowners had computers, but only ten percent took advantage of online services. Even so, the Web was well on its way to becoming a mass medium. For non-PC users, the biggest obstacles for going online have been the high cost of computers, the availability of relevant information, and the complexity of the Internet. According to one recent study, seventy-five percent want the Internet to be easy to use and lead them on a pursuit of their personal interests.

With the introduction of WebTV, Internet access has become available to nearly every home in the United States—dramatically changing the profile of the typical Internet user. The latest Nielsen studies, which were based on the PC-using population, showed the typical Internet user to be a male between 25 and 44 years of age, with thirty-four percent college graduates and twenty-five percent with household incomes of $80,000 or more, These statistics will change dramatically as the daytime TV watching consumer audience logs onto the Internet. What kind of online traffic jam this will create is anybody's guess. . . but one thing is certain—it's serious business where big money is being spent.

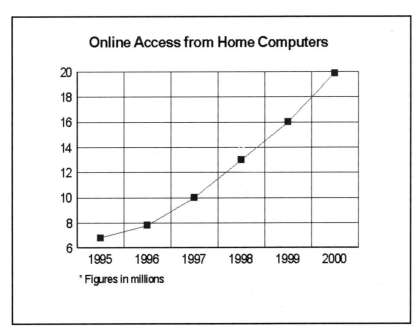

Online Access from Home Computers

* Figures in millions

At-home demand for online access explodes as American households log onto the information superhighway.

In 1995, an estimated 6.8 million American homes used their PCs to access online services and entertainment. Online access from PCs is projected to grow to 19.9 million households by 2000.

—LINK Resources

Voices from the industry:
Kevin Hopkins, Web Entertainment Producer

Bio

Kevin Hopkins, president of Skylight Entertainment, served as Director of Technology and Telecommunications for San Diego Mayor Susan Golding. In 1995, he was named "Marketer of the Year" for his innovative use of virtual reality to bring the 1996 Republican National Convention to San Diego. He has served as executive director of California's "Smart Communities" project, staff director for San Diego's "City of the Future" project, communications adviser to the International Center for Communications at San Diego State University, and technology consultant to AT&T, *Business Week* magazine, *Computerworld* magazine, Ford Motor Company, and Science Adviser to the President and the White House.

Q: How is the convergence of broadcasting and the Web changing the global market?

A: The coming convergence is the most profound technological change of the 20th century and is also one of the most confusing. Politicians and scholars throughout the world have heralded the emergence of the "Information Superhighway" and the "Global Information Infrastructure" as events that will revolutionize the ways in which we live, play, work, and do business. And yet, even today, few people truly appreciate what these changes mean or how they will affect their lives.

Most of us know this phenomenon has something to do with computers and telecommunications. Many are aware that it involves the Internet and the Web. And quite a few have used some of its first-draft applications, like electronic mail, online shopping, and electronic chat rooms. But the Information Superhighway remains an adjunct to most people's lives, a supplement to traditional ways of doing things, a recreation. Its potential to transform still waits in the wings.

Q: Will the Internet transform our cities into "smart communities"?

A: Transform it will. San Diego Mayor, Susan Golding, whose city launched once of the earliest "Smart Community" initiatives, recently noted that "the planetary equations of wealth and power are tilting more swiftly and profoundly than anyone could have forecast just a few years ago. Those prepared for this titanic shift will become the world's next superpowers. Those that are not may well be condemned to electronic obscurity."

History here is a useful instructor. In the early days of the American West, many once-booming communities became literal ghost towns when their gold or other resources dried up. More than a century later, cities unprepared for the emerging technological changes may suffer a similar fate, becoming "electronic ghost towns" on the virtual frontier, abandoned by corporate and human citizens seeking a more enlightened leadership and a more electronically hospitable environment.

If that happens, the urban problems of today—so pressing, even overwhelming to many local leaders—may become very small indeed.

Q: **Who is driving the technological convergence?**

A: Techno-visionaries. This technological convergence can be seen in what we'll call "The Three Ms of the New Millennium." The Means. The Money. And the Message.

What is driving these technological changes is something futurists have long referred to as "convergence"—the melding of television, telephony, computers, and the Web into a single global communications network. Even a few months ago, the forecasts of convergence would have struck all but the most fanciful as events destined for another lifetime. But that convergence is no longer the futuristic dreamstuff of technovisionaries. It is here—today. And it will transform our lives as has no political or technological development in the last fifty years.

Q: **What is the means?**

A: Since the dawn of convergence-think, the technology of convergence has fallen far short of its dreams. No longer. The first affordable television set-top boxes now have arrived that make it possible for people with no computer experience and little technological sophistication to navigate the Web on an ordinary television set. Internet for the masses is here—today.

Of course, anyone who has used the Web knows that sometimes it seems to take forever to download even simple graphics. But again: no more. Cable modems and other high-speed digital modems are now being marketed that are from 100- to 300-times faster than conventional modems, using the same coaxial cable and copper telephone wires that are already in or near almost every American home.

The expanding network of Internet-capable satellites and fiber-optic cable will boost transmission speeds even higher. The result: real-time, theater-quality video, audio, and virtual reality soon can be delivered to almost every home, business, and institution in America—not over network television or cable TV or VCRs, but by means of the Web. In fact, by the year 2005, MIT's Nicholas Negroponte predicts that more Americans will be on the Web during prime-time than will watch network television.

Q: **Is there money to be made?**

A: Just over a year ago, Netscape Communications, maker of the world's most popular Web browsing software, tendered an initial public offering on the U.S. stock market. Here was a company with no corporate track record, no profit, not even any income. Yet it earned $2 billion in a single day in what at the time was the largest IPO in U.S. history.

Netscape isn't alone. Sony, Time Warner, Fox, Paramount, NBC, Intel, DreamWorks, Viacom, and scores of others are collectively investing billions of dollars into convergence technologies and content—today. Microsoft alone is spending nearly $1.5 billion over the next five years. And that's only the beginning.

Q: **What's the message?**

A: What are the great technological giants doing with all this bandwidth and billions of dollars? A lot of guessing, to judge by their own confessions. Apple founder Steve Jobs recently remarked that "the Web reminds me of the early days of PCs. No one really knows anything." The head of Microsoft's Interactive Division admits: "We don't kid ourselves that we know what's going to happen. If someone told me they did know, I'd say, 'Sign 'em up.'"

As a matter of fact, a few smart companies do know. Microsoft, long the world leader in computer software, is "morphing into a media company for the new millennium," in the words of *Wired* magazine, devoting more than a third of its research and development staff to convergence technologies and content.

NBC early in 1996 joined with the computer giant to form the world's first global interactive news network, MSNBC. And dozens of thriving start-ups, from San Diego's DigitalTalkTV and Soular Intentions to Hollywood's "Late Net" with Tim Conway, Jr., to New York's American Cybercast, are getting into the act.

Q: **Will the entertainment industry dominate the Web?**

A: Skylight Entertainment is one of the companies leading the way into the new world of real-time online interactivity. As a developer of entertainment content for the Web, we believe that entertainment will be the application that finally brings the masses to the Web— establishing the cultural foundation for what experts predict will be a $6.5 billion market for online shopping by the turn of the century.

Skylight is working with a number of other companies, including Sony Television Entertainment, Soular Intentions, DigitalTalkTV, and Skylight's own global Internet network, Millennium Worldwide Entertainment Broadcasting Company (MWEB), to create the first-ever entertainment properties wholly integrated with commercial marketing applications and designed exclusively for complementary broadcast over both regular television networks and the Web.

5 Where are journalists working online?

There are many opportunities for writers to work for online publishers or to become online publishers, producers, or broadcasters themselves.

One of the early newspapers that bridged the gap between print and electronic publishing was the *San Jose Mercury News* in California. That newspaper—in the heart of Silicon Valley—kept pace with the early adopters who were ready for interactive electronic publishing.

The *San Jose Mercury News* provides a news forum on America

Online as well as a news-clipping service, *NewsHound*.

Many writers today who have been downsized from the print dailies are finding work with the digital news publications. One of the biggest attractions of online journalism is that it often doesn't matter where you're located. Writers for the new media can submit all the news that's fit to e-mail. You're never too far away to write for a digital publication, whether you're telecommuting from home or sitting in a telecenter.

http://www.itp.tsoa.nyu.edu

Students seek new ways to use technology at NYU's Interactive Telecommunications Program. The program works in collaboration with NYU's Center for the Advancement of Technology (CAT) to develop multimedia technologies and relationships with business and industry.

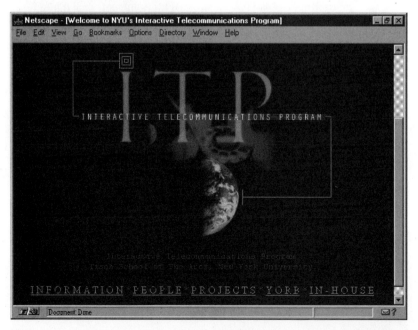

The Web offers the writer unlimited research resources—just a click away—ranging from online publications to entire libraries whose doors are always open. One of many resources is *Computer Mediated Communications*, a magazine that reports about people, events, technology, public policy, culture, practices, research, and applications of computer-mediated communication. It's free and comes to you on the Internet.

The Web is leveling the field of publishing and broadcasting for creative writers and journalists the world over. For many, the Web is the only open channel of communication able to bypass the control of an oppressive government.

All writers have—or should have—an equal right to express themselves, whether they are home-based, physically challenged, over the "age of retirement," or just out of college and starting their career. The Web is making us rewrite the rules and rethink employment requirements and opportunities.

Let the global writing talent think for itself, question all authority, and deliver verified information in a timely, compelling, and aesthetic manner. That's the whole idea.

http://www.cjr.org

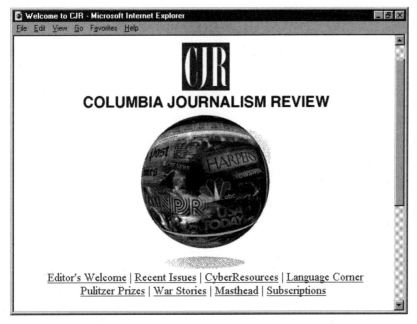

The *Columbia Journalism Review* includes a section called *Cybersources* that's full of online research resources for journalists who want to go fishing with the Net.

Who are the serious investors?

Joint ventures and strategic partnerships between software companies, news organizations, and movie studios are changing the face of the Internet. Some of the largest companies are making serious investments to create a new hybrid online broadcast medium for news and entertainment.

Broadcast News Ventures

Merrill Brown is the chief journalist in charge of MSNBC Interactive, the Internet side of the ambitious new joint venture between NBC News, a unit of the General Electric Company, and the Microsoft Corporation. The venture went on screen in July 1996. So, what happens when the out-going news media culture collides with the introverted corporate culture of a software developer?

"They love e-mail at Microsoft," David Corvo, an NBC News Vice-President in New York, told the *New York Times*. "We're reporters. We use telephones all the time. We've had to learn more e-mail; they've had to learn more telephone."

Furthermore, Microsoft Network's newsroom is almost free from television sets. News is pulled from wire services for MSN's online service. In contrast, Microsoft visitors to NBC News in Manhattan found computers being used almost exclusively as word processors.

"We talk about customers; they talk about viewers," a Microsoft executive told the *New York Times*. "They talk about content; we talk about journalism," Mr. Corvo said. "It's important to make sure we mean the same thing."

"Part of Merrill's charge," Andrew Lack, president of NBC News, told a reporter from the *New York Times*, "is to raise the bar for the people working on the online side so that their skills and experience and journalistic sensibilities match those on the NBC side."

"Some of the younger people who aren't steeped in journalism may sometimes get cockamamie ideas about it," Mr. Brown told the *New York Times*. "We're working on being very careful about what we put out, and not abusing the fact that we can gather tons of information on the Internet, some of which may have limited value."

An example, he said, was polling data that crops up all over the Internet, and may look intriguing but turn out to be flawed. Still, he said, the cultures over all can be melded.

"Superficially, of course, they are very different cultures, referring to the difference between Microsoft and NBC," Mr. Brown told the *New York Times* in a recent article. "But fundamentally, it's a media-news-information culture we're dealing with. For the interactive side, we've hired people from CBS News, from *U.S. News & World Report*, from *Time*, and from the *Far Eastern Economic Review*."

Mr. Harrington has hired people from print journalism as well as television for MSNBC Cable. The 24-hour news and talk channel uses NBC reporters, as well as some special contributors, and in prime time will have news and interview shows using some of NBC's best-known journalists—Tom Brokaw, Bill Moyers, Jane Pauley, Brian Williams, Katie Couric, Bryant Gumbel and Bob Costas, among them.

http://www.nytimes.com/web/docsroot/library/cyber/week/0708msnbc.html

CyberTimes reporter Lawrie Mifflin wrote about the joint venture between NBC News, a unit of the General Electric Company, and Microsoft Corporation.

*The verbal artist
must also be
a verbal mechanic.*

Together, the two enterprises have hired about four hundred people. On June 3rd in Fort Lee, about three hundred people reported for work for the first time, in a broad, sunny newsroom where each desk has a Hewlett-Packard computer and tiny RCA television set on top.

"It's a tremendous population explosion within NBC, no question," Mr. Lack said. "And I'll tell you candidly, I've been disappointed in my search within electronic journalism for enough capable colleagues to meet the challenge. I've increasingly turned to reporters who have come through the kind of training you get at a major newspaper."

The *New York Times* article reported that "the majority of newcomers are young, in part because they can be paid lower salaries and in part because younger people tend to have more computer knowledge."

"But the primary criteria," Mr. Harrington told the *Times*, "were journalistic skills and interests, and the ability to work together. These are people who want to do news—not entertainment programs, not sports, not talk shows, not television in general, but news."

All new staff members are employees of NBC News, not MSNBC specifically. "This is NBC News on cable, not some parallel universe," Mr. Corvo said.

So, where in this convergence of big business and technology is your next career move? Perhaps one of the most important questions to ask is how will you fit into the group as a writer. If you're an introverted technical writer, will you be able to make the shift to a bustling newsroom or entertainment atmosphere? Or if you're a journalist—will you fit into the corporate culture of a software developer as a content writer creating interactive instructional material for employee training? Will you be happier writing news and nonfiction or writing scripts for computer games or interactive comic books?

The type of writing you like most and the companies that buy most of your articles, stories, or books will give you clues as to where you belong. Emerging Internet technology makes it possible to find the businesses that use the kind of writing you do best. As long as there's a wide enough audience to read what you write, there will be a market to sell the type of writing that most becomes you. Write for the needs of your audience and they will create your niche. 🐦

7 Is print dead?

Trends say there won't be less print publishing, but rather, there will be more of a variety of print publications and books, many about the new electronic and online media. The *New York Times*, *Newsweek*, and *Time* have Web sites and produce both printed and online versions. As a result, there are more publications and book publishers available to absorb writer's works.

The Web has redefined publishing and creative, business, science, and technical writing. New media publishers think differently and the way they think is changing again. This change is affected by the fact that the way we perceive the media has taken an electronic leap forward so that now anyone can have a global voice and address. Not only has everyone a subject about which to speak, but now a pipeline to instantly bubble it to all the world.

Hidden jobs in online journalism are plentiful. New J-school graduates are finding work with the major media outlets in cyberspace. An estimated 775 publications worldwide have put up online sites.

The boom has created a common ground where non-media software companies can join forces with traditional print and broadcasting organizations. These companies are actively looking for reporters whose journalistic skills are combined with a knowledge of a desktop broadcasting, Web authoring, and interactive media development skills.

Most journalism schools are incorporating new media software and Web authoring into their core programs. They are teaching courses online and in classrooms on how to develop Web content, format manuscripts for online publishing, and work with Internet-based software—from news to movie-making programs.

Training in technology now goes along with teaching journalists how to write well. The goal is to have writers cope with rapid technological changes as they move along. At the Columbia School of Journalism, a course called "Tools of the Modern Journalist" includes instruction on how to write com-

One the "first" Web, everyone became a publisher.

On the "second" Web, everyone became a broadcaster.

puter programs related to Web content development and interactive media.

Writing or using hypertext is a necessary skill for journalists who wish to compete with content developers for jobs in online journalism. The focus on the state-of-the-art technology (at the time of this writing, HTML, CGI, and *Java*) is necessary to keep abreast of developments online.

At the University of Missouri's School of Journalism, the new media is emphasized. Students run a Web site called *Digital Missourian*. It's similar to a wire service

with updated news stories of the region. Journalists must be both creative writers and technicians. The journalist who is also a technocrat will have no trouble finding work in today's market.

Computer skills plus journalism training and experience will help anyone land a job quicker than having only one of those skills—whether it be as a Web content developer, a content writer, editor, or indexer/librarian. Students with these skills have been offered starting salaries higher than those earned by writers with degrees in comparative literature or writing.

A scanned version of the front page of the *New York Times* can be displayed in both headline and digest form, with links to the articles. (Compare this front page to their interactive front page on page 6. It's the same issue—one in hypertext and the other in print.)

http://www.nytimes.com/yr/mo/day/front/scan.html

cyberscribes.1: The New Journalists

According to the *US News and World Report,* one recent graduate student was offered a $60,000 a year job designing a Web site for a newspaper. So journalists who design Web sites for magazines, newspapers, book publishers, or scriptwriting departments of new media companies can demand higher pay than someone with 'only' a liberal arts education and experience in creative or news writing.

Most companies developing online news networks prefer to hire journalism school graduates. You need to be able to reason logically and objectively about how you are presenting the news, and be able to separate online fact from fiction.

Last year, one well-known newspaper hired about twenty people, although none had a journalism degree. The people employed had computer knowledge and experience working on college campus newspapers. In contrast, MSN News at Microsoft hired only journalism school graduates.

As the field evolves, rules and roles are being rewritten. One of the problems is that journalism schools are following the online movement, rather than leading it. As a result, employers are willing to hire non-journalism majors who know something about technology and creative writing, but lack editorial experience.

If you are a professional journalist seeking to strengthen your ties to the computer industry, you may begin by joining professional associations such as the Computer Press Association or the Digital Multimedia Association. Check the job listings that can be found in most of the major electronic publications.

Writers, your new medium is here, but it won't be new for long. At one time, writers made a fortune in radio—before Ernie Kovacs started working with a television camera. Today, individual writers and artists can take their digitized video clips and combine them with sound bites to produce a desktop broadcast of their own design.

The time for change has come and you can be among the first to branch out into interactive intuitive writing and broadcasting on the Web. 🐾

What changes will the "third" Web bring?

Voices from the industry:
Ralph Izard, Ph.D., Director, School of Journalism

Bio

Ralph Izard is Director of the E.W. Scripps School of Journalism at Ohio University.

As an educator, author, and journalist, Izard has a broad range of experience with a special interest in issues related to ethics, the First Amendment, public affairs reporting, and news writing.

Recent changes in communication technology promise major overhauls in journalism and thus in journalism education. It may or may not be true that traditional media, especially print media, are doomed. But it certainly is true that those of us involved in journalism at all levels are challenged to adapt our traditional values and skills to new means of information delivery.

It's both frightening and gratifying to see journalists devoting significant effort to make their respecting media fit the newer forms. At first these changes will simply be add-ons to what we've done for years, but then we'll be challenged to find a synthesis that maintains many of the older values of journalism within the new electronic context. Some media are ahead of others, but it will be a slow process for most.

It's going to be especially necessary that professional journalists and journalism educators work together in full cooperation if we are to meet the challenge. We must help each other if, collectively, we are to continue to provide information in a form that is useful to the society we serve.

In journalism education, we are fighting to keep up and to move ahead. Our young people, the journalists of tomorrow, must be equipped for the communication revolution that we all see on the horizon. This is not simply a matter of helping students find jobs. It is more important that they understand the newer forms of communication technology because that technology will result in different methods of information retrieval and distribution.

Journalism schools must provide education, not simply training. Our students must be part of the change, not simply challenged by it. And we in education must move quickly to provide them with opportunities to understand both the technological and social implications of the journalism that will become dominant during their careers.

In the E.W. Scripps School of Journalism at Ohio University, we are working hard to find both the economic and human resources to create such opportunities for our students. We know that budgets will be stretched, and faculty members will be forced to learn new techniques.

We now offer several new classes and hope to modify our entire curriculum. Among classes added has been one that helps students gain usage of electronic data bases and other sources of information and one that is devoted specifically to Web pages and journalism. We will have other new classes, but it will be more important that we analyze our entire curriculum and find ways to integrate the newer forms, not simply add them to what we've done for years.

At the same time, it is crucial for journalism that we not pay too much attention to technology. Technology remains a means to an end. If our students are to succeed, they must fully appreciate how important journalistic values may be woven into newer forms of distribution. We must give our students the ability to distinguish themselves from the millions of others who will use the technology to communicate but will not understand or appreciate the distinction between true journalism and simple communication.

http://www.scripps.ohiou.edu

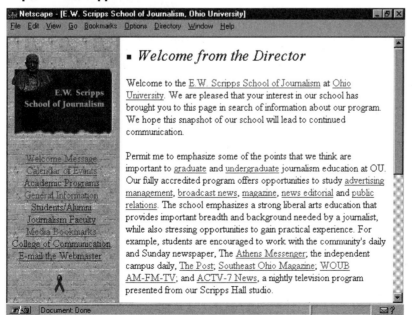

The E. W. Scripps School of Journalism offers academic programs in Advertising Management, Broadcast News, Magazine and News Writing, Editing, and Public Relations. Their site includes a wealth of information, including hot links to online resources.

Will journalism survive?

In a speech to a near capacity audience at UCSD on May 8, 1996, veteran journalist Daniel Schorr, 81, stated that the media and the public have split.

"Journalism has been absorbed by a vast entertainment industry controlled from the corporate boardrooms of giant conglomerates."

If this is so, then will the Internet reunite them? When seasoned journalists downsized from dailies enter new careers, will it be as fiction writers of computer game scripts or as producers of digital and immersive video or interactive programming? Can three-dimensional writing skills be interchangeable with visionary writing and reporting the news?

Schorr said that the press has somehow lost its relationship with the American public, that the media is perceived as another anti-people institution, like government or business. Schorr explained, "No one looks at journalism anymore as a separate entity. It's now a part of something else."

If it has become a dangerous hybrid appearing in the form of such programs as daytime talk shows, then why are the ratings so high? When the hoards of television viewers invade the Internet, will it become the Interknot—offering the same kind of immersive dumbed-down tabloid programming that is so popular on daytime TV?

It's up to the writer to determine what online journalism and interactive storytelling will become— writing from the bones or writing to make an impact on the emotions. Will writing that appeals to the heart find a larger audience than writing that appeals to the head, to logic and reason? Does propaganda as fiction sell well to the emotions? Yes! But, is that the world we want to build?

The fate of online journalism is up to the writer and producer as a team. What you get is what you write or design, and what sells is what the audience demands— or is it?

Documentary Script

YOU AND ERIC:

THE EDUCATIONAL RESOURCES INFORMATION CENTER

by Anne Hart

VIDEO	AUDIO

Segment 1:

Introduction to Eric.

Narrator shows chart reading:

What is Eric?

- National Information System.

- Source for obtaining documents on education.

- Network of decentralized information centers.

Montage:

Music, futuristic. Show information overload.

TODAY'S PREDOMINANT THEME IS CHANGE. THE EDUCATIONAL COMMUNITY INCESSANTLY PRODUCES AND USES INFORMATION. NEW CURRICULA, NEW MEDIA, AND NEW TEACHING METHODS ARE BEING DESIGNED IN CLASSROOMS THROUGHOUT THE NATION. THESE ACTIVITIES ARE HAPPENING AT A RATE UNPRECEDENTED IN THE HISTORY OF EDUCATION.

ALL THIS RECENT EXPANDING ACTIVITY HAS PRODUCED THOUSANDS OF VALUABLE DOCUMENTS, MANY OF WHICH HAVE NOT REACHED THE PEOPLE WHO NEED THEM. AS RECENTLY AS 1964, LIBRARIANS WERE FINDING THEIR SHELVES CHOKED WITH A PROLIFERATION OF PUBLICATIONS. TEACHERS WERE STUNNED BY THE DELAYS IN MOVING DOCUMENTS FROM ONE READER TO ANOTHER. BY 1965 THE NEED FOR A SOURCE FOR OBTAINING DOCUMENTS ON EDUCATION WAS SO URGENT, THAT ERIC--THE EDUCATIONAL RESOURCES INFORMATION CENTER-- WAS DEVELOPED.

This script was written in 1976 by Anne Hart for one of the first computer-related TV shows. ERIC, the topic of the show, has its place in cyber history as an early component of what we now call the Internet.

Perhaps the concepts of new media, multimedia, search engines, collaborative computing, and decentralized networks aren't so new after all.

VIDEO	AUDIO
	ERIC'S SYSTEM WAS DESIGNED TO OPERATE THROUGH A NETWORK OF SPECIALIZED CENTERS WHERE INFORMATION ON EDUCATION WOULD BE ACQUIRED, INDEXED, MONITORED, EVALUATED, ABSTRACTED, AND LISTED IN ERIC REFERENCE PRODUCTS.
Graphics follow narration with speaker and charts describing Eric's objectives. . . .	TODAY ERIC IS A NATIONAL DECENTRALIZED INFORMATION SYSTEM DESIGNED AND DEVELOPED BY THE UNITED STATES OFFICE OF EDUCATION. IT IS NOW OPERATED BY THE NATIONAL INSTITUTE OF EDUCATION.
History segment:	ORIGINALLY ORGANIZED AS A PROGRAM OF THE BUREAU OF RESEARCH, ERIC BEGAN WITH THE SUPPORT OF EDUCATION FOR THE DISADVANTAGED UNDER THE ELEMENTARY AND SECONDARY EDUCATION ACT OF 1965. A PRELIMINARY EFFORT INVOLVED THE ORGANIZATION AND DISSEMINATION OF WHAT HAS BECOME KNOWN AS THE "DISADVANTAGED COLLECTION" OF 1,740 DOCUMENTS TO THE VARIOUS STATE EDUCATIONAL AGENCIES AND TO CERTAIN LOCAL SCHOOL DISTRICTS. ERIC WAS ORIGINALLY CONCEIVED AS A SYSTEM FOR PROVIDING READY ACCESS TO

VIDEO	AUDIO
	EDUCATIONAL DOCUMENTS. DR. LEE BURCHINAL, ONE OF ERIC'S EARLIER DESIGNERS, DEVELOPED ERIC IN 1966.
	BY THAT YEAR, FOUR MAJOR OBJECTIVES HAD BEEN DEVELOPED FOR THE ERIC PROGRAM. . . THEY ARE STILL THE SAME TODAY. . . .
Transition from history segment to Eric's objectives.	THESE OBJECTIVES ARE: TO MAKE UNAVAILABLE OR HARD-TO-FIND SIGNIFICANT RESEARCH AND DOCUMENTS EASILY AVAILABLE TO THE EDUCATIONAL COMMUNITY. . . TO PREPARE INTERPRETIVE SUMMARIES OF INFORMATION FROM MANY REPORTS FOR USE BY EDUCATION DECISION-MAKERS AND PRACTITIONERS. . . TO STRENGTHEN EXISTING EDUCATIONAL RESEARCH DISSEMINATION CHANNELS. . . AND TO PROVIDE A BASE FOR DEVELOPING A NATIONAL EDUCATION INFORMATION NETWORK THAT CAN EFFECTIVELY LINK KNOWLEDGE PRODUCERS AND USERS IN EDUCATION.
History segment:	AT THE TIME ERIC WAS FIRST DISCUSSED, THE LITERATURE OF EDUCATION WAS UNCONTROLLED. RESEARCH REPORTS, SUBMITTED TO THE OFFICE OF EDUCATION BY THEIR CONTRACTORS AND

VIDEO	AUDIO

GRANTEES, RECEIVED AN INITIAL SCATTERED DISTRIBUTION AND THEN DISAPPEARED. REPORTS FROM OTHER SOURCES GENERALLY REMAINED EQUALLY INACCESSIBLE. ERIC WAS INTENDED TO CORRECT THIS CHAOTIC SITUATION AND TO PROVIDE A FOUNDATION FOR SUBSEQUENT INFORMATION ANALYSIS ACTIVITIES IN AN ATTEMPT TO SPREAD THE USE OF CURRENT DEVELOPMENTS.

BECAUSE OF THE DECENTRALIZED NATURE OF AMERICAN EDUCATION, THE MANY SPECIALIZATIONS, AND THE EXISTENCE OF NUMEROUS PROFESSIONAL ORGANIZATIONS, ERIC'S DESIGNERS OPTED FOR A NETWORK OF ORGANIZATIONS RATHER THAN A SINGLE MONOLITHIC INFORMATION CENTER LOCATED IN WASHINGTON, D.C. ERIC WAS CONCEIVED, THEREFORE, AS A NETWORK 'CLEARINGHOUSE', LOCATED ACROSS THE COUNTRY IN 'HOST' ORGANIZATIONS THAT WERE ALREADY NATURALLY STRONG IN THE FIELD OF EDUCATION IN WHICH THEY WOULD OPERATE.

Transition to Clearinghouse segment.

A CLEARINGHOUSE CONSISTS OF A GROUP OF PEOPLE DEDICATED TO HUNTING DOWN, CATALOGING, AND MAKING AVAILABLE ABSTRACTS OF USEFUL DOCUMENTS OF EVERY SIZE AND TYPE: BOOKS, PERIODICALS,

VIDEO   AUDIO

RESEARCH REPORTS, THESES,
CONFERENCE PROCEEDINGS,
PROJECT REPORTS, SPEECHES,
BIBLIOGRAPHIES, CURRICULUM-
RELATED MATERIALS, AND
INDUSTRY-PRODUCED REPORTS, TO
NAME A FEW. THESE ABSTRACTS
ARE MADE AVAILABLE THROUGH THE
MONTHLY CATALOGS. IN MOST
CASES, MICROFICHE AND XEROX
HARDCOPIES OF THE ACTUAL
DOCUMENTS ARE MADE AVAILABLE
FROM A CENTRAL COPYING
FACILITY.

CONTRACTS ISSUED BY THE
GOVERNMENT GAVE THE
CLEARINGHOUSES RESPONSIBILITY
FOR ACQUIRING AND SELECTING
ALL DOCUMENTS IN THEIR AREA
AND FOR PROCESSING THESE
DOCUMENTS. 'PROCESSING'
INCLUDES THE FAMILIAR
SURROGATION ACTIVITIES OF
CATALOGING, INDEXING, AND
ABSTRACTING. THIS SCHEME
WORKED OUT VERY WELL.

VIRUTALLY ALL OBSERVERS OF
ERIC HAVE CONCLUDED OVER TIME
THAT THE NETWORK OF
CLEARINGHOUSES DOES A BETTER
JOB OF FERRETING OUT THE
CURRENT DOCUMENTS OF EDUCATION
THAN ONE SINGLE INFORMATION

VIDEO	AUDIO

CENTER IN WASHINGTON COULD
EVER DO. WITH THEIR
SPECIALIZED SUBJECT EXPERTISE,
CLEARINGHOUSE RESEARCH
ANALYSTS ARE WELL QUALIFIED TO
MANAGE ERIC DOCUMENT SELECTION
FUNCTIONS. DECENTRALIZATION
HAS PAID OFF AS WELL FOR
INFORMATION ANALYSIS AND USER
SERVICE ACTIVITIES.

THE CLEARINGHOUSE COLLECTS
INFORMATION ON RESEARCH AND
TECHNIQUES WHICH ARE
OUTGROWTHS OF TECHNOLOGY.
INFORMATION CONTAINED WITHIN
THE ERIC SYSTEM INCLUDES
MATERIAL PROVIDED BY THE
GROWING NUMBER OF TECHNOLOGY-
BASED MEDIA CENTERS AS WELL AS
MATERIAL FOUND IN SCHOOL AND
COMMUNITY LIBRARIES.

BUT DECENTRALIZATION WAS NOT
THE COMPLETE ANSWER. IN ORDER
TO GENERATE PRODUCTS THAT
INCLUDED THE OUTPUT OF ALL
NETWORK COMPONENTS, SUCH AS
REFERENCE SOURCES, INFORMATION
GATHERED BY THE CLEARINGHOUSES
HAD TO BE ASSEMBLED AT ONE
CENTRAL PLACE.

ERIC'S FINAL DESIGN,
THEREFORE, INCLUDED

VIDEO	AUDIO
	DECENTRALIZED CLEARINGHOUSE OPERATIONS INTEGRATED AROUND A CENTRAL COMPUTERIZED FACILITY WHICH SERVES AS A SWITCHING CENTER FOR THE NETWORK.
	THE DATA RECORDED BY EACH OF THE CLEARINGHOUSES IS SENT TO THE FACILITY TO FORM A CENTRAL DATA BASE FROM WHICH PUBLICATIONS AND INDEXES ARE PRODUCED. THE COMPUTER IS THE MOST POWERFUL TOOL IN OPERATION TODAY FOR THE FAST HANDLING OF LARGE QUANTITIES OF INFORMATION.
Transition: How are documents made available?	HOW ARE DOCUMENTS MADE AVAILABLE TO THE PUBLIC? ERIC WAS TO MAKE DOCUMENTS AVAILABLE FROM A CENTRAL SOURCE INSTEAD OF JUST INFORMING USERS THAT A GIVEN DOCUMENT EXISTED. IT WAS DECIDED, THEN, THAT EACH CLEARINGHOUSE WOULD GENERATE NEWSLETTERS, BULLETINS, BIBLIOGRAPHIES, RESEARCH REVIEWS, AND INTERPRETIVE STUDIES ON EDUCATIONAL SUBJECTS TO SATISFY THE NEEDS OF THE EDUCATIONAL AREA IT WOULD SERVE. IT WAS, THEREFORE, NECESSARY TO PROVIDE A DOCUMENT REPRODUCTION SERVICE WHERE ANY

VIDEO	AUDIO

NON-COPYRIGHTED DOCUMENT
ANNOUNCED COULD BE OBTAINED.
COPYRIGHTED MATERIALS ARE ALSO
REPRODUCED, WITH PERMISSION.
ERIC WAS DEVELOPED AS A
DOCUMENT ANNOUNCEMENT AND
RETRIEVAL SERVICE.

Transition: Cost

WHO PAYS FOR ERIC? WHAT DOES
IT COST? THE GOVERNMENT COULD
NOT SUBSIDIZE EVERY USER'S
DOCUMENT NEEDS. THE DOCUMENT
REPRODUCTION EFFORT HAD TO
BECOME SELF-SUPPORTING.
THEREFORE, USERS HAD TO PAY
FOR REPORTS THEY WANTED.
DISSEMINATION OF THE DATA IS
NOT SUBSIDIZED BY THE
TAXPAYER. PERSONS WANTING ERIC
MAGNETIC TAPES ARE REQUIRED TO
MEET TAPE, DUPLICATION, AND
PROCESSING COSTS. THE FEDERAL
GOVERNMENT LIMITS ITS
INVESTMENT IN BOTH AREAS BY
GENERATING A FUNDAMENTAL DATA
BASE AND THEN PERMITTING THE
PRIVATE SECTOR TO MARKET IT AT
PRICES ADVANTAGEOUS TO THE
PUBLIC.

Segment:

ERIC EMERGES AS A NETWORK WITH
FOUR LEVELS. THE GOVERNMENTAL
LEVEL IS REPRESENTED BY THE
NATIONAL INSTITUTE OF
EDUCATION. CENTRAL ERIC IS THE
FUNDER, POLICY SETTER, AND
MONITOR. THE NON-PROFIT LEVEL

VIDEO	AUDIO
	IS MADE UP OF 18 CLEARINGHOUSES LOCATED AT UNIVERSITIES OR PROFESSIONAL SOCIETIES. THE COMMERICAL LEVEL CONSISTS OF THE CENTRALIZED FACILITIES FOR MANAGING THE DATA BASE, PUTTING OUT PUBLISHED PRODUCTS, MAKING MICROFICHE, AND REPRODUCING DOCUMENTS. FOURTH AND LAST ARE THE USERS WHO RECEIVE THE BENEFIT OF THESE ACTIVITIES.
Transition: Segment: What ERIC can do	ERIC CONTAINS INFORMATION PROVIDED BY THE GROWING NUMBER OF TECHNOLOGY-BASED MEDIA CENTERS. SOME OF THE FIELDS OF INFORMATION ERIC COVERS ARE: INSTRUCTIONAL FILMS, LEARNING RESOURCE CENTERS, EDUCATIONAL TELEVISION, PROGRAMMED INSTRUCTION, LIBRARY TECHNOLOGY, COMPUTERS, SIMULATION AND GAMING, MICROFORMS, INSTRUCTIONAL MATERIALS CENTERS, RADIO, COMMUNICATIONS SATELLITES, INFORMATION SCIENCES, AUDIO AND VIDEO RECORDING, MULTIMEDIA, EDUCATION AND TRAINING OF LIBRARY PERSONNEL, MICROTEACHING, SYSTEMS, APPROACHES TO TEACHING, INSTRUCTIONAL DEVELOPMENT, THE OPERATIONS OF SCHOOL AND UNIVERISITY LIBRARIES. . .THE

VIDEO	AUDIO
	EDUCATION RELATED RESEARCH COULD GO ON. IF YOU'RE SETTING UP A LEARNING RESOURCE CENTER, IF YOU'RE USING COMPUTERS IN INSTRUCTION, IF YOU'RE PRODUCING INSTRUCTIONAL MATERIALS OR MAKING AN INSTRUCTIONAL FILM OR TV PROGRAM, OR TRAINING LIBRARIANS OR MEDIA SPECIALISTS. . .ERIC CAN HELP YOU. OR MAYBE YOU'RE LOOKING FOR TRADITIONAL UNPUBLISHED DOCUMENTS IN EDUCATION RESEARCH. YOU CAN USE ERIC'S TOOLS AT OVER 500 ERIC RESOURCE CENTERS THROUGHOUT THE COUNTRY.
	WHO CAN USE ERIC AND HOW?
	ERIC CAN HELP SCHOOL ADMINISTRATORS: TO IDENTIFY NEW AND SIGNIFICANT EDUCATIONAL DEVELOPMENTS, TO APPLY NEW MANAGEMENT TOOLS AND PRACTICES TO THE LOCAL SITUATION, AND TO BASE BUDGET ESTIMATES ON THE LATEST RESEARCH DATA. ERIC CAN HELP TEACHERS OBTAIN THE LATEST INFORMATION ON PRESERVICE AND INSERVICE TRAINING, LEARN ABOUT NEW CLASSROOM TECHNIQUES AND MATERIALS, AND DISCOVER "HOW TO DO IT" PROJECTS FOR PROFESSIONAL DEVELOPMENT. ERIC

VIDEO	AUDIO

CAN HELP RESEARCHERS KEEP UP-
TO-DATE IN THEIR FIELD OF
INTEREST AND OBTAIN FULL-TEXT
DOCUMENTS ON RESEARCH. ERIC
CAN HELP INFORMATION
SPECIALISTS COMPILE
BIBLIOGRAHIES ON SPECIFIC
EDUCATIONAL TOPICS. . . TO
SEARCH ERIC PUBLICATIONS FOR
ANSWERS TO INQUIRIES. . . AND
TO LOCATE AND ORDER DOCUMENTS
FOR LOCAL INFORMATION CENTERS.

ERIC ASSISTS PROFESSIONAL
ORGANIZATIONS KEEP ABREAST OF
RESEARCH IN A SPECIFIC AREA OF
EDUCATION. . . TO INFORM
MEMBERS OF DOCUMENTS IN
PERIPHERAL AREAS OF EDUCATION.
. . TO KEEP MEMBERS UP-TO-DATE
ON INFORMATION SYSTEMS. ERIC HELPS
STUDENTS TO GAIN ACCESS TO THE
LATEST INFORMATION FOR
PREPARING TERM PAPERS AND
THESES IN EDUCATION, TO OBTAIN
INFORMATION ON CAREER
DEVELOPMENT IN EDUCATION, AND
TO BUILD A PERSONALIZED, LOW-
COST LIBRARY ON EDUCATION.

Transition:

Segment: How?

HOW DOES ERIC DO ALL THIS? BY
MAKING AVAILABLE AN EXTENSIVE
DATA BANK OF 'FUGITIVE'
EDUCATIONAL MATERIALS--
MATERIALS THAT TEACHERS AND
RESEARCHERS WOULDN'T EASILY BE

VIDEO	AUDIO
Show Materials:	ABLE TO FIND THROUGH STANDARD REFERENCE SOURCES. ERIC'S SPECIALTY IS NONCOPYRIGHTED, UNPUBLISHED EDUCATIONAL MATERIALS SUCH AS PROJECT REPORTS, SPEECH TEXTS, RESEARCH FINDINGS, LOCALLY-PRODUCED MATERIALS, AND CONFERENCE PROCEEDINGS.
Show Services:	WHEN ERIC'S CLEARINGHOUSES THROUGHOUT THE NATION SEEK OUT, GATHER, COORDINATE, INDEX, AND CATALOG THESE MATERIALS, TWO UNIQUE SERVICES RESULT: FIRST, ERIC PROVIDES READABLE ABSTRACTS OF ALL MATERIALS. THESE ABSTRACTS ARE AVAILABLE IN MONTHLY CATALOGS AT INFORMATION CENTERS, SUCH AS THIS ERIC RESOURCE CENTER. THE MONTHLY CATALOGS ARE AVAILABLE AT DEPARTMENTS OF EDUCATION, EDUCATIONAL LIBRARIES, INFORMATION CENTERS, AND SOME UNIVERSITY CAMPUSES. THE CATALOGS ALSO ARE AVAILABLE ON COMPUTER TAPES. SECOND, ERIC PROVIDES INEXPENSIVE MICROFICHE OF THE COMPLETE TEXT OF MANY NONCOPYRIGHTED AND UNPUBLISHED MATERIALS. THE MICROFICHE CAN BE ORDERED FOR LIBRARIES AND INFORMATION CENTERS.

VIDEO	AUDIO
Transition:	A WORD OF WARNING. . . . ERIC IS NOT FOR EVERYBODY. ERIC IS DESIGNED FOR THE MOTIVATED PERSON WHO IS WILLING TO SPEND TEN MINUTES TO LEARN HOW TO BENEFIT FROM A SYSTEM THAT OFFERS ACCESS TO A COLLECTION OF OVER 100,000 DOCUOMENTS WHICH GROWS AT A RATE OF 1,000 EACH MONTH.
Segment: What ERIC cannot do	WHAT IS THERE THAT ERIC CAN NOT DO FOR YOU? ERIC IS NOT AN HISTORICAL LIBRARY. ERIC'S COLLECTION CONTAINS CURRENT, NEW INFORMATION, GATHERING IT AS IT HAPPENS. ERIC DOES NOT CONTAIN ANSWERS TO QUESTIONS OUTSIDE OF EDUCATION-RELATED RESEARCH. IT WON'T HAVE NEWS OR POLITICAL OR ECONOMIC RESEARCH, NOR WILL IT TELL YOU FACTS ON STONEHENGE, ASTRONOMY, OR PHYSICAL SCIENCES. BUT IF YOU'RE A PHYSICAL SCIENCE TEACHER SEEKING CURRICULUM OR PROGRAM EVALUATIONS OR TECHNIQUES, ERIC WILL HELP YOU TO FIND SUCH EDUCATION-RELATED INFORMATION.
Transition:	TO RECAP SOME OF THE IMPORTANT POINTS ABOUT ERIC: IT IS FOR THE MOTIVATED EDUCATOR WHO'S WILLING TO

VIDEO	AUDIO
	LEARN SOME SIMPLE SEARCHING TECHNIQUES.
	UNLIKE MANY INDEXES TO MATERIALS, ERIC ACTUALLY GIVES YOU ACCESS TO MANY OF THE DOCUMENTS THEMSELVES AT LOW COST. THE OPTIMUM VALUE OF ERIC IS ACHIEVED WHEN YOU ARE WILLING TO USE MICROFICHE, WHICH INVOLVES A MICROFICHE READER.
	IN THE UNITED STATES AND, INCREASINGLY ABROAD, ERIC USERS RECEIVE A PHOTOCOPY DOCUMENT PAGE BY PAGE FROM A MICROFICHE READER/PRINTER AT AN ERIC CENTER. MICROFICHE IS THE PRIMARY MEDIA FOR STORAGE AND DISTRIBUTION OF THE COMPLETE TEXT OF DOCUMENTS IN THE ERIC COLLECTION.
Output microfiche or hardcopy photocopies	MICROFICHE, OR SHEET MICROFILM, IS A COMPACT 4" BY 6" CLEAR ACETATE CARD, ECONOMICAL, EASY TO STORE AND REPRODUCE, CRISPLY IMAGED, AND EASY TO HANDLE. IT IS THE PRIMARY MEDIA FOR STORAGE AND DISTRIBUTION OF THE COMPLETE TEXT OF ERIC DOCUMENTS. ONE MICROFICHE CAN CONTAIN FROM 48 TO 100 PAGES OF A DOCUMENT IN REDUCED FORM. IT IS AN INEXPENSIVE ALTERNATIVE TO HARDCOPY OR PHOTOCOPY.

VIDEO	AUDIO
	TO USE MICROFICHE, YOU MUST HAVE A MICROFICHE READER, OR READER/PRINTER TO ENLARGE THE PRINT TO A LEGIBLE SIZE. EACH ERIC RESOURCE CENTER CONTAINS A MICROFICHE READER AND A PRINTER. YOUR MICROFICHE READER ENABLES YOU TO VIEW YOUR DOCUMENT ENLARGED, BEFORE YOU ORDER YOUR PRINT-OUT.
Transition:	ERIC HAS MATERIALS THAT YOU CAN'T EASILY FIND ANYWHERE ELSE. ERIC ENABLES TEACHERS AND ADMINISTRATORS TO LEARN FROM OTHERS LIKE THEMSELVES IN THE FIELD. ERIC EMPHASIZES A PARTNERSHIP BETWEEN IT AND THE EDUCATOR. THIS PARTNERSHIP EXTENDS TO THE RESEARCHER SUBMITTING MATERIALS FOR INCLUSION INTO THE ERIC SYSTEM. ANYONE WHO USES ERIC REALIZES THE VALUE OF LEARNING FROM OTHERS' EXPERIENCES. TO KEEP THE ERIC SYSTEM ON TARGET, EDUCATORS, RESEARCHERS, YOU. . .MUST BE ENCOURAGED TO WRITE AND SUBMIT YOUR PROJECTS, SPEECHES, AND OTHER MATERIALS TO ERIC.
Segment: Document search and retrieval functions.	THE PRINCIPLE REFERENCE TOOL IN THE ERIC SYSTEM IS THE THESAURUS. IT MAINTAINS THE SOURCE OF SUBJECT HEADINGS USED BY THE INDEXES AND

VIDEO	AUDIO
Show Retrieving:	PROVIDES THE SYSTEM FOR RETRIEVING DOCUMENTS AND JOURNAL CITATIONS IN ERIC COLLECTIONS. TO INSURE THAT ERIC SYSTEMS USERS ARE NOT REQURIED TO LOOK UP FOUR OR FIVE SYNONYMS FOR THE SAME CONCEPT, ERIC'S DESIGNERS DEVELOPED A CONTROLLED VOCABULARY. TERMS,SOMETIMES
Show Descriptors:	CALLED DESCRIPTORS OR SUBJECT HEADINGS, WHICH APPEAR IN THE THESAURUS ARE VALID FOR CONDUCTING AN ERIC SEARCH. IF YOU WANT TO LOOK UP ADDITIONAL CONCEPTS FOR YOUR SEARCH OF ERIC HOLDINGS AND REFINE ONES YOU HAVE ALREADY INDENTIFIED, THE THESAURAUS CAN BE USED.
	USING A COMPUTER TO HELP SEARCH THROUGH THE THOUSANDS OF ENTRIES IN THE ERIC DATA BASE CAN PROVE TO BE A COST EFFECTIVE AND POWERFUL WAY TO RETRIEVE INFORMATION. THE RESULTS OF A COMPUTER SEARCH LOOK MUCH LIKE A BIBLIOGRAPHY.
Show Basic Components:	IN ORDER TO HAVE AN EFFECTIVE SEARCH PERFORMED, YOU SHOULD BE FAMILIAR WITH THE BASIC COMPONENTS OF THE PROCESS. THE FIRST COMPONENT IS THE "SEARCH STRATEGY," WHICH INCLUDES THE STATEMENT OF THE RESEARCH PROBLEM FORMULATED IN TERMS

VIDEO	AUDIO
	THAT THE COMPUTER CAN RECOGNIZE AND DEAL WITH.
	THE PROBLEM MUST BE TRANSLATED INTO ERIC DESCRIPTORS AND SET UP USING AN ERIC SEARCH TECHNIQUE. TAKING THE DESCRIPTORS FROM THE THESAURUS, THE KEY TERMS USED FOR THIS SEARCH TECHNIQUE ALLOW THE COMPUTER TO SORT OUT ONLY THOSE CITATIONS WHICH SATISFY THE NEEDS OF THE PARTICULAR RESEARCH PROBLEM.
	ERIC IS MOST EFFECTIVE WHEN THE SEARCH IS CONDUCTED BY THE 'DIALOGUE' APPROACH, IN WHICH THE COMPUTER USES A SERIES OF THESAURUS DESCRIPTORS WHICH SCAN THE 180,000 ITEMS IN ERIC'S FILES.
Transition:	ANYONE WHO USES ERIC REALIZES THE VALUE OF LEARNING FROM OTHERS' EXPERIENCES. THE RETRIEVAL OF DOCUMENTS IS ONLY THE FIRST STEP IN THE APPLICATION OF INFORMATION.
	IN ORDER FOR INFORMATION TO BE USEFUL TO A WIDE AUDIENCE, DATA MUST BE REPACKAGED INTO ABSTRACTS, REVIEWS, AND A VARIETY OF FORMATS. WHILE ERIC HAS MANY FEATURES IN COMMON WITH OTHER LARGE NATIONAL INFORMATION SYSTEMS, IT IS SET

VIDEO	AUDIO
	APART BY THE BROAD RANGE OF SOURCES FROM WHICH DOCUMENTARY MATERIALS ARE ACQUIRED. AUDIENCES HAVE DIVERSE INTERESTS, THEREFORE, THE CONCEPT OF THE DECENTRALIZED INFORMATION SYSTEM AND THE PRINCIPLE OF CENTRAL LEXICOGRAPHIC CONTROL WITH CLEARINGHOUSE PARTICIPATION SET ERIC APART. THE USER OF SUBJECT SPECIALISTS, WORKING IN THEIR OWN PROFESSIONAL ENVIRONMENT WHILE PERFORMING DOCUMENTATION FUNCTIONS, IS THE KEY TO UNIQUE STRENGTHS IN THE ERIC SYSTEM.
Conclusion Close-up of on-line computer	IN SUMMARY, ERIC IS AN ANACRONYM FOR EDUCATIONAL RESOURCES INFORMATION CENTER-- A NETWORK OF 18 CLEARINGHOUSES LOCATED THROUGHOUT THE COUNTRY, EACH SPECIALIZING IN A PARTICULAR FIELD OF EDUCATION. ERIC IS FUNDED BY THE NATIONAL INSTITUTE OF EDUCATION. ITS SERVICES ARE FREE TO EDUCATORS, RESEARCHERS, AND OTHERS INTERESTED IN THE FIELD OF EDUCATION.

# # #

CHAPTER TWO

Casting Your Net Beyond the News

*T*he Web has become a high-frequency broadcasting giant whose potential has big companies tuning in. Netcast technology that is pushed to the desktop or pulled from a Web site is a powerful tool in the hands of the writer. It's the most intimate visual medium that can invade the home, school, or office.

In the near future, rich media netcasts will be widely embraced as a standard training vehicle on the Internet , Intranet, and Extranet. Interactive online events that allow people to teleconference in real-time over the Internet will become an integral part of employee communications, marketing, and customer support programs.

Writing for Web publications and streaming media productions are lucrative markets for freelance writers. It's a natural for those who have an interest in both writing and commercial art and who like to work

with computer graphics and video. The demand for professional media scriptwriters and content developers will continue to increase as the communications, entertainment, and software industries converge to bring interactive content and distance learning to the home, school, and corporate boardroom.

Writing for public and private Web networks, hybrid parallel broadcasts, and interactive news services requires many of the same skills needed by those who write for print, radio, and broadcast TV. Think all of the above and take one step more.

As the print, radio, and television news media converge on the Web, they each bring formats and styles characteristic of their field. These disciplines, when applied to the Web, define a new medium for communication and create a wealth of opportunity for journalists and creative expressionists.

In the emerging push-pull broadcast evolution. the next step is a metaphorical shift from page to channel.

9 Can local print publications compete with online news providers?

The quantity and quality of e-zines and interactive newspapers appearing on the Web is creating a field day for writers. Everyone with print, broadcasting, or silicon in their veins is getting into the act. Call it news with an attitude.

In November 1996, the publisher of *Wired* magazine launched *Wired News*, an around-the-clock online news service that taps news from the cutting edge of the digital revolution. One of the top stories the first day the service was launched told of the executive order issued by President Clinton to shift control of encryption technology from the State Department to the Commerce Department. This story, which was buried on page ten of many print newspapers, paves the way for secure electronic commerce on the Internet.

The same week, Microsoft announced *Sidewalk*, an online entertainment media e-zine with localized content. The 1997 rollout includes editions for Washington D.C., San Diego, Minneapolis/St. Paul, and Sydney, Australia.

http://www.wired.com/news

Wired News provides instant news about the people, companies, and the technologies that are driving the digital revolution. Targeting a broader than Generation-X audience, this around-the-clock feed of original stories chronicles the ways technology is changing business, politics, and culture.

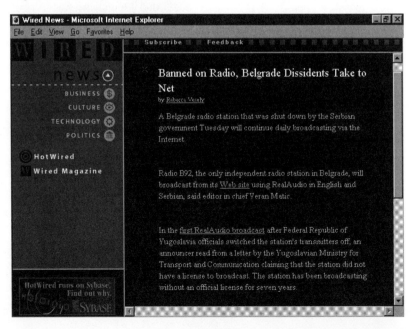

Michael Goff, editor in chief, described *Sidewalk* as, "the next generation of city media, combining distinctive local editorial with new technologies to deliver timely, comprehensive and customized insights that capture the essence of each city."

The strategy behind Microsoft's *Sidewalk* is to "hire proven, top-notch editors, producers, and contributors who have pushed traditional media to the limit, give them another dimension to explore with new tools and toys, and set them loose on their cities."

The demand for customized news with local content is driving the industry as Internet news providers compete with print dailies to establish their presence in local communities. Microsoft is offering fulltime and freelance positions in editorial, media, and design to writers in cities across the United States and beyond. Other ventures, such as Time Warner's RoadRunner and WebTV Networks are seeking to establish their local presence by linking to sites that showcase their technology while offering quality content.

All this attention to local markets translates into increased competition for print publications as everyone targets the same reading, viewing, and clicking audience.

http://cnn.com/TECH/9611/16/internet.intrigue/index.html

The alliance between CNN and Time Warner promises to create an interactive media giant with vast resources and high-speed connections to local cable television markets.

Voices from the industry:
Hoag Levins, Editor & Publisher magazine

Bio

Hoag Levins is the editor of *Editor & Publisher Interactive*, the Web site of *Editor & Publisher* magazine. Based in New York City, E&P is the 112-year-old weekly journal of the North American newspaper industry.

Mr. Levins spent more than twelve years as an award-winning staff reporter for the *Philadelphia Daily News*, the *Philadelphia Inquirer* and the *Courier Post* of Cherry Hill, N.J.

Levins is author of six non-fiction books, including, *AMERICAN SEX MACHINES: An Engineering History of Sex In American as Told From the Files of the U.S. Patent Office*, published in 1996 by Adams Publishers.

If you're getting ready to put your newspaper on the Internet and looking forward to reaching as many readers as possible, you probably ought to give some thought to the peculiar concept of invisible ink.

For instance, the technology now exists to print paper newspapers in special inks visible only under certain kinds of lights. It's an impressive achievement, really, involving genius levels of chemical engineering; but no newspaper has yet adopted the system. And no wonder.

Why would any publisher print with ink that is readable in less than 15% of all homes and offices of his circulation area? Imagine going to the news stand in the lobby and finding the racks filled with perfectly folded but completely blank newspapers— because the place has the wrong kind of fluorescent bulbs. Crazy, huh?

Yet this same bizarre approach to mass communications is what many are adopting when they mount World Wide Web sites constructed around Java, Shockwave, animated GIFs, streaming video, and the spreading tangle of other incompatible standards now creeping across the Web like virulent growths of electronic kudzu. Each day, millions of users attempt to access sites only to encounter the digital equivalent of pages printed in invisible ink. Either their browsers can't access the site at all because of its oddball standards, or the congestion of its advanced structure makes it impractically slow to load, or worse yet, the site 'locks' or 'freezes' the user's machine.

When the World Wide Web first caught fire in the public's imagination there was an elegant simplicity to its single standard: Pages of text and graphics constructed in HTML 2.0 could be quickly accessed by any browser software on any computer, period. And that was the true beauty of the thing: A new medium with a single common dialect linking computer users around the planet over standard phone lines. Elegantly simple universal communication was the main promise and most intoxicating lure of the Internet's graphic interface.

But now that same electronic matrix is being balkanized by the frenzied war for proprietary advantage between Microsoft and Netscape and the proliferation of 'improvements' in Web technologies that actually serve to lock out increasingly larger segments of the overall audience.

What is evolving is a Tower of Babel laid flat across the phone networks. And this muddle of incompatibility needs to be taken into careful account by any publishing company that hopes to reach the maximum number of people through a new Web site.

So when that hot-shot Web development firm you just retained sets up a Sun SPARC station on your boardroom table and demonstrates screen wizardry that looks like something out of Walt Disney studios, stop and ask yourself: "Yes, but how will it play on Mr. and Mrs. Normal's computer out there in newspaperland?"

http://www.mediainfo.com

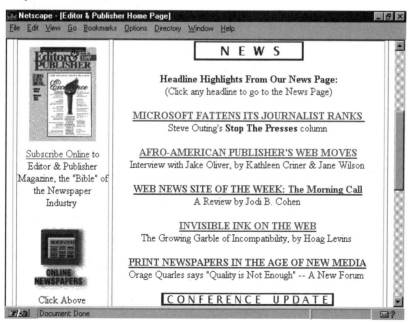

Editor & Publisher magazine sponsors a series of seminars on interactive technology for the newspaper industry. Their site provides late-breaking news, editorial features, and research references for writers in the new media.

Levins' point is well-taken—that some versions of software or code that is considered by some to be obsolete can often be used as a common denominator to reach a broader audience on the Web.

Chances are, it won't. Mom and Pop Normal are probably among the large numbers of the people accessing the Web with browser software that is, to say the least, not the latest version, and on computers that are, at best, of middle-level speed hooked to modems of 14,400 or even 9,600 baud. It's estimated that less than 15% of all Web users have the browsers, high-powered computers or high-speed modems that would allow them to enter or operate sites constructed with much of the high-tech gimmickry now being so heavily promoted in the trade press.

If you're planning your first Web site, here's a good exercise: Design the entire thing HTML2.0 and test it with NetScape 1.1. This is the last format that remains a reasonable common denominator across the entire Internet. It allows the creation of slick, magazine-like page layouts with text, photos, graphics, columns and intricate interconnectivity. Before you worry about glitzy packaging, work out the editorial strategy and content of your Web site: The logic of its segments, focus of its stories, the sharpness of its

headlines, the muscle of its facts, and the cadence of its text. Once you have it all operating as an effective communication in HTML 2.0, you have a structure that will be accessible by most any browser in the world. Add additional gimmicks with great care and the knowledge that each new feature of "advanced technology" you incorporate eliminates another segment of your potential total audience.

At the same time, think about making your publication an advocate on the issue of coherent Web standards. In fact, if they coordinated their efforts as a group, American newspapers could project a loud and influential national voice on this issue.

In the name of the public they serve, the papers could use their combined clout to send a message to the techno-geek software moguls who are either too greedy to understand, have lost sight of, or simply don't give a damn about the original promise that should be the sacrosanct touchstone of all Web technological developments: Elegantly simple universal communication.

How is audio broadcast on the Web?

Today's Web is full of radio broadcasts, Web telephones, and live chats that take advantage of streaming audio technology. You will find everything from alternative rock to author interviews and news commentary on the Internet.

The Cybercasters is an Internet audio site produced by Jan Ziff and Allan Davidson. Jan Ziff is also the writer, producer, and host of "Sound*Bytes"—an award winning daily computer radio program now in its sixth year. She delivers

insights regularly on the U.S. computer industry for the BBC and also presents software reviews on NPR's "Morning Edition" and "All Things Considered."

The combination of browsers and plug-in software required to play Internet audio varies from site to site. Many sites require a specific version of browser to be used with a combination of players and plug-ins. Although the required software can be downloaded for free from most sites, it may be frustrating at first.

Without the Web, what I say would be only words. The proof is on the Web!

—Art Bell
ArtBell@aol.com

http://www.cybercasters.com

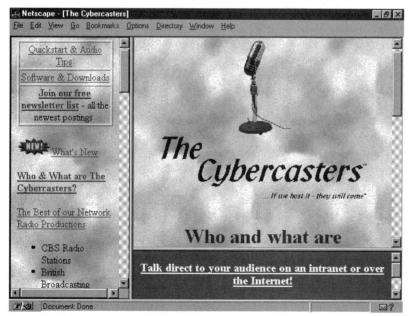

"The Cybercasters"is an Internet audio show produced by Jan Ziff and Allan Davidson that brings high-quality radio content to the Web.

Streaming audio and video technologies have opened new markets for road-tripping virtual scouts.

However, once everything is in place you will be able to enjoy a new dimension of the Web.

If you are more aural and oral than print-journalism oriented, you too can host interviews, roundtables, and live chats from your living room studio or salon. Whether you're a seasoned journalist and broadcaster or just a "wannabe," you can now have your own Internet "media" station or channel on the Internet. RealMedia Server from Progressive Networks allows you to transmit on-demand or live audio sychronized with simultaneous media streams of video or animated content. The software is licensed by the number of streams that can be played at the same time, (which makes the price to reach a mass audience quite high without additional revenue from paid advertising). However, you can start with a small number of streams and expand as your audience grows. There are also alternative audio resources on the Web that operate in the public domain such as Internet Relay Chat (IRC) and the Undernet.

Writers with a commitment to excellence will find rewards in broadcasting on the Internet. It's one more niche where your research, analytical, and writing skills, combined with your media relations and people skills will be appreciated and rewarded.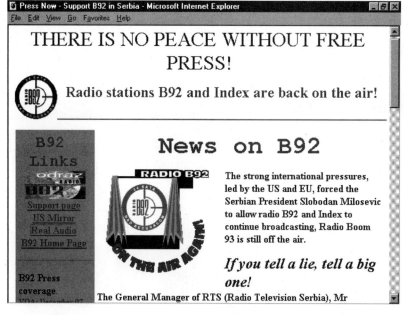

http://www.dds.nl/~pressnow/b92.htm

When the Serbian government forced independent radio station B92 off the air, its Web site took over reporting the news with RealAudio links in Serbo-Croatian and English. The Internet makes it possible for local stations to bypass government transmitters and official news agencies to bring their stories to the world.

THERE IS NO PEACE WITHOUT FREE PRESS!

Radio stations B92 and Index are back on the air!

News on B92

RADIO B92

The strong international pressures, led by the US and EU, forced the Serbian President Slobodan Milosevic to allow radio B92 and Index to continue broadcasting, Radio Boom 93 is still off the air.

If you tell a lie, tell a big one!

The General Manager of RTS (Radio Television Serbia), Mr

B92
Links
odraz
B92
Support page
US Mirror
Real Audio
B92 Home Page

B92 Press coverage.

Voices from the industry:
Nels Johnson, Download Recordings

>Date: Sat, 4 Jan 1997 15:49:53 -0800
>To: anne hart <scribes@ellipsys.com>
>From: Nels Johnson
>
>Anne,
>
>My basic feeling is that writers are going to be very important, because content is king. Stories are going to be told in all kinds of new ways, but they will start out linear/passive in the new media environment and evolve from there. Digital storytelling is going to be big.
>
>I think the main point is that writers don't need to be programmers or digital authoring tool experts, but they do need to see what these tools are capable of as they write their stories and scripts.
>
>As for my thoughts on electronic journalism, they are less focused than my feelings about digital storytelling, but I believe that is because there are more forces in conflict in this area. For instance, I would rather read the daily paper than subscribe to PointCast and its unrelenting barrage of unfiltered news.
>
>In a way, the job of the electronic journalist is going to be harder (at least until the dust settles) than that of the digital storyteller. Because of the overwhelming volume of raw news, much of it contradictory by nature, the electronic journalist will have a much bigger pile of data to sift through to develop the story. Electronic search tools will help find some of the important elements, but the truth, like the devil, is usually in the details.
>
>And the story, after all, is what people want to hear/read even in their news consumption. Good stories are put together by good reporters and good editors, whose jobs will be secure even though they'll have to work faster in more flexible environments to make electronic publishing deadlines. In a way, electronic news publishing is going to be more like traditional radio news than print journalism.
>
>I'm glad you liked the book.
>
>--Nels Johnson

Bio

Nels Johnson is president of Download Recordings, a Bay Area consulting and production firm specializing is desktop video and multimedia software development.

He is the author of *How to Digitize Video* (John Wiley 1994), *Web Developer's Guide to Multimedia and Video* (Coriolis 1996) and the *Web Developer's Guide to Multicasting* (Coriolis 1997).

Voices from the industry:
Simon Croft, WWBC, U. K.

Bio

Simon Croft is the content controller for the pro-audio web site *ProStudio & Live Audio* and a founder of World Wide Business Communications. Simon is a regular contributor to pro-audio and broadcast magazines distributed in Europe, North America and the Asia Pacific. Formerly an audio equipment sales & marketing manager, he has been a full-time writer since 1985.

(www.prostudio.com)

Q: **How did you get started in your writing career?**

A: Writing started as a part-time interest, until someone called me in 1985 and asked if I would like to edit an audio magazine. This type of background is quite common in pro-audio. That is to say, a lot of us were already in the industry. I am not convinced that there is an art to writing for the Web as such. In fact, much of the material on *ProStudio & Live Audio* has appeared in some form in print. Re-purposing it for the Web was more a question of structuring to be less linear.

Q: **What is your opinion of the Internet audio technology?**

A: That is quite strange because I was just posting an article to Asia Pacific Broadcasting on that very subject when your email came in. I've certainly written a lot about Internet audio, but for the printed medium.

Although there are some broadcasters using the tech-

nology, it is pretty peripheral to the pro-audio industry as a whole—for the moment.

People active in pro-audio are reluctant to have Internet audio delivery from their site. This is because the performance of pro-audio products is a magnitude higher than is possible over the Internet. It's a very clever technology but it is still at the mercy of a transmission medium not designed for real-time continuous data transfer.

So although we are writing about audio and using the Internet as a way of providing access to that material, I do not believe that there is any sense in which the contributors to PS&LA are writing specifically for Internet audio.

We have talked about the possibilities of providing radio-format audio in the future but we are not convinced that it is necessarily a better way than the printed word for meeting information needs. However, the field of entertainment is another issue entirely.

Can advertising support a Web broadcast?

11

PointCast is an example of a push-technology-based news network on the Web. It delivers customized advertisement-supported content around the clock—both news and entertainment—displayed as a SmartScreen™ screensaver when the computer is idle.

Each channel features a selection of rotating animated advertisements that can be targeted to user preference. Users can select a specific channel for news, sports, weather, entertainment, even the horoscope or lottery results.

PointCast uses a proprietary front-end that replaces the *Windows 95* screensaver. It then downloads news and advertisements, storing personalized data on the user's hard disk according to the user's preference.

By allowing users to read the stories offline, *PointCast* makes effective use of broadcast downtime and the limited bandwidth of the Internet. During periods of keyboard inactivity, the *PointCast* SmartScreen kicks in, displaying a random selection of news and current events.

http://www.pointcast.com

PointCast users can customize their news preferences by industry. The frame in the upper-right corner rotates a selection of animated advertisements, many with hot-links to the sponsor's own Web site.

What is an "Internet appliance"?

The term, "Internet appliance." represents a new category of products that provide Internet access without a computer. One of the first products on the market was developed by WebTV Networks, Inc. and provides high-quality access to the Web by remote control through a television set. The technology was licensed to Sony Electronics and Philips/Magnavox who now sell their respective WebTV Internet applicances through consumer electronics stores. Internet access is then provided to WebTV purchasers for a monthly fee.

WebTV was developed to provide a secure platform for electronic commerce and for a while, was actually classified as a weapon by the U.S. government. The encryption technology used to code all transactions was considered too powerful to be exported out of the country. Shortly thereafter, the Clinton administration issued an overnight executive order to liberalize long-standing government policies regarding encryption technology.

WebTV Networks, Inc. was founded by Steve Perlman, Bruce Leak, and Phil Goldman. The three had previously worked together at Apple Computer and General Magic. Perlman holds eleven patents in the areas of graphics, video, animation, modems, communications and telephony, and has ten patents pending in related technologies in conjunction with WebTV.

WebTV has struck a chord with the investment community. By the end of September, 1996, Paul Allen's Vulcan Ventures Inc. , Asia Pacific Ventures, Microsoft, Citicorp, VeriFone, Times Mirror, Lauder Partners, and Brentwood Venture Capital had signed up to support the debut. The investors were attracted by a number of factors, including the patent-pending TV image-enhancement technology, the consumer-focused user interface, and the enthusiastic advance response at retail. The potential for secure banking and transactional activities via the SmartCard slot in the WebTV box, as well as the open standard design offers significant opportunities for collaboration.

WebTV Networks developed a proprietary browser especially for the non-computing user. The company held focus groups with members of their target audience to determine which features and design elements were most effective. The result is a slick interface that works well within the constraints of a television screen. The company plans to integrate elements of Microsoft's Internet Explorer technology into future releases of the browser.

Aragon Consulting Group predicts that the market for Internet appliances will fall short of expectations. Their study questions whether today's computer-literate children will be satisfied with Internet access that lacks the ability to run programs and store data. They also anticipate a resistance from parents who are not eager to enhance the capabilities of their TV sets.

According to another study by Yankelovich Partners, Inc., the greatest perceived value of the Internet from the standpoint of consumers is its capacity to simplify and enhance their lives. Sixty-four percent were interested in pursuing personal interests and viewed the Internet as a strong addition to a child's education. According to industry analyst Gary Arlen, "Bringing the Internet to television must be part of the mix if the Internet is to grow into a true consumer resource."

WebTV Home Page

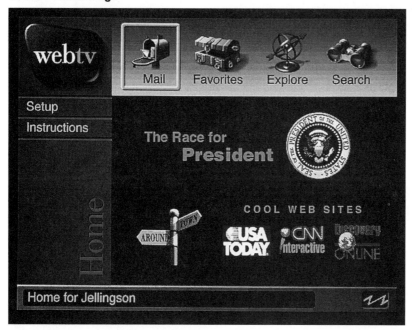

The WebTV interface more closely resembles a CD-ROM application than a Web site. The display is visually appealing with text that is larger and used sparingly. Unlike most computer displays, the status bar appears at the bottom of the screen rather than the top.

Voices from the industry:
Bob Lawrence, Broadcast Journalist and Producer

Bio

Bob Lawrence spent twenty years in broadcast journalism, primarily as a TV news anchor, producer, and reporter. He has won awards for both commercial and documentary production. Lawrence has personally interviewed four of the past five U.S. presidents and spent a month in the Persian Gulf. Lawrence's reports have been carried by all three networks and CNN.

Bob and his wife Donna Lawrence operate a video production company with international clients—including one of Mexico's major independent broadcasting, production, and cable companies.

Q: **Has the broadcast industry tried the Web concept of 'narrowcasting'?**

A: For a long time, TV people felt that computers had their place but that television could serve the public interest and make a profit just fine as it was—with limited ownership of facilities that made pictures fly through the air to receivers with twelve reliable channels and a whole bunch of other fuzzy channels called UHF, which few people cared about.

Then came the explosive growth of cable, creating a level playing field for both UHF and VHF stations and providing amazing potential for choice and options. But cable has fallen way short of expectations. When the concept of 'narrowcasting' (programming tailored for specific groups rather than the least common denominator) proved unable to attract sufficient viewership and revenues, most cable channels retreated to the tried and

tested formulas of old movies, sitcom reruns, and new low-budget, hip, titillating shows.

Q: **How is the computer industry reacting to digital TV?**

A: Meanwhile, the computer people, who knew TV could not win in the delivery system race, saw the potential for using coax, phone lines, fiber optics, microwave—anything that will carry digital data—to fulfill the promise that cable made and then broke. But in addition, computers offered one other major enhancement. . . interactivity.

Q: **How will digital TV broadcasting offer more choices?**

A: Digital TV will offer a degree of freedom that no other mass communications form has ever offered. In the future, pontificating anchormen, cock-sure reporters, micromanaging news directors, and omnipotent general managers will have to do something that big money, community influence and TV deregulation have shielded them from doing. They'll actually have to listen to the public.

Q: **How does the government fit into the equation?**

A: This has to make them uncomfortable and you can expect a backlash of proposed regulations, criticisms, and power plays to try to rest this kind of power back from the public. Will they be able to stuff all of the pickles back in the jar? You can bet they'll try because no one gives up power and the resulting money easily.

Q: **Who are making and breaking the rules?**

A: I think the convergence of TV with the Internet will cause significant chaos. Those frequent, rhetorical questions. . . who owns the Internet, who controls it, who regulates it, and who sets the standards are frightening because the answer is always 'nobody'. Can it stay that way? Nothing in the history of human experience has. Meanwhile, the struggle between those who want the Internet to be untamed for freedom's sake, those who want it

to remain untamed for profit's sake, and those who think nothing should escape the tight control of the government and social convention will go on. All we can do is hold on for the ride, learn as fast as we can, and hope the process can be simplified and costs brought down, so the Internet can become a so-called, "big tent" and not the limited resource it is today. The more, the better because the ultimate future of the Web hinges on access for everyone.

Q: **What will come out of the convergence of video and TV on the Web?**

A: The convergence of video production and the Internet is inevitable. It is cyber-Darwinian evolution. Shouting became telegraph. . . telegraph became radio. . . radio became television. . . television becomes digital, and digital becomes. . .??? It is far from over and the people who are now finding their comfort zone in the Internet better not get too comfortable because something else they never imagined will evolve and they'll either embrace it—with all of its uncertainties—or live in denial and be left behind.

13 Who's developing programming for Internet TV?

The technologies of television broadcasting—particularly cable TV—have merged with digital communications on the Internet. The result is an exciting mix of all the technologies and services we have come to rely upon as the telephone, TV, and computer become a single information appliance.

It was inevitable that TV broadcasting—particularly cable TV—and online communications would converge into a new hybrid media. Television shows that link live to the Internet are a model for the future where studio multimedia presentations, recording, production, and distribution of television news, entertainment, and education is spun on the Web. The idea and goal is convergence.

An involved audience can now ask who, what, why, when, where, and how—instead of being told. If education is the key, then a TV talk show format with multimedia performance piped through the Internet is an ideal forum to learn by doing. The solution embraces convergence, context, control, and communication technologies—the four C's.

DigitalTalkTV is the result of a collaboration of talent from complimentary technologies and resources. The logistics are no small undertaking—a production that combines elements of a live news broadcast, TV talk show, and radio interview with a parallel interactive experience on the Web. Each *DigitalTalkTV* show is hosted by Roger Hedgecock, former mayor of San Diego and radio talk show host.

The producers of *DigitalTalkTV*, including Thomas Kihneman, Mike Larsen, Douglas Foxworthy, and Edward J. Keyes, have successfully combined multidimensional hypermedia models with television production methods, techniques, and technology. The result is an entertaining and informative forum where timely topics can be presented, explored, and discussed. The concept and content is original and the shows have been sold into syndication.

Voices from the industry:
Jeff Kelley, DigitalTalkTV

As vice president of technology at DigitalTalkTV, I keep the board members, creators, and producers aware of the daily trends and events to determine the best mix of underlying technology that will support our vision of the future of television. I designed and built the initial web site as a proof-of-concept intended for investors.

The tools we use are traditional broadcast television and Web multicasting features, as limited as they are. Not unlike cable providers offering phone service and the phone service offering movies, TV tuners will become standard PC gear while Internet TV set-top boxes will appear in homes nationwide.

There's a need for quality programming that takes advantage of the potential this technology offers. *DigitalTalkTV* is an evolving model for Web programming of the future. Although for a time, the communications technology may take center stage as the topic of discussion, it will ultimately be the open forum that captures the hearts and minds of the audience.

Bio

Jeff Kelley is a multimedia producer, digital artist, and musician. After graduating from Drake University, Kelley pursued a career in music technology and digital media communications.

http://www.digitalktv.com

DigitalTalkTV is a new breed of broadcast that integrates a live radio talk show with cable TV and the Web.

DTTV has come up with some creative job descriptions and titles for those on their team, including, "Media Jockey," "Cyber Czar," and "Techno Scribe."

Voices from the industry:
Edward J. Keyes, Interactive Producer

Bio

Ed Keyes is Executive Vice President of Inspired Arts Entertainment, co-founder of DigitalTalkTV, and a founder and director of the San Diego Digital Multimedia Association.

Keyes has produced and directed hundreds of video promos, ads, training, marketing and instructional programs. He has taught classes in programming and production, and has helped develop live-action animated educational tools for interactive multimedia products.

A native of New York City, Keyes graduated in 1977 from Holy Cross College in Massachusetts and is currently pursuing a Doctorate degree at USIU in Interactive Multimedia and Instructional Technologies.

Q: **Is it premature to look for work as a content writer for Internet-related TV?**

A: At the present time, searching for work in the content writing field for Internet TV broadcasting business is like trying to convince 19th century society that humans will soon fly! Amusing to some, interesting to many, unbelievable to most—the future of communication and information technologies will by necessity be interactive; it is what we as creatures of continual progress want.

Change occurs slowly in the mass market—it is natural and expected. Early adopters of new technology and methods drive the assimilation. Digital television is inevitable, but it won't look like it does now. It's therefore not unusual to experience massive resistance and snail-paced forward movement. Most of society is comfortable, slightly uneasy with change, willing to experiment (with little risk involved) and utterly skeptical. But, when convinced of something new, hip, and trendy (and often useful!), the human tendency is to embrace it and not return to the old—except in a nostalgic longing for the "good old days." In fact, those who resist so vociferously the new, but later adopt it, tend to hit hardest onto those still struggling—almost as if to say, "C'mon, can'tcha keep up? Get with it!"

Q: **What kind of content will the audience want?**

A: Content for the emerging interactive communications era (and the Internet is only one of many mediums which will reflect and mirror these longings of the mind) will by a natural course of evolution and experimentation, belong to the worlds of exploration and discovery. Humans delight in an environment which compels the mind to investigate and search, but that ultimately rewards the effort.

The reward is particularly interesting—there is a natural desire for recognition and payback for exertions contributed. Folks want something back, even if it's to see their names on the screen, or spoken, or singled out. Content, therefore, should present the information of a business or organization in a way that is almost game-like. The more we can encourage participation and a sense of discovery in a non-threatening playful and supportive manner, the better visitors will feel about the connection with the host (although they may not know why).

There is no scarcity of ideas or potential content for the interactive era. Content will be reconstructed from information in every field, topic, subject matter, lesson plan, and human notion. How it is sculpted, in context, is the key to it being useful, relevant, and reused or recombined with other iterations. It is a non-stop integration of the brilliance of human creativity and innovation— whimsical or drop dead serious.

Q: What adjustments will writers need to make to enter this field?

A: For successful integration of the Internet with interactive television, writers will want to expand their "bird's-eye-view" of the information and stories they write. Imagine the landscape available from the aerie point of view, and writers can build upon this analogy to fashion storylines with multiple paths to the final goal (or episode break).

Always, writers will want to think 'holographically' and in many dimensions, so that the work necessary to process the information (story) is attractive, challenging, and involved. In-depth character histories, relationships, and conflicts add to the broad nature of interactivity. Build pause-points for visitors to choose a direction, make a commitment, or explore a new uncharted area. Expand the story.

Cooperation is an expansive trend—building bridges between complimentary paths and finding common ground between separate goals.

Q: **Will there be an renewed demand for artists and other creative expressionists?**

A: Artists of all kinds will want to understand that in the near future, visitors will want to become 'immersed' into virtual environments, and travel alongside—within and among—the graphics and landscapes of the Internet realities while exploring and interacting with the sites. Artists will do well to reach beyond standard flat art and become familiar with techniques that elevate their work to new multi-dimensional heights. Color and light is constantly changing in these environments—just as in the outer world. Users want to see this organic nature reflected in their virtual worlds.

Q: **What age group will be targeted for the Internet TV audience?**

A: Youngers will always want to push the extremes of style and sound, even just for the experience of creating and identifying something not yet accepted into society. They own it, and stuff it if you don't like it! If Olders do not approve, all the better!

With interactivity, exploration and discovery, it's as if we all cooperate to return to a common ground of connected experience—as when a child learns by touching, that's pure interaction with environment. We've all done it, no exceptions! The next generation of interactive communications will reach out to all ages, perhaps—strangely enough—to Olders more intimately at first. Age becomes less and less significant. Difference in cultures, social standing and ethnicities no longer weigh so heavily. In fact, we'll find an increase in celebration and acceptance of diversity, while strengthening our commonalities and bonds.

Q: **Does growth in this market rely on the availability of high speed Internet connections?**

A: By the time higher bandwidth capability in introduced into homes and businesses (allowing more robust and dynamic interaction along with full screen, real-time, true-motion video, graphics, and animation) there will be a mere percentage of the expected early adopters, cutting edgers, and techno-brilliants on board. Within eighteen months, we'll see the most incredible evolution of interactive Internet integration with virtual, immersive experience for medicine, training, gaming, advertising, research, politics, and education (likely in this general order).

Q: **How can writers position themselves for success in this emerging field?**

A: Writers are the heart and sole (yes, think about it) of interactive multimedia. Nothing of substantive value is created without the glue of story, relationship, scene, open, intro, meat, conflict, resolution, close, and options.

The elements writers bring to the equation are unparalleled in any other field. Independent writers want to remain so, and not be shackled to a company (unless that company is highly evolved, allowing and encouraging the writer to work at different hours, places, and assignments). It is art in its truest form, and must not be restrained or too heavily monitored. But writers must realize that this is also a business, and they must perform on time and come in under budget. Discipline is the key—focused attention and wildly unfettered imagination make for a valuable asset in a writers' team.

Q: **Is the model for interactive business built upon competition or collaboration?**

A: Cooperation and alliances among groups is the model for the next generation of successful interactive business. No one entity shall emerge as the victor; there are no such spoils. The results are organic, malleable, and ethereal. The rewards are infinite, for they connect hearts and minds to one another. There may be no greater joy or purpose—when all is said and done in these lives—than to have acted toward our higher good, to bring together different people in a common task, so that we may all benefit. It can become a springboard for great change in the world. 𝄐

Collaboration is a reductive trend— reducing the number of paths through the convergence of technology and the merger of goals.

What are the most popular programming formats?

Cyber cafés are free-thinking and distinctive haunts where fact trails off into fantasy.

Where do you begin if you are hired to write a script for a netcast, panel discussion, interview, or online moderated chat? A non-fiction script should always prove a point. Depending on the framework chosen, you may use graphics or special effects to drive your point home.

Think of the audience watching the program and visualize them asking, "What's in it for me?" When a writer, a producer, and a viewer or reader can answer that question, positively, the script is marketable.

The goal of writing a commercial non-fiction script may be to close a sale, show the benefits and advantages of whatever idea is being sold or presented. The point of the sale is to sell escape as entertainment, to train, inform, or demonstrate.

Unlike dramatic and fictional scripts which use the single-column, master-scene format, non-fiction scripts are typically written in a two-column format as shown in the sample at the end of Chapter One.

Newscasts

The newscast format enhances credibility. Scripted facts about the client or a product can be discussed in a simulated newscast format on closed-circuit or cable TV which is simulcast or mirrored on the Web.

Actors, professional speakers, and even students can be hired to play the part of the newscast anchorperson. This works well for personal interviews, controversial discussion videos, personal and corporate backgrounders, or any other news magazine format.

The newscast style is similar to an infomercial and can even be used in place of a resumé when applying for jobs where you'll be spotlighted as a trainer or public speaker. The newscast format can be one of the least costly ways to present information for decision-making or to introduce a new personality to the public. The professional broadcaster, perhaps a recent graduate from a speech or broadcasting school, does an "on the scene" editorial to introduce the interviewee and to give a summary at the end of the script.

Some high schools have fully equipped closed-circuit TV studios that are used to teach video production. The studio may be available for a small fee, or you may use the studio of a local public access cable provider or a private videographer who has the necessary equipment.

Video Magazine Format

In a video magazine format, many segments are highlighted with terse interviews and examples of a personality in action on the scene. A video magazine may include several interviews with musicians, singers, personalities in the news, entertain-ers, and business people. It focuses on one segment of the society or one age group and may report on the entertainment, fashion, food, health, and career news for that age group. A good example would be an e-zine for teenage girls who are interested in music, fashion, movies, school, and boys.

The video magazine format is similar to the newscast format with an anchorperson conducting interviews and hosting the show. The style promotes visibility of the person, product, or service featured, and the scriptwriter, as well. A video magazine both publicizes and entertains in a newscast format. The magazine style offers facts with fantasy in a fast-paced action docu-

The cyber café audience wants road-tripping content writers in designer genes who can deliver news in electronically freeze-dried time capsules of emotion.

http://www.hyped.com/index.html

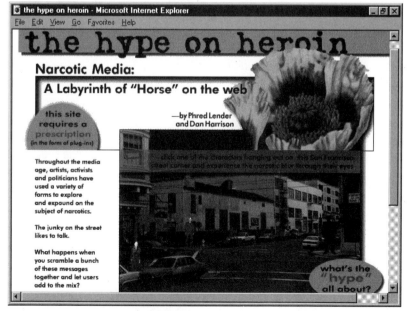

The *hype* is an experiment in multimedia storytelling, produced for "PlanetNews" at San Francisco State University. The piece mixes mainstream and educational media about narcotics with quotes from junkies and random user responses.

The *hype* was produced in 12 weeks by Phred Lender and Dan Harrison for under $100, and nominated as ""Cool Site Script of the Year" by Infi-net—Gala, People, and Apple.

mentary style combined with newscast, lighting, infomercial cut technique, and lots of action. It's primarily entertainment sold as news in the style of shows such as "Prime Time," "Sixty Minutes," "20/20," "48 Hours," and "Real People."

Electronic magazines can be 'webcast' weekly like a TV show or published monthly like a magazine. The production can be supported by paid advertising or made available to users by subscription. Both models are being used on the Web.

In a simulated newscast, interviews are used to both inform and entertain the audience with a variety of visual images. Shows can be designed with statistics and imagery that startles the audience and moves viewers to action.

Avoid using talking heads for more than a brief ten to fifteen seconds. Cut to the visual, music, special effects, or another person at a different location doing something more active. Panel discussions become dull after fifteen seconds.

The average viewer's attention span while watching a single scene in an instructional video is three minutes long. The attention span of an average adult watching a non-fiction video is seven minutes. In a feature film, the average attention span per scene drops to two and one-half

minutes. The average attention span of a child watching cartoon animation is shorter than an adult's, so animation scenes typically run one-half to one minute in length. It's recommended that you avoid long scenes and cut to a new location or change visual images every two to three pages (or minutes) in a script for anyone over twelve years of age.

Stop-Tape Discussions

The stop-tape discussion is good for handling controversial issues or personal experiences shared befor a live audience. The stop-tape discussion format that combines prerecorded matierial with live audience discussion and feedback is frequently used to raise funds for nonprofit organizations. The stop-tape format that combines real-life experience plus discussion also works well with a live audience at a workshop or seminar.

To stage a stop-tape discussion, you must first allow the audience to watch a prerecorded video. Then, stop the video to allow the audience to give their views. The audience may even share their views in a live chat over the Internet.

Next, the audience watches a prerecorded panel of experts give their opinion on video tape. The resulting audience discussion is a reaction to the emotion evoked by viewing the stop-tape discussion.

You may have the issue presented on one tape and the panel members reflecting their opinions on another. First show the controversy, then have recognizable people or experts comment on the controversy. If it's a fund raiser, have a professional panel of experts ask for donations for the worthy cause.

A stop-tape consisting of case histories, a dramatization, and discussion panel travels well around the country. Clubs and schools will use such a tape to stir the live audience into discussion or to raise funds.

Panel Discussions

Whenever a panel is used in a simulated newscast, e-zine, or other format, make the topic one of high controversy with the leading personality in the middle. Choose highly recognizable people for the panel—those who are hot issues in the news.

Keep the panel moving. Never show someone making a blackboard or chalk lecture. Blackboard-style lectures belong on audio tapes and are frequently packaged with a book, software disk, card deck, or board

game. Don't tape a client lecturing as a "talking head" and expect people to get involved—unless the talking head is an avatar.

Interviews

The most effective interviews use timely, startling statistics or events to discuss a point. The producer may hire a professional interviewer, public speaker, or "voice-over person" to interview the client on screen. The scriptwriter may list the questions and also provide alternative questions.

The interview format works well when there's information so new that the media hasn't yet picked up on it. Use testimonials about the person or product that jump off the screen.

Viewers look for recognizable people in an interview. What important facts will be given? Plan the questions in advance and rehearse them before, if possible. However, sometimes a spontaneous reaction is desired with no prior rehearsal to capture a reaction to a controversial question.

Give both the interviewer and the interviewee the list of questions in advance to avoid any hesitation on screen. The interviewer should always be in control of the conversation. During rehearsal, time the Q&A session so the interviewee doesn't leave out important statements.

The interview can be scripted on paper with camera cuts and time allotted for questions. Figure out how long it will take to answer each question and what should be emphasized. Tell the interviewee how long he has to answer before the recording begins.

The interviewee needs to be reminded in advance to keep eye contact with the camera. Have the camera operator cut to the interviewee's face when the interviewer looks down at notes, or vice versa. After the interview is over, make sure to obtain feedback from the interviewer and camera crew.

Montages

Great interviews are peppered with quick cuts called *montages*. A series of visual images, often with musical background, explains the message in a way that no dialogue could do.

As an experiment, turn off the sound while watching a video-based presentation. If you can't follow the logic, then re-arrange the visual images so anyone can tell what's going on without a sound. Does the action still reveal what's going on when the sound is shut off?

Don't use a voice to say what can be shown visually. Set the montages to music using voice-over to show the passage of time. Perhaps the pictures have multiple meanings.

Camera Angles

Scriptwriters frequently write camera shots into the video script for clarity. For example, to emphasize a particular point of view, try a *subjective* camera shot. The point of view is from the camera's eye. The camera sees what's being taped or filmed from one person's (e.g., the hero's) point of view. Use subjective camera whenever you want to enlist a reaction or point of view.

The camera's lens may follow an object at low or near-ground level. To see from a dog's point of view, a trail can be followed from the back door to a bowl of dog chow. That's called the *camera's eye shot*.

Most productions have budgetary or technical restrictions that limit them to a "one-camera" show. However, even a one-camera show—or on the Web, a "no-camera" show can cover a lot of territory. Many producers' budgets are not geared for extravagant special effects. However, today, affordable special effects can be achieved from the desktopusing digital video and animation software.

15 How do you choose questions for an interview?

The best interviews showcase the leading character in a real-life drama. The most compelling articles present different points of view. As a general rule, four people should be quoted for a 2,000-word article or its electronic equivalent.

To begin, first state the problem. Show how it came about, and last, find out who's going to solve the problem. Use dialogue to help the audience experience—rather than read—the story.

Research

To broaden your perspective, fill in the background of the person by interviewing the people around that person. The people in the background who know the person can lead you to the best questions. To begin, go to the Internet and check the local newspaper files. Then broaden your online research through databases to compile information on the scope of your article. Finally, narrow your research to three fresh angles on current news,

history, or the topic of your story. It doesn't matter whether you're writing late-breaking news for an online service, a docudrama for virtual theater, or a training script.

Obtain biographies from everyone you interview, as these will be needed by your publisher's fact-checker. You will need all these references to compile your list of resources. Always keep your notes and audio tapes from interviews. Someone ten years down the line may call you regarding a quote.

Mind Mapping

Rather than simply report from a laundry list of facts, use the technique known as "mind mapping" to uncover the deeper story. Use inner-space imaging to draw a wheel or hexagon to illustrate three different angles of the same story. Rotate the angles in a circle and turn them upside down and from side-to-side. Your goal is to sneak backstage and find the supporting roles hiding behind the obvious story.

One step past Web channeling is innerspace imaging.

Don't expect the public relations people to lead you the deeper story. It simply won't be found in a canned press release. Ask yourself questions before the interview. Then, find the spokesperson who leads you to the deepest angle. Often, the tangents they embark upon will be more important than the original story. Each spinoff can then be developed and sold as a different piece. The surface of the story is only one article. Dig deeper to find the serial saga, novel, play, or virtual docudrama. Flesh out the sidebars into new stories and articles.

Keep moving out in a circle like the ripples in a pond to find more background interviews that can be developed into new articles. Then, shift your focus. That's how my article on fish ponds spun off into an article about building topiaries, which in turn, circled outwards into more interviews with people who started a variety of outdoor backyard businesses. Work your way around the perimeter of your mind-map circle. After you've interviewed people who are involved in what you are writing about, then interview those indirectly affected or changed by the outcome.

You may begin by writing about how the job market has changed as a result of the Internet. . . which in turn, spins off an article about how distance education courses help train corporate employees to write better business communications. . . which spins off an article about how publishers using interactive training to teach employees with low reading levels. . . which may uncover a new trend in education—novels for adults with first-to-third grade reading levels. . . and so on.

Back up your interviews with statistics. If you're writing about swing shifts, get the statistics on how the domestic violence rate goes up every time spouses are shifted from working nights one day to working days the next few days, or how the substance abuse rate goes up when employees are shifted back and forth between working nights and days.

Let the spinoff subjects whet your curiosity. Interview volunteers and people in career transition to find out what it's like to search for a job in multimedia when you're coming from a screenwriting background or what it's like to go back to school in mid-career to learn the new media.

The range of experiences is wide. How do they cope, live, and go beyond coping to find fulfillment in their career search? Ask those whom you interview to connect you with others who may see a different angle of the subject. Then, ask those people for the names of still other people to interview. Try not to miss anything that may be of value.

Ask for the names of professionals who deal with similar situations. Look for diverse views and opposite agendas. After you have interviewed the experts, interview those who disagree with them. Interview introverts who look inside for depth and extroverts who hunger for external feedback.

E-mail Interviews

An e-mail interview may provide more facts that a phone interview which can easily become social or limited by time constraints. E-mail interviews are often full of important ideas, points of view, and facts that you won't find in an off-the-cuff, superficial phone conversation. The interviewee uses a different thought process when writing and it's also cheaper than a phone call. After the e-mail interview, follow-up by phone to ask more in-depth questions. Then, give the person time to respond. An introverted person may prefer to respond by e-mail so they can think through what they want you to put into print, whereas, extroverts think as they talk. Give the introverted interviewee the time needed to pause and write out the interview and answer questions when not under pressure to perform.

After conducting the series of interviews, you'll find the real story to be a human experience resulting from an external event—whether it's a trauma or joyous celebration. Use your mind-map circle to get to the real story.

An introverted person will interview differently than one who is extroverted. As introverts seek the cause, extroverts will more often seek the story behind the scenes and create spinoffs based on the divergent interviews from people who are seemingly unrelated to the topic. The extrovert may then try to converge the tangent interviews into one topic. Introverts are more likely to work from inside out, creating the spinoffs first, and interviewing fewer people with the goal of drawing together divergent anecdotes into seemingly related topics.

Key words for introverts:
1. *Depth*
2. *Vertical*

Key words for extroverts:
1. *Breadth*
2. *Lateral*

*Quotes belong
in time capsules—
they are the promise of
premise.*

The introvert will look for what each person expresses differently—whether it's fear, love, joy, or anger. Extroverts write about the saga of rebuilding lives from the outside inwards.

An introvert may write an investigative piece on what caused the event, focusing on the cause, testing its values, and looking for contradictory answers. Extroverts seek innuendo and the tone of voice in the interviewee, expanding their questions to cover the expanding circle of contacts and spinoffs of the original story.

Be careful not to water-down your original story. The more expansive the story is, the weaker it becomes. Interview only those who know what they are talking about before you interview your lead characters or interviewees. That way, you'll learn about the subject and be able to compose relevant questions on a topic for which you have not been trained.

Having a clearly-defined premise is every bit as important to writers of nonfiction material as it is to storytellers and screenwriters. Your original premise should remain stable and in focus as your list of questions and people to be interviewed expands.

If your interviewee refuses to talk on the record, go to the public records. If your questions are good, you'll find someone who is willing to talk. Trace your story to its causes. When people tell you the same thing, follow up on that repetition to its core. File your statistics by separate subject categories.

Let the story marinate for a few days. Make a list of quotes that support each of your most important points or causes and expand them. List the quotes in order of how critical or important they are to the story. It may help to color code your quotes in your word processor according to their value.

Use facts to support the quotes. Put your most powerful quotes first to accommodate those who skim the article. Then, run bridges between your quotes to smooth out the transitions.

Go backstage and get behind the scenes. The real story is lying there somewhere on the fringes, in the margins, and on the cutting edges of technology.

Voices from the industry:
Lynn O'Shaughnessy, Freelance Writer

Q: **How did you get the assignment to write content for Time Life Medical?**

A: I found it through the Journalism Forum on CompuServe. I try to check the job listings in the Journalism Forum at least once a week. Most of the time, the online and print jobs aren't worth applying for—the pay is minimal. But every once in awhile I find a gem like this one. I was hired to help convert two Time Life Medical videos on pregnancy and colorectal cancer into a form suitable for the Internet. You can find the videos in just about any pharmacy. The Internet project should be online during the first quarter of 1997.

Q: **How does writing for an interactive publication differ from writing for print?**

A: You have to think in more than one dimension. I had to decide where the graphics and photographs that Time Life Medical had prepared should go. I also had to provide links to different sites in the material.

For instance, if I mentioned 'trimester' in the pregnancy text, I needed to link that term to the glossary I had written. The type of people who will read educational materials on the Net is also more sophisticated than your typical newspaper or magazine audience. I'm not sure if it was reflected in my copy, but I think you can present materials on the Net on a slightly more sophisticated level.

Q: **What existing skills were required and what new skills did you acquire?**

A: The editor in New York who called me with the assignment said he was really attracted to my writing samples. He liked the way I could write about health without getting bogged down in medical language. So I guess it was my eighteen years of experience as a newspaper reporter—the last six and a half years at the *Los Angeles Times*—and then as a magazine freelancer that helped me land the job. I needed to learn minimal

Bio

Lynn O'Shaughnessy spent twelve years of her career as a newspaper reporter. Since 1991, she has been a freelancer writer for national magazines and a copywriter for financial businesses. As a new media journalist, Lynn has written online content for *WOW!* and Time Life Medical.

HTML skills and I was flown to New York for a one-day orientation.

Q: **Was there any technical experience in your background to help you land this assignment?**

A: From 1984 to 1990, I was a reporter with the *Los Angeles Times*. Since then I have written primarily about health and personal finance as a freelancer for national magazines. My only other online experience came when I wrote dozens of articles on mutual funds for WOW! (CompuServe just announced it was shutting WOW! down.)

Q: **What advice can you offer to writers who want to reposition their careers for the new media?**

A: First, don't assume that you aren't qualified to write for the new media because you have little or no experience at it. Hardly anybody does. Since it's such a new field, people in need of writers are having to look to professionals with expertise in traditional media.

To find jobs, I'd suggest checking out the many appeals for

writers that you'll find on the Internet and to network online. The leads you find and the contacts you make could be invaluable.

While the experience was great, the story didn't have a completely happy ending. I never received my final payment for the work I did on the colorectal project.

As it turns out, the Time Life Medical videos were not produced by Time Warner, the parent company of Time Life. For the first time in its corporate history, Time Warner had sold the use of its brand name— Time Life—to an outside company. This company, Patient Education Media, Inc., incurred millions of dollars in debt when the original videotapes did not sell. Alarmed, Time Warner pulled its backing and its permission to use its brand name in December, 1996. Without the Time Life name, the venture collapsed. About ten freelancers were owed money when the project ended. Many of us are now suing Time Warner in small claims court. 🐊

16 Can previously published material be repurposed?

When adapting a story from a book or a news page to the new media format, you should ask the same six reporter's questions that every first year journalism student is taught in order to write a news article: Who? What? Where? When? Why? and How?

- **Who** did this happen to?

- **What** startling events occurred?

- **Where** did it take place? Can the story be told within a reasonable budget and made in a single location with few characters? Can it be adapted to the stage or virtual theatre? Can it be filmed at home or abroad?

- **When** did it happen? It should be contemporary, because most producers don't have budgets to recreate the past, except for public television.

- **Why** did this event occur? Answering the reasons why it happened will expose a premise, a plot, and a structure within the story.

- **How** are the events portrayed?

Some sensational story lines may ask startling questions such as: Were you abducted by a UFO and impregnated with an alien child? Perhaps this story tells the world that aliens are real and the CIA has planted disinformation. Why? Why should anyone be interested in this story?

The answer is, because it contains a universal message that is every adolescent's story of growing up. Or the story may be one of every working woman's experience of climbing the corporate ladder and fighting stereotypes. To be marketable, an adaptation must answer these basic questions and at the same time offer a fresh news angle on a unique and universal story.

You may remember seeing a feature article in the newspaper that you think a producer might consider. How do you get the rights to a story that has been covered in the news? Before writing the script, the writer should always obtain a letter of permission from the individual or family involved. You may discover that they are happy to be tell their story, or on the other hand, they may want to preserve their privacy. Here is where you need the legal advice of an entertainment attorney to be sure you're not mentioning the names of real people in a story without their written permission.

Material for adaptation might come from unpublished manuscripts, tapes, or diaries of retired investigators, soldiers, commandos, police, and foreign agents. Perhaps a story based on a unique and controversial issue in the news will have enough commercial value to become a feature film or documentary.

Take the story about the Jewish woman from Brooklyn who married an Arab Moslem from the Middle East. She married him because the Arabs and Jews are historical cousins and she said she wanted to make peace in the Middle East, starting at the family level.

Five years and two children later, the marriage goes sour and the father takes the children out of the country to be raised by a grandparent in the fundamentalist Islamic tradition. Without the financial means and political influence necessary to pursue them, the mother is unable to kidnap the children back. So, twenty years go by without com-munication between the mother and her children—until they show up on her doorstep demanding college tuition and housing that she can't afford. The plot is hot and contemporary. It's an issue in the news. It's a true story.

There have been many movies like this made from true stories, either from personal accounts, newsclippings, or novels sometimes written by the person to whom the adventure or experience happened. The State Department has interesting true stories and case histories on file that are ripe for adaptation.

What if the writer is unable to gain rights to the story? One answer is to create *faction*—fiction that is based upon facts. You can still have a hot script based on a true story, but the facts have been fictionalized.

You may not want anything you write to be related to the real story in any way. However, you do want to drive the point of the story home.

The possibilities for dramatic conflict and subplots are as endless as the stories in the news. Focus most of all on the structure of a drama or true-life story. Some stories are so bizarre, they can only be true.

A Factionalized Story

Shackled by a Sheik

by Anne Hart

At dawn I rose on October 25, 1963 to see the salmon slit that ripped the East. My eyes were weary, but the day had to begin. Above, a jet cracked the sky, leaving a feathery trail of scattering wisps of smoke. These clouds soon parted. And by the time the sun melted into the hot winds and its streams radiated to push the thermometer up to 120 degrees, I had packed and unfolded the first flaps of tent to start the new day.

I had been visiting my mother-in-law, a Bedouin woman, one of three wives of a local Saudi-Arabian sheik. Her name is Amina. Amina, innocent as Eden. This was my first day in Arabia as the Norwegian-American wife of a Bedouin sheik. I emerged to squint at the rocky landscape and high stone tenements down the path. Around me pilgrims thronged--wearing their white djellaba and turbans or long, flowing robes and headdresses wound with goat's hair and gold tinsel thread. "La, Ahlaha, Ahlah, la ("There is no God but Allah") is followed by "Alla ou Akbar, ou Akbar Allah ("God is greater") translated by modern Saudi teenagers as "God is the greatest." The shouts were loud enough to awaken even the soundest sleeper.

Do you have a story that could be re-purposed and adapted as an interactive, episodic, streaming media adventure on the Web? This article by Anne Hart was originally published in 1967 by *Saturday Review Magazine*. That article, "On Being a Sheik's Wife," was written under the author's pen name "Anne Shammout."

The streets in Ridyadh, Saudi's capital, are filled with taxis, Fords, all kinds of diesel trucks, buses, Cadillacs, and donkeys. I preferred the donkey-cart, a wedding present from by my brother-in-law, ten-year-old Faruk.

My husband was one of many Arabs who quit secondary school at fifteen to go to work in West German factories as a machinist. After six years he came to the United States on a 60-day visa. Making up the lie that he was an engineer with a job, he talked me into marrying him within six weeks of our meeting at a foreign student dance at a New York YMCA. He looked like Omar Sharif and told me he would take me around the world. I was only twenty-one at the time and became pregnant within a few months. Soon we had two children--a girl and boy.

My mother-in-law was at the airport to greet me when I stepped off the plane, dressed in shocking chartreuse pumps and gloves, a white linen suit and wide-brimmed hat. Mother Amina, and her two younger wife-sisters, Hamdia and Su'ad, kissed me and my children and slung gold bracelets on my arms and pushed a horde of rings on all of my fingers with squeals of "ya aini, ya rouhi ("my eye, my soul"). My father-in-law greeted me with "Ya binty, ya noor el ain" ("My daughter, the light of my eyes"). All twenty-two brothers-in-law were present to kiss me on the hand and touch my hand to their forehead, gently murmuring, "achteck" (sister). O "nightingale of Norway, "salamoo aleikum." I replied, "Wa' aleikum ou slaam," returning their welcoming-home greetings. Then they kissed my son and daughter.

Master-Mama Amina strode forth with a gleam in her dark, oval eyes and patted me gently on the shoulder. "We are making a wedding for you now, Arab style. It is to begin tomorrow at 4 o'clock." We were to be wed and feasted over again in a proper Moslem Arab ceremony.

Arab wives are young at marriage, usually twelve to fifteen years old. The most common statement I heard was that a girl was married at thirteen, a mother at fourteen, and a grandma at twenty-nine, a great grandma at forty-four, and a great-great grandma at sixty or less. Child marriages are fairly common, although the U.N. Commission on Human Rights had asked that fifteen be the minimum age for marriage in the world. All my female in-laws were married between the ages of thirteen and sixteen.

This contrasts with the age of thirty-six for my Norwegian/Icelandic mother and forty-seven for my father, after both obtained their Ph.D's in plasma physics. I was born when my mother was thirty-eight.

Arabs constantly protest that girls are ready for marriage at twelve or thirteen, although boys can marry in their middle twenties. Dating and courtship are unknown, since the parents arrange a marriage between cousins, usually when the girl reaches puberty. How this elimi- nates the stress of competition, wallflowers, and frantic beauty surgery that we have in the West--but it shortens a woman's life through continuous pregnancies and nursing.

In this hot land, the temperature at night stood around 90 degrees, so there was little activity. We sat and talked about our children as in any small American town. What I missed most was not having a supportive family of my own--from my own culture. I was always an "outsider" and it was the family against my individual rights. The family was all--a universe unto itself.

Those of us who read, read. We ate and folded clothing and used our fine motor coordination to do needle work. Our lives were stitched in tiny golden petals on lacy pillows, fringed and perfumed. Most of us could read at least the Koran. We prayed, too, like the men, only separately.

The Koran says, "If a wife disobeys you, beat her and send her to rooms apart." We shed our shoes and donned comfortable robes and sipped tea and laughed about babies. And when it was late and the moon transfixed its silvery fangs on the balcony, the women departed together, and then the men, and they closed with: "Peace be with you, our family, be yours: God grant you life." I replied, "And with you, my family, be peace!"

I passed my wedding night silently at home with the women, preparing a trousseau, folding and partaking of baklava pastry, coffee, nuts, and honey dip.

After the festivities, a small Moslem ceremony united bride and groom. I remember writing in

my diary on my honeymoon the words, "Tonight I
died."

From a distance, on a balcony of the women's
quarters, I looked down and whipped out my pen
and notebook and scribbled a poem which just
had to be born:

> Down Sa'a's snake-rimmed breasts
> Burst ripe chestnut locks,
> Innocent as Eden and just as moot.
> Men still toss money, but I will throw rocks;
> War has sapped and cankered my root.
> She draws her own blood as part of the act,
> And each man views the other with mistrust.
> From her ruby navel poems contract.
> In labor Shakespeare settles to brown dust.
> Then, under nutmeg's banner visions waft.
> Impurities cover smiles like dead bones.
> She rips her skirt to show how she is cleft
> Like the hoof of the devil crushed by stones.

Finally, when the wedding drew to a close, in the
henna glow of dawn on the fourth day, we left the
whirling dervishes and returned to the tenement Mama
owned but lived in only occasionally. We slept
through the heat of the day in separate rooms. The
Arab comes alive only at sunset when the heat begins
to settle.

In ancient Egypt,
a smart woman was a
toot (owl).

In ancient cultures, the
wedding ring sybolized the
rope that bound the bride's
wrists as well as the circu-
lar rhythm of nature.

At dusk the cry, "Salat, Salat"--prayer time--
was echoed through the winding alleys as a
green-turbaned policeman thumped on windows to
be closed for the sunset prayers. So ended a
typical day in the life of an American wife of
a Bedouin sheik. Outside waves of sand lapped
at the shores of my city and wind-whipped
sculptures stood in the desert contemplating
nature's dappling. Once I sought art in the
aristocracy of museums. I now gazed on the rare
simplicity of the clay and stone folk.

Ten years later, I found myself divorced and
alone. The children were now in the custody of
my ex-husband. Under Arab custom, the children
and money, property and moral support go to the
husband. I lost everything and gained only
seven years experience as a battered wife.

It was then that I decided to become a poetry
therapist. As a poetry therapist, my mascot has
gone from hare to owl. As a battered wife I was
like the rabbit. In nature's order of things,
predators, and warm-blooded predators in particular, are a distinct minority. There are
many more rabbits than there are wise old owls.

# # #

CHAPTER THREE

Adapting to the New Media

*T*he new media demands writers with scriptwriting skills because writing for the new media is scriptwriting—whether you are writing interactive articles, how-to books for CD-ROM, or commercial autobiographies.

The ultimate purpose of a script is to "close a sale"—just as if you were selling a product or service. However, the point of this sale may be to train, inform, or demonstrate. You may be trying to 'sell' an idea. Regardless of what you're selling, your script must be a story worth telling, worth listening to, and worth buying. Scriptwriting and screenwriting are all about human action and reaction.

If you don't like the idea that a print journalist should study scriptwriting to improve the chances of finding work in the expansive new media,

then think again. Consider the big picture. Journalists and other writers—especially those who consider themselves to be creative nonfiction writers—will find more openings in the field of digital media if they understand the basics of good story structure. To choose your media is to choose your weapon and come out broadcasting on the Net. It will go far before returning full circle.

In this chapter, we will examine some of the techniques used by scriptwriters and screenwriters to construct and refine a story. These strategies will help you adapt any book, novel, article, event, or story to a script or screenplay for any media—old or new. After you understand the basics of writing a linear scriptwriting, you will be ready to break all the rules and write a three-dimensional nonlinear script for an interactive story.

The bottom line is that a writer may wear many hats in the new media. You're no longer only a journalist—you're a scriptwriter, too.

17 Why should I learn scriptwriting?

Scriptwriting is a verbal art, whereas writing news is verbal mechanics.

As dailies downsize and companies merge, journalism and English major graduates are finding fewer job openings in the traditional print media. At the same time, more jobs are opening in the new media for content writers, editors, Web site designers, and administrators. The journalism graduate who can create an HTML document for an interactive newspaper has a better chance of being hired—and at a higher salary—than the journalism graduate with no new media skills. Journalists are doing everything from designing training materials to writing interactive scripts for electronic publications.

Your background may include journalism, corporate communications, advertising, public relations, and even video and film production. You may have majored in English with an emphasis on nonfiction, essay writing, or fiction and poetry. However, writing for the new media requires a hybrid mix of these skills that have been traditionally segregated into different schools of thought.

In the past, more professional opportunities may have been found by working within one organization and moving vertically up the corporate or educational ladder. However today, the new media allows you to combine your skills and transfer laterally as a horizontal expression of your vertical desire.

Writers are scrambling for jobs in PC wire news, Internet audio, and in the entertainment/edutainment industry. Teachers, librarians, and journalists today compete for the same content writing jobs in educational technology. There are unlimited opportunities for scriptwriters who create the industrial and training films and videos used for immersive simulated training.

The writer's profession has become a hot-linked how-to experience written in frames and screens. The bottom line is that writers wear many hats in the new media. You're no longer strictly a journalist reporting the news—you're a creative scriptwriter, too.

Voices from the industry:
Aaron Heinrich, Vice President, McQUARTERGROUP

Q: **What skills will writers need to succeed in the new media?**

A: There is—and hopefully always will be—a need for people to write effectively. A compelling story doesn't become less so just because it's on the Web and the Web doesn't make a noncompelling story any more so.

The new media isn't changing the need to be concise and informative in the messages you deliver on behalf of the client. Since most companies post their press releases verbatim to their web sites, the traditional execution of press releases and related materials is still relevant. However, the Web is still the purview of programmers and graphic designers. Until the Web becomes driven by content rather than hype, the role of the true writer will be practically nil.

Interactive CD-ROMs and DVD presents a whole different opportunity and group of necessities. I believe it is extremely important for writers to be familiar (notice I did not say expert) with a variety of graphic software. This includes Macromedia Director, Adobe Photoshop, Illustrator, etc. These are all tools being used to create the interactive content that may eventually end up on the Web or some iteration thereof.

Traditional storytelling (with a beginning, middle and end) will still be a necessary skill, but it will become equally important to develop and convey a plethora of variations of the middle and end. Very linear writers will have a difficult time of it. But writers who enjoy constantly asking themselves "what if. . . " and who don't abhor the rewrite process will find themselves better off with the various new media.

Bio

Aaron Heinrich is Vice President and General Manager of Public Relations for the McQUERTERGROUP—San Diego's largest high tech advertising and public relations agency.

Heinrich is also a free-lance writer with an undergraduate degree in journalism from Arizona State University and a graduate degree in screenwriting from the University of Southern California.

18 How do you begin a scriptwriting project?

The virtual casting couch features avatars applying for screen tests of the imagination.

Your project may be to adapt an existing story into a format suitable for CD-ROM or for serialization on the Web. The producer may ask for a specific genre, or the writer may scan the market to select the genre that is popular at the moment. A premise is written, then a one-page synopsis, then a treatment of fifteen pages, then an outline of forty-five pages, then a script of 90 or 120 pages. Each page in the script represents approximately one minute of screen time.

The premise and plot are then summed up in a single, short sentence. This is called a *high concept*.

Ask how the story will benefit the audience. Don't tell the audience or producer what the script will do for the writer. Show the benefits.

What makes a great story commercial? What makes characters charismatic? Ninety percent of all writing for print, video, and film involves psychology—writing to the type and temperament of the audience. An ideal script, one most likely to sell, is one in which the story shows a range of change or personal

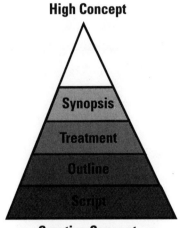

High Concept

Synopsis

Treatment

Outline

Script

<—Creative Concept—>

growth in the characters. Write each character according to a specific personality type and temperament. This will help you portray the larger patterns in society. Whatever is concrete is universal. Shift to the right hemisphere of the brain. Write dialogue in caricature to be visual.

Then, separate the high concept from the broader, whole-story-based creative concept. The creative concept is like an all-encompassing net that catches the important events of the story. Think of your creative concept as a Native American dream catcher with feathers and beads woven into the memories and facets of your story.

19 How can I give my story commercial appeal?

One of the best ways to give your story commercial appeal is to study the work of professional script and screenwriters. There are many tried-and-true formulas and techniques that can be applied to your writing for the new media.

Here's a simple formula that will help the audience become emotionally involved in the journey of your story:

1. Start out on a positive note.

2. Sweep the audience to a negative place. Use startling facts or statistics to give your sources credibility and visibility.

3. Finish by bringing the audience back to a positive place—not the starting point, but a better place where they feel important, empowered, and good about themselves. Leave them a step higher in mood than when they started the journey. Every script is a journey and the final scene should "close the sale."

Building Frameworks

A framework provides a platform for the inner mechanism of your story or presentation. The story becomes a structure of carefully selected frameworks, edited, and dove-tailed together like bridges that lead from the beginning to the end.

A single script may incorporate several frameworks, including streaming audio narration, animation with voice-over, and montage. Other often-used frameworks—including comedy and drama—can be applied to new media presentations, as well.

The frameworks may vary from one category of facts or segment of the story to the next. In a documentary-style biography, you might include simple animation, back-lit negatives, artwork, photos, or a narration to bridge the transitions. The completed project should flow like one piece of cloth with no seams or hanging threads—like liquid, visual music. Using a varied selection of frameworks will help keep the attention of the audience and give the writer more options to set up a mighty conclusion.

Be sure the frameworks don't overpower the information with too vivid an impact. You want the audience to remember the benefits derived from the information rather than the device that was used to present the material. The viewer will remember the message if it isn't overpowered by a special effect or personality.

The Audience Setup

To smooth the transition between scenes, there must be a logical reason for what will come in the following scene. The audience set-up incident is a commercial and excellent technique for bridging scenes.

For example, if one character does something that comes as a surprise, set up the audience with a visual clue in the preceding scene. Show a logical reason why the event in the next scene should happen. Give a preview. It's all right to throw in a surprise, but the surprise or new clue must be believable. The audience should be prepared or set up to learn the new fact.

Using Sight and Sound

It is also important to determine whether your new media application is to be sound- or visually-oriented. On the Web, the trend is moving away from stone-silent HTML-based presentations toward online productions with streaming audio and video.

Today's verbally-oriented text-based Web sites offer information that enables viewers to make intelligent decisions about a product or service. This approach works on the left hemisphere of the brain—the logical, analytical, decision-making side that seeks verbal information. The ultimate purpose of a sound-oriented or verbal presentation is to persuade, to inform, to warn, to obtain feedback, or to close a sale.

Visually-oriented presentations, on the other hand, rely on symbolism and metaphor rather than facts. A visually-oriented script is there to entertain, evoke emotions, and imprint the imagery on a viewer's brain to be recalled later.

Visually-oriented scripts work on the right hemisphere of the brain which controls emotions and imagery—the same place where advertisers imbed subliminals and where art forms evoke feeling.

Writing in Caricature

In the same way that an artist draws a face in caricature to produce a cartoon, you may write in caricature with sly, adult wit to present a point, message, or demonstration in a humorous script. Writing in caricature—or in a different voice—gets attention and makes an impact.

To write great dialogue, you must learn to write in caricature. This means selecting the highlights and details of the personality exuded from each character and bringing forth their charisma, their exaggerated stereotypes, their animated exuberance, and above all, their concrete details pulled out of the abstract concepts. You must pare down to bare bones the most important point you want your character to say.

The reason why so many thousands of TV and film viewers, radio listeners, and computer game players can remember the jingles to commercials so easily is because of the power of caricature in copy writing and scriptwriting. You use the exaggerated or ludicrous to get to the abstract, and you use the concrete detail to reach the universal—that which applies to all of us.

It's a pas-de-deux, a two-step dance between the speaker and listener. Writing in caricature is the essence of great dialogue writing. No one did it better than William Shakespeare, who was a master of writing dialogue in caricature.

As your audience experiences the script during its performance, your writing will leap from two-dimensional text to the three-dimensional world of your audience's imagination. As you write this way, fit your dialogue into imaginary dialogue bubbles above the heads of your characters. they begin to vibrate with charisma. The goal is to give each character the ability to influence, charm, inspire, motivate, and help the audience feel important.

Using Humor

The more important you make the audience feel, the better chance humor has of conveying a message of value. You may use carefully chosen humor with serious topics to hold the attention of the audience and to prevent the material from become too dry, abstract, or technical. Humor works well when it reveals pitfalls to be avoided. Your ability to make an audience laugh will increase the marketability of your script.

Humor teaches hindsight— the best framework is one's peer group caricatured online.

Using Drama

Drama is one of the best frameworks to use for non-fiction and instructional scripts—however difficult to do well. To incorporate drama into a non-fiction script, include a story with subplots framed like those in one of the fiction genres such as romantic comedy, adventure, mystery, or suspense.

Ask how the inner mechanisms work. Are facts readily available? Or does the script allow the leading character or narrator to share only one experience as an interlude of inserted drama in a training video? Educational scripts, sales demonstrations, documentaries, and children's programming can all benefit from contrasts shown between the frameworks of dramatization, re-enactments, and demonstration.

Choosing a Marketable Topic

If you're looking for a marketable topic, try writing a collection of case histories with a point that leads to a universal application that all businesses in that industry find valuable. Case histories sell to trade magazines. The trade magazine video and new media script is dramatically increasing as videoconferencing grows more popular. Networking, really working a room

of corporate case histories is excellent material to write and sell a first script in the case where nobody hires you as a beginner, to write a script before they see what you can do first.

Of all the topics that could waste your time, the least likely to remain on your shelf are timely case histories applied to lessons of hindsight, forecasting, and advice of pitfalls to avoid and strategies or tips to show how a group of entrepreneurs share "lessons learned" with those about to open their first business in a niche industry.

A good script will take the concrete detail and show how to arrive at the universal application. You may use this concept to write a premise in less than ten words. Write a springboard of two pages to outline your point with more detail—and finally, a formal outline that tells the beginning, middle, and end of your story.

Whether the story is based on truth or imagination doesn't change its purpose of empowering the audience to make better decisions from timely information. Put the prophet in the profit, the retail in the detail, and the good in the "should."

Here's how to:
Adapt to the 'old' media

Here's how to adapt any book, novel, story, news article, comic book, tape recording, popular-song lyric, stage play, or biography from its original format into a ninety-minute script or two-hour screenplay.

1. Organize your notes.

If you don't have a computer, you will need a looseleaf binder and a package of notebook paper (200 sheets will do). With a colored marker, number the first 55 sheets from 1 to 55. Place these numbered sheets into the binder. These sheets correspond to the 55 scenes in a feature film.

Starting at the beginning of the notebook, insert two blank pages behind each numbered page until you have 55 sets of three pages. Each set will become one scene from your script. Each scene will be approximately 2 1/2 pages long, but not necessarily of equal length. Some scenes may be only half a page, while others scenes will be one, two, or even three pages long. The ideal scene length is 2 1/2 pages.

On these blank pages you may glue or tape the scenes—or, if you're working on a word processor, you may type them in. Do whatever works. However you do it, you should come out with a 90- to 120-page script, depending on your choice of format. Although you may prefer to do this work on a computer, it's still a good idea to keep a hardcopy notebook of your work in progress.

2. Summarize the story.

Sort the timely and important facts into the introduction, middle, and ending. (The introduction will look a lot like the final scene at the end.)

The techniques described in this section were adapted from *The Screenwriter's Workbook* by Syd Field. Copyright © 1988 by Syd Field. Used by permission of Delacorte Press, a division of Bantam Doubleday Dell Publishing Group, Inc.

3. Identify the major events.

Pick the twelve most important events in the original format. List them as the highlights, emphasizing the most important scenes. Each event is a stepping stone to the most important goal. List them. These will later form the basis of the script.

Make the individual events so universal that the viewer won't ask whether the script appeals to the masses. They are stepping stones to the path to be taken—or not taken. Think of an adaptation from a book to a screenplay as covering twelve events of the hero's life that the writer considers to be important. In a biography, the major events can correspond to the transition points of life. In a true-life adventure, they could correspond to the natural sequence of events that takes place. The duration between the stages of life, in turn, can be tied to the five turning points of the story.

1. Infancy

2. Childhood

3. Teen Years

4. Young Adulthood

5. Mid-life

6. Maturity

Be careful not to write an episodic script of unrelated events that can't be smoothly strung together. Avoid a "string-of-pearls" story where the previous scene has no relation to the one that follows. Create smooth transitions, like liquid visual music, that logically relate one event to another.

With a long story, you may start by writing song lyrics in twelve stanzas about the most important point or message in the story. Then, expand the song lyrics into a script. The act of tightening the 100,000-page book into a page of song lyrics focuses the highlights of the plot on what will happen in the three acts.

4. Form a creative concept.

Study books that have become scripts and also popular song lyrics that have evolved from scripts. Then, form the *creative concept*. The creative concept is the basic framework like an umbrella that encompasses all the important events of the story. The creative concept holds the audience's attention. It's the hooking device.

5. Summarize the highlights.

Summarize each highlight into a premise of a single paragraph that tells it all in a nutshell.

6. Divide the story into three acts.

Divide the paragraphs into Acts I, II, and III. The story, which was previously organized by chapter, is now arranged by event and act.

Script	120pp	90pp
Act I	1	1
Act II	25	45
Act III	90	75

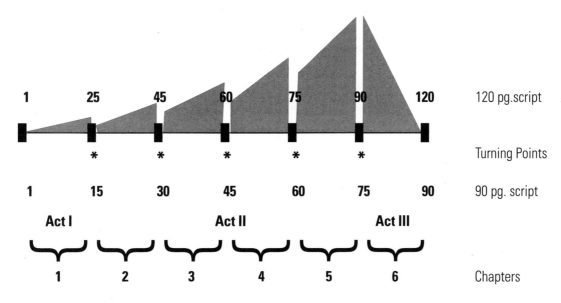

7. Identify five major turning points in the story.

Color-code the paragraph at each turning point.

In a 90-page script, the significant events will be scaled back thirty pages because the script ends sooner. In a 120-page screenplay, Act III begins on page 90. The resolution of the conflict and quick ending appears by page 120, leaving pages 90 to 120 to work on the outcome.

8. Divide the story into six parts.

Divide the story into six parts, or chapters, separated by the five major turning points in the story.

9. Write the premise.

Make the first chapter (which is an expanded hook) into the premise. The protagonist, the hero, heroine, or best character will be introduced in the first act. Then work in the protagonist's allies. In the second scene of the first act, develop an important point about the antagonist and his allies.

10. Pinpoint the significant events.

From these main parts of the story, lay out the twelve most important events. These can be pinned up on a cork bulletin board or highlighted with a marker. At each turning point in the story, another crisis will happen that propels the action forward in another direction.

11. Summarize each chapter.

Write a paragraph summary of each chapter. The following examples are based on a 120-page screenplay.

- Paragraph #1 (pp. 1-24)

  The premise tells the plot and introduces the hero. A critical situation is in motion. The hero and heroine are attracted to each other. Or some crisis occurs. Suspense begins to build.

  Conflict and physical attraction create crises at the cliff hanger on page 25-27 that spins the action forward in a new direction. Layer in the physical background. Draw storyboards to visualize the action scenes. Write the visuals first. The dialogue will come later.

- Paragraph # 2 (pp. 25-44)

Continue the hook and develop the critical situation further. Develop the hero's own moral code based on the hero's type and temperament. Use strong suspense or strong sexual tension depending on genre—action or love story—or both.

Bring in the subplot and the antagonist's strengths, but don't give too much information yet. Foreshadow the crisis to come by giving clues to the antagonist's allies. End with a cliff hanger to move the action further, faster, with each new crisis.

- Paragraph #3 (pp. 45-59)

Enter the antagonist and all his allies. Tell how the antagonist comes into conflict with the protagonist for equal goals. What or who does the antagonist hate and why? What does the antagonist do?

Introduce a whopper of a new event. It could be a big fight, adventure, or sexy love scene. Call into question whether the hero will be able to reach his goal due to the strong resistance, combat, or opposition from the antagonist and betrayal by his own allies.

If the goal will ultimately be attained at the end, then make the goal more impossible to reach than ever. The hero withdraws from the heroine. Success withdraws at this point.

- Paragraph #4 (pp. 60-74)

What does the protagonist do to take action against the antagonist? What adventure does the hero embark upon and what happens on this excursion or experience? The action can be either internal or external. What happens when the hero finally reaches the destination? What happens to the hero's allies? How does the hero lead the allies?

Page 60 is the midpoint in the script and where the background, suspense, and relationship conflicts increase to the breaking point. This would be an opportunity to use a flashback or a time travel sequence in *one surprise scene* only. However, the majority of commercial linear scripts do not use flashback because it fails to move the action forward. Producers often reject scripts with flashback due to the increased production costs and the interruption in the plot that slows down the story.

The trend is for tightly written, shorter scripts where the suspense increases as the countdown grows more intense as the deadline approaches. The hero's goal is to squeeze every challenge out of life in the time left before the explosive climax. The opposition is busy trying to diffuse the hero before disaster occurs.

- Paragraph #5 (pp. 75-89)

Continue developing the tension and suspense—even with comedy—until the end of Act II.

- Paragraph #6 (pp. 90-120)

There are now thirty pages left to finish the final act. What do you write in these final pages? The action and suspense must increase. Everything is now at its most critical boiling point of action. In the final act, which corresponds to the final chapter of the novel, the biggest crisis occurs. The biggest crisis has the strongest barriers and the most conflict between the hero and heroine, between the protagonist and the antagonist. Betrayals from the past come to fruition between allies.

End the script with the most important action of the story. Build the adaptation around the twelve events, each with increasing drama, conflict, crises, tension, and suspense. Then bring the hero and his goal together at the end.

If it's a love story or romance, bring the hero and heroine together. If the hero has led a miserable life and lost out on love, end the script with something good happening through the efforts of the hero, rather than by random coincidence. Show that the hero has the power of choice and control over his life. The opening scene and the last scene should be similar in visual tone. If you start with a horizon at sunset, end with a horizon at sunset. Use visual symbols and follow the circular patterns found in nature.

The survivor wins, but that doesn't necessarily mean he's right. However, upbeat endings are popular because the audience wants to be cheered up. Bring people into a positive light and leave them there at the end, feeling good about themselves. People grow towards the light, towards love, and towards whatever feels good.

12. Fill in the details.

Now that you have an outline of the basic building blocks of the story, you can draw a flow chart or storyboard for your main characters. Define your main character's strengths, and then begin to fill in the details and dialogue.

13. Shuffle the deck.

After you have constructed a linear version of your story, try shuffling your narratives like a deck of cards. Create an interactive piece where all odd-numbered chapters make up an entire free-standing story and the even-numbered chapters make up another. Then merge the two—interspersing chapters from both pieces into a new whole with multiple pathways, sub-plots, and endings.

Ten tips for:
Writing an audio script

1. Write for the ear.

Linear writing is required for both radio and streaming Internet audio because the ear hears from beginning to end in a straight line. If you write your script out of order, it still must be organized to be read in linear chunks. Audio writing is conversational writing. Make sure it can be understood by the average ten-year-old. Read everything out loud before you write your final draft. If it's not written solely for the ear, with sound effects instead of visual shots, it won't be clear.

2. Say it, don't read it.

Write the way conversation is said, not the way a script is read. Use large type and spell out phrases like "three-feet-by-two-inches." Never write 3'x2". Never make the script reader guess what you mean. Say what you mean and mean what you say.

3. Write out numbers.

Spell out numbers one through nine, but use numerals for 10 through 999. Spell out words such as 'hundred' or 'million'. Use numbers above 10 combined with billion-dollar worlds such as 25 billion or 60 thousand. Write out ten thousand sea shells instead of 10,000 sea shells.

4. Don't use symbols.

Spell out names for symbols—otherwise, they may be mispronounced. Write 'dollars' instead of '$' when you want to say one hundred dollars or 100 dollars. Write the full name first if you're talking about an acronym or an abbreviation, as in World Wide Web (WWW).

5. Write in segments.

Audio scripts are written in segments rather than pages. The audio can be played in sixty-second segments until action takes over. Don't write audio by the page because it's heard by the segment.

6. Write the action.

Write about the action in your story. Back the speech by text and voice, music and visuals. We learn better that which we see and hear at the same time. When text and audio are played together, it becomes a closed-captioned sequence that may be read by those without audio capability.

7. Write for the narrator's personality.

Keep the narrator's personality in mind when writing an audio script. Let the narrator preview the script and offer suggestions that will make the presentation feel more natural.

7. Create a friendly avatar host.

Avatars are the animated characters used in 3-D worlds to represent the participants and visitors to the site. On the Web, an avatar can easily become a newsanchor or talk show host. Create an interesting personality and animate the avatar so it is perceived as you, your alter ago, or any other person, real or imaginary. To make the listeners feel more at ease, your avatar may say 'we' rather than 'I'. Your avatar will be the listener's host, guide, and guardian angel, walking the listener through the talk and talking him through the walk.

7. Coordinate the visual and audio effects.

To make your presentation look and feel less like a Web site, combine your message with supporting sound effects, simple animation, and illustrations within your chosen framework.

10. Be consistent.

Be consistent. It's better for the eyes and ears to work together.

20 How can I learn to write in three dimensions?

To write interactively means to write outside of structure and tradition. Write in returning cycles, in rebounding rhythms, like the seasons, the orbits, and the love handles of revolving galaxies. Don't leave unused your vital components.

Interactive writing and reading is about finding unexpected connections, to voyage freely over everything that's new and to broadcast it in different channels. Find new routes and meanings, new uses for old stories, and fresh angles on the news. Work freely with precon-

scious metaphor, as Lawrence Kubie writes in his *Neurotic Distortion of the Creative Process*.

Writing in two dimensions and adapting one medium to another is directed originality. Writers can make a list of 'excursions' to be followed by comments in their margins. The excursion may be a trip into the preconscious mind of metaphor.

As a writer, you may find ideas by rotating an object in space, turning it upside down or inside out. Look at

A Nonlinear Three-Act Story Structure

In this example, the story moves along a linear path according to a three-act structure. However, within each act, the reader can choose different paths or excursions. You might add to this structure the possibility of three different endings.

the inside out from a new angle, and come up with fresh ideas to make it real. The writer rotates all facets of human experience in time and space to find a fresh angle.

Before you can learn to think and write in three dimensions, you must to learn to write in two dimensions. Picture a square drawn on a flat sheet of paper. That's two-dimensional, linear writing. However, even when writing at the two-dimensional level, you can begin to experiment by giving choices to the reader or audience.

Nonlinear Writing

All stories have a beginning, middle, and end that are tied to what came before and what comes after. Writing in flat, linear time—from beginning, to middle, to end—is only the beginning. In nonlinear writing, beginnings, middles, and endings are interchangeable like plug-and-play computer peripherals.

To adapt a two-dimensional story to a nonlinear script, all you need is the flat square—the linear time. The pop-up cube will appear as you create branching narratives. Picture a cube or a pop-up book that snaps into three dimensions by extending the lines along the corner. Three-dimensional writing is in circular time with branching narratives ending in leaf nodes like the curving tree of life.

A Parallel Story Structure

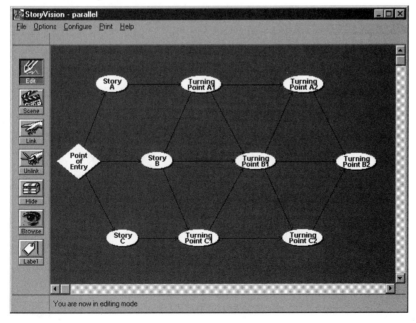

In a parallel structure, you may follow separate linear stories or take an excursion to another story at a turning point. This technique may also be applied to show the perspectives of different characters within a single storyline.

Think of your story as a stack of cards—a metaphor used by many authoring tools.

1. Take a deck of blank cards and divide it into thirds—one for each part of your story. On each card, write a different beginnings, middle, or ending for each part of the story.

2. Shuffle the each pile of cards so the reader can choose multiple pathways to interact within the story. Instead of linear time, you now have a three-dimensional parallel structure that goes back and forth like a time-travel novel.

3. Let the reader choose a different path, or return to the beginning to start a different story.

The most important rule to remember when designing an interactive story is that there are no rules. Start with a diagram and define the widest categories. Then, refine the story diagram, getting more specific as you go deeper into each story level.

Interactive writing uses metaphorical thinking to stimulate creative response. The interactive writer becomes a master of flexibility and a weaver of ideas, pictures, and sounds.

A Web Story Structure

A web structure is ideal for handling topics that are interconnected. Examples include a role-playing game, relationships between people or places. The interconnections between the scenes form a web. You have to think and feel in three dimensions to visualize the connections between the scenes.

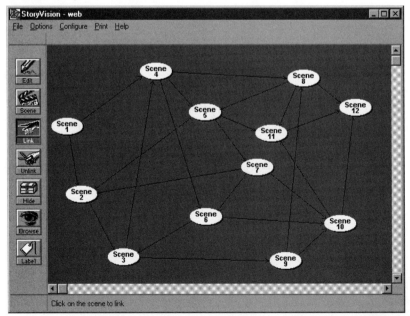

An Audio Script

The Cyberscribes Show

SFX: Musical introduction: Zamba Mora
Narrator: Dr. Aniba Merimdeh, Avatar

ANNOUNCER

BROADCASTING LIVE FROM BEAUTIFUL
DOWNTOWN CYDONIA, IT'S TIME FOR THE
CYBERSCRIBES SHOW. . .AND HERE SHE IS,
CRUISING DOWN THE NILE IN STYLE, YOUR
MISTRESS OF CYBERSPACE, THE HOSTESS
WITH THE MOSTEST AND THE GODDESS WITH
THE BODICE, DR. ANIBA MERIMDEH!

SFX: Wild audience applause, music, and
chimes as Dr. Aniba rises with arms
outstretched as if casting her net.

ANIBA

GREEETINGS CYBERSCRIBES! AND THANK
YOU, GREAT ONE, FOR THAT MARVELOUS
INTRODUCTION. MAY THE PIGEONS AWAKEN
YOU.

SFX: Audience laughter and sound of gong.

ANIBA

ARE YOU HAVING A GOOD TIME?

SFX: Wild audience applause.

ANIBA

IT'S TIME TO PLAY STUMP THE SCRIBE!

SFX: Wild audience applause.

OUR FIRST CONTESTANT HAS TRAVELED FROM
A DISTANT LAND TO BE WITH US TODAY.
LADIES AND GENTLEMEN, LET'S GIVE IT UP
FOR AUTHOR, ANNE HART.

SFX: Wild audience applause. Musical
transition as Anne Hart is beamed to the
contestant's podium.

                    ANIBA

    HAIL TO YOU, ANNE HART! A GREAT
    PLEASURE TO HAVE YOU ON OUR SHOW
    TODAY. ARE YOU READY TO PLAY STUMP THE
    SCRIBE?

                    ANNE

    YES ANIBA, I'M READY.

                    ANIBA

    THEN LET'S GET STARTED! ANNE, YOU MAY
    BEGIN THE GAME BY CHOOSING A CATEGORY.

                    ANNE

    ANIBA, I THINK I'LL CHOOSE CATEGORY
    NUMBER ONE, "A DIGITAL RENNAISANCE
    WHERE ART MEETS TECHNOLOGY.'

SFX: Audience applause.

                    ANIBA

    MAY I HAVE THE FIRST QUESTION, PLEASE?

SFX: Sound of tinkling chimes.

                    ANIBA

    HOW ARE BUSINESSES USING THE NEWEST
    MEDIA?

SFX: Sound of ticking clock.

                    ANNE

    NOW IS THE TIME TO START WRITING FOR
    THE NEWEST MEDIA, WHETHER IT'S NEWS,
    EDUCATION, ENTERTAINMENT, OR A HYBRID
    MIXTURE OF ALL OF THE ABOVE. THE
    TECHNOLOGICAL WORLD IS UNFOLDING IN
    WAYS THAT ARE GREAT FOR WRITERS.

    ART HAS OVERTAKEN COMMERCE AND WRITERS
    ARE BEING RECRUITED AS CONTENT
    CREATORS BY THE DESIGN-BASED

INDUSTRIES AND MANUFACTURERS OF THE
DIGITAL ERA. IT'S AN OPPORTUNITY FOR
WRITERS TO REACH A BROADER MARKET,
MAKING MONEY IN CREATIVE EXPRESSION.
THE DIGITAL INFRASTRUCTURE HAS CREATED
A FUTURE IN WHICH THE ARTS AND
TECHNOLOGY WILL WORK AS A UNIT AND BE
CHANNELED DIRECTLY INTO PEOPLE'S HOMES.

SFX: Sound of symbols and applause.

                    ANIBA

CONGRATULATIONS, ANNE! THAT'S CORRECT!
HERE'S QUESTION NUMBER TWO. . .

SFX: Sound of tinkling chimes.

                    ANIBA

WHAT IS A CONTENT CREATOR?

SFX: Sound of ticking clock.

                    ANNE

THE WEB IS NOW THE CENTER OF ATTENTION
FOR CREATIVE WRITERS, ARTISTS,
COURSEWARE DESIGNERS, REVIEWERS, AND
WRITERS OF TECHNICAL AND BUSINESS
RELATED MATERIAL. TOGETHER, THEY ARE
BUILDING THE BODY OF INFORMATION WE
CALL THE WEB.

SFX: Sound of symbols and applause.

                    ANIBA

CONGRATULATIONS AGAIN, ANNE! ARE YOU
READY FOR THE FINAL QUESTION?

SFX: Sound of tinkling chimes.

                    ANIBA

QUESTION THREE: WHO ARE THE NEW
JOURNALISTS?

SFX: Sound of ticking clock.

                         ANNE

        THOSE WHO MAJORED IN COMMUNICATIONS,
        JOURNALISM, CREATIVE WRITING, ENGLISH,
        SCRIPTWRITING, OR RELATED SUBJECTS
        WILL FIND AN ABUNDANCE OF
        OPPORTUNITIES IN ONLINE JOURNALISM.
        JOURNALISTS MUST NOW TRAIN IN MORE
        THAN THE "BIG FIVE" COMPUTER
        APPLICATIONS. COMPUTER APPLICATIONS
        RELEVENT TO THE FIELD OF ONLINE
        JOURNALISM SHOULD BE CONSIDERED A CORE
        SUBJECT BY COLLEGES, UNIVERSITIES, AND
        WRITING SCHOOLS SEEKING TO PREPARE
        STUDENTS FOR THE WRITER'S MARKET OF
        TODAY AND TOMORROW.

    SFX: Sound of symbols and applause.
    Musical interlude three to five seconds.

                         ANIBA

        CONGRATULATIONS ANNE HART, YOU ARE THE
        QUEEN OF ALL CYBERSCRIBES! GREAT ONE,
        WILL YOU TELL ANNE WHAT SHE'S WON?

                      ANNOUNCER

        ANNE, YOU HAVE WON A ROUND-TRIP TICKET
        TO COME BACK ON OUR SHOW!

    SFX: AUDIENCE APPLAUSE

                         ANNE

         THANK YOU, I'LL BE BACK!

    SFX: MUSIC begins as ANIBA stands with arms
    outstretched.

                         ANIBA

        THAT'S ALL THE TIME WE HAVE FOR TODAY
        FOLKS. THANKS SO MUCH FOR JOINING US.
        AND WE'LL SEE YOU NEXT TIME ON STUMP
        THE SCRIBE!

    SFX: Wild audience applause. Fadeout music to
    the end.

                      # # #

CHAPTER FOUR

Understanding Your Writing Style

Some writing jobs are better suited to one personality or temperament over another. Different writing jobs can have varying effects on your health, physiological responses, feelings, behaviors, emotions, and stress levels. In short, certain jobs fit individual writers better, in the long, run than others.

Personality characteristics are frequently measured with tests such as the *Myers-Briggs Type Indicator* (MBTI™) which lists sixteen universal types, the *Enneagram*, which lists nine types, and psychoanalyst C.G. Jung's eight types. Each of these are methods designed to measure the personalities of relatively mentally-normal people.

The MBTI™ was developed by Katherine Briggs and Isabel Myers, based on Jung's research into the personality. Personality preferences have also been classified into four temperaments by Dr. David Keirsey. There are thirteen normal personality styles discussed in the excellent book, *Personality Self Portrait (Why You Think, Work, Love, and Act the Way You Do)*, by John M. Oldham, M.D. and Lois B. Morris.

There are many other personality inventories that measure levels of creativity, intuition, original thinking, and the balance of anger, harmony, and similar tastes. The *Cyberscribe's Career Classifier* in Appendix A of this book is a simple test that will help you identify your personality type and temperament based on your preferred style of writing and relationships in the workplace.

On the Internet you will find many Web sites, newsgroups, and mailing lists devoted to the study of the personality. You can find these and more by searching on the word "personality" or by your specific type.

Emerging Internet technology makes it possible to find the businesses that use the kind of writing you do best.

21   What are the sixteen personality types?

According to the MBTI, the sixteen personality types are combinations of the following characteristics:

I   Introverted.

E   Extroverted.

S   Sensing (practical, realistic, and down to earth).

N   Intuitive (insightful, imaginative, fanciful, seeing possibilities rather than realities, what *could* be instead of what is).

F   Feeling (basing decisions and values on reactions to inner feelings, personal likes and dislikes).

T   Thinking (logical, listening to the head and not trusting the heart in decision-making).

P   Perceiving (understanding through the senses, a playful, free spirit remaining open-minded with tolerance for ambiguity, waiting for more information before deciding).

J   Judging (coming to quick closure, a need for structure and decision-making).

Before 1996, approximately 72% of the U.S. population was considered to be extroverted and 28% introverted. Seventy-six percent was thought to be sensor, whereas only 24% intuitive. Feelers and thinkers are split 50/50 as are perceivers and judgers. However, the most recent studies indicate there are more introverts in the U.S. than previously thought.

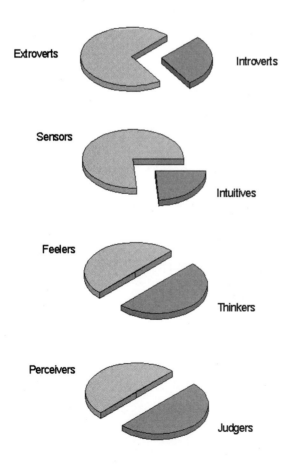

Extroverts   Introverts

Sensors   Intuitives

Feelers   Thinkers

Perceivers   Judgers

What should I know about the four temperaments?

Besides the sixteen personality types, there are four temperaments which David Keirsey wrote about in his best-seller, *Please Understand Me*. The four temperaments are:

SP   Sensing Perceivers (38%)

SJ   Sensing Judgers (38%)

NT   Intuitive Thinkers (12%)

NF   Intuitive Feelers (12%)

When each of the sixteen personalities are taken by themselves, apart from introversion and extroversion, four distinct kinds of temperaments emerge.

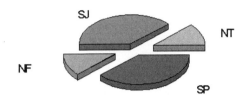

Sensing Perceivers

The SP leaps before he looks, and he looks to make an impact. He looks for excitement. Typical examples are the artisan rock star, gambler, promoter, stock broker, motorcycle stuntperson, or weapons master. The motto of the SP is to "send shock waves through America (making an impact on all of you out there and in the family, too!)"

Sensing Judgers

The SJ is traditional and seeks to belong to traditional groups and have a secure, steady, routine job, preferably in a large company. The typical example is the secretary, clerical supervisor, accountant, or elementary school teacher. The motto of the SJ is to "protect and serve, guard tradition, laws and rules, and fulfill duties with a smile in order to ensure security from change and scarcity."

The ultimate J is one who organizes and gives structure to everything and makes decisions for all. In exaggeration, the J temperament, particularly the SJ, is what some would describe as a "control freak."

Intuitive Thinkers

The NT combines imagination with logic. A typical example is the NT who is driven to conquer or control nature and ideas—the computer 'nerd', analyst, physicist, theoretical scientist, or mathematician. An extroverted NT could be a manager, a field marshall, or a military genius. The NT is an analyst who likes to put things and people into categories and design models on paper. The motto of the NT is to "achieve control through questioning authority, being skeptical, and thinking about how to improve things. If it's not broken, I'll break it to make it work better." These people consider ideas to be more important than facts and see patterns and branching pathways in everything. Is it any surprise that Microsoft is known as an "NT" company? As an outside observer looking in, it looks like NTs rule the roost at Microsoft.

Intuitive Feelers

The NF is the social worker, personnel manager, psychologist, psychiatrist, or creative writer with a gift for language and the arts. The essence of the NF temperament is communication, to relate to and understand people and relationships. The motto of the NF is to "grow to my maximum potential while expressing my creativity through speech, writing, or the visual arts." The extroverted NF is a great networker who brings people together and really knows how to work a room.

This book was written, edited, designed, and published by a team of intuitive, feeling, perceivers. Stacy, the copy editor, and I are introverted-feeling types, while Claire, the designer and publisher is an extroverted-intuitive type.

An NF reading this book will delight in its many layers of innuendo, and its focus on ideas and imagination. A detailed-seeking sensor will target its practical application to the fast track in new media careers.

If keeping track of the sixteen personality types is too complicated, try focusing on the four temperaments: NT, NF, SP, and SJ. Put these four together in a story or workplace and watch the dramatic conflict unfold as each does his own thing in a different way.

Temperament Key

SP Sensing/Perceivers (38%)

SJ Sensing/Judgers (38%)

NT Intuitive/Thinkers (12%)

NF Intuitive/Feelers (12%)

How does my personality influence my writing?

It's not surprising that corporations have personalities just as people do. How do you know which company matches your style and which new media writing career will make the most comfortable fit for you?

Is there a fundamental conflict of workplace style between the software industry and established news organizations from the broadcast TV and print media? Let's examine how these professions compare typologically, as the e-mail-sending introverts from the computer world meet the phone-gabbing extroverts from the newsroom.

Screenwriters

Screenwriters and scriptwriters operate in an environment where team work and collaboration are mandatory. A script will be revised and reworked many times by many voices. It's essential that the writer be able to work with others on a team or production crew. ENFPs are well suited to scriptwriting, careers in production, storyboarding, animation, and new media production. Why? Because you need the quality of extroversion to reach the top levels in the scriptwriting and production fields. Most of all, you need the extroverted intuition in order to work with many people and to tolerate having your script changed so many times by so many hands.

Content Writers

Writers from the software industry are usually referred to professionally as "content writers" or "documentation analysts." Their work atmosphere is complimentary to the intuitive/thinking" (NT) personality types (INTJ and INTP).

Journalists

Writers from broadcast journalism communicate most often by telephone and are usually trained journalists by profession. They work in an intuitive/feeling (NF) atmosphere, where communication equates to:

Feeling + Perception = Experience

or,

Intuition + Feeling = Judgment.

This work style is suitable for the intuitive/feeling personality type.

Temperament Key

SP Sensing/Perceivers (38%)

SJ Sensing/Judgers (38%)

NT Intuitive/Thinkers (12%)

NF Intuitive/Feelers (12%)

The Work Environment

Information that makes an emotional impact is retained the longest. However, at a typical software or computer company, information is focused on logic and analysis rather than emotion and feeling. Ease of use takes priority over emotional sensations from audio/visual news flashes and soundbites.

Introverts may prefer getting news from wire services, whereas extroverts may prefer speaking to the source or watching television to experience the visual effects and sound bites. What do intuitive/feeling companies have in common with intuitive/thinking companies? Both are forward-looking, visionary firms. In contrast, a company like IBM might be considered to be a benchmarking firm, one based on tradition. Microsoft is a visionary firm looking to the future, which is an intuitive/thinking character trait.

For the new media, intuitive/feeling writers can combine journalism and computer skills to bridge the transition between writing content and journalism. It's a matter of using double skills—newsgathering (intuition with feeling) and computer excellence (intuition and thinking with sensing and logic). An alternate career for content writers and new media journalists with artistic talent might be digital animation and photo-journalism.

Extroverted speakers are often found in front of the camera or as a featured speaker at computer industry events. Introverts prefer writing behind the scenes, but may sometimes be persuaded to participate on a panel of speakers. Extroverted/thinking personalities such as ESTJ and ENTJ like to run and organize the show from the administrative side, letting others do the creative writing.

Cognitive Styles

Every type has a personal writing style that is best served by a perfect match between the writer and the subject, and between the writer and the publisher or producer. The brain has four cognitive styles and writers should strive to match their style to that of their employers and collaborators.

1. Reductive (ISTJ, ESTJ).

2. Allusive (INTP, ENTP).

3. Metaphorical (INFP, ENFP, INFJ, ENFJ).

4. Ironic (INTJ, ENTJ).

The Introverts (and how they might describe themselves)

INFJ   1%

"To word pages properly and perfectly."

INFP   1%

"To sell escape as fiction and report the non-fiction with a cause, mission, or quest. To take on new long-term projects. To be oceanic, rather than volcanic in feeling."

INTJ   1%

"To keep an open mind (as long as it's my own opinion) and let people know when they are being illogical. To organize business and nature."

INTP   1%

"To think for myself and question all authority. To be independent and to analyze. To build models of theory and prove them to be true."

ISFJ   6%

"To be of service without making waves, do the grunt work, be a 'guy or girl Friday', fix it with a smile."

ISFP   6%

"To be humble while having fun making music, keeping shop, or sculpturing my art or craft, and to be modest and follow the leader. To be in rapport with nature, animals, and people. To insist on sensitivity to all things beautiful and serene."

ISTJ   6%

"To supervise and monitor details, to work as long as possible at being precise and to tell you what's wrong with anything you asked me to look over. I will find the flaws in it for you, for a fee."

ISTP   6%

"To fly the skies with tactical turns, put out the fire, design the product, engineer the program, build the cabinet, repair the appliance, master the weapon, race the track."

The 1% Club

The 6% Club

The Extroverts (and how they might describe themselves)

The 5% Club

ENFJ   5%

"To speak the speech trippingly on the tongue, preach the sermon, manage the people, and tell the story to evangelize and convince with volcanic feeling."

ENFP   5%

"To conceive another great idea, even if I'm distracted while doing more than one thing at a time. To rescue, counsel, coach, design, create, and spread the news to all time zones."

ENTJ   5%

"To quickly commandeer, organize, and start a business, to group people together, to co-produce or anchor the show (although I cannot not lead). To take charge."

ENTP   5%

"To break away from established rules and traditions that limit our rights. To be an entrepreneur's entrepreneur."

ESFJ   13%

"To base my values on tradition and family togetherness, to reminisce and continue the line. To sell well but be less impatient with those who are idealistic and creative, because I'm realistically conventional."

The 13% Club

ESFP   13%

"To have fun, enjoy good company, good games, good food, and merriness as everyone watches me perform with a smile. The show must go on—with me (and the costume counts)."

ESTJ   13%

"To run the household and the business like a general. To help people organize and be the administrator. To serve my country with patriotism. To control my home and all in it and eliminate weakness."

ESTP   13%

"To avoid responsibility, get myself free, and enjoy the fun that business and entertainment brings me by promoting the game. To be a radio talk show host or work in real estate or travel. Have I got a deal for you!"

24 Is one personality type more creative than another?

There is no personality type that can be described as more creative than another. However, there are different styles of creativity that may be expressed in concrete or abstract ways. Sensors are often creative with tangible, concrete situations, whereas intuitives are more often creative with intangible and abstract situations. However, it's a mistake to say that sensors are less creative than intuitives.

Sensors and Intuitives

A sensor may be very creative in fashion design, music, or art composition and be able to pick a note or color out of hundreds of shades and variations on a theme. Or a sensor may be creative in finance, in surgery, engineering, dentistry, in dexterity—working with the concrete and expressing the concrete or photo-real picture of objects in the present time.

An intuitive will be creative in the way imagination takes the person away from the real and into the surreal or hyperreal world of fantasy and abstraction. It is a form of abstract creativity that allows the intuitive to see the big picture, spot the trend, grab an abstract idea out of time and space, and take the conceptual leap. An intuitive might turn a trip to a strange city into a good interactive adventure.

Abstraction is at the core of the intuitive personality. Their creativity deals with the intangible—like writing advertising copy. The sensor deals with the concrete and sells the steak while the intuitive sells the sizzle. One is reality-focused and the other is creating spinoffs of the imagination, seeing what could be rather than what is.

Thinkers create the technology of the art and feelers create the art of the technology. Judgers create the organized model and matrix, and perceivers create the spinoffs of what could be made from turning the model inside out.

Styles of Re-Creation

Sensors

Sensors re-create in miniature to emphasize precision.

Perceivers

Perceivers re-create with startling, spontaneous statistics.

Judgers

Judgers re-create to slow the persistence of time.

Thinkers

Thinkers re-create mechanically wholistic models with hair-splitting accuracy.

Intuitives

Intuitives re-create on a gigantic scale by simulation.

Feelers

Feelers re-create to give more drama to their story than their research.

How do "thinkers" and "feelers" write differently?

Would you rather write for a person who first looks for the flaws in your work? Or would you rather write for someone who praises your work, titillates your personal feelings, and rarely sees your errors? Would you like a polite lie about how great your piece is, or the brutal truth of propitious hair-splitting logic about your shortcomings? Someday either a thinker—as in tinker—or a feeler —as in dealer—is going to decide whether to buy, evaluate, shape, or carve up your writing. Someday you'll ratify both characters before you stumble over your words or recapture your composure.

Thinking Writers

Thinking personalities are most likely to critique and evaluate first and praise only when it has been earned by a wide margin. Thinking writers may justify what they write with detailed anecdotes about cutting expenses, increasing efficiency, copying the smart habits of the successful, and considering rights rather than circumstance. Books

about lateral thinking, working smarter, and learning how to manage in one-minute segments are all written for a thinking audience. Writing is part of the science of business.

Thinking writers use logic and rationality to justify what they create.

- Concrete Thinkers (SJ)

    Concrete thinkers focus on reductive language by reducing a sentence to fewest literal words. They say what they mean by using a concrete symbol as in "all hands on deck."

- Abstract Thinkers (NT)

    Abstract thinkers create writing that focuses on how logic leaps toward big-picture concepts. . . as in "why follow a leader when I can take responsibility for myself?"

Science fiction writers are overwhelmingly intuitive thinkers. Intuitive/feeling science fiction writers focus less on the technological con-

Temperament Key

SP Sensing/Perceivers (38%)

SJ Sensing/Judgers (38%)

NT Intuitive/Thinkers (12%)

NF Intuitive/Feelers (12%)

volutions of their outworlder chronicles and more on the relationships, values, and morality of the individual characters in their stories.

The 'why' and 'what' that sometimes causes thinking writers to lose control or lose their place in a creative project is because they expect those whom they interview to behave logically—just as they expect the technology to behave logically. They expect that business, the environment, government, and human nature will bend to their logical expectations.

Concrete-thinking writers want the world to act like it's supposed to—from CEOs to dish washers. It's that SJ "ought to and should do" mentality that shows up in creative nonfiction writing from essays to reports on polls. Financial writers who are concrete thinkers expect a logical response from the markets—even though the markets are full of intuitive/thinking forecasters, gurus, and trend watchers. Intuitive/thinking writers look at the forces and write about the concept, while taking the intuitive leap. Concrete writers simply report the profits and losses.

Feeling Writers

Feeling writers consider creativity to be a goal and process.

- Intuitive Feelers (NF)

    Intuitive/feeling writers can jump in the middle of a project and start writing as a process that targets the act of creativity as a living organism. It's the force that drives the grass up through the mud.

Intuitive/feeling writers focus on the creative force by "growing toward the light" and using metaphor or simile. An intuitive/feeling writer will create a guide for searchers of self-identity. The intuitive/feeling writer may focus on the inner self. When an intuitive writer creates the "*World's Most Powerful Money Manual*," the emphasis will be more on matching what you are to what you do.

- Sensing Perceivers (SP)

    Sensing/perceivers tackle the goal first and never worry about the process. A sensing/perceiving writer will be less interested in looking deep inside and searching for identity.

Thinkers create the technology of the art and feelers create the art of the technology.

A creative piece written by a feeling/sensing/perceiver will more likely be about how to correlate than how to navigate. A feeling/sensor would be more interested in writing about how to use the turbulent currents of rising interest rates, whereas an intuitive/feeler would be more likely to write about a universe of potential clients or how to creatively profit from falling interest rates.

Intuitive/feeling writers search for fluidity while sensing/feeling writers look for familiarity and tradition. A sensor is a more likely to imitate the success of others while trying to look original. Intuitive/feeling writers seek originality, but when they can't find it (as in few ideas are original) will seek future possibilities and hidden markets waiting to be uncovered.

An intuitive/feeling investigative reporter is naturally drawn to search out the hidden story, while a sensing/feeling writer may prefer to mind his own business and be reluctant and uncomfortable conducting an in-depth investigation. A sensing/feeling writer works from the limbic system before writing from the bones or emotions. However, the writing of a sensing/feeler can be volcanic—as explosive as extroverted feeling in an introverted super sensor.

The creative intuitive/feeling writer may first seek to bring the reader to a positive place by taking the individual through a labyrinth of negativity. Intuitive/feeling writing is oceanic, as doled out step-by-step as the writer seeks the novelty in the subject.

Extroverted feeling in an intuitive writer may be explored as introverted intuition—such as writing about the inner workings of the mind or how to avoid the pitfalls of relationships.

The main difference in creative expression between feeling writers and thinking writers is that thinking writers question and evaluate, while feeling writers seek identity and personal values in the subject of their creation. 𓅓

Temperament Key

SP Sensing/Perceivers (38%)

SJ Sensing/Judgers (38%)

NT Intuitive/Thinkers (12%)

NF Intuitive/Feelers (12%)

26 How can I target the personality of my audience?

Writers who want to create a best-seller must write for a sensing/thinking or sensing/feeling audience. Their range of interest falls on the practical side of creativity. If you write for an intuitive/feeling audience, you'll miss 70% of the audience.

At one time, I was a member of a group dedicated to the study of personality type. The INFP facilitator eventually started showing Sally Field movies, asking everyone to guess the personality type of the supporting characters. The group had been led by two INFPs in succession, neither of whom wanted to continue after the membership dwindled from several hundred down to ten members. (The sensing, thinking, and judging members left as soon as the movies started.)

The point is, that most writers are intuitive/feelers, and most readers are sensing/thinkers. If you write for people like yourself, you might miss a wide range of readers, the major-ity of whom are sensing/thinkers looking for practical advice, information, and examples of successful people to imitate.

Too many INFP and INFJ writers are writing books for other NFs and then wonder why they sell to only 5% to 10% percent of the population. If they looked at what sensors—the majority—want in a book, they would see the need to write for the sensing market where STJ and SFJ are a majority and NFP is a minority. An example of a story that might appeal to an NF audience is the time-travel romance. Meanwhile, science fiction stories are popular with a small number of NTs—usually INTJs and INTPs. However, the most popular spy novels and western novels sell to SJs.

The largest market of readers in the United States is composed of ESFJ and ISTJ women. These people seek out practical how-to books or escape fiction in true-love contemporary romance, sports, and entertainment-oriented novels about real

To master metaphor is the mark of genius.

—Aristotle

people doing practical things. History puts ESFJ and ESTJ types to sleep. An ESFJ woman would rather read *Hollywood Wives* and *Boss Lady* type romances or stories about men meeting women who are raising small children alone, and other immediate problem-solver romances about life issues or practical jobs. *First Wives Club* is an INFJ fantasy.

To prove the point, look at the best-sellers today. They all hit hard at sensing types, especially ESFJ and ESTJ readers—books about athletics, sports, and entertainers. The average woman in the U.S. is an ESFJ who will never buy a book on Jung's life theories. NFs read an average of nine hours a week in addition to work-related materials. Since most writers are INFP, INFJ, or ENFP (speakers tend to be ENFJ), when they write for their own salon audience, they limit their readership.

The key to wide appeal is to aim for the sensors and write about their immediate needs. Note the best selling books are about cooking, sports figures, entertainers, thrill-

ers and spies, military combat, and romance—all dealing with critical issues in the real world.

One of the best-selling nonfiction books was about travel (but not *time* travel). Sci-fi and time travel books are bought mostly by intuitive/feelers and thinkers. Sensors are distracted by theory and imagination because fantasy, to sensors, is often associated with something "kooky, sexual, or weird." To a sensor, NF-type books are for 'flakes'. Exceptions to this rule are Isaac Asimov's sci-fi novels that target the NT introverted audience and have attained wider appeal with all types as comic books modeled after the robot novel series.

If you want a bestseller, write for the sensors. They don't like it when you write in parables (with the exception of the Bible, perhaps). "Say what you mean, and mean what you say," is a quote from one of the questions on the MBTI to reveal a sensor's preferences in written or spoken communication.

Remember that sensing types are more often audio-oriented and kinesthetic learners, and intuitive

Temperament Key

SP Sensing/Perceivers (38%)

SJ Sensing/Judgers (38%)

NT Intuitive/Thinkers (12%)

NF Intuitive/Feelers (12%)

types are more often visually-oriented in their reading, listening, and hands-on learning styles.

More choices in everything is what the design of information industry has given publishers and writers. Shall you publish books of romance or computers? Entertainment or news? Perhaps your temperament will give you a clue. As you learn more about your type and temperament, you will be able to use the knowledge to make better decisions in your writing career.

Understand the market before you begin. If intuitives buy more books than sensors, but sensors make up the majority of the population, should you write for intuitives or for sensors? Who are the majority? If you write for sensors, and less sensors buy books, are you missing the mark for intuitive book readers?

And if more sensors buy books, should you write or publish market-driven books, even though as an intuitive/feeler, it soon becomes dry and boring? How can you make it come alive for all audiences? The widest market appeal combines the reading habits of SJs with the buying power of NFs and the rave reviews set by NTs along with the promotion-by-impact of SPs.

http://www.ellipsys.com/test/tester.html

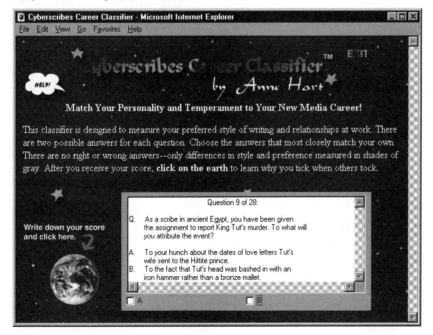

An interactive version of "The Cyberscribes Career Classifier" from Appendix A of this book is on the publisher's Web site. This version, which was written in a combination of Java and HTML, automatically calculates your score and provides additional information about your type and potential career opportunities in the new media.

27 How can I find the right publisher or producer?

In writing for the new media, your preference as a publisher or writer determines, to some extent, what kind of material you'll publish and how you'll seek to teach and entertain. You may be a stiff lit, an explosive dramatist, a receptive novelist, or a retentive intuitive thinker who needs to organize and control.

As do all people, publishers come in four basic temperaments. These four temperaments influence how they select a genre or find a niche.

- NTs like books on strategic planning and theory.

- SJs prefer how-to books broken down into a few easy steps for practical people who dislike theories and complexities.

- NFs love to merge art with technology and nature.

- SPs like travel books, adventure, gaming, sports, recreation, and celebrities.

Publishers focused on intuition, feeling, and perception are at opposite corners with those focused on sensing, thinking, and judging with their emphasis on organization, methodology, bigness, tradition, and fear of change. Thinking/intuitive publishers typically keep 'stables' of writers while intuitive/feeling publishers prefer 'teams' of writers. The sensor looks for the consequences while the intuitive looks for the possibilities.

Traits of Intuitive Publishers

In publishing and writing, the belief that you never can predict the future by looking at the past, is an intuitive, feeling, visionary stance that focuses on living for change rather than changing to live. The visionary intuitive lives from project-to-project looking forward to change and adaptation and is likely to read futuristic magazines such as *Psychology Today, Omni, Discover, Wired*, or *Internet World*.

Temperament Key

SP Sensing/Perceivers (38%)

SJ Sensing/Judgers (38%)

NT Intuitive/Thinkers (12%)

NF Intuitive/Feelers (12%)

Intuitive publishers are more likely to focus on visionary topics with people-using-technology and technology-using-people themes. Playology is the NF's way to approach a how-to subject. For intuitives, the idea is to learn through fun and play. Although an INFJ may work well a technical project, many would prefer a subject more about people, ancient history, and even new age spirituality.

Traits of Sensing Publishers

The tradition-based sensor's view is that history will repeat itself. The sensor's benchmarking, traditional slant is based on imitating successful giants of the past, where change is eschewed—particularly in publishing and writing formats. Sensors believe that what worked well once will work well again.

The sensor may read history-based magazines like the *Saturday Evening Post* or savings-oriented publications such as *Forbes*, *Money*, *Smart Money*, *Worth*, or *Fortune*. Sensing publishers of newspapers and periodicals typically focus on the immediate present patterned after the past.

Information Designers— Past, Present, and Future

In the not-so-distant past, SJ vendors created the industrial revolution and the manufacturing industry. Prior to that, SP artisans developed the high craft of the medieval world (particularly ISFP stone artisans and fine artists like Rembrandt). During the last decade of this millennium, intuitive thinkers and feelers (NT and NF) are overtaking the manufacturing industry with the information design industry.

In all forms of information design, sensor/judgers are more the uptight and retentive "stiff-gumshoes" for whom the intuitive's message is to "lighten up!" On the other hand, the information design of explosive intuitive/thinkers and receptive intuitive/feelers is to "spread it thickly through the news." Intuitive information designers treat fiction or other entertainment as news and write news as entertainment, with startling hooks. The hooks are the cash-cows.

NT publishers and writers may design information that tells a niche audience how to achieve power and control through quantitative research and by building models, matrices, and tables. Retentive NTs shrink from the socially bold SPs whose tactic (rather than strategy) is to meet crises head-on spontaneously without preparing for the trouble-shooting situation.

In publishing, the ENTP entrepreneur works well with the ENFP adventurer as long as the NF is allowed to be the center of attention. The NT will naturally seek power over the NF by finding the flaws in a plan or project before praising it. The NF will praise first to get attention, and then find fault later in the project design. NTs design in the model-making two-dimensional sense of quantitative research, while NFs build the 3-D model and bring pages and people together interactively.

Sources of Power

When working within the information design sector, smooth teams run well when each understands where the other seeks power:

*   Intuitive/Thinking Publishers

    NT publishers find power through control over nature and the physical world of science and technology. The NT seeks to organize and present logical thought. Many publish books on self-help and the analysis of why people learn, why history happened, why nature acts as it does, why crimes happen, and how to control these things through technology.

The more confident INTJ/ENTJ makes quicker decisions than the questioning, less confident INTP, talkative ENTP, or reclusive INFP.

Today's publishing industry calls for issues management, and nowhere is there more an issues-management type than INTJ or ENTJ. You'll find the NT writer working as a professor in schools of management and writing about competition as a management strategy.

NT publishers and writers may seek the answers to what two or more events have in common and focus on forecasting, anticipating, and analyzing future trends. The psychological motivation for focusing on issues

Temperament Key

SP Sensing/Perceivers (38%)

SJ Sensing/Judgers (38%)

NT Intuitive/Thinkers (12%)

NF Intuitive/Feelers (12%)

management (NTJ) is to ask what events have in common and what they mean for the future.

- Intuitive/Feeling Publishers

NF publishers find power while seeking to be the center of attention. NF has a high tolerance for ambiguity and lives for change while changing to live. The NF is a "big picture" person and believes in planning beyond the next two generations—but never for today.

For the NFP publisher, the formula is, if you want power, get attention. Nothing gets attention faster than entertainment, and that's the way the news and books are sold.

ENFJs often combine book publishing with a speaking career. NFs are most often found in training departments, with INFJ and INFP writing training material and ENFJ and ENFP taking the show on the road. ENFP is more of an entrepreneur than ENFJ who is more of a preacher.

The INFP may write about future implications, convergence and cooperation. The ENFP, about collaboration.

Introverted intuitives (INTP and INFP) are happy to work in seclusion until their work is perfected. At that time, the INF will team up with the ENF to get the work out to market. Introverted/feeling personalities like to work alone whenever possible, often assuming two hats as publisher and writer, and focusing on books about insight, almost exclusively.

- Sensing/Perceiving Publishers

SP publishers find power from bold performance or composition as an artisan or troubleshooter—at all levels from surgery to firefighting, piloting to patrolling the back alleys, entertainment to programming code. SPs plan for the present. In writing, SFPs and STPs tend to design information that troubleshoots present-moment crises, spontaneously, adapting as trouble arises, using tactics, not strategies to solve problems. SPs are the spontaneous promoters, performers, paparazzi photographers, and publicists of the moment, on the spot, getting the shot.

- Sensing/Judging Publishers

  After finding NT-style strategies too abstract, an SJ publisher will settle on SP-style tactics—troubleshooting tempered by duty.

  SJ publishers find power by imitating successful giants in history and believing they always can predict the future

by looking at the past. SJ doesn't think we're running out of resources or that we won't find a way to solve problems when they come up. The "one day at a time" approach leaves little room for planning for future change.

The SJ seeks power by proving responsibility to duty and dependability in a crisis. The SP heads off the crisis and moves on with boldness to make an impact or extract revenge, using anger to get power—or if anger is disallowed, tactics and courage under fire.

http://www.aptcentral.org/apttype.htm

The Association for Psychological Type, founded in 1979, is an international membership organization open to qualified individuals interested in personality type. APT members come from a variety of professions. Members seek to extend the development, research, applications and the ethical use of type theory.

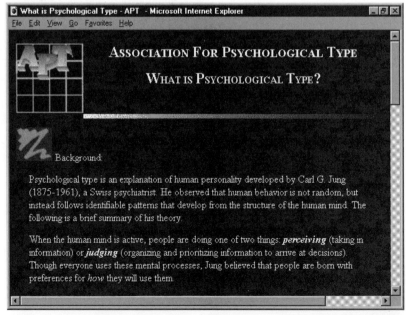

28 How many computer book publishers does it take to change a lightbulb?

Computer book publishing is driven by frantic software release dates and a price-per-pound approach that appeals to buyers who judge a book by its cover, trendy topic, and width of spine. Most computer books publishers follow the trends by watching what other publishers do—which is evident from the number of similar books on the same topic.

The software industry moves so fast that authors are forced to learn by the seat of their pants so they can write about a topic so new that there are no experts on the subject. Writers work under terrific time urgency stress to produce a book of 600-800 pages that in six months will be pulled from the shelf as obsolete. Youth is targeted in these software manual writers because few older writers would take on such a grueling project—often for little reward.

In mainstream computer book publishing, seeking the 'it' means finding out what appeals to the reductive speech of the STJ, the majority of the population in this country. When ESTJs told ESTJ, Harry Truman to "Give 'em Hell, Harry," as the campaign buttons said, they were reducing all meaning to the fewest words possible. That's the point computer book publishers need and want to make. Say it, teach it, in as few words as possible. That's the secret of making the complex easier for the SJ to understand.

Reductive speech saves time and gives the impatient learner cause to master the skill—but it takes a lot of reductive speech to fill a 1000-page book. All messages are compressed to as few words as possible to hit the reader hard with SP impact and boldness in a predominantly ISTJ/ESTJ or ISFJ/ESFJ world of computer industry workers.

Everything is reduced to whatever conveys the meaning in action verbs. This is where it's at in the computer publishing field. Give them. . . not hell, Harry, but facts.

It is our policy that we not enter any business where we would not be number one. Unless we see a clear path to being number one, we do not enter.

—Masayoshi Son, CEO Softbank Corp.

Temperament Key

SP Sensing/Perceivers (38%)

SJ Sensing/Judgers (38%)

NT Intuitive/Thinkers (12%)

NF Intuitive/Feelers (12%)

The Leaders

Microsoft, an NT company, ensures its success by seeking the visionary future based on forecasting and trend watching. If Microsoft had been more impulsive by nature, they would have jumped in early on the Web like the ENFJ and ENFP companies who saw that the Web had arrived.

It takes an NT to work the enormous number of hours writing code or to plot the strategy behind the next maneuver. In fact, it takes precisely an INTJ to be the most preferred type that Microsoft employs. . . and an ENTJ to deal with the public. The 'ideal' Microsoft employee would probably be INTJ. The ENTPs wouldn't be willing to put in the extra hours and the rest would be exhausted by the hard driving INTJ who's in charge.

NFs are willing to take risks to explore parts unknown, whereas NTs will jump in later after others have made the intuitive leap into financial risk. They just can't waste a dollop of that power to seek control over nature or technology.

In the end, the INTJ will run the giant company based on innovation and new ideas, as long as the other types continue to do their jobs. No other type is more fiercely competitive or more confident than the INTJ. He is not likely to pursue a win-win situation. However, his blind spot is that he will often tell you more than can be verified, so look to another type for proof of every idea offered. The INTJ is as overconfident as a megalomaniac in Shangri-La, as Saddam Hussein at Sheila Levine's Seder table, and as Microsoft at Netscape's Christmas party.

How-To Books

"How-to books" are often written by SPs and published and read by SJs. The most popular selling book of all time—the cookbook—is written for SJs, by SJs. In the past, Betty Crocker's sensible, practical, useful, and very SJ approach has sold more books than the Bible (which also is SJ and based upon tradition). The bread basket of America, the midwest, is SJ in its book buying habits. Interestingly, the vast majority of computer books are published in this part of the country. Computer book buyers who are SJ buy how-to-use-the-software or how-to-configure-the-hardware 'cookbooks' and computer 'bibles'. The favorite SJ computer book might be something like "*The Ten Commandments of Computing in Ten Easy Steps.*"

Books On Theory

NT systems analysts buy books on artificial intelligence, virtual reality, and theory. Engineers who eschew theory are typically sensors (ISTJ, ESTJ, or ISTP). Among computer publishers, the vast market is for SJ readers with a smaller audience of NTs looking for new theories in programming and systems analysis. The core ISTP programmer may not ever read the book. The ISTJ publisher is a super sensor, and introverted sensing is what propels and moves the large majority of computer book readers.

Books for People of "Limited Intuition"

Introverted sensing is what this most popular trend in computer book publishing is all about. Reading *The Complete Bimbo's Guide to SpamPerfect"* is the ultimate SJ (particularly ISFJ) experience in humility.

Publishers of computer books for people of limited intuition have an incredibly successful market—

especially with SJ personality preference styles—because SJs feel humble. They are intimidated by anyone praising them and calling them intellectuals or experts outside of their work specialty. Many SJs feel incompetent and struggle with low self-esteem.

When an SJ sees a book from the "*Dumb Bimbo"* series, they say, "Gee, that's for me. Nobody could be more of a dumb bimbo than I am when it comes to using this software." What sells best to the SJ audience, particularly the ISFJ and ISTJ, is "*How to Learn 'XyzAbc' Software in 10 Easy Exercises.*"

Making it easy means making the SJ feel dumb. When he feels dumb enough, he'll sink to a level of welcomed humility and humbleness that feels familiar. The familiarity will then cause him to feel proud of the accomplishment of mastering the "10 Easy Steps." Buying into the self-doubt and low self-esteem of the ISFJ allows the reader to realize that somebody has written a book especially for him. Now he can learn the nitty gritty step-by-step without the fuss or frills that make him feel out of place and humiliated. This approach works wonders with the SJ and that's the secret of its success.

There's one very important personality trait that I think is imperative for any good writer—especially a writer of how-to books or instructional material: Empathy.

If you're able to *be* your student or *be* your reader when teaching or writing, your instructional style and content will reach your audience.

—Nan McCarthy

Publishers who may be sensors themselves also learn best in this way. They avoid theories and don't demand intuitive leaps of imagination. There is no emphasis on forming concepts or reading between the lines. They simply go from one step to the next, reading in sequence. They say what they mean and don't theorize or add extraneous material. Bare-bones hands-on instruction is what the SJ wants. However, this approach seems shallow to the NF because it doesn't call upon the reader's intuition—an essential for the NF reader.

The Followers

Copycat time-urgency publishing is the ultimate in banal retentiveness. These publishers make copycat rip-off versions of best-selling books. If the "*Dumb Bimbo's Guide to Java*" sold a trillion copies, then the "*Babbling Bimbo's Guide*" will sell more. They'll assemble a force of anonymous work-for-hire writers and turn out a book in thirty days. It's an SJ personality style to copy what has worked well in the past. IBM is the epitome of the SJ corporation and a model for other SJs to follow.

User Friendliness

The intuitive-feely user-friendliness emphasized in computer book pub-

lishing is a typical NF trait. It must have been an NF forecaster and publisher working with an NT programmer who kept repeating loudly that more people will buy more products andsign up for more services when the complex becomes simple. The payoff for an NF is to get attention through rapor.

It turns out that a large proportion of journalists, advertising copywriters, and communications specialists are intuitive feelers. Is it only a coincidence that when journalists began flocking to the Internet in droves and complaining in print about how hard it was to use that suddenly browsers appeared with point-and-click ease-of-use? It is adaptation and survival of the fittest.

True Confessions

Intuitive and empathic NF computer book authors and publishers may teach you how to use the software with love, fun, sex, greed, fear, and mischief in a framework that broadcasts to the world. Leave it to the bubbling fountain of ENFP computer book publishers to reveal the untold story behind the software publishing empire. They are the ones most likely to sell Hollywood screen rights to a computer book. The NF may write about what people confess to in public places like taxicabs at Comdex, parties at MacWorld, or behind the anonymous safety of their e-mail account—as in Nan McCarthy's trilogy of cybernovels, *CHAT, CONNECT, and CRASH*. On the other hand, the volcanic ENFJ when observing the same trends, may critique the industry from the pulpit in an outspoken expression of inner conviction.

Convergence

The number crunching SJ world of computer books for bean-counters is diverging from the need of NT and NF readers for books that bring together computers, people, and the arts with technology and innovation. For intuitive feelers and thinkers, cyberware is now cyber-wear. We wear and bare our souls, not in public places, but in global spaces on the Web—a place where true confessions have a place far from the number-crunching world and closer to the seat of NF novelty of values, NT artificial intelligence, SJ responsibility for skill mastery, and SP boldness of impact.

So, to answer the question, "how many computer book publishers does it take to change a lightbulb?"

The answer is four:

1. An SP to stand on the highest rung of the ladder (while everybody watches);

2. An NF to empathize with the situation ("Remember—it goes lefty-loosey, righty-tighty!"), suggest an appealing new color, and dream up innovative ways to use the discarded lightbulb;

3. An SJ to supervise and explain (in ten easy steps) how to prevent the new light bulb from breaking, and. . .

4. An NT to install solar panels on the roof.

Voices from the industry:
Ed Tiley, Author

Bio

Ed Tiley is author of over a dozen computer books, including *Windows Stuff Microsoft Forgot*, *Windows After Hours*, *Tricks of the Windows 3.1 Masters*, *Using MS-DOS 6.22 Special Edition*, and *Using Clipper*.

His latest book, *Personal Computer Security* takes a user-level look at what must be done to protect users and data in the everyday world.

Tiley makes occasional appearances on the lecture circuit, writes freelance magazine articles, develops custom software for business and government, and plays a mean game of 8-ball.

>From: Ed Tiley

>Subject: Re: Computer Book Publishing Digest for 08/15/96

>Date: Fri, 16 Aug 1996 02:13:59 -0400

>

>OK, kids, it's off the wall time.

>

>I've been writing computer books and the odd bit of half-assed software since 1988, when I called Que to order some books, joked to the saleslady about writing a Clipper book, and they signed me to do it. In that time I've pumped out something like 19 books, counting major revisions. I've lost count since they quit giving out plaques.

>

>At the moment I'm taking a sabbatical from the book biz because I'm frankly a crispy critter. Burnt. So I'm taking a year to live and work on the Net. My latest is http://www.fla-beach.com, which is new, has a couple of small problems, but I think I'm getting the hang of it finally.

>

>Point is, I'm not looking for a book contract; and have genteelly deflected a couple of inquiries. In fact, if I could swing it, I'd never do another computer book in my life. I'm getting old, and beta testing is a young man's game. Women too. What I want to do is write a book that won't be obsolete in six months. Like every one of you, I'd like to do (drum roll please) FICTION. Tada! The ultimate F word! To be immortal and have high school students curse your name because they are assigned to read the F word. Fiction.

>

>The mere sound of the word is appealing. Anybody got a take on how to make the transition and still earn 70-80k a year until Hollywood drops a big wad on your agent?

CHAPTER FIVE

Writing the Story of Your Life

The art of autobiography has become interactive in the virtual theater of docudrama. Writers, who at one time or another have considered writing their autobiography will find many avenues of expression in the new media.

Writing an autobiography involves the never-ending search for identity. It's a photographic plate of the mind—an introverted, sensing experience painted in the textures, touch, sounds, scents, and voices of your life. Animate your memories with interactive illustrations, photos, music, and narration. You may begin as simply as recording your story on audio tape to accompany a slide show. If you have a multimedia-capable PC, record your soundtrack to a digitial format using your microphone and soundcard. From there, you may take one step further by broadcasting your story on the Web.

Practice creative introspection and imaging to recapture the vivid details from each scene in your life. A new sense of self will grow from your research. Focus on the allocation of your talent instead of the allocation of your capital. Define and design yourself as if you are a product to be sold. After you have defined yourself, build a working model of your story that allows you to rework your past, present, and future. You can either stay with your design or change it as new information is perceived.

Listen for feedback and write it down for future reference. The feedback will let you know how to build upon your strengths and learn from your weaknesses.

Don't worry about becoming self-absorbed when working on your story. Your autobiography is your own personal network—a gesture of giving and sharing.

Your autobiography is your own personal network— a gesture of giving and sharing.

How do I start writing about myself?

As you write your autobiography, you will rediscover and redefine your core competencies. Core competencies define the essence of what you are. They are not superficial like one's transient job or career. Your core competencies are the things that you have a natural talent for. Innate creativity, intuition, and imagination are examples of core competencies that can be transferred to many fields. Take away your ability to write or paint, and at once your creativity and imagination of the possibilities are transferred to another endeavor. If you lose your sight and can no longer paint, you will find another way to express your core competency of artistic expression.

Another example of a core competency is sensing, and then creating, the real instead of the possible using textures, sounds, tastes, aromas, and pictures that are firmly planted in the real world.

In the research and development phase of organizing your autobiography, manage your competencies rather than your objectives. Focus on your internal skills and values regardless of your type and temperament. Make a list of all the core competencies that define who and what you really are.

Take off your tinted glasses of self-delusion and preconceptions to uncover skills which may, as yet, remain undiscovered. You may worry that you have lost some of your talents over the years through disuse. Take action to rediscover your innate skills by doing the things that feel most comfortable and natural.

Competence comes from understanding how to identify, enhance, develop, and nurture the things you're really good at and from sharing them with others. Assert your competence through the art of interactive autobiography.

Where does my story begin?

Focus on the bridges and transitions in your life. Instead of starting with your birth, start with the high points of action and work backwards to the bridges that spanned the gaps and arcs between major events in your life. For example, if the highlight of your life was your graduation, marriage, or divorce, start with the first day of your new life—when your life turned over or made a transition.

Write about how you bridged the gaps in your life. Most of all, write about how you grew from one point to another—or took a fork in the road, a path less stampeded—or why you chose to skate to the tune of a different harpist rather than run with the herd. Write about the diversity and adversity in your life—how you grew from a sheltered beginning to full bloom—or what it feels like to age with grace—or in disgrace—or come of age in the information age. Conference with yourself by looking in the mirror and let your memory be your search engine. Take your vital signs and write about them.

Your personal journal is your little black box—an interactive legacy of of memories that measures your growth from one event to another. Your autobiography will record the pulse of your entire lifespan.

Consider your autobiography to be your human 'net' connection. Your life—like the Internet itself—follows a path of zigzagging routes and interconnected hubs. Just one of many pathways through which data is routed from birth to death and perhaps beyond.

An autobiography shares inner experiences from the storyteller's personal point of view. It's your chance to tell it your way. Instead of writing about how you got screwed by the "industry," show each experience as connected to the next and explore the reason why. Focus on the connections we all have and—most of all—use the concrete facts to get to the universal. Everyone can relate to something that is universal—like wanting to be the captain of your soul or fate or taking the path less traveled.

Everybody's life is good for at least one story. Make it your own. Write so it can be understood by someone from another land, or planet—using crop circles as visual fractals. Create tantalizing descriptions of your life experience arc with multiple endings.

Use your autobiography to design your life and plan your future—just as you would plan your past, if you could. Let the readers choose which way they'd like to conclude each phase of your life at a selected point—an exercise that might be fun and most revealing. In your interactive autobiography, there is always a second chance to start a new page.

To find an idea that is great enough to become a story, start by keeping a daily log. Then, turn the idea into dialogue. First write the action, then sell it as faction. Write about:

- **Who** you are;
- **How** you work;
- **Why** you work that way;
- **What** makes you tick.

Then, develop the story by stating how you grew from one point to the next, as well as who measured you and why.

Your story is about your connections and relationships. Its goal is to make you choose and grow. You see, we really are the only net around—the human one.

http://www-csli.stanford.edu/user/jbgalan

J.B. Galan uses his Web site to tell the story of his life and travels in hot-linked hypertext, pictures, and newsclippings. The initial "J" in his name rotates in three-dimensional space, changing from a "J" to a "B" with each rotation. As a survivor of a spinal chord injury, J.B. uses an "assessor" to control his computer by pointing his head and voice commands. (See also page 191.)

How should I organize my information?

Since you will be gathering information for your autobiography from many different sources, it may be easier initially to organize your notes in a notebook rather than in a word processor.

Follow the steps below to create a notebook for your research or adapt them to create an electronic notebook on your computer:

1. Photocopy your notes if you're gleaning facts from many different sources.Then, organize the events and facts into categories.

2. Color-code each category with a felt pen or colored dot.

3. Choose the most important events to emphasize as the stepping stones in your story.

4. Color-code each fact to identify each in its proper category.

5. Weed out what isn't important. (You may be able to use it later.)

6. Write the name of each category at the top of the page on a blank sheet of paper. Then, cut apart the photocopied set of notes. Tape, glue, or staple your notes into a logical, chronological sequence.

7. Staple the pages from each category into neat packets of notes organized in a logical, chronological order.

—or—

Use index cards and shuffle the deck in any order you like. The color coding will let you easily group similar information together under one heading.

8. Look for gaps in your research and fill in the holes. Then, recheck your notes and gather more information.

You now have the beginning of a notebook from which you can develop your true story. The information is sorted logically and your important life events are color-coded for easy reference.

Try writing scripts for family and corporate biographies.

32 How should I view criticism of my work?

Honest feedback will help you build upon your strengths and learn from your weaknesses. Listen for feedback and write it down for future reference.

A good evaluator will help you discover untapped pathways, new ideas to consider, more choices, and alternative routes to arrive at your goal. If the critic has your success at heart, that person will tell you what pitfalls to avoid and offer his experience and hindsight coupled with your foresight. Look for a warm, nurturing book doctor who is willing to share writing secrets and tips.

For a "feeling" writer, constructive criticism never feels very constructive. However, for a "thinking" writer, a good debate and the argument that ensues allows the logician to seek improvement. (However, only *if* the evaluator is judged competent will the terms for improvement be considered.)

Learn from feedback, yes, but watch out if you get more than you asked for in response. It's the key to hostility based on a payoff of power and control. When your writing comes under attack, consider the possibility that the critic must consider your work of considerable value to have spent their time blasting it page after page. If the response is overly hostile, the payoff is about getting power—the power they want to take back from you. If your writing is "really, really bad stuff and a disservice to all people everywhere," then why would they spend so much time to reply at length with such vehemence?

If the criticism makes you feel more invaded than pointed in a better direction, ignore it. The minute you start to feel indignity instead of improvement, the criticism has stopped being constructive and will become a waste of everyone's time.

Here are a few questions to ask the next time your work is evaluated:

1. Does the evaluator offer solutions to problems or suggest alternatives?

—or—

Is the criticism harsh, crushing to your ego, and offering no solutions to your omissions or misdirected references?

2. Are the suggested changes truly constructive?

    —or—

    Are they meant to tear you down?

3. Does the evaluator approach the subject as a battle to be won?

    —or—

    Does the evaluator make an effort to understand?

5. Do you feel treated with respect?

    —or—

    Do you feel invaded after being criticized?

Criticism is a highly subjective. If ten critics were given one piece to evaluate, you would receive ten very different replies. Few have the knowledge, experience, or desire to help you to improve your writing and most will dish out praise in tiny slices. It's much easier (and more satisfying for some) to tear down rather than build up. Try not to take it personally—afterall, it's just your life's work they're tearing apart.

Consider the personality and temperament of both yourself and your critic. If you are an intuitive person being evaluated by a practical, down-to-earth sensor/judger, then they may miss what you have intentionally written between the lines. On the other hand, a highly intuitive critic may find your work boring.

Instead of looking for criticism, invest some time to study the styles, habits, and techniques of the most successful writers. Ask yourself for feedback before asking others for theirs, but be willing to roll with the punches. Let yourself fall out of love with your work—just a little.

The moral of this story is to welcome constructive feedback based on experience. Remember, your audience is the final judge. You can't please everybody and a little controversy can be a good thing. Look at disagreement as an empowering wave. It's all right to agree to disagree. Go your way and believe in yourself, knowing that what you write works right for you. In the valley of the Internet, every scribe's a monarch.

What's the payoff?

NT - Power.

SP - Revenge.

NF - Attention.

SJ - Exemption.

33 How do I find the storyline of my life?

Perhaps something happened in your childhood that is worth sharing with all people. You may want to trade the wisdom of age for the energy of youth.

- You have survived a disaster and have built a successful career helping others.

- You have led a glamorous life meeting the rich and famous and now want to tell all.

- You were kidnapped and held captive for ransom by aliens.

- You adopted a houseful of children in need.

- You dropped out of college and became the world's richest man.

- You lost your executive career in midlife and became a homeless street poet.

- You killed your spouse in self-defense, were sent to prison, and then acquitted at the last hour.

- You run a matchmaking service for lonely hearts on the Web and arrange authentic repro-

ductions of ancient wedding ceremonies and coronations.

- You rent yourself out as a freelance corporate battered spouse to speak out against the swing shift.

- You traveled where no man has gone before and came back to tell the story.

- You developed multiple personalities due to a traumatic childhood experience and as a result, your journalism always has a fresh new angle.

- Your children were kidnapped by your ex-spouse and raised as fundamentalists in a foreign land.

Your agent may tell you that it has all been done before. Although they reject your work, you know that your story is unique. You know that what's been done before will be done again and again in other countries. That's how *Lethal Weapon* became *Fatal Weapon* in Japan and how *Fatal Attraction* became a hit in Japan's home video market as *Lethal Attraction*. Your unique story is universal.

Dialogue Sequences

PLAYPEN HOSTAGES

CHILDREN KIDNAPPED AS TODDLERS
RETURN AFTER TWENTY YEARS TO FIND A SHOCKING
SURPRISE ABOUT THEIR UNKNOWN MOTHER

by Anne Hart

FADE IN:

TITLE SEQUENCE - SLITSCAN EFFECT

1.INT. ANNE JOAN LEVINE'S HOME - NIGHT

Anne Joan Levine, an organizational development consultant in her forties, is sound asleep
in her parent's home in a quiet Canadian sub-
urb.

PAN
from front cover of her new book. (The cover
will have a photo of her talking into a radio
station microphone. The title will be *Choose
the Work You Love According to Your Personality
Temperament and Get Rich Quick.*)

ANGLE ON
her book which stands on a night table next to
her bed. Next to her book is also a clock radio
on the same table.

PAN
from her book on the night stand next to a
clock radio to ANNE as she sleeps alone in a
king-sized bed.

The Web is like the early days of radio all over again. Try converting your story to dialogue and have students or friends play each part. Add some background music, a few visuals and sound effects, and then broadcast it to the world.

2.EXT. JUST OUTSIDE ANNE'S DOOR

ANGLE ON ALI

ALI is a Middle-Eastern looking young man in
his twenties. Next to him stands his sister,
SAMIRA, a year older, and well-hidden behind
Islamic dress, including head scarf that covers
the neck. On her hands are a multitude of Middle-Eastern ethnic jewelry: rings covering all
fingers, jangling bracelets. She is tall and
dark with long hair. They speak with an Egyp-
tian/Arabic accent. ALI looks at his sister,
pauses a beat to sigh with tension, and then
reluctantly knocks on the door.

3.INT. ANNE'S HOME

Anne rushes to answer the door.

ANNE swings open the door in anger, but is
stopped in her tracks, surprised and shocked by
the appearance of her two children whom she
hasn't seen in twenty years.

                    ANNE

What the hell???

4.ANGLE ON ANNE'S FACE

as she stares in awe, surprise, and shock at
Ali and Samira. She pauses, speechless, her
mouth open wide.

CUT TO:

ALI as he smiles a wide grin and nervously extends his hand to grab Anne's. He lifts her hand to his forehead and kisses it, then placing her hand over his heart, he holds on for a moment. Are you our mother? We got your address from our uncle.

                    ANNE

Not one of my letters was answered, not for twenty years.

Anne reaches out to Samira and Ali and hugs them both. Anne pulls the headscarf from her daughter's face to look at her for the first time in twenty years.

                    SAMIRA

I'm getting married, but you're not invited to the wedding because you're Jewish, and if you tell my husband's family you're Jewish, you'll never see us again. You'll lose us.

Anne walks around Ali and looks at him.

                    ANNE

I already lost you twenty years ago when your father kidnapped you both and took you out of the country. What was it like growing up in Egypt?

                    ALI

Can we come in your house?

                              ANNE

Yes, of course.

PAN
Messy room. A stack of her own books is piled
high in the middle of the floor. Her photo on
the cover is visible.

CUT TO:
Anne as she scrambles to pick up stuff and
neaten the room.

                           SAMIRA

Weren't you expecting us?

                              ANNE

No. No one called me.

Anne runs around the house, waking her elderly
parents. Her mother and father come out of
their rooms. Everyone sleeps in a separate bed-
room in the house. They all file into the living room. Ali and Samira follow Anne around
the house, trailing behind her as she rushes
into the kitchen and faces a stack of dirty
dishes that sway, rattle, and fall on the floor
before she can catch them.

Her pace quickens as she searches for something, leaving no pillow unturned. Anne dives
under tables, running like a rat in a maze
throughout every room. As she searches, she
tosses pillows, books, and other household
items randomly about so that the house ends up
looking ransacked.

ANGLE OVER ANNE'S SHOULDER as she finally
locates an old scrapbook of children's photos
under a table. She rushes into the living room.

                        JOAO

How come we got company so late on the eve of
Passover?

                        ANNE

It's my kids, Moses and Zipporah. They've come
back from Egypt.

                        JOAO

But he kidnapped them when they were only four
and five years old. It's been twenty years
without a word. Twenty years wandering in the
wilderness.

                        ALI

We lived in a noisy Cairo apartment and I'm
here to ask you for money so I can go to medical school.

ANGLE - OVER ANNE'S SHOULDER

Everyone in the family looks at Ali. He grins
while Samira looks down.

                       SAMIRA

We are very religious, good Moslems. We want to
go to school in America. Our father told us
that our mother was a rich American doctor,
and....

                        ANNE

Wait a minute. I'm not a doctor. Your father
told me he was a doctor, but after the marriage
I found out he never finished high school. He
worked as a machinist until I bought him a res-
taurant. Just where is your father, anyway?

ALI

We need a house to live in. Our father is sick,
he can't pay rent. We want him to live with us.

JOAO

And you expect my daughter to provide you with
a free house and support you and your father?

SAMIRA

So we can both go to medical school.

ANGLE ON

dirty dishes full of gravy lying in the sink.
Anne laughs viciously. Samira turns around to
Ali and Anne's parents. Valivanda and Joao look
them over.

Joao walks around the kids, touching their
hair.

JOAO

They both look exactly like you, Anne.
Who are you staying with tonight?

ALI

Our uncle, Abdul. But it's tight living with he
and his wife and six children. Also, our father
has been living there for many years.

ANNE

You mean your dad dumped you on his mother in
Egypt for twenty years and came back to Canada
to live with his brother?

                    SAMIRA

That's correct. We only saw him for two years.
He spent some time in jail and has lived here
ever since. We came to live with him but heard
you own real estate all over Canada.

                     JOAO

I own one house besides this and it's rented.

                    SAMIRA

So kick the tenant out.

                     JOAO

It'll make me poor in my old age.

CUT TO:

Anne as she overhears the conversation in the
kitchen, hurriedly washing the dishes. She gri-
maces, tears welling up in her eyes.

ANNE carries the scrap book back into the living room. She opens it to pictures of her children from infancy to age four and five. She
shows the album to them.

                     ANNE

I bet you like surprises, that's why you didn't
call first.

                    SAMIRA

No, you're phone number's unlisted.

                     ANNE

I've been sending letters to your grandma in
Egypt for years with my phone number. Why do
you think I still live with my parents? I've
waited for you for twenty years to return.
Nothing's changed in my life.

CLOSE-UP ON

Anne as she pours fruit juice from a bottle
that looks like wine.

                    ALI

We don't drink alcohol. We're Moslems.

                    ANNE

It's mixed fruit juice. I'm a strict vegetar-
ian.

                    SAMIRA

Why did you never come to visit us?

                    ANNE

I'm afraid to fly. I've been agoraphobic most
of my life. . . and what would a little Jewish
girl be doing in Egypt during the '67 war? A
rabbi's daughter, yet.

                    ALI

Why would a rabbi's daughter marry a Moslem
student from Egypt on a thirty-day tourist
visa?

                    ANNE

Because I really believed that in a past life,
I belonged in Egypt.

                              To be continued. . .

                         # # #

CHAPTER SIX

A Palette of Authoring Tools

*T*he interactive software market is fast becoming one of the most exciting segments of the software industry. What has happened is similar to when word processing matured into desktop publishing. Only today, desktop publishing has evolved into something new: interactive hypermedia publishing on the Web.

There are several types of software products used by content creators for the Web and CD ROM. There is software for collaboration, idea generation, flow charting and storyboarding. In addition, there are numerous hypertext editors, Internet browsers, hypermedia authoring tools, graphics and animation packages. Most developers use an assortment of products, sometimes several in each category.

When choosing an authoring tool, you should consider whether you want the completed application to be both CD-ROM and Web compatible. Some packages support both formats and others do not. Also— and this is a "biggie"—ask if there is an additional license fee to distribute the application commercially.

Look for companies who develop products based on open standards that are compatible with related technologies. Find out if the company is moving ahead with technology or lagging behind.

Writers need to understand the basic capabilities of the software, regardless of they intend to hire a developer who specializes in interactive media or learn to use the software themselves.

In this chapter, we will examine some of the newest media authoring tools, techniques, and trends with the help of Claire Condra Arias, book publisher, interactive producer, and digital artist.

No one democratizes the Web more than writers and artists. most of whom work for the news media. entertainment. advertising. and educational industries.

34 Which platform should I choose?

Although the Web is essentially platform-independent, there are several distinct platforms and methods of distribution used by designers and writers for commercial and non-commercial applications. Let's take a look at the newest technologies and also the more common platforms in use today:

Personal Computers

At this time in the U.S., most commercial interactive applications are developed on the Mac platform, but for users of IBM PC compatible computers. Although today, a multimedia-capable Pentium PC is a viable development platform, the most advanced 3-D animation and virtual reality applications require the power of a Unix workstation such as those manufactured by Silicon Graphics or Sun.

DVD (Digital Video Disk)

CD-ROM will soon be replaced by DVD as the media of choice for not only the distribution of hypermedia titles, but for data storage, as well.

Developed jointly by Philips and Toshiba, DVD offers read/write capability with a storage capacity of up to seventeen gigabytes. That's enough space for an entire full-length feature film—in multiple languages and multiple endings. It's fifteen times the storage capacity of today's standard Pentium PC. The small, square DVD disk will ultimately replace both CD-ROM and VHS and become a universal standard format for hypermedia applications, film, and video.

Internet Broadcasting

Much of the current interactive Web technology—including the *Java* language—was originally developed for interactive TV. The latest trend is "push technology" that delivers customized interactive content to the desktop over netcast channels of streaming media. Included in this category are tele- and video-conferencing, e-mail casting, and real-time online events linked worldwide by digital satellite and high-speed fiber optic.

The newest wave in PC hardware is the "Internet appliance," a machine that provides Internet access without a computer. Soon, Internet-enabled TVs will be everywhere, followed by a flurry of interactive network programming. This is the beginning of the wave that the entertainment industry has been waiting for.

CD-ROM
Compact Disk Read-Only Memory)

The compact laser disk is played on a CD-ROM drive and is standard equipment on most computers sold today. CD-ROM has nearly replaced the diskette as a distribution medium for software products. CD-ROM drives are versatile devices, able to quickly read multimedia data from a disc and also double as musical CD players. They have also been mistaken, on occassion, by new users as coffee cup holders. Despite its versatility, the days of the CD-ROM are numbered, as it is gradually phased out over the next few years to make way for its successor, DVD.

Publishing on CD-ROM is one of the biggest markets, but has been difficult for small and large publishers, alike. Retailers still haven't decided whether a CD-ROM is fish or fowl— a book or a software program. Should it be packaged in a box as a software product, in a jewel case as a musical CD, or pasted inside the back cover of a book? In spite of a recent distribution shake-out, sales of commercial CD-ROM titles constitute a multi-billion dollar industry.

CD-i (Compact Disk interactive)

CD-i is a significant technology developed by Philips in the Netherlands. CD-i applications are computer independent and run on special players which are similar to inexpensive game machines. CD-i was an early venue for high-quality, full-motion video and stereo, which made it well-suited for touch-screen kiosk and corporate training applications where the complexity of a computer and keyboard were an unwelcome intrusion.

For years considered a standard in Europe, CD-i failed to capture the attention of the U.S. consumer market who were already too deeply entrenched in Microsoft products to embrace an alternate platform.

In any event, the advances made in CD-i technology will soon be rolled over into a new generation of even more advanced interactive products running on DVD.

Videodisk players

Videodisk players are dedicated machines that combine interactive video with optical laser disk technology. A wide variety of videodisk players (such as the Imagination Machine from Philips Interactive) have been developed to keep pace with the explosion in electronic entertainment.

3DO (Three-Dimensional Optics)

3DO systems include virtual reality, and other three-dimensional optical technologies. This technology offers a combination of three-dimensional technology, video, and animation.

Interactive Movies

Interactive movies allow the audience to participate in the story through personal computers or simulation machines. The audience may choose alternative plots, branches, and movie endings. It lets members of the audience get inside of the story and become one of the characters.

Because of its nature, this technology seems to be best suited for an online experience or a one-on-one production on DVD. With so many options, a theatre audience must vote to choose the most popular ending. This is how they solved the problem with the first movie ever produced in this category; *I'm Your Man,* by Controlled Entropy.

Computer Game Players

Computer game designers evolved from the old video arcade games that were around for decades. The electronic entertainment industry is a hot business with companies like Nintendo and Sega producing games for both dedicated game player machines and PC/Mac formats. Some popular games have even evolved into animated or live action television programs and movies.

Board games or games combined with books are included in the game players category. It also may include live games similar to psychodrama acted out by a group at parties or in virtual theatre on the Web.

35   What is hypertext?

In 1965, a computer visionary, Theodore Holm Nelson, coined the term, 'hypertext'. He described it as the way everyone would write in the future and called it 'nonsequential' writing. With dialogue, you write sequentially. But, ideas are not sequential. They have a structure that is out of sequence, or they wouldn't be ideas. Ideas are tied together nonsequentially.

What hypertext does is to tie together chunks of text so they can be explored out of sequence. To write in hypertext, you should break down the information you want to present into chunks. The reader can quickly find and jump to the topic of interest without having to follow a sequence dictated by the author.

An HTML document is essentially a dynamic online book. Writers and readers can select a particular page to read, flip page-by-page, or let the book turn the pages by itself. If you plan to write hypermedia books, this is the way to start. Playing a docu-

ment gives you a live presentation of mixed video, audio, image, and text objects.

Hyperlinked publishing is where the writer's profession is heading. Internal document links provide powerful mechanisms for feature articles, training material, and research.

Web writing is multilevel publishing. It's a series of levels, a hierarchy. Now add interactive, three-dimensional writing with branching narratives and you have a complexity of writing that encourages critical thinking and consideration.

Even those in non-writing professions use interactive writing to stimulate creative thinking. According to Karl Mettke of the USDA Forest Service Regional Office in Milwaukee, Wisconsin, in 1991 they initiated a computer-generated internal network, or *Intranet*, to spark creativity and new thinking within the Forest service. Called "Dreamers," the network helps facilitate discussion and interaction related to organizational change and creativity both within and outside the Forest Service. It evolved slowly within one region of the Forest Service to gradually encompass the whole agency. Their publication, *Creativity Fringes,* is used to publish and share information related to creativity and new thinking.

Writing for the Web means taking into consideration the differing capabilities of users' systems—such as screen resolution ,modem speed, version of browser, etc. You should write for the lowest possible denominator to reach the widest audience. This is why many sites include a message saying, "Works best with Browser Ver. X." Many users still have only text-based access to the Web—especially those using computers in librar-ies—so make sure to include a text description of every graphic used in the site.

Don't go hog wild with the special effects or assume that everyone has the same setup as you do. If you're working on a hi-res monitor with a high-speed modem, your page won't load or look the same when read by a person with a slower modem and low-res monitor.

During peak traffic periods, servers are slower and it's going to get worse. If your reader has to wait more than ten seconds for your page to load, chances are that they'll give up before transfer is made. Only the most patient few will read your written material.

Presentations are dynamic, in both temporal and spatial dimensions. If you put up HTML fiction on the Web and want to go beyond to hyperme-dia writing or publishing on the Internet, create virtual pages within a document. All HTML objects are grouped by virtual pages. HTML pro-vides an easy way to publish your writing online.

Just as tag lines add descriptive features to dialogue, so does adding hyptertext tags to Web documents enhance their visual impact. Line breaks, heading levels, bullets, tables, and rules are all determined by hypertext commands. Other hypertext commands can be used to add special features such as graph-ics, animation, and sound.

In a script, short sentences used for visual impact are called "tag lines." In an HTML document, the markup codes are called 'tags'. Tags define the structure of your document. The text is enclosed in a set of matching tags that represent a specific formatting attribute. For example, you would use the tag <H1> to denote a large headline (level one head). When formatting an HTML document, you may use either upper- or lower case characters.

To create an interactive document, you add may add links to other pages or documents on the Web. You can present the reader with multiple choices and let them decide which path to follow in the story or lesson.

If the information isn't easy to digest at first glance, the majority of people will tune out or click off. That's why the first step you need to take is to outline your storyboard flow chart so you'll know where your links end up and you can see the big picture—with the forest detailed inside, too.

Web writing is both time- and space-based writing. Use links to create different levels of writing.

Your flow chart or storyboard will help you to see the relationship between linked scenes or pages. Try to keep a one-page Web experience to thirty seconds of reading. Time your events. Don't ever let anything go beyond sixty seconds. For that long, it better be the most important part of the story.

One of the most important and challenging issues is to keep the time required to load a page to a minimum. It's tempting to load the site up with fancy graphics and animation, but you may leave a large part of your audience in the dark.

Hypertext isn't the best solution for every type of writing. Don't expect someone to sit there and read through pages and pages of information on their screen while their telephone line is busy. You can save the long linear documents for the printed page—or encourage the reader to download the file or print it out to be read offline. Remember the story of the Internet. Until the Web made it easy to browse, the Internet remained underutilized. Keep the users' interests in mind by designing pages that are easy to use and easy to load.

A Hypertext Document

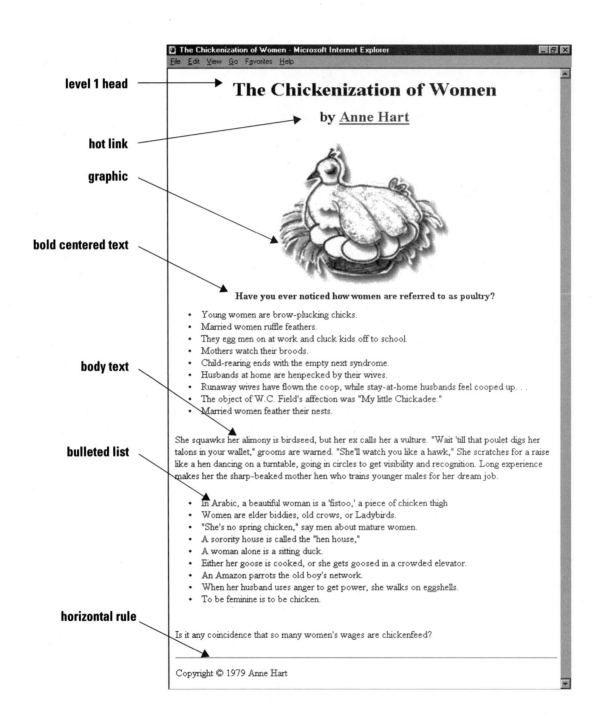

level 1 head →

The Chickenization of Women

hot link → by <u>Anne Hart</u>

graphic →

bold centered text → **Have you ever noticed how women are referred to as poultry?**

- Young women are brow-plucking chicks.
- Married women ruffle feathers.
- They egg men on at work and cluck kids off to school.
- Mothers watch their broods.
- Child-rearing ends with the empty next syndrome.
- Husbands at home are henpecked by their wives.
- Runaway wives have flown the coop, while stay-at-home husbands feel cooped up. . .
- The object of W.C. Field's affection was "My little Chickadee."
- Married women feather their nests.

body text →

She squawks her alimony is birdseed, but her ex calls her a vulture. "Wait 'till that poulet digs her talons in your wallet," grooms are warned. "She'll watch you like a hawk," She scratches for a raise like a hen dancing on a turntable, going in circles to get visibility and recognition. Long experience makes her the sharp-beaked mother hen who trains younger males for her dream job.

bulleted list →

- In Arabic, a beautiful woman is a 'fistoo,' a piece of chicken thigh
- Women are elder biddies, old crows, or Ladybirds.
- "She's no spring chicken," say men about mature women.
- A sorority house is called the "hen house,"
- A woman alone is a sitting duck.
- Either her goose is cooked, or she gets goosed in a crowded elevator.
- An Amazon parrots the old boy's network.
- When her husband uses anger to get power, she walks on eggshells.
- To be feminine is to be chicken.

horizontal rule →

Is it any coincidence that so many women's wages are chickenfeed?

Copyright © 1979 Anne Hart

Here's how to:
Create a simple HTML document

1. **Enter the basic HTML document code.**

   Using any text editor or HTML authoring tool, enter the following code to mark the main sections of the document. Notice how the commands come in matching pairs and are enclosed brackets. The closing command always begins with a forward slash. Also, HTML code can be typed in either upper- or lowercase characters. (We use uppercase in these examples to make it easier to read.)

   ```
   <HTML>
   <HEAD>
   <TITLE>
   </TITLE>
   </HEAD>
   <BODY>
   </BODY>
   </HTML>
   ```

2. **Enter the title.**

   Enter the title of your page between the <TITLE> and </TITLE> tags. This text will appear in the title bar of the browser window. The title and tags can appear on the same line, as follows:

   ```
   <TITLE>My Page</TITLE>
   ```

3. **Set the background color.**

   On the first line after the end heading marker </HEAD>, enter the following line of code to set the background color to white (rather than grey).

   ```
   <BODY BGCOLOR="#FFFFFF">
   ```

This essay by Anne Hart, originally written under the pen name "Anne D'Arcy" was widely circulated in the late 70s—even appearing in the syndicated column, "Dear Abby."

Here's how your completed project will look when viewed on the Web through a browser. (Chicken not included.)

3. Enter the heading.

On the first line after the <BODY> tag, type these two lines of code:

<CENTER><H1>The Chickenization of Women</H1> <P>

<H2>by Anne Hart</H2><P></CENTER>

This will create two centered headings, separated by a blank line. (There are six sizes of headings available, numbered from H1 to H6.)

4. Make a link.

To create a hot link to another document, such as a page that contains the author bio, you would enclose the text to be linked (which in this example, is the author's name) within the following code:

<A HREF="Anne.html">Anne Hart</A>

This code creates a hot link out of the author's name, Anne Hart that will load the associated file (anne.html) whenever the user clicks on the link. (The referenced file must exist for this example to work.)

5. Enter the body text.

Type the following line of text, inserting the tag <P> at the end of the sentence. (This tag inserts a carriage return and skip a line.)

Have you ever noticed how often women are referred to as poultry?<P>

6. Add a graphic.

The following line of code would display a graphic image of a chicken, centered on the screen and followed by a blank line.

<CENTER><IMG SRC="chicken.gif"></CENTER><P>

The most common type of graphic files used in Web pages are .GIF and .JPG. Since graphics take a while to load online, they should be used sparingly in Web pages.

7. Create a bulleted list.

The user list tags <UL> </UL> mark the beginning and end of an indented list. The <LI> tag (with a letter 'i') places a bullet at the beginning of each item. Type the following lines of code into the body section after the previous line:

<UL>

<LI>Young women are brow-plucking chicks.

</UL>

Complete the bulleted list by adding the following lines between the beginning and end user list tags.

<LI>Married women ruffle feathers.

<LI>They egg men on at work and cluck kids off to school.

<LI>Mothers watch their broods.

<LI>Child-rearing ends with the empty nest syndrome.

<LI>Husbands at home are henpecked by their wives.

<LI>Runaway wives have flown the coop, while stay-at-home husbands feel cooped up. . .

<LI>The object of W.C. Field's affection was "My little Chickadee."

<LI>Married women feather their nests.

</UL>

8. Add a paragraph of text.

Type the following paragraphs, placing a <P> carriage return tag at the end of each:

She squawks her alimony is birdseed, but her ex calls her a vulture. "Wait 'till that poulet digs her talons in your wallet," grooms are warned. "She'll watch you like a hawk,"<P>

She scratches for a raise like a hen dancing on a turntable, going in circles to get visibility and recognition. Long experience makes her the sharp-beaked mother hen who trains younger males for her dream job.<P>

9. Add another bulleted list and conclusion.

Type in the following to create another bulleted list and conclusion.

```
<UL>
<LI>In Arabic, a beautiful woman is a 'fistoo', a piece of chicken thigh.
<LI>Women are elder biddies, old crows, or Ladybirds.
<LI>"She's no spring chicken," say men about mature women.
<LI>A sorority house is called the "hen house."
<LI>A woman alone is a sitting duck.
<LI>Either her goose is cooked, or she gets goosed in a crowded elevator.
<LI>An Amazon parrots the old boy's network.
<LI>When her husband uses anger to get power, she walks on eggshells.
<LI>To be feminine is to be chicken.
</UL>
Is it any coincidence that so many women's wages are chickenfeed?<P>
```

10. Add a horizontal rule and copyright statement.

At the end of the body section, just above the end body tag, add the <HR> tag to create a horizontal rule across the page, followed by a copyright statement. The © command inserts the '©' copyright symbol.

```
<HR>
Copyright &COPY; 1979 Anne Hart
</BODY>
</HTML>
```

11. Replace special characters.

Special characters such as quotation marks, ampersands, are interpreted differently by some systems. To make sure they are displayed correctly, these characters should be replaced with their corresponding HTML code before the document is uploaded to the Web.

Use the find and replace function of your text editor to replace each quotation mark in the document with the following code:

```
&QUOT;
```

12. Save the file.

Save the file, giving it the three-letter file suffix "HTM." You have now created a simple HTML document that can be loaded onto the Web and viewed through a browser such as Netscape Navigator. The document can also be viewed offline by loading it into your browser from your hard disk.

If this file were to be uploaded to a UNIX server and published on the Web, it would be necessary to rename the three-letter .HTM suffix to the four letter .HTML suffix. However, on a DOS-based system running Windows, this final step can only be completed after the file has been copied to the server.

An Opening Scene

"The Chickenization of Women" for CD-ROM might begin with a scene like this.

This scene was drawn in Fractal Design's Painter with a Wacom tablet.

Which HTML editor should I use?

Today there are many good HTML editors and Web authoring tools on the market. It doesn't really matter which program you use, unless you intend to develop a commercial site with advanced functions such as online database access and order entry.

If you prefer to coordinate your software into compatible suites of complimentary products, you may want to choose an HTML authoring tool from a company whose software you already use—such as Microsoft, Adobe, or Macromedia. On the other hand, if you like to mix-and-match your software, you will find many innovative and affordable programs by doing a search on the Web.

Backstage Internet Studio

Backstage Internet Studio is an authoring tool for database-oriented Web applications. More than an HTML page layout program, Backstage provides a library of ready-made objects and management tools for the professional developer.

FrontPage

FrontPage from Microsoft is an easy-to-use page layout program that supports a broad range of plug-ins and advanced functions including ActiveX, Java, and PowerPoint animations.

HotDog

HotDog from Sausage Software is the brainchild of a 23-year old Australian programmer. Unlike other products featured in this category, HotDog is a simple menu-driven text editor. It doesn't attempt to shield you from the HTML code, but keeps you in the code—helping you to learn HTML as you use the program.

PageMill

PageMill from Adobe offers a WYSI-WYG point and click, drag and drop interface. its layout and graphics handling are superb, as would be expected from Adobe; the industry leader in desktop publishing software.

Trial versions of all of these programs can be downloaded from the Web.

Is one browser better than another?

As browser technology evolves, the market seems to have split into three camps: those who use Netscape Navigator, those who use Internet Explorer, and those who use both. Web site developers are well advised to have both browsers installed on their system so they can test their work for compatibility.

Time Warner and WebTV Networks have selected Internet Explorer as their "browser of choice." Meanwhile, Netscape is focusing on the corporate Intranet market and has recently landed plum accounts with major telephone companies.

Basic browser software can be downloaded at no charge from the Web and is often preloaded on computers at the factory. Computer magazines sometimes include a CD-ROM of free software which may include a browser or two.

Netscape Navigator

Netscape Navigator is only one component of a suite of software designed to let users communicate, share, and access information.

If you're interested in the politics of technology, Netscape should be commended for their leadership in promoting open standards on the Internet.

Internet Explorer

Internet Explorer is a very slick and pleasant-to-use browser. However, don't confuse it with their pay-by-subscription online service, the Microsoft Network (MSN). You may inadvertantly be led to subscribe for the service while installing the browser. (You can just skip over that part of the installation.)

3-D Browsers

The most recent versions of Netscape Navigator and Internet Explorer offer 3-D browsing capabilities. Netscape's Live3D is an extension to Navigator that provides access to 3-D worlds, animation, sound, music, and even video. Other 3-D browsers include Cosmo from Silicon Graphics, Inc. and Worldview from Intervista Software, Inc.

The most recent version of these products can be downloaded from each company's respective site.

Voices from the industry:
Dana Todd, V.P., Sales and Client Services, Bien Logic

Bio

Dana Todd was working as a 'serious' journalist and editor when she caught the advertising bug writing advertorials for special newspaper sections. After completing a degree in Advertising from the University of Georgia, she worked as a consultant and account executive for a small agency in San Diego, California.

Upon discovering the Internet, she promptly ditched it all to join Bien Logic (then a start-up company and now a major Web site developer). In addition to her duties as Vice President of Advertising and Client Services, Dana is a chat room diva for Bien Logic's ongoing cyber-party at FLIRT.COM.

She'll never go back.

When designing a Web site, you have to assume first that the user is confused and has low-end equipment. If you can design effectively within these limitations, you can design for any bandwidth (hardware, software or brainware).

Think first along the same lines as designing a building: what is its function, who will visit, where is it located, does it need to follow a certain artistic style, etc. For instance, you wouldn't design a school building as a glass-paned high-rise unless you're in New York. A library needs to be arranged in a certain way to invite people to read while still addressing security and archiving concerns.

To use the Web simply as an advertising tool is to waste the medium.If you had to build a cathedral with words, how would you go about it?

Try it as an exercise. Write a cathedral in one long stream of consciousness, as if you had never been

in a cathedral before. Now, break it up and edit it down: limit yourself to one hundred words per page. Next, take all the pages and mix them up, then spread them out in a web pattern. Find a way to link them all, and you've written a virtual cathedral. Remember when linking the pages, that the body doesn't travel to this building—the mind and spirit do. Logic should always prevail in leading the viewer from one page to the next, but not as a way of limitation. Surprise the adventurous and reward the curious and illogical traveller.

Next step, add graphics. Once the metaphor is set, this should be almost easy. Graphics can also incorporate written text and dialogue so that the words are not lost. Once upon a time, the Internet was strictly text-based. Now, with the option of full color graphics and multimedia, your choices are limited only by imagination and your audience's average bandwidth capabilities.

How do you create graphics for the Web?

Graphics can be used to illustrate a Web page, as background 'wallpaper' or as a hot link to jump to another location in the document or site on the Web.

Most graphics used in HTML documents are bit-mapped images composed of tiny dots or 'pixels'. Virtually any type of two-dimensional image—from photographs and line drawings to paintings and cartoons—can be incorporated into an HTML document. The two most common bit-map file formats are .JPG and .GIF, both of which can be readily transmitted through telephone lines. The .JPG format is generally preferred for photographs, whereas the .GIF format is usually preferred for line art. Until the availability of streaming media, graphics were used sparingly in HTML documents because of the time it takes to transmit and reassemble each image at the other end.

At the very least, you should have a good graphics program that is capable of importing and exporting files for the Web (.GIF and .JPG) as well as the standard graphics formats

used for print and CD-ROM production (such as .TIF, .PCX, .BMP, .PICT, and so on).

Painter

If you are an artist, you will love Fractal Design's *Painter (ver. x)*. The program emulates every type of media imaginable, from crayons to oil paint—including onion skin cell animation. To get the most from the program, you should purchase an graphics tablet. Those on a tight budget may consider Fractal Design's entry-level product, *Dabbler*, which can often be purchased bundled with a small graphics tablet for a reasonable price.

Photoshop

Photoshop from Adobe Systems is considered a "must-have" by professional designers. Photoshop allows you to combine images and special effects from most any source—photos, clipart, scans into a composition that meets professional production standards. If you're in the market for a scanner, you may be able to find one that comes bundled with *Photoshop*.

How do you create animation for the Web?

File size continues to be one of the biggest obstacles to using animation freely on the Web. If a single bit-mapped image takes a while to load, how long will it take to transmit and view a multi-image animated sequence? The problem has been addressed in part by a technique called 'streaming' that allows portions of the animation or video to be displayed while the rest of the file is loading into memory.

Animated GIFs

Another approach—and perhaps the easiest and most affordable—is to create an animated GIF. No special player software is required to view them and the software needed to create them can be downloaded from the Web.

GIF Construction Set from Alchemy Mindworks, is a full-featured GIF utility that lets you to combine separate GIF files into a flip-book style animation. The shareware program can be downloaded from the Daily Download site (see facing page).

Here's how it works:

1. Use your favorite paint program to save each image for the animation as a separate GIF file.

2. Use the GIF Construction Set (or a similar program) to stack the GIF files in sequence. Then, add timing to control the speed and number of times the animation will play in a loop.

3. Save the file as an animated GIF and refer to it as you would any other GIF file from your HTML document.

The four images above were combined to create an animated GIF for the *Cyberscribes* Web site. It's easy and fun to do.

Vector-Based Animation

Macromedia Flash is a Web-based animation tool that uses vector rather than bit-mapped images. Vector-based graphics are drawn from mathematical calculations and are much smaller and download faster than bit-mapped graphics. Images may be drawn freehand using the program's drawing tools. Also, bit-mapped images can be imported and used as backdrops for Flash movies. You can use Flash to create animation, interactive interfaces, animated buttons, scrolling banners, and zoomable graphics.

Flash movies can be viewed online with the Shockwave Flash player which may be downloaded at no charge from Macromedia's Web site. (See Appendix D for product information.)

Less is More

Simplicity almost always works to your advantage when designing for the Web. Ask yourself if a visitor to your site will be willing to wait patiently while your graphics load or will want to download any special software that may be required.

As people switch to high-speed broadband connections, we'll see more animation and video on the Web. Many developers now maintain two versions of the same site: One for those running in the fast lane with streaming video, animation and sound, and another for those still travelling in the slower lanes of the Internet.

http://www.ellipsys.com

Animated GIFs gave life to this interview by Paul Howell of KTEN News in Denison, Texas with Aniba Merimdeh, avatar hostess of "The Cyberscribes Show." This segment was part of a four-part series in which Aniba discussed the future of the Internet and the latest in broadcast technology on the Web.

40 What should I look for in a hypermedia authoring tool?

Hypermedia describes the way multimedia objects such as text, graphics, sound, and video are combined to create a full-featured application. Hypermedia applications tell the story in sights and sounds and allow the user to participate. Because hypermedia involves more of the senses, it is ideally suited for instructional applications and sales presentations.

Most any type of document can be adapted to hypermedia. Ask yourself, "How can I tell this story in pictures?" A few examples of nonfiction applications would be newsletters, catalogs, sales presentations, guidebooks, technical or marketing reports, and any type of lesson—from music to surgery.

The good news is that it is now possible for a freelance writer working from home to create affordable interactive hypermedia applications that can be distributed on either CD-ROM or the Web. Furthermore, the Internet offers these creative people immediate access to an international market.

We evaluated several authoring tools while researching the material for this book—products with a price range between $200.00 and $10,000. Here are the basic features we were looking for:

- **Portable**
  PC/Mac cross-platform compatibility.
  The ability to export HTML and *Java* files for the Web.

- **Programmable**
  Scripting language and/or database access.

- **Free runtime**
  The ability to distribute your completed application as a commercial product without additional licensing fees.

- **Customer support**
  Does the company support the product? Are they moving ahead with technology?

- **Easy to use**

- **A good value**

Authoring Tools

Whether you decide to mix and match your software or go with a coordinated suite of products from a single vendor, you will find many exciting authoring tools for creative expression.

The two hypermedia authoring tools that we believe to the best in this category are Macromedia *Director* and *HyperStudio* from Roger Wagner Publishing, Inc. Each of these programs fills a different need in the marketplace.

Macromedia Director

Director has earned its position as the industry standard in this category. A knowledge of *Director* is nearly a prerequisite for employment in the interactive multimedia field.

Director is based on the metaphor of a major movie studio production. The media elements to be used (such as graphics, animation, and sound) are first assembled as members of the 'cast'. Members of the 'cast' are then presented on the 'stage' as specified in the 'score.'

Director gives the developer explicit control over every aspect of the production. Because of its wealth of features, *Director* takes a while to learn, however the time invested is worth the effort. The documentation is well written and supported.

Other complimentary products include Macromedia's *Shockwave* which allows a movie created in *Director* to be viewed on the Web and their HTML authoring suite, *Backstage Internet Studio*.

HyperStudio

HyperStudio from Roger Wagner Publishing is less complex and less powerful than *Director*, but is easy to learn and affordable—which makes it a favorite in the educational community.

HyperStudio is based on the concept of a stack of cards where each screen page of your application is one card in the stack. An application may incorporate a variety of multimedia objects such as text, graphics, animation, sound, and *Quick-Time* movies that are arranged on the cards. The user can move from page to page, or respond to prompts by pressing buttons that are set to perform various operations. A button may play a sound file, run another program, display a new page, or jump to another location—which may be another stack of cards or even an address on the Web. *HyperStudio* is easy to learn because it allows the user to take a less structured approach.

Because it is a less complicated program, the product documentation is not as extensive as that of *Director*. However, the company is friendly and willing to answer questions.

If your needs are not too sophisticated and you are on a limited budget, you will find this program to be a good value. (With the money you save, you can buy yourself a nice graphics package.)

QuickTime

QuickTime is a line of products based on video playback technology developed by Apple. When Microsoft and Intel were still showing slide shows on their PCs, Apple was off and running with immersive video. The QuickTime family of software has grown to include products for virtual reality and live conferencing on the Web. QuickTime movie

files can be readily incorporated into applications developed with authoring tools such as Macromedia Director and Hyperstudio. QuickTime from Apple is available for both the Mac and PC.

How much should you spend?

While evaluating software in this category, we also examined two authoring tools in the $10,000 price range. Each of these products was developed by a company outside of the United States, originally for their own in-house use. Each company later decided to sell their software as an authoring tool for the "high-end" market. Although they considered their products to be authoring 'engines' rather than "shrink-wrapped" products, neither program could meet our minimum requirements for functionality and support.

The fact is, you don't have to spend a small fortune to gain entry into the new media market. Although you may need to invest in several software programs, most products in this category have a retail price between $300 and $700.

A Hypermedia Script

THE CHICKENIZATION OF WOMEN

by Anne Hart

VISUAL AND USER INTERACTION	AUDIO
INTRODUCTION:	
Title Screen	Sound of crickets chirping.
Hen flutters in and settles on nest.	VOICE-OVER: Have you ever noticed how often women are referred to as poultry?
Hen ruffles feathers as she lays two eggs.	<cluck. . .cluck. . .cluck>
The eggs roll to the bottom of the screen and become 'Yes' and 'No' buttons.	
USER RESPONSE:	
YES or NO: Egg wobbles and cracks and out pops a chick.	<peep. . .peep. . .peep>
TRANSITION TO: Through the barn windows, the sun rises over the barnyard. . .	Music. . . The chicks <peep> and the hen <clucks> as a rooster <crows> to begin the new day. . .

How would you present "The Chickenization of Women" as a hypermedia script? How would you illustrate each scene? How can you tell the story in sights and sounds?

This script shows one approach for the opening scene.

How do you design a user interface?

The interface of most interactive applications is defined by a series of templates that determine the screen layout. This stage of the process deals with the presentation of the information rather than the content.

Your project may be to publish an electronic magazine on CD-ROM, design an interactive sales presentation for a kiosk, or to prepare an educational tutorial to be distributed on the Web. In each of these applications, a screen template can be used to coordinate the presentation and interaction of the text, graphics, animation, sound, and video clips. The best presentations are simple and straight-forward.

In each case, information supports learning through the instructional frames or "screen shots" that the users read as they flip through pages on the computer screen by clicking on buttons or icons.

Think of a frame as a template designed for a specific purpose. When you design a frame, you are actually designing the way information is presented to the user on the screen. You are designing the user interface of the program.

Each area on the screen should have a special function with consistent locations. For example, you may choose to present new information in the center and supporting information about the lesson at the top. Consistency will help the user know what to expect and to understand what you're trying to show.

Whatever you do, define the location for each type of information and use these locations consistently. Patterns that are easily recognized and remembered work the best. . . like imprinting white on a black background or using colors that go well together.

You should design a variety of templates for different purposes, and then use them consistently throughout the application.

Presentation Screens

Presentation screens show the basic lesson information to the user or student. Each screen may present new instruction or information in a story or give examples and guidance. Say what you have to say in easy to understand, ten- to fifteen-word sentences.

Instructional Screens

Instructional screens introduce the relationship between the former and current learning subjects or parts of a story.

Instructional screens may alert the user to the need for different skills before the lesson starts. Use instructional screens to raise a flag or to get attention. Instructional screens also help identify relationships among past and present learning and can be used to bridge the transition points in your story or lesson. Information contained in different locations of each frame will be consistent from beginning to end of your project.

Question Screens

Use question screens to get input from the user. In many cases, students can learn from their own responses. In the case of a lesson, the only information that will change from frame-to-frame will be the question. All other information will be identical, including the directions for answering the questions, the location of the routines, borders, and options.

Dialogue Screens

A dialogue screen asks a question and provides feedback in the same frame. You may use a show-and-hide technique to display the question and then the answer or feedback.

Transitional Screens

Transitional screens may be used to introduce a reading comprehension lesson, present short reading material of any kind, or to view video clips.

Prompt Screens

Prompt screens help the user to understand the information and give them the opportunity to respond.

Help Screens

Help screens guide the user step-by-step to produce a correct response or to provide additional information about a topic.

These techniques can be applied to the interface design of any interactive application, regardless of the purpose of the application or the authoring tool you use.

Ten tips for:
Designing an interactive story

1. **Determine the content.**

   Prepare the outline of your story or script.

2. **Choose the concept and framework.**

   Determine the creative concept and the framework that will serve as the umbrella for the presentation or story.

3. **Choose the platform.**

   Choose the platform(s) the application will be designed to run on. If the program is designed for CD-ROM, you can more be liberal in your use of media elements such as graphics, animation, and sound than you would be for the Web.

4. **Choose the media types to be used**

   Choose the type of media elements to be used—whether graphics, animation, video, or a combination of all of the above. Make sure that these support rather than overpower the main message and concept and work within the system limitations of your platform.

5. **Design the look and feel of the program.**

   Design the layout of each type of type of frame to be used, based upon your creative concept and overall framework. This will determine the "look and feel" of your application.

5. **Choose the system of navigation.**

   Choose the navigation tools the user will need to move throughout the application. These should be located in the same place on each frame.

6. **Determine the level of user interaction.**

   Choose the level of interaction the user will have with the application. What input and decisions will the user be required to make?

7. Draw a flow chart.

Prepare a flow chart to illustrate the logic of the program and the paths the user may take from the beginning, through the middle, to the end.

8. Draw a storyboard.

Draw a series of thumbnail sketches, or storyboards, to illustrate each step in the flow chart. Each sketch should be based upon one of the screens or templates you have designed.

9. Insert the content into each frame.

Insert the lesson information or story segments into each frame, following the outline of your story or script and flow chart.

10. Use the authoring tool of your choice to create the application.

Using the authoring tool(s) of your choice, combine your text-based content with the visual presentation and media elements you have selected to create your presentation.

Letters from Beyond the Sambatyon: The Myth of the Ten Lost Tribes

Maxima New Media's *Letters from Beyond the Sambatyon: The Myth of the Ten Lost Tribes* weaves a mysterious tale of history and myth from a collection of ancient letters, maps, art, and interviews with possible modern-day descendants of the ten lost tribes.

Based on an exhibition at the Beth Hatefutsoth museum in Tel Aviv.

42 Do I have to think like a programmer?

You don't have to be a programmer, but it will help to map out the logic of the application with a simple flow chart. A flow chart will provide an aerial view of the logic, user interaction, and structure of the program. After you've drawn a flow chart showing the physical branching, different parts, and procedures that are necessary, you can focus on each specific component. A flow chart is like a roadmap to the application that shows everywhere the user can go.

Jumping Ahead

In a forward-moving program flow, the user may skip over information he already knows. The next information presented in sequence will always be found between the user's current position and some point ahead.

You may place the navigation under the user's control rather than the program control, unless the user must progress to a specific place in the program or lesson—as when learning a foreign language. An embedded forward flow can be used as a feature to keep the program or lesson moving along.

Jumping Back

Use backward branching to jump back to an earlier portion of a lesson or game. This technique may be used to repeat a lesson segment, return to the main menu, or start again.

You may use this technique in training or instructional applications to return the student to an earlier point before the error was made. Until the correct response is selected, the program will jump back to repeat the lesson until subject is understood.

Predefined Jumps

When something predictable always happens at a specific point, you may save the user extra steps by "hard-coding" the jump into the application.

Conditional Jumps

Conditional expressions may be incorporated into the logic of the program to give the instruction:

"If this is the case, do this. Otherwise, do that."

Some authoring tools include high-level programming languages that provide additional control over the logic of the application. Macromedia's *Lingo* and HyperStudio's *Hyper-Logo* allow you to incorporate conditional expressions and advanced features into the program. A timer can be combined with a conditional expression, causing the program to return to a menu if there is no response from the user within a reasonable time.

Conditional statements offer more possibilities for the user to interact and exercise their imagination and individuality. You may offer different levels of mastery for a lesson or creative writing project, each which results in a different ending or experience.

Conditional logic allows for more sensitivity to the differences in each person's performance ability or experience and gives the user more control over the program. Let the user respond to a menu item based on a conditional expression. It's an intersection in the flow of the program. The program will respond based upon the individual's answer and originality.

User Prompts

Answers most likely to be entered can be anticipated in advance and presented as the 'default' selections. In other cases, you may create a condition that lets the user respond with a unique simple answer. Their answer may be saved and used later to create a personalized dialogue with the user.

Make the program intuitive by giving the user clues and guiding them to the type of response needed. Be consistent and keep detail to a minimum.

Try designing a story from a flow chart using linear forward and backward branching. As an exercise, design a flow chart for a short story that requires the user to click on a button to flip the pages from start to finish. For more advanced practice, design a flow chart for a story that branches backwards in a loop. Then, use all the branching options to create clues to solve a mystery or explore different endings. The flow charts on the next pages can be easily adapted for any lesson or story.

Linear Structure

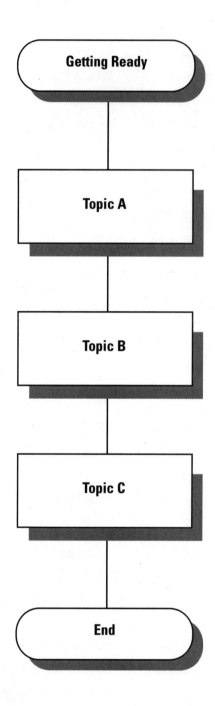

Conditional Structure

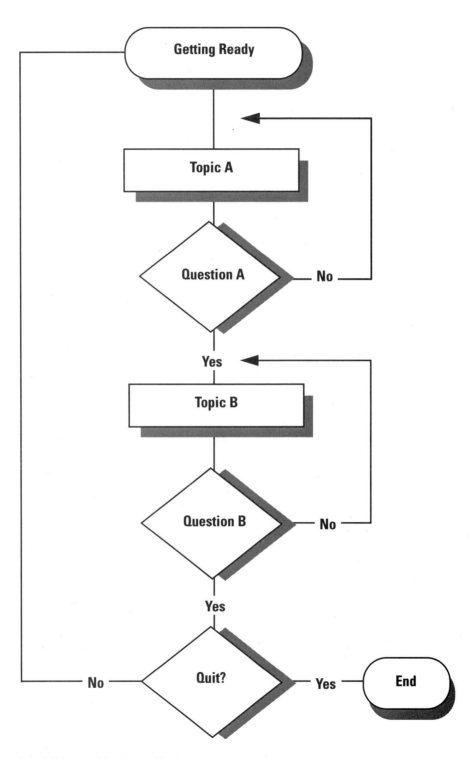

43 Is there flow charting software especially for writers?

StoryVision is a tool for writers and developers working on interactive media projects. It allows the writer to create a detailed blueprint for interactive products such as educational and reference applications, advertising kiosks, and interactive online presentations.

Each balloon in the diagram represents a single scene from the story. The scenes are linked to form a hierarchy, following your story structure.

The script for each scene can be typed into a master screenplay template, using either Microsoft Word or Microsoft Write. Each balloon can be linked to the corresponding script (or other media) file for the scene.

StoryVision is easy to learn and takes about 2MB of storage on your hard disk. The program's printed diagrams are useful for documenting a project and will help when making a presentation before potential investors or producers.

StoryVision

StoryVision helps you plan and organize interactive presentations and applications for the Web and CD-ROM.

The program is available for both Windows and Macintosh.

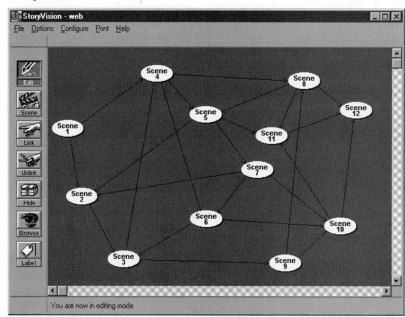

Voices from the industry:
Aron Trauring, Maxima New Media, Israel

Q: **How difficult is it to break into the CD-ROM market?**

A: The key issue before you undertake publishing a CD-ROM title is to understand the complexities of the multimedia CD-ROM market. This market is saturated and totally dominated by giant companies that will effectively make it impossible for you to sell your product in software channels.

Bookstores hate CD-ROM. First, there is the problem with 'shrinkage'—people steal CDs out of books. Second, many bookstores owners think the CD will cause the demise of books. So there's an emotional anti-technology reaction to it. Third, many early CD-ROM titles were garbage, so people didn't buy them or bought and were disappointed. Booksellers, burned out by the hype, have developed an antipathy for the whole category. Some of the many quotes I have heard this past year include:

- CD-ROM doesn't add anything to the store.

- We won't carry CDs on principle.

- We had some but they didn't sell so we won't carry them anymore.

- We love your product, but . . . (I wish I had a dollar for every time I've heard this) we're not yet ready to handle CD-ROM.

The largest distributor, Ingram Book, no longer carries CD-ROM (or rather carries very few). The CD-ROM division of every major publisher has either been closed, downsized, or transferred to other divisions of the corporation.

If despite all this you think you have some guaranteed niche, be prepared to budget anywhere between $150,000 and $400,000 for the development of your title by an outside contractor. $400K is the industry average for development cost. Excluding the top thirty titles, the average revenue is— ta da—$7,000. I kid you not.

Bio

Aron Trauring graduated from Columbia College in New York with a degree in Urban Studies and the Carnegie Mellon School of Urban and Public Affairs with a Master's degree in Public Management.

Trauring has worked in software development and project management to develop sales and distribution networks for companies in the U.S., Europe, and Japan.

In 1994, Trauring co-founded MAXIMA New Media with his wife Simcha Shtull. Together, they have developed several award-winning multimedia CD-ROM titles and are involved in educational projects with museums and foundations in Israel and the U.S Their sixteen-year-old son Itamar is MAXIMA's programmer.

Q: **How can a small company survive?**

A: Our company has survived by being far below average on development costs and far above average on revenues, with a lot of luck and help from good people. I can think of very few examples of people who have made money in CD-ROM—and those were people who sold out at the top of hype frenzy. People's lives have been ruined by this industry.

Q: **What about the Internet?**

A: The Internet has moved into the useful realm for the average businessmen far quicker than I thought possible. It will soon move into that category for the consumer, quicker than I thought even six months ago. Those who hate big brother may not like this, but the primary reason that the Internet will become "the" dominant information appliance of the next decade is the recent Telecom Act which guarantees universal Internet access to all U.S. schools. Research indicates that the time kids spend on computers is at the expense of—TV time!

Before you get too excited about the endless possibilities of the Internet, you should be aware that the big boys have already positioned themselves for dominance of this media.

Q: **Are there any advantages to publishing on the Internet?**

A: The Internet offers the possibility to form alliances with major networks. (This is the model that the big boys are fashioning.) Unlike TV, bandwidth on the Internet is not limited and networks will be looking for diverse content. A friend of mine in the industry told me that small information providers of all sorts should be thinking of a syndication model on the Internet. Also, an opportunity to sell direct and bypass the middle man and the potential for direct contact with your audience. This requires building a community on the Internet around what you have to offer.

Having said all this, the new media in general still has a bright future—as does CD-ROM—but the pitfalls are enormous. The bottom line is: I wouldn't recommend a novice to get in at this stage.

Voices from the industry:
Ron Mann, Documentary Filmmaker, Canada

Q: How did you get started writing nonfiction CD-ROM titles for Voyager?

A: Bob Stein and I met at a screening of my films *Imagine the Sound* and *Poetry in Motion* at Pacific Film Archives (PFA) in Berkeley, California in 1982. He bought me a hot dog and also bought the VHS and laserdisc rights to the films. *Poetry in Motion* was the first title released by Voyager. That film made many firsts. For instance, it was the first VHS to be distributed in a book store (Rizzoli's in New York), and it was one of the first films to be converted into a CD-ROM. Voyager felt that since it was their first VHS/laser title it was appropriate to select for QuickTime release. (Note: *Hard Days Night* came after PIM). Anyway. . . I became friends with Bob and Aleen and their kids and I slept

Bio

Ron Mann, who has made the documentary films *Comic Book Confidential*, *Poetry in Motion*, and *Twist*, is an inspired observer of popular culture. A new film and CD-ROM in production called *Grass* is a feature documentary about the history of marijuana. He lives in Toronto, Canada.

Poetry in Motion, **Voyager**

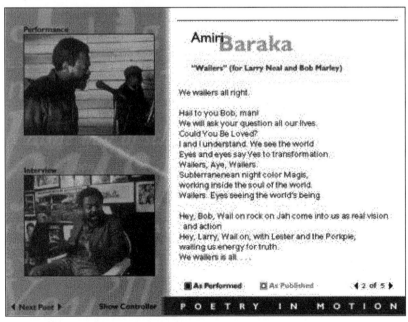

on their floor when visiting L.A. and helped package the 1st Criterion discs *Kane* and *Kong*. Technically I never had a job at Voyager—I was a friend whose work they liked and distributed.

Q: How do you go about developing an interactive title?

A: Steps? First content, second content, third content. . . then a design document to show people what is in your head and how you think the resources fit together. Usually this is worked out with the producer and designer and then eventually completely handed over to programmers.

The most recent disc is *Painters Painting*. My mentor on the project was the filmmaker Emile de Antonio who made what is considered to be the most important film about American artists. I thought that de's film would make a wonderful art disc—using the film as a resource that could be expanded. I spent time researching de Antonio's archive and pulled together the

original transcripts, out-takes from the film, and other related artifacts. I wanted the disc to be very accessible too. I had commissioned Douglas Kellner, a cultural critic, to provide the introductions and edit de's unpublished journals. Then, I worked with Peter Girardi, the talented Voyager producer and designer to find the right form. The whole process took about two years. . . and I'm pleased with what we did— with the exception of the quality of the *QuickTime* transfer. . . Until *QuickTime* improves, I don't think movies on discs will work except as a visual reference.

Since this interview, Apple has announced major enhancements to QuickTime, including the QuickTime Media Layer, a technology designed to provide Internet content creators with a way to manage a broad range of media types, including audio, video, animation, three-dimensional objects, speech/voice recognition, and virtual reality.

CHAPTER SEVEN

Exploring the Newest Realities

*V*irtual reality applications are merging with the animation industry to create three dimensional worlds where the business of learning will thrive. The challenge of virtual reality is to find unique, new ways of human-machine communication to transcend space.

One of the biggest differences between multimedia and virtual reality has to do with the cost of creation. In multimedia, a viewer watches a small square of digital video on a computer screen while listening to sound and reading narrative text below. In high-end virtual reality, a viewer assembles complex 3-D environments or navigates through territory, without having to stare at a computer screen and touch a keyboard. The user can walk, drive, or fly through a world of unlimited possibilities.

Virtual reality must accommodate the senses. Matching the user's needs with technology, allowing the user to keep the normal single point of view above ground level, and achieving awareness of realistic movement, are necessary goals.

Historically, virtual reality has focused on three goals:

1. To find new ways to make the keyboard and computer screen disappear;

2. To take people places they couldn't go before;

3. To make learning more entertaining.

Those who pioneer virtual reality study how the mind is oriented to a new world—and a new media.

The challenge of virtual reality is to find unique, new ways of human-machine communication to transcend space.

What is the history of virtual reality?

As the control of the old analog machines of the seventies were taken over by digital circuits in the nineties, the computer's ability to control video made it an ideal medium for building simulated cities and creating virtual worlds.

By the late eighties to early nineties, multimedia using graphics, text, video, and sound on CD-ROM flooded the PC market, creating the homebased electronic desktop publishing and desktop video industries, designers, developers, and animators.

The mid nineties brought garage VR and immersive virtual reality at a variety of levels and costs. CD-ROM photo and textures databases of images or animation. Today's high-end animation software has built-in tools to photorender and animate walk-throughs and fly-throughs for virtual museums, trade shows, and other events.

Also by the mid nineties, software authoring tools allowed users to publish narrative text on CD-ROM or the Web. Ultimately, interactive media and high-end virtual reality, both spin-offs of space industry training simulations, filtered down to PC users.

Socially correct virtual reality includes "garage VR," a lower-end virtual reality and 3-D modeling that is affordable for personal computer owners. Garage VR is popular. People are seeking low-cost 'garage' VR solutions. One of the biggest stumbling blocks to the home-based VR lab is the cost. The headgear alone that is required to experience many VR applications can cost several thousand dollars.

With the authoring tools appearing on the market today, you don't need a great deal of technical experience to break into the field of virtual reality. There are a variety of opportunities creating animation or writing environmental impact reports. Anthropologists, fiction writers with master's degrees in creative writing, and archaeologists are often hired to develop those reports.

45 What is "armchair travel"?

The Virtual Art Museum at Carnegie Mellon University is networked so that users can walk through and experience total immersion in a digital representation of the ancient Egyptian Temple of Horus, built between 300 BC and 300 AD.

The goal of a virtual museum like the one at CMU is to be used for distance learning by network. Viewers use a head-mounted display and jiggle a joystick to travel back through time and navigate from the exterior of the virtual art and architecture museum into the lobby and then into the Temple of Horus Gallery.

Outside the temple, the viewers experience the open-air courtyard. Sculptures and murals are interactive. Inside the inner sanctuary, they can experience the ambiance of ancient Egypt.

Three virtual tour guides document the history of the temple. The space is modeled accurately. Rooms are studded with giant columns and open ceilings. In October, 1994, the virtual exhibition opened to sellout crowds at the Solomon R. Guggenheim Museum SoHo, in New York.

Carl Loeffler and Lynn Holden developed the virtual temple at the Studio for Creative Inquiry at Carnegie Mellon. Loeffler is project director of telecommunications and virtual reality. He contributed the technical expertise, and Holden, an Egyptologist, authenticated the realism.

The virtual museum uses a distributed client/server architecture. Its potential is to allow unlimited viewers to interact in the same virtual environment.

Is the virtual museum a symbol of what future museums will be like—a form of interactive entertainment as distance learning? Will the future virtual museum be available to all—architects, students, all of the public—on line? Who will put virtual museums on the Internet? The developers look at it as a point of origin, a starting gate. Who will pick up this idea and expand it further? Why not other virtual museums for a variety of ancient cultures, religious groups, and ethnicities?

To what extent will distance learning be made available to students and armchair travelers? Will it be available to home-based senior citizens, the physically challenged who can't travel, or children who are too young to visit the actual sites?

Telepresence is a form of virtual travel that uses video cameras and remote microphones to project the viewer into a different location. NASA Ames is using telepresence for planetary exploration. Architects use telepresence to see areas inside structures that are not visible to the eye.

Telepresence is also used by architects who design hospitals and by medical product designers who create the surgical instruments that use robotic control. Telepresence used in surgical procedures permits the surgeon to peer inside the patient's body.

Architects apply the same principles to seeing inside of structures to inspect whether they are sound. Telepresence is the future of virtual reality. By matching the person with the contact surface, telepresence can help identify differing needs by measuring the accessibility of an area for physically challenged people.

Teleworkshops and virtual classrooms can now be set up to broadcast anywhere. The virtual office, security, trends, and the impact of the Web on global communications has is creating the virtual classroom of the future, based on resource learning. Writers can teach through tele-workshops, and organizers of such workshops can make a new communications business out of delivering teleworkshops that deliver briefings by satellite and through the Web.

Voices from the industry:
J.B. Galan, Stanford University

>To: scribes@ellipsys.com

>Date: Fri, 13 Sep 1996 16:10:14 -0700 (PDT)

>Hi Anne,

>

>As you may know from our research description, we have developed a system called an accessor that can be modified to an individual's particular needs. This accessor then transports whatever form of data a disabled person can enter over to a host machine. The host machine can be any off-the-shelf Macintosh, IBM or compatible, SUN, or Silicon Graphics computer. In other words, there are absolutely no modifications made on the computer which you wish to access. The accessor is portable and can be taken to any computer at home, work, the library, etc. . . I often say that the accessor is merely an alternative keyboard and mouse because anything and everything that can be done with the keyboard and mouse can be done with our system just as easily.

>

>My accessor is designed to accept speech input and head pointing because I am unable to use my hands to type or move a mouse. A blind person would obviously need different modifications but their accessor would still operate in the same manner.

>

>As far as working at home, our system gives the freedom to access technology wherever one may want to work.

>Thanks,

>J.B.

>http://www-csli.stanford.edu/user/jbgalan/

Bio

J.B. Galan recently graduated with honors from Stanford University with a BA in Psychology. Born in Guadelajara, Mexico, J.B. grew up in Walterville, Oregon.

J.B. works on the Archidemes Project at Stanford's Center for the Study of Language and Information (CSLI) to develop special technology for the disabled.

He also coordinates the production of a database to assist in the accurate portrayal of disabled individuals in films.

46 What is VRML?

Virtual reality and the simulated life for the writer has come to the Web. It's up to individuals to find more creative ways of applying virtual reality—artificial experiences—to literature, art, music, entertainment, training, armchair travel, and the rest, so the energy of technology can merge with the creative expression of the poet, artist, and scientific researcher.

VRML (pronounced vur'mel) stands for Virtual Reality Modeling Language. VRML grew out of the art and science of 3-D modeling and is now the open standard for 3-D on the Web. VRML provides a framework for presenting multimedia data, which means there will be more live action and more Web publishing that animates text with motion and realism.

Back in 1993, when Internet users were surfing the Internet with the Mosaic browser, thinkers were already tired of staring at two-dimensional text and objects on the screen. At the First International Conference on the World Wide Web

in March 1994, a meeting launched a "back-to-the-drawing-board" movement to bring a common virtual reality language to the Web. Suddenly, VRML became a buzzword for writers, publishers, designers, and animators.

Now writers, publishers, and designers could speak 3-D on the Web. For the designer, artist, or animator, VRML gave the Web the capability to render complex 3-D images. Markup instructions are plat-form independent and similar to HTML. The key to making VRML documents easy to render lies in defining 3-D objects in ASCII characters.

The Web address of a VRML documents looks exactly like an HTML document, except for the extension. HTML documents have an extension of either .html or .htm. However, VRML docments use the .WRL extension to identify the document as a "world file."

Writers can use VRML for Web publishing to build complex 3-D scenes or models without expensive equipment. VRML defines polygonally rendered objects and special effects for lighting, realism, environment, atmosphere, ambiance, and mood. Now you can illustrate your stories and books on the Web with complex special effects and other graphics. With clip art and scanned images, you don't have to spend years in art school to illustrate your written stories, if you are looking from the writer's angle on Web publishing.

For the artists, designers, animators, and special effects developers, VRML is graphical in nature. The only text in a VRML document is shown as an object or inside a VRML image. The VRML specification focuses on how 3-D scenes are rendered on your Web site.

VRML includes facilities for linking objects and scenes. As VRML evolves into later upgrades, it will link more types of objects with scenes. For example, you can design an illustration for a children's book, advertisement, cartoon, or greeting card and insert your text or spoken dialogue in an interactive comic book as an object inside your VRML

image. Put all this on the Web, and let everyone sample your talents. Make your resume 3-D and combine it with your writing and art portfolio.

VRML is excellent for model rendering. Designs you render in 3-D are called 'nodes'. The nodes create three dimensional images such as cylinders, cones, spheres, and cubes. You can define a shape and add texture, lighting, special camera angles, object transformations, and other effects.

VRML gives the writer advanced layout ability. Simply put, VRML lets you manipulate three dimensional images on your Web page, Web book, or script. Inline sound and video capabilities are necessary for full 3-D presentation. Internet Explorer extensions support inline video in Microsoft .AVI format and sound in .WAV, AU, and MIDI formats. The current version of Netscape supports the embedding of multimedia objects.

Web publishing changes by the week. A writer can become a Web self-publisher with mark-up languages such as HTML or VRML with plug-in extensions for *Netscape* or

Internet Explorer. Off-the-shelf authoring tools like *Pioneer* from Caligari make it possible for anyone to publish in three dimensions on the Web.

Three dimensional authoring tools allow an author to create virtual worlds that map the imagination and the universal mind. The author may add plug-in scripts to their world to reference additional VRML extensions directly. A language like *Java* may show how things behave but it's up to the writer to define how things appear. VRML is all about appearances. Here, the writer needs to convey both how things appear and behave.

Virtual reality publishing on the Web gives a writer tremendous versatility. True cyberscribes are explorers and communicators of the imagination. Intuition is taken to a higher octave when combined with the textures of the senses. The goal is to create stunning worlds to be experienced by as many senses as possible. A writer's ultimate refer-ence guide and most useful tool for creating fiction down-to-earth non-fiction. For inspiration, view a docu-mentary, then project it into the future to create fantasy.

http://www.caligari.com

This virtual world was created by 23-year old Italian artist Eolo Perfido using Caligari 3-D software. This and other award-winning worlds are on display in the art gallery at the Caligari Web site.

Voices from the industry:
Chester Dent, VR Producer, U. K.

>Date: Sun, 22 Sep 1996 13:18:57 +0100
>To: anne hart <scribes@ellipsys.com>
>From: chester@easynet.co.uk (Chester Dent)
>
>Anne:
>
>I always imagined interactive telly would mean that you could take the camera and swing around to look at whatever took your fancy. Sadly, the reality stops at single level options: playing a pre-edited bit of video returning you to the same dull (or jazzed-up) main menu. Setting your wake-up call or gambling with your choice of awful pay movies in a hotel room, is about as interactive as it gets. And let's be honest, 90% of multimedia is basically just page turning. Granted, you can jump directly to what you want to look at. But then books do that.
>
.>QuickTimeVR is the most genuinely interactive medium to emerge in years. You can play it like video: with Director running the VR and sound, your bite-sized guided-tour looks much like TV. But the beauty of QuickTimeVR is that you can interrupt and take off on your own, go back and look at something again, or just wander around listening to the audio as you go, like a museum tour.
>
>This has been perfect for everything from communicating the use of retail space to staff at M&S to selling accommodation at the Savoy Hotel.
>
>Authoring software like Macromedia Director is crucial to exploit the full potential of QuickTimeVR. Naturally, clients want to be sure of communi-cating everything they want to get over in their interactive presentation. The viewer may give up without seeing everything, so a guided tour option and navigation aids are essential to help the viewer find their way about. And

Bio

Chester Dent is an award-winning director with broad experience in film, television drama and commercials.

In 1995, he founded Spacexploration, Europe's first production company for QuickTimeVR. Clients include Marks & Spencer, Saatchi & Saatchi's Facilities Group, The Savoy Group and Nikkei Architectural Review in Japan.

sound adds a new dimension to the VR experience. Programming maps is fiddly but very worthwhile: nothing worse than getting lost in space, as you do.

>

>Hardware Spec:

>

>Spacexploration has developed a HighRes version of QuickTime VR playing in a 500x300 window and offering four-times greater detail than the original Apple demos when zoomed in. This makes greater demands on the RAM in the playback machine requiring a minimum of 16MB but we always provide StandardRes version which will play on lower-spec hardware.

>

>We originate on 35mm film and scan to PhotoCD. The fast turn-around required by retail end-users means we also shoot on the Kodak DCS 460 digital camera with Nikon lenses. And our object movies are now exclusively shot on the Kodak digital set-up.

>

>London based Spacexploration provides QuickTimeVR production, post -production and multimedia solutions to clients world-wide.

>

>Regards

>

>Chester Dent, PRODUCER
>http://www.spacexploration.com/

_____

s p a c e x p l o r a t i o n

47 Is the virtual reality market ready for professional writers?

VR scriptwriters are called 'virscriptors' and 'content writers' by multimedia industry staffers. VR scriptwriters offer fantastic imagery by sending the viewer flying through models and simulations. However, to compel the viewer to stick with the story, the writer needs to define the problem and show sequentially, step-by-step why and how the problem is solved.

If a concrete step is missing, the viewer will feel at a loss or 'experience missing time.' The viewer won't be able to navigate the map. A VR scriptwriter learns to think in three dimensions.

The writer who sees patterns in everything makes giant leaps. There is a conceptualization that the viewer won't see. Show the viewer concrete, step-by-step solutions with the benefits and advantages.

The concrete detail organized in a step-by-step order, showing the problem and each detail of the solution makes a compelling story in

virtual reality as learning enhancement, interactive feedback, demonstration, and marketing.

The applets of *Java*, HTML, VRML, and what ever evolves after all relate to better ways to publish your writing and graphics on the Web. It's all about making what you write three dimensional and animated.

Virtual reality is no longer only for robots, animated cartoons, digital cockpit games, or medical telepresence monitoring. Virtual reality and three dimensional modeling have become the domain and multi-user domain of creative writers. More writers are taking art training to become dual-skilled in creative writing and design, using both the left and right brain hemispheres on one project. They're finding creative skills are transferable, if training in both takes place together.

Writers today are engaged in electronic commerce. Repackaging a former journalist or reporter for a career in dynamic, animated writing on interactive Web pages is a whole new industry filed under 'software talent management.'

Virtual reality content writing is not bound by gender, age, or former training. Imagery for visual impact is everything and everywhere. It's the writer's job to create mental impact out of visual splines and textures. It's all grouped under object-oriented writing. You rely on the concepts of objects, properties, and methods, exactly like in object-oriented computer programming.

Properties such writers work with include the color of an object, where its located, attributes, in short details. Events trigger objects to do something. Writers react differently to different types of input. A *Java* applet also can react differently according to the variety in types of input. Both object-oriented writers and object-oriented technology are moving in a parallel line together.

Writers' jobs are becoming more like programming languages. The writing tasks are growing more object-oriented in direction. Those who hire writers increasingly want news journalists and computer game scriptwriters, alike both to know how to run complex Internet applications on a computer.

http://www.netaxis.qc.ca/wth/ood.htm

The MARS Virtual Reality Simulator (VRS) is a navigational training application developed by WTH Systems Inc. for the Canadian Department of Defense.

Users wear a head mounted display while participating in training of formation exercise maneuvers for ships at sea.

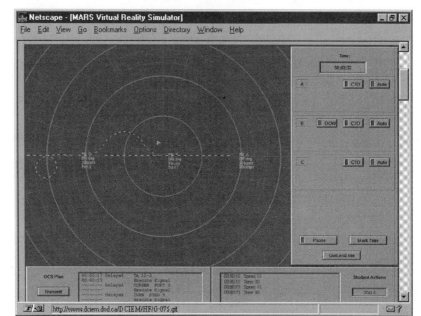

The career path for a content writer follows the evolution of Web publishing: On the first Web, everyone became a publisher and now on the second Web, everyone is becoming a netcaster.

New languages for the Web mean new jobs for a different kind of writer—a more technical one—but still telling the same great story. Good storytelling is the base line that will land you a job. However, to compete for the highest-paying positions, you must learn how to how to write the waves like a cyberscribe. (It won't hurt to learn Java—with today's authoring software, you may not need it, but it looks good on a resumé.)

Advertising copywriters will also find a niche creating environmental advertising for virtual worlds. These soft-sell ads for products are strategically placed as objects in a virtual world and come alive when selected.

VR script writers take advantage of 3-D to organize space, writing in virtual reality and sometimes in hypereality. Otherwise, it's the same old stuff as usual—reporting the news made compelling as a drum tattoo.

http://www.netaxis.qc.ca/wth/ood.htm

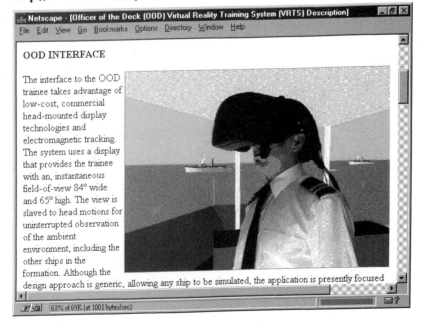

The Officer of the Deck Virtual Reality Training System consists of three components: the interface, the bridge team, and instructional facilities. Lesson plans provide a script for the training exercise.

(Screen shots courtesy of the Canadian Department of National Defence.)

Voices from the industry:
David A. Wagner, VR Developer

Bio

David A. Wagner is a special effects photographer and producer of virtual reality applications. David's "Virtual Liberty" is on permanent exhibit at Liberty Science Center in New Jersey. David sits on the FIT photo advisory board and is a graduate of the Fashion Institute of Technology.

Q: **How did you first discover virtual reality?**

A: Discovering QuickTime VR was a profound experience. As a special effects photographer, I had a sense of what Virtual Reality was supposed to be; the headgear and the gloves, grasping at air while looking at images. When I first saw QTVR demonstrated, it was nothing like I had imagined. It was simple. No gloves or headgear. It worked on almost any home computer. A sense of being there. Instantly, I had a headache from all the ideas running through my mind. I ran right back to the studio and ordered all those things I needed to get going. I couldn't wait to start producing virtual images.

Q: **Is the market ready for VR?**

A: The market was wide open and ripe for the technology. I pulled in my very first QTVR job after my first presentation to the Liberty Science Center. They were amazed at what they could do with this stuff—look around in 360 degrees; look up and down in a photograph that wrapped around the viewer; or "hold" objects and rotate them to look them over or under, like holding them in your hands. Right there on the computer's monitor was a full representation of quite a number of the museum's rooms and objects.

It wasn't long before the simple, 360 degree view was placed into a series of connected points, or nodes, that allowed the viewer to travel from place to place within the room. Very engaging.

That was six months ago. Now I am working on a full-fledged museum title that tours the entire museum.

48 Is "Big Brother" watching?

In the 1700s, Jeremy Batham designed the panopticon. It was an imaginative all-seeing machine that was used to scare prisoners into thinking the all-seeing eye was on them. The panopticon had a special design that produced an 'asymmetrical gaze.' Prisoners became objects of their own subjugation.

The panopticon emphasized the atomization of power. It had 360° visibility night and day, and its job was the separation and categorization of people. Today, the Internet is a type of panopticon. Computers are gathering information about all types of people. In the workplace, monitoring includes smart badges, e-mail, keystroke counting of word-processors, and viewing computer files—even retrieving e-mail long since erased, but hidden in master computers and networks. The three main features of a panopticon is the ability to atomize power, the ability to see anywhere, and the ability to separate and categorize individuals.

Time Magazine's recent poll revealed that 70 to 80 percent of people are deeply concerned about information being collected about them in databases. Computers have the greatest power to concentrate and control information about people.

One in five companies in the U.S. admits to eavesdropping on employees, according to sociologists. Trust is the most important trait you want to build in a virtual or long-distance business partner, editor, artist, or co-author. In order to find out whether you can be trusted, your potential partner may decide to screen you by placing a 'cookie' on your hard drive. Screening potential business partners by sending cookies into their hard drive is becoming increasingly popular.

According to Bob Hawkins' weekly *Computerlink* column in the *San Diego Union-Tribune* on cookies in your computer, this type of electronic snooping to screen you without your permission violates your privacy, but increasingly is being done on the Internet to track clients and measure an audience's buying and living habits. If you use the Web frequently, chances are a cookie is bugging your computer right now.

```
if (cookieFound){
    start = end + 1;
    end = document.cookie.indexOf(";",start);
if (end < 0){
    end = document.cookie.length;
}
else if (end < start){
    end = document.cookie.length;
}
else if (oven=350){
    cookie = oatmeal+raisins.bake;
}
return document.cookie.substring(start,end);
}
return ";
```

A cookie is technically referred to as a 'persistent client-state hypertext transfer protocol cookie.' According to Hawkins, You may never suspect that you are being checked out when you visit a Web site. However, when you register, a 4 kilobyte cookie is sent to your hard disk with encoded information. Each time you return to the site, the cookie sends back all your personal data. Since the release of *Navigator 1.2*, Netscape has made cookie technology available to Web designers. Most recently, Netscape has taken a step back to offer users a measure of protection from those who might misuse the technology.

More and more Web sites are requiring visitors to register before entering. The information entered in saved in a database and accessed next time you visit the site. Each time you pay a return visit to the site, you'll be greeted by name. It's a friendly place to be—but that is not all. They may be gathering information about you, including all the Web sites you have visited, your favorite search parameters, passwords you use, and even what software you have on your computer. *Windows 95* has a cookie that can send back a list of all the programs on your hard drive.

Hawkins suggests ways of finding out whether someone has crumbled a cookie into your hard drive. According to Hawkins, you should do a search for the file, "cookies.txt." On a Mac, the key words are "Magic-Cookies."

There have been articles splashed all over the *London Financial Times* about the space-eating storage occupancy of cookies seeking out business information or personal data from your computer files.

Cookies can collect information about you behind your back. If you sell your compute—or share one with another at work—your profile information will be combined. Only a few cookies can occupy as much as four megabytes of space.

On the shadow side, this snooping could easily be used for industrial espionage. On the sunny side, you only have to register once.

cyberscribes.1: The New Journalists

49 Is there a dark side to virtual reality?

In 1994, Art Bell received a fax from a former virtual reality project advisor at the University of California, stating that "The technical problems in virtual sex have been worked out. The working prototypes have been developed. The experience so frightened me, that I left the project."

Russ Wagner, who later appeared in a two-hour interview on Art Bell's radio show, was indeed very much involved in the project. "When I ventured my ideas on the subject of virtual reality at UCSD, I had very little first-hand knowledge of the current techniques being employed in virtual reality hardware. My ideas involved the manipulation of the human nervous system, and a new approach to controlling the sensation of impact and pressure via a liquid substance.

"Unknown to me at the time, my ideas were unheard of at that date. I had actually invented a practical, working, theory base for three of the hardest to implement facets of virtual reality—movement, the sensation of impact, and injury simulation. I was literally in shock when I found out that nobody had thought of using electrical impulses similar to the TENS system to simulate pleasure or pain sensors in the body."

"We put one of the hardware designers into a simulation," said Wagner. "One of the computers malfunctioned and shut down. The audio portion of the simulation completely turned off. We shut off the temperature and pressure. He didn't realize it. He'd been walking around in the simulation for a little over twenty minutes. In his mind he was still hearing the simulation.

It's hypnosis," Wagner said. "You hypnotize yourself with the aid of hardware. You need to be brought out of it. If you're not brought out of it in a certain manner, the result can be disastrous. We finally had to go out there and pull the helmet off. His eyes were shut. He so became

This interview was originally broadcast on Art Bell's national radio show on September 12, 1994. The excerpts from the interview that appear in this article have been reproduced with permission.

accustomed to the images in the helmet, that he didn't need them anymore. VR hardware is the solution, not the problem. It puts you under and trains you to respond—unless you walk in and say, 'this is not real'. If you don't do that, when the sounds shut down, you keep right on going."

Defining virtual reality "is like asking what is hypnotism," Wagner stated in the interview. Russ Wagner defined virtual reality in laymen's terms as, "any hardware or software system capable of stimulating your nervous system through all, if not most of your sensory organs to place you sensually in a scenario that is not in keeping with the scenario you are truly in, hence creating a new environment, a new reality contained within the one you are truly experiencing."

Art Bell mentioned that he heard in the media that "VR is going to make crack cocaine seem like candy." Wagner responded, "VR is destined to be the drug of 2000 and beyond, because, quite frankly, let's say someone who experiments with a hallucinogenic drug has no idea what the outcome is going to be. With VR, you have the ability to create a scenario of almost anything

http://www.artbell.com/art/space.html

These NASA pictures show the infamous face formation in the Cydonia region of Mars. The face is close to the "D&M" five-sided pyramid, named after the two researchers who discovered the formation. The pyramid is said to defy the laws of geological process and is thought by some to have been intelligently designed.

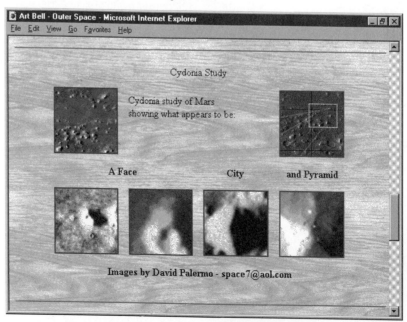

you could want to do in your lifetime and then live it in a comfort level that is appropriate to you."

"If you're going to get in the ring and box with Mike Tyson, and you have the appropriate VR hardware, you're going to get hurt. You're going to feel the impact."

"Some people don't recover from this (VR)," Russ Wagner stated. "There's a thing that says the weak minded are easily influenced. Some people have been shown to have a serious problem realizing that their virtual reality is not reality."

"It's a form of hypnosis that is so all-condensing, that once the stimulus is removed some persons will actually continue in the artificial environment. They'll still be in the scenario. That's the part of this that is so frightening."

On the good side, a disabled person in a wheelchair was able to walk for the first time in his life, actually feeling what it's like to walk in virtual reality.

"Basically you can fix anything in your life in VR," said Wagner. "If you think you're fat, you can put yourself in a VR scenario where you have the body of Arnold Schwartzenneger."

How good is VR? "It's fantastic," said Wagner. "We discovered what we were doing wrong. We were basically trying to pull out all the stops with the hardware. We were trying to allow impact sensation images that would blow your mind.

"The latest technical specifications call for twelve screens stacked, layered, basically pancaked and laminated on top of one another. They can be turned translucent. You can literally pass an object—one in front of another. It also gives a sensation of depth. By the time you get to the twelfth screen, you are so convinced that object is moving away from you, that if you don't know what's happening, you're already falling down." Virtual reality plays games with all your senses.

What about the darker side of virtual reality—such as fantasies of violence? "Yes," said Wagner. "The potential for dark simulation is incredible. You'll be able to walk around in your virtual environment. Virtual reality is hypermedia. Once VR is induced, it's very much like astroprojection. When you pull your fist back to slug somebody, the computer simulation would block. It's like computer speech recognition."

When Art Bell asked Wagner whether virtual sex is the same as having sex, Wagner replied, "Yes. Indeed it is. . . from stimulation of glandular function in the male or female, everything including orgasm is achieved through nervous stimuli. This is where those more susceptible to hypnotism can be affected. You have to really screen your "test pilots" before you actually put them in the cockpit."

'We were experimenting with hardware and still working with electrical nerve stimulation and trying to elicit responses from certain nerve centers in the pubic regions (using student volunteers). People put in a VR trance, still don't realize when the VR simulation is over. 'The people who have experienced this have the most vivid dreams,' Wagner told Art Bell. 'You return to the entranced state when you dream. It makes your dreams so realistic because you're used to controlling your action in the dream, not the

effects. The hardware was almost not necessary. I think the key to this lies in how the person is placed under the trance. The trance process the second time around is almost instant.'

There's one regulation or restriction Wagner places on VR. 'I never want to see it fall into the government's hands,' Wagner told Bell. 'It'll turn you into the perfect damn near anything you want to be.' The question is, once you see a VR simulation, will you never again unsee it?

Who's watching the watchers?

The future of publishing, broadcasting, and entertainment is moving toward three-dimensional worlds as seen in virtual reality. The question is, will the future of Web publishing move entirely into an interactive graphics-based medium? If so, will print publishing follow and also evolve into a graphics-based medium?

From the writer's view, writing itself is becoming more visual, more right-hemisphere. Mind mapping, use of more graphics and less text, flow charts and storyboards instead of premises are rapidly replacing text-based learning and entertainment experience. Children who grew up on Saturday morning cartoons, videos, and films and less on books are designing today's three-dimensional Web publishing environments.

The former generations who grew up without television, radio, or video, were text-based learners. Visual learning for writers used to be kept to looking at woodcut prints and illustrations of children's books or the occasional photo or fine art print, or comic book cartoon. Visuals in newspapers were called "the funnies." This generation of writers have moved into the visual. In a screenplay, one test of marketability is to shut off the sound and see whether the action will tell the story without a word of spoken dialogue. Even Woody Allen tried making the film in which no words are spoken. Dialogue is moving toward more action and three dimensional visuals and less verbiage, less spoken.

In books, the long-winded passages of dialogue are cut to ten-word sentences, with visual tag lines used to allow the reader to see an image of the action in the mind's eye, to visualize more and read less text. Children are more visual in their choice the younger they are. Children's picture books have little text. On the Web, we're moving closer to that format with less text-based information, more storyboard, and less rambling. People want to hear the story and be part of the action.

On the "third" Web, will we become part of the Net through micro appliances and bio-technical applications?

Virtual reality allows people to be projected to invisible and unreachable locations. For architects or physicians, this may be inside buildings, pipes, microscopes, or arteries to make necessary repairs. People will be going to different virtual locations to look, select, fix, enjoy, and buy.

Research in virtual reality has been conducted since the early nineties at the National Supercomputing Center in Ohio, using Cray supercomputers. Supercomputers make it possible to see what couldn't be seen before and compare what couldn't be compared.

New virtual environments will also bring computers into the street and living rooms of the noncomputing public. Home shopping by interactive digital television will help people choose their programming and products, while remote computers linked to home entertainment centers track the buying habits of consumers.

Virtual reality will be used to chart future trends in branching and interactive parallel worlds, using audience-capturing visual narratives to sell a concept, or revise the past. It's

the art of inclusion. The future of virtual reality, like the future of anything else, involves taking two very different objects and combining them in new ways to form another.

There are questions about virtuality that futurists, trend forecasters, industrial anthropologists, androidologists, psychologists, science fiction writers, and venture capitalists would ask, such as where is it heading? What's the prime directive (in the Star Trek definition)? Where is its place in the cyberlife?

Teams of futurists are assembled to study virtuality from the psychology and anthropology researcher's point of view. Is it a new artificial and international language? Are we what our virtual reality makes us? Where does the task force on virtuality meet?

Sherry Turkle's *Life on the Screen* is not about computers, but rather, about how computers cause people to reevaluate their identities in the age of the Internet. The changing impact of the computer on our psychological lives and about our evolving ideas about minds, bodies and machines. Turkle says that what's emerging is a new sense of identity that is decentered and multiple.

These experiences formed in virtual environments are causing a dramatic shift in our notions of self, other, machine, and world. Technology bring postmodernism back-down to earth.

Faith Popcorn is another trend watcher who observes behavior and thinks up catchy phrases for the things people do. Popcorn reports that while trends are going in the "bigger is better" direction, that 'small' is preferable in business because small companies have the potential to grow.

To apply this idea to the new media, a small company may find it easier to identify and move quickly to take advantage of trends in technology and society—combining both to create something new.

Today it's not only writers and artists who desire to express their individuality, but the consumer audience who expresses its individuality through customized preferences of virtual environments.

You don't have to be a professional intuitive to see what's happening on the Internet today. However, once a trend hits the market full force, it's no longer simply a trend in the making, but a trend in the passing. Once a subject has made the talk show circuit—like a smiley face on the surface of Mars—it's probably too late to start a writing project based on that subject. Many trends go in cycles like the seasons—like 'good' and 'bad' aliens from outer space. Trends are eventually recycled like the products they spawn. You don't have to be a marketing genius to see that people on the Internet are more interested in aliens than angels. The trick is to spot a trend in the making before the merchandisers step in and make a lapel pin.

What does this all mean for the writer? It means there's a market for topics and products that combine individuality with emerging technologies and a sense of our place in the universe—whether it's the armchair traveler visiting exotic places and shopping in virtual bazaars or the erotic traveler looking for the virtually bizarre. The Web is the ideal

But who's watching the trend-watchers? They are all, quite obviously, watching each other.

—Ann O'Tate, Suck
http://www.suck.com

place to identify emerging trends in issues and entertainment.

Intuition and creativity are the writer's tools for survival. Just as sure as the novelty of silent two-dimensional Web sites will ultimately subside, people will begin moving into their own three-dimensional virtual worlds full of sound, motion, and experiences customized according to their preferences. Virtuality is a real estate boom waiting to happen for the designers and architects of three-dimensional worlds in cyberspace.

The newest technologies represent a high-growth market with many opportunities for writers who can create the copy and scripts to drive the applications. But what kind of programming skills will be needed to captivate the next generation of cyber-fried couch potatoes? One universal theme that people are repeatedly drawn to identifies or reaffirms who they really are and shows what they could be doing better with their lives. That's the ticket to the trend.

No one is watching the watchers, so we have to watch ourselves. Virtual reality reminds the senses that we're only an emotional arc— a minute—evolved from our pale-olithic past.

http://wpmc1.wpafb.af.mil/hideout/neo/mars1.jpg

This site, called 'the Hideout' is part of a larger project called "First Team" that uses surplus government computers under USAF administration to connect seriously ill children in medical centers via e-mail, BBS, and chat.

The goal of the project is to prove that connectivity improves patient morale and assists the healing process.

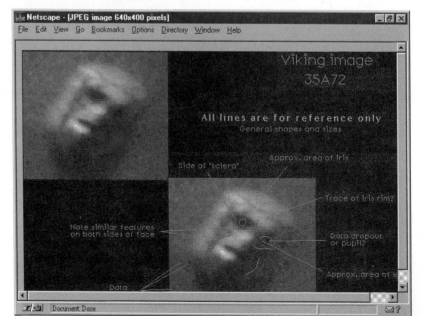

CHAPTER EIGHT

Internet Direct Response, Cyber Malls, and Virtual Trade Shows

Over the past two decades, the mediums of television and radio have not dramatically altered the way we conduct business. Contrast this with what has happened on the Web over the past few years: Each day, 45,000 entrepreneurs bring their businesses online. In 1994, only 5,000 Web sites existed. Today, the Web consists of hundreds of thousands of linked sites—and growing.

Perhaps the most exciting recent development is the combination of streaming multimedia content combined with high-speed access—making possible the ability to broadcast real-time video, TV, and radio over the Internet and re-purpose existing creative commercial content. These streaming media sites will be largely supported by paid advertising, monthly access fees, and subscriptions—much like a magazine, newspaper, or cable TV service. The Web has been trans-formed into a viable venue for professionally-produced commercial content. For the writer, this will bring an increased demand for high-quality interactive content from online broadcasters, advertisers, and their agencies.

The future Web—for better or for worse, depending upon your point of view—will be a powerful forum for the promotion and distribution of products sold direct to the consumer. Unlike the Old Web, where early commercial sites resembled high-volume, low-margin data warehouse stores, the commercial sites and boutiques of the New Web offer a soft-sell approach supported by personalized service, entertainment, and informative content. Hunter-gathers on the Web have evolved into a global village of settled farmers and traders. The flow of capital into the Web has begun the evolution from gatherer, to farmer, to barterer and trader—and trading is what the New Web is all about.

The flow of capital into the Web has begun the evolution from gatherer, to farmer, to trader.

211

Is there a market for direct response on the Web?

Commerce on the Internet is only now coming of age. Although the sales figures of some pioneering entrepreneurs have fallen short of expectations, Internet commerce is expected will soar over the next three to five years. The Web has finally come into its own.

According to a recent study by The Arthur D.Little/Giga Information Group, almost 30 percent of respondents credit the Internet with increasing sales of products and services. However, 90 percent of the respondents said that current sales from their company's Web site account for less than 20 percent of their total sales. Respondents believe a radical shift will take place over the next three to five years, with almost 35 percent expecting Internet sales to exceed 40 percent of their total sales.

The study found that many organizations now use the Internet for marketing, rather than sales, activities. Over 13 percent of the respondents said that providing information about products and services was the main reason for developing a Web site, but enhancing market image and selling products and services ran a close second.

According to a study by Yankelovich Partners, men still hold the dominant position in terms of Internet usage (57%), but women are quickly closing the gap (43%). Their study revealed the average new female online user to be 34.7 years old, married (52%) and with a household income of $55,500. For both sexes, 22% make online purchases online in the categories of software (80%), airline tickets (47%), computer hardware (46%), clothes (39%), and gifts under $50 (37%). These figures translate into big opportunities for writers of marketing collateral, sales letters, direct response scripts, promotional copy and online advertisements.

Internet Direct Response, (IDR), is the application of direct response techniques to the interactive world of the Web. IDR will offer kiosk-style hypermedia presentations over high-speed lines where the viewer can read interactive text, see the video, hear the audio, and even order directly from the site with digital cash. Internet direct response sites will take a soft sell approach by offering chat rooms, cyber cafes, and discussion groups where people with related interests can meet online. Orders will be placed by audio e-mail and paid for in digital cash. It's more than a new channel of product distribution.

The Web makes it possible to develop an ongoing relationship with your customer. Although it is easy to gather the e-mail addresses of each visitor to your site, it is imperative that you resist the temptation to flood cyberspace with unsolicited junk e-mail. People consider junk mail on the Internet to be an unwelcome invasion of privacy. Never send unsolicited commercial notices to an individual or "spam" a newsgroup or listserv.

Instead of "putting your foot in their door," let them come to you. Establish reciprocal links with sites of related interest and make sure your site can be readily found by the most popular search engines. If you have not already done so, register your company or product name as your Internet domain. Make yourself easy to find through search engines and reciprocal links.

The Web is a random house, an unabridged direct response to TV rather than of TV. It's the whodunit genre that kicks in by offering interactive multiple endings. The customer can not only buy the product, but interact by questioning the manufacturer about individual applications of the device, service, or item advertised. The IDR kiosk may combine syndicated columns with direct response and multimedia attractions. Visitors should be able to ask questions at your Web kiosk and know the benefits, advantages, and contraindications of the service or product being advertised.

The field of Internet direct response is an emerging market that demands the skills of creative expressionists. Interested writers should first learn the basics of commercial infomercial scriptwriting for cable TV. Then, take the best of those skills and techniques and apply them to the Web.

The Internet is made for direct response in a way that is measurable and quantifiable. The very term interactive implies a response from the user. The ultimate purpose may not simply be to sell a product, but to gather information, generate leads, or to build good will and brand name recognition.

Voices from the industry:
Deborah Morrison, Ph.D., Associate Professor of Advertising

Bio

Deborah Morrison. Ph.D., is Associate Professor in the University of Texas Department of Advertising at Austin. She teaches portfolio development for copywriters and art directors, creative strategy, and advertising as popular culture.

She has received teaching awards for her work and has placed nationally in The One Show in New York City, the International Newspaper and Marketing Executives competition, and in regional art shows. Her teaching and research focus on creativity as a social process and as a dynamic function of advertising; social communication and advertising; and American advertising as a perpetuator of myths.

>Date: Mon, 16 Sep 1996 10:42:09 -0600
>To: scribes@ellipsys.com
>From: dkmorrison
>
>Anne:
>
 >Good rich topic --
>
>The language of web advertising is vital. The audience embodies adjectives that paint a focused picture: savvy, smart, cynical, adopters, explorers. They don't believe old adspeak, they want information and entertainment, each category relevant to who they are and how they think.
>
>They have an ear, an eye, a bead on b.s. We could make a good case that this grand pronouncement works for any medium. It does. However, emerging electronic advertising shows a stormtrooper mentality; do it this way or become not just ineffective, but a laughingstock in the cyberworld.
>
>The easy answer and, it would seem, a valuable perspective on this is: good writing is good writing. It should engage, inform, pull and push the reader. With an understanding of format and audience, a good writer should be able to adapt to the medium at hand, probably develop a specialty where the voice created is perfect for that media selection. Indeed, in this era, who you're speaking to is the ultimate guideline, prioritized with how you're communicating that message. That's what brings us to a take on emerging media such as the Web.
>
>Deborah Morrison, Ph.D.
>Associate Professor
>Texas Creative
>The University of Texas at Austin
>http://advertising.utexas.edu

What are "virtual trade shows" and "cyber malls"?

Virtual trade shows and infomarts at multimedia-driven Web sites are a new way to make money from travel downtime. Virtual trade shows offering virtual conferencing and chat systems bring together more people from more places on Earth than could ever fit into a convention center. Without the pressure of time or the expense of travel, attendees can focus on any business or area of interest.

An Internet search on the words "virtual trade show" found 700,000 documents matching the query. Companies such as Apple Computer, Hewlett Packard, D'Animation, and Digital Media Performance Labs provide around-the-clock expo time to virtual trade show visitors. The Internet has become an important adjunct to both the exhibition floor and the conference program of many trade shows. Patrick Patterson, director of multimedia for Coe-Truman Technologies, Inc., of Savoy, IL, is a purveyor of virtual

trade shows. He says, "The role of virtual trade shows is to complement and support regular trade shows."

The Trade Group is an exhibition design company that considers virtual trade shows to be the way of the future. They have experimented with new technologies and their Web site is a valuable resource for anyone wishing to learn more about the virtual—and even the traditional—trade show industry.

Virtual trade shows enlarge the personal worlds of the global business community. *Virtual Places*, a software program developed in 1994 by Ubique Ltd. Of Rehovot, Israel, was one of the first authoring tools designed to produce virtual trade shows on the Web. It was first shown to the public at Networld+ Interop in Atlanta. The software allows Internet users to visit vendor booths, work the show floor, and study product demonstrations without leaving their computer. The software makes it possible for those who can't travel to visit trade shows, from the home based to those without the funds or time to travel. *Virtual Places* was used to create online versions of Networld+ Interop trade exhibits.

Last March, N&I Online had 9,995 attend their Las Vegas virtual trade show. Another show opened in Atlanta. N&I Online's seven 1996 international trade shows will all be held online.

Attendees may register for free at most virtual trade shows, but as with any trade show, revenue is generated from exhibitor fees.

http://www.tradegroup.com

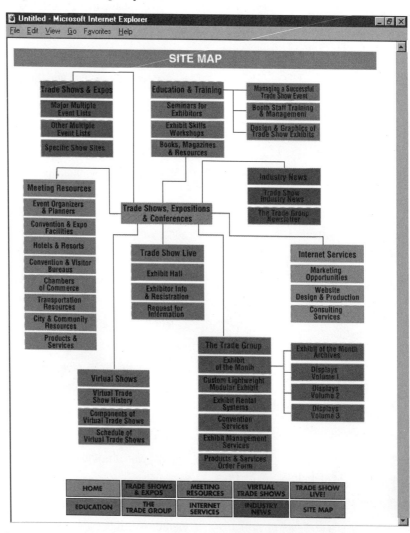

This map shows an aerial view of the Trade Group's Web site. (The portion relating to virtual trade shows is in the lower-left corner.) Aside from helping you navigate within their site, this map gives an overview of the different components of a trade show.

Booth fees at a major virtual trade show can run up to $3,000—as much as a 10' x 10' booth at an actual show. Most businesses willing to pay this much for a virtual exhibit are already targetting the online audience and have allotted a budget to attract the attention of people who do business on their computers. Quite frequently, the technical trade shows have the best turnout for online events. However, virtual trade show audiences are not limited to high-tech people, because attendees are buying lots of low-tech products, such as jewelry, books, and even pets.

Book publishers have literally filled the Web with exhibits, cyber book malls, and reading rooms. Many publisher sites offer searchable catalogs with online excerpts of publications that may be downloaded from the Internet.

Web TV Internet appliances are a new and affordable venue for author tours. *The Cyberscribes Show* is an animated talk show on the Internet, hosted by avatar hostess, Aniba Merimdeh. The show includes a cybercafe-style chat that links similar events in different cities. The WebTV units provide an easy and affordable way to combine a kiosk-style menu-driven presentation or

http://www.interop.com:80/vrml/atlanta96/mall.wrl

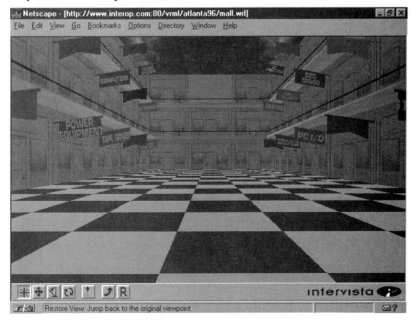

This scene shows the entrance to a virtual mall at the 1996 Interop show in Atlanta. This virtual world was designed by Planet 9 Studios of San Francisco.

demo with a live online event. This cybercafe-style event dove-tails nicely with the trend in bookstores toward author events with a café ambiance.

Tracking a targeted audience is easy with virtual trade show attendees who are required to register before gaining entrance to the exhibit floor. Most sites have sophisticated referral tracking and automated response systems to bring back targeted customers.

InterAct '96, sponsored by *InfoWorld*, Stratus Computer, and *Time* magazine was the world's first online virtual reality conference for distributed computing staged exclusively on the Web. Visitors could choose between a hypertext-based information path or a 3-D virtual reality world in the main hall. The main hall featured three-dimensional booths, multimedia theaters, and interactive product presentations. In that virtual world, visitors could mingle with avatars representing other attendees and exhibitor personnel. Unlike most trade shows, when your feet got tired of walking, you could do a fly-through down the aisle, instead. Or, as SignWeb boasts of their virtual trade show for the sign industry, "You can walk this trade show in your underwear. "

http://www.sbexpos.com

Softbank Corporation— a Japanese-owned company which dominates the computer book publishing industry also controls a large segment of the computer trade show industry. Their most recent venture into digital satellite broadcasting promises to bring new innovations to trade show conference programming.

Voices from the industry:
Mary Westheimer, President, BookZone

Q: How were you, as a print journalist with no technical background, able to start an Internet service for book publishers?

A: I have been in the publishing business in one capacity or another for more than two decades. My father published books as an avocation, and I helped him proofread and organize files. I've also worked in three bookstores as well as written, designed, edited and promoted titles. I've also worked with hundreds of authors and publishers as executive director of the Arizona Authors' Association and as a founding member of the Arizona Book Publishing Association.

So when Laurence Palestrant, who is the technical side of the BookZone equation, came to me in 1994 and said he wanted to start an Internet service for publishers, I was intrigued.

When I saw the Web and its potential, I was hooked. I realized that this new technology afforded independent publishers the opportunity to break through the distribution bottleneck and sell direct to their readers. Both publishers and readers would benefit from this new freedom.

Q. Is the Internet changing the balance of power in the book distribution system?

A: The balance of power in book distribution has indeed begun to shift. With the current distribution system's apparent inability to improve availability, publishers have turned to other methods.

Web sites as direct sales vehicles are, I believe, the business model of the future. Distributors in a number of businesses, including publishing and real estate, can no longer control the marketplace. Suddenly, pro-

Bio

Mary Westheimer is president and cofounder of BookZone, one of the first book-related sites on the Web. Mary serves on the board of directors of the Publishers Marketing Association (PMA), is a former executive director of the Arizona Authors' Association, and is a founding board member of the Arizona Book Publishing Association.

ducers can reach their audiences directly, cutting out heretofore necessary monetary, time, and resource costs. As the Net matures and people discover its ease of use and huge, sometimes instantaneous results, direct sales of many products—especially books—will grow. That may cut into the traditional distributors' piece of the pie—even though many of them are jumping to take advantage of the Net's remarkably wide reach and relatively low cost—but bodes well for publishing companies, which will reap greater profits.

The Net will most likely supplement—but not replace—traditional sales methods. After all, traditional bookstores offer an incomparable sensory experience. The Net also offers an opportunity for them to broaden their own stock, through distributors who are establishing their own sites and through innovative solutions designed to improve distribution of independent publishers' lines.

I firmly believe that books have the right to succeed or fail on their own merits, not because distributors and wholesalers are inefficient. The virtually limitless envelope of the Net permits that to happen.

The Net's influence on the balance of power will be indelible, but may take a few more years to come into its own as a commercial channel.

Q. **What is BookZone?**

A: We call BookZone "Home of the Net's Most Interesting Books" because you can find books here you might not find anywhere else. BookZone features titles of more than 600 presses and authors in well-conceived custom and packaged sites as well as cost-effective single-title listings. BookZone has many other attractions that make it one of the Web's most popular book sites for publishers, authors, and readers alike.

We encourage diversity and in fact, have more than ninety

subject categories in our Super Catalog. You will also find a great deal of information about the books, which is especially important when the books are not as well-known as, say, a James Michener release.

Q. How does BookZone manage seemingly competing interests in the publishing field?

A: Much of our success has come from building alliances—we're the home of the Audio Publishers Association and the 3,000-member strong Publishers Marketing Association as well as associated with more than a dozen writing and publishing groups in North America— offering real value and top-notch customer service. We really want to help publishers and readers, who need to know about each other.

BookZone has come a long way in a short period of time. When we first launched our site we had to explain what the Web was, but now most publishers who call us have their own dial-up service. It's been exciting to

be a pioneer in this business. We firmly believe that the Net will help independent publishers prosper—and that helps us prosper, too.

Q: What do you do during a 'typical' workday?

A: We have a great team here, and most of us are prepared to "do it all" (except for the highly technical programming, which is done by our systems administrator, Mike Howerton). I do everything from customer support to promotion to sales to HTML coding and graphic manipulation. I also do most of the writing for the site, handouts and promotional material.

Q. How is the Internet changing the writer's profession?

A: I don't think most people yet grasp the impact the Net is going to make on our lives. I still write for an in-flight magazine quarterly and did my research on the Web for the most recent piece. It almost made me want to go back to freelance writing! What a joy to find such a wealth of information literally at my fingertips. Whether you're just gathering facts or finding interviewees on mail lists and in newsgroups, the Net immeasurably broadens your scope.

Materials can be submitted in a flash by e-mail, which saves time, money, and resources. The Net also opens new markets for writers. After all, "content is king," which makes writers' contributions valuable.

A writer I met through one of my mail lists once told me that he realized that most of his clients came to him through the Net. "That means I can live anywhere," he mused. The Net enhances your ability to work from anywhere with anyone.

Q. **Can writers expect to find equal employment opportunities in the new media?**

A: One of the beauties of this new medium is that you are judged by your work and your professionalism. The color of your skin, your age, religious beliefs, height, etc. don't matter as long as you can deliver. That's one reason I believe the Internet may well save the world.

Q: **What's the best way to prepare for a job in this field?**

A: I think it's important to understand the technology. Learning to run a printing press helped me understand my work as a print writer, so I think the same facility applies here. Learning how to best gather information—which means familiarity with search engines, directories, etc.—also is important.

As someone who had to be dragged kicking and screaming into cyberspace, I'm gripped with the need to communicate the value of this new world. The Internet has the power to transform our world into a place where we better know our neighbors (which often makes them harder to hate!) share ideas with people we might never have otherwise met even though they have a missing piece of our own puzzle, as well as save resources.

Yet we are only in the Gutenberg stage of this remarkable era. Once I saw the value of the Net I was an immediate convert. I urge others to get online and become familiar with what will inevitably become a part of their careers and their lives.

53   What is a "rocket pack"?

Web-based trailers for films and television shows are called "rocket packs" in the Hollywired industry. E-zines that contain trailers for films are also becoming a popular way to promote products for profit on the Web—especially when the site is supported by paid advertising or sponsored by the producer.

A traditional film or video trailer ranges in length from thirty to ninety seconds. These previews for promotion compile various scenes on tape like a coming attraction preview that's shown in theatrical films. Wholesalers sample the tapes in order to decide whether they want to sell the video. Studios now consider the Web to be part of the standard promotional mix for a film.

For entertainment enthusiasts, archives of films and videos could be started with links to demographics related to the films, the trailers, or the advertisers who put their links on sites that promote films or

http://www.virtualfilm.com/TIFF/Home.html

The *Virtual Film Festival* presents netcast events for the international community of film lovers and those involved with the production, marketing, distribution and communication needs of independent film, video and mediamakers.

videos. For beginners on the Web, starting a filmographic site and selling promotional content to film makers and video producers provides an opportunity to promote yourself as a resource, critic, or industry observer. You may write about the personalities in the industry or evaluate films and related productions. Put out-takes on the Web, even your own or those yet unproduced.

You may invite other film critics and reviewers to contribute content, as well. Another resource would be to place reciprocal links to film and video schools. After developing a following, you could sell advertising on the site and launch a direct mail campaign to your targeted list of film buffs.

Once a promotional site for a film has been placed on the Web, it will continue to generate interest long after the season has ended. The site will be catalogued in the online database of film archives and search engines, which in turn, will create untold links to the site. It will become a part of the Net. 🐾

http://www.actwin.com/ITVS/programs/USofP

The United States of Poetry was produced by Washington Square Films for the Independent Television Service (ITVS), with funds provided by the Corporation for Public Broadcasting. Although the five-part series premiered on public television in February 1996 this preview remains on the Web to this day.

Voices from the industry:
Michael Bugeja, Ph.D., Professor Journalism

Q: **How important is paid advertising to the success of an online publication?**

A: For e-zine writers to support themselves as freelancers, they will have to rely on electronic publications that understand advertising. Right now most contributors on the Web receive nothing but exposure, although a few paying e-zines—Spiv.Co, for example—do pay good rates.

The first hurdle concerns e-zines that appeal to segments of society with narrowly defined concepts, much like print magazines have. Then, once the audience is established, an advertising base must be found to support the electronic publication. Only then will freelance writers benefit from the Web, other than via research and fact check.

Q: **Will content continue to be distributed for free?**

A: The trouble lies with establishing an audience that assumes info will be free or that fears paying for info, because of security considerations. Because of these lingering concerns, I think the future of e-zines is in doubt. You'll find many print magazines on the Web purely to garner subscriptions for the real thing on paper. But the medium is richer than that.

We need fewer technicians and more marketers who understand how to reach audience electronically. Right now, like writers, marketers are going where the money is, where the advertising base is, and where the security—financial and otherwise—is and probably will continue to be until a Bill Gates-like genius resolves the dilemmas.

Bio

Michael Bugeja teaches magazine writing at the E.W. Scripps School of Journalism. Michael is a former UPI correspondent, TV talk show host, and award-winning author with a special interest in ethics and music.

What are the basic formats of sales scripts?

Desktop distribution presents a new opportunity for content writers to reach a target market on a one-to-one basis. It's customization that's king, not content anymore. One of the easiest ways to attract mainstream advertisers to the Web is to repurpose their existing creative content. With today's streaming media technology, a thirty-second commercial created for TV can be easily incorporated into a Web page. Others are creating banner ads and netfomercials especially for the Web.

A sales script writer may use numerous testimonials, endorsements, and product claims highlighted by music, hundreds of cuts to the product, to users of the product, to satisfied customers amidst a background of special lighting and entertainment to maintain the viewer's attention for the half-hour commercial. The average adult's attention span for viewing a nonfiction video is only seven minutes.

The video script format for infomercials uses the two-column format. Video (visuals) is typed on the left. Audio (sound, music, speech, and special effects) is typed on the right.

The video directors are given in upper and lower case letters. The audio or speaking part is typed in capital letters so the narrator or actor can see the speaking parts stand out for easy reading or memorization.

The visuals show the product demonstration. The narration tells the viewers the unique features and benefits of the product. Don't tell how good it is, tell how it will benefit the viewer.

The ending makes the most impact. A play on words can lend humor to the script if it also lends credibility to the product and emphasizes how the customer will save money and get superior merchandise. There are many categories of infomercials, including the following:

Product Demonstration

Scripts for trade show exhibition often play in a continuous loop. The sales demonstration video for a trade show is like a department store product demonstration. The demo says to passersby: "Here's what we can do for you." Demonstrations can tie in the product with any viewer's unique, yet universal experience. "We all have had this problem. Here's how to solve it."

Testimonial

Let real people tell success stories to add credibility to a product.

Pitchman

A straight narrator delivers a sales pitch on the product to give factual information in the shortest period of time. This is a talking head short that should only be used for brief commercials or a scene in an infomercial of less than 10 seconds.

Slice-of-Life

This is a dramatization between two people and a product. In an infomercial or training script, the dramatization is a framework that can be used to portray true-life events to teach people how to make decisions or how and where to get information.

Socio-Economic Lifestyle

The social class of the user is emphasized to show how the product fits into a certain economic class such as blue collar, yuppie, new parent, career woman climbing the ladder, or senior citizen retiree. Examples are Grey Poupon, the upper-caste mustard selling to social climbers and Miller Beer, dedicated to blue collar workers celebrating the idea of the working man and woman being rewarded for hard labor with a cold beer.

When the product offered is more expensive than comparable products available in the store, the customer may be persuaded by being told that "he (or she) is worth it." The emotional impact hits home by asking, "Don't you think I'm good enough to deserve this product?" Those who decide to do something special for themselves for a change, will find themselves calling the toll free number with credit card in hand to order something they otherwise never would have purchased.

Animation

Cartoon infomercials sell to children in school and at home. Adults become impatient watching a cartoon demonstration. Animation is expensive to produce for cable television. Use it only to sell to children or to sell supplies to professional animators in non-broadcast demonstration video tapes used to sell products through mail order or at an animator's trade show or exhibit.

Jingles

Lyrics work in short commercials because they are remembered. A best-selling board game called 'Adverteasements' makes players recall all the advertising jingles and trivia information from their past. Ask any person in the street to sing the jingle of an advertisement, and chances are he or she will remember the jingle.

Humor

In a short commercial, humor such as, "Where's the beef?" can be very effective. However, in a long infomercial, it can detract from the primary message—which is to convey information. Humor can be used to prove a point and break the monotony of a long commercial but can undermine credibility if overused.

Serial Characters

Fictional character who appear in print ads and short commercials, such as "Mr. Whipple" or the "Pillsbury Doughboy" are very effective. However, in a longer commercial, viewers may soon tire of the fantasy character and change the channel. Infomercial viewers often want to see real people's testimonials, people like themselves with whom they can identify. Keep the fictional character out of a true-story informational commercial. People want references. Give them references who testify why the product works so well.

Tell-Me-Why

Give people reasons why the product works as it does and why they should buy it. Reason-why copy works better in print than in a short TV or radio commercial. However, in an infomercial for cable, obtaining "tell me why" information is the reason people watch in the first place. Viewers want the writer to go ahead. Make their day.

How-To

In any bookstore the how-to books dominate and appeal to the mass audience reader. People come in for straight information when they want to make decisions on what to buy or how to build it.

Escape doesn't work in a how-to infomercial. A viewer watching a tape on how to buy real estate doesn't want to be swept away to a castle in a fantasy setting for long. It might work in an infomercial selling a general idea or theory that applies to many people in many jobs, such as how to get power and success in relationships or careers.

Feelings, Intuition, and Sensation

Tug at my guilt-strings. Persuasive infomercials use feelings backed up by logical facts that prove a point about a product. Move the viewer by writing genuine emotional copy. A dramatization showing a person shedding tears of joy that someone has telephoned long distance is persuasive. It makes viewers feel guilty they haven't called their mother in years. Infomercials emphasize dem-

onstrations, testimonials, pitchpersons, and straight-sell formulas.

A little emotion within a dramatization can be very persuasive. It may have a positive effect and sell the product or evoke guilt and anger in the viewer for not having lived up to expectations. The viewer may have conflicting feelings. A whole slew of nasty or sentimental feelings totally unrelated to the product can be unleashed by one emotional scene in a commercial.

The emotional, "tug at my guilt-strings" approach works when selling nostalgia. Emotion persuades people to make more telephone calls, or send more candy and flowers by wire.

Using the emotion strategy works well for selling sentiment and can be applied to fields as far reaching as telecommunications, knitting machines, charm bracelets, products or services for the elderly, and greeting cards. Consider the success of the long-running AT&T commercial, "Reach out and touch someone." Who doesn't remember that command to extrovert?

What qualities should I look for in a copywriter?

Who makes the best ad copywriters for the Web? Do you think it's the expressive, creative NF (intuitive/feeling) type, eager to be a designer? Nope. It's more often the INTJ (introverted/intuitive/thinking/judging) type searching for conceptual complexities. The most important thing about writing effective marketing copy for the Web is to see the underlying patterns from many different perspectives, The INTJ naturally uses that introverted intuition with extraverted thinking to solve problems and forecast how the future will affect the present in any situation—especially in the area of how design changes marketing habits.

Traits of Intuitive Thinkers

NTs are often attracted to careers in ad copy Web design for different reasons than ENFPs and INFPs (intuitive/feeling/perceivers) who strictly enjoy the feeling that aesthetics give them, or the energy of extroverted intuition that sends them seeking variety of visual impact. The INTJ makes the ideal Web designer because INTJ is attracted to complexity. The kind of ad copy and Web design the NT will do depends on whether they are an introverted or extroverted (INTP or ENTP) perceiving type who defines the problem based on marketing research analysis, or a judging type (INTJ or ENTJ) who needs to define the solution and actually solve the problem.

- The INTP will see the "big picture" and point out areas to be addressed.

- The INTJ will give you the specific solution.

So, when an INTJ goes into designing ad copy for the Web, or the art and design end of this marketing career, the INTJ will actually solve the marketing problem for you and tell you why. The NTP may give you a list of how many problems you actually have to be solved. And the NFPs—the most creative of expressive artists and designers with words or visuals—will give you lots of information and ideas. . . all the resources you need to find someone else to work out the implementation.

The INTJ will analyze any product or design idea and find out anything that's unique. This is what is meant by defining problems, and INTJ is expert at defining and solving problems, whereas the INTP will define the problem but not want to solve it unless forced to do so. The INTJ foremost will want to solve the problem but may have trouble defining it. If you were to assemble a creative team of people, balanced by personality traits, you could have:

- An INTP define the problem;

- An INTJ solve the problem;

- An INFP to express the solution creatively;

- And an ENFP to market the design and make it interactive so people will engage in rapport, recognition, and interact with it—publicizing, promoting, and selling the big picture of how edutainment, infotainment, and application can bene-

fit the consumer, increase productivity, and offer advantages leading to more ideas.

However, if you're working with a limited budget and can hire only one person to design your Web site and write your ad copy, make that person an INTJ. He'll address your specific issues in concrete terms and tell you how to address them. The other types may express the concept when first you need to define the problem.

If you want someone to explore a scenario from all angles—without regard to budget, look to the NTP (intuitive/thinking perceiver). However, if you are in need of a creative strategist who can identify specific practical solutions to your marketing problems, look to the INTJ.

How can I give my writing "sense appeal"?

Proven direct response techniques from the world of print and television can be applied directly to the Web. However, you won't have to announce, "Get your pencil and paper ready to take advantage of this one-time offer!"

Think of the Web as one big direct response sales letter rather than a TV show. Picture a couple sitting across the table from one another with an object on the table between them. It could be anything from a bowl of chili, to a cake, a package of condoms, or a can of corn. The people and the product form a triangle, and the customer becomes the couple sitting equidistantly from the product.

The script reads, "Nothing can come between us, dear, but this gadget in the spotlight." The product is now the center of attention as the viewer is the center of gravity. Thus, sense, sex, and sell appeal converge, bringing two loving people closer in bonding. That sells anything—interactively or interstitially—by narrowing the space between two people.

To write a message that sells, first find out the client's budget. Then deliver a selling message within their budget and time frame.

As with any multimedia application, keep the pictures simple. Use words to make an impact, but the fewer the words, the better. The more complex the graphics, the fewer words are needed to explain them. Turn the sound off. Can you still understand what is being sold? Sight and sound work together. Use sound only to explain what the picture is demonstrating.

Ninety words can be spoken in sixty seconds. Forty-five words can be crammed into thirty seconds. Many thirty- and sixty-second commercials contain far less words so the viewer can really get the information. Compare this to the print ad which usually runs 1,500 words in a thirty- to sixty-second read.

Sell every second the script is on the cyberwaves. The first four seconds are the same as the headlines of a print ad. Don't waste that time waiting for graphics to load. The viewer will use those four seconds to decide if it's worth the wait.

You may open with a real-life situation to hook the viewer in the first four seconds. The music and visuals can add the background. The opening is called the "cow-catcher" because it's supposed to grab the viewer. The average attention span wanes quickly. People want to read less and see more. They need to hear enough within their seven-minute attention span to keep focused on the subject. (The attention span of a child is four minutes.) Compare this to the traditional info-mercial script that is 28 1/2 minutes long with more than 400 cuts of graphics and montages. Make your Web intermercial or presentation one quarter the length or less.

Use motion to keep attention riveted. Show the syrup pouring, the machines working, the demonstrator demonstrating. Let the viewer hear the whirr of the machine as it moves forward. The sound is more appetizing than the look—and sound is more "do-able" on today's Web than video.

Use titles superimposed over the picture to reinforce a sales point not covered in the narration. An info-mercial typically repeats the product name and selling point several times because most viewers aren't paying attention when the infomercial comes on. The product name and selling point is repeated at the beginning, middle, and end of the presentation.

Show people using the product throughout the presentation. Product neglect is the primary reason why infomercials don't sell. Show people demonstrating, talking about, and using the product in different scenarios. Use a child to sell a product emotionally. Have an adult present the facts and logic behind the demonstration for credibility.

Use a celebrity to do a voice-over or on-camera narration. Identify the celebrity by name and superimposed title. In local retail infomercials, give the directions or address of the store.

Emphasize believability, clarity, and simplicity over creativity. Don't write confusion into a script by putting in too much dazzle, sensation, and entertainment that overpower the information and message.

The emphasis is on making information available to help the customer reach a buying decision and keep them coming back for more. This wait-and-see soft-sell approach is referred to as the "pull" model, where the user initiates the contact by visiting the Web site.

The Campbell Soup Company has built an entire culture around their brand. A visit to their site evokes warm childhood memories and makes you wonder what you're going to cook for dinner tonight. It's not about soup—it's about family and togetherness. Their site is a nice place to visit and the next time you need a casserole recipe, you'll know where to find one.

In contrast, the in-your-face "push" model delivers information directly to the desktop of the consumer. The face of the Web will be transformed as sites evolve into advertising-supported netcast channels that deliver rich media experiences with streaming, synchronized audio, video, and animation. This is where the industry is heading and where the money is flowing.

Regardless of which model you choose, bringing people together is the primary appeal of the Web and the very nature direct response. Remember—bonding and branding sell. Sell intimacy made practical. Nothing can come between us dear, but this can of chowder.

http://www.campbellsoups.com

The Campbell Soup Company Web site is full of menu planning tips, a searchable database of recipes, activities, and projects to benefit your family, your school, and the entire community.

This shopping list calculates your total order and then can be printed out and mailed to the company.

57

Where can I find professional resources and guidelines?

Infomercial producers have set their own guidelines to establish professional standards and battle a poor public perception of the long-form commercials. The National Infomercial Marketing Association (NIMA), requires members to produce programs based on truthful information in compliance with current laws and regulations. These guidelines, which can be directly applied to developers of commercial Web content, cover such crucial issues as sponsorship identification, program production, product claim substantiation, testimonials and endorsements.

The National Infomercial Marketing Association's guidelines for members include ordering guidelines. Writers need to work into the script the ways in which customers can order and pay for the product. What is a fair price? Can the customer buy it cheaper in a discount chain? If so, why would he order from the Web and pay more? Are similar and competing products available in stores or on other sites? Is there a benefit to purchasing the product online?

A writer may be hired to write copy to sell at the client's prices, sometimes knowing in advance that the customer can get it cheaper in the store than by ordering from the site. Also, what warranties are on the product? What guarantees have been made and are there guidelines for refunds?

As a condition of NIMA membership, guidelines on refunds, guarantees, warranties, and prices are required. However, not all infomercial producers are members of NIMA, nor are all clients of infomercial producers members either.

It's the client who makes the product, then hires an infomercial producer as an independent contractor or freelancer. The infomercial producer either hires a freelance infomercial video scriptwriter or Web site designer for the project. Some producers specialize only in making commercial Web sites.

Among NIMA members, if a guideline is violated, a complaint is presented to a review board—two NIMA members and three consultants. If the board finds a violation, the program must be removed from the airwaves within ten days.

Members in good standing can certify TV station and cable networks that each infomercial complies with the guidelines. NIMA provides telecasters with a list of members in good standing every six months. By codifying the conduct of infomercial producers, the infomercial industry can be lead out of a difficult period when many viewer's attitudes toward infomercials were low.

Regulations set by NIMA state in part that each video will be preceded and followed with a clear announcement that it's a paid advertisement. There must be sufficient product to meet the demand within thirty days. There must be reliable evidence for all claims made and testimonials from consumers must to be voluntary from bona fide users of the product. The stated price of the product must disclose all additional costs, postage, and handling. These are just a few of the issues Web marketers should be sensitive to as online marketing and advertising comes of age.

As a trade association, NIMA promotes the growth, development, and acceptance of electronic retailing worldwide, including infomercial, television shopping, and short form direct response companies and their suppliers as well as other interactive media marketers.

http://www.nima.org

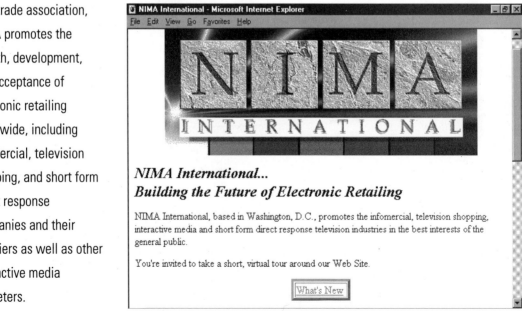

CHAPTER NINE

Understanding Your Electronic Rights

As money flows into cyberspace, the right to profit from electronic use of articles has become a growing concern. New technology has extended the shelf-life of freelancers' work making some articles perpetually available for resale anywhere in the world.

One issue is whether the publisher has the right to license to database producers articles by freelancers in online and CD-ROM formats without permission of the authors. Some Web publishers maintain that no permission or extra payment is needed. However, writers may argue that since, under the law, freelancers own the copyright in their work, any unlicensed use of the material constitutes infringement. This is an area where old rules are being broken and new rules are being written as we speak.

According to *Contracts Watch*, a bulletin published by the American Society of Journalists and Authors to keep tab on freelance rights issues, some periodicals have begun to split with authors the royalties received from such ventures as the Nexis and UMI databases while others pay fees for the rights.

The Authors Registry was established to collect electronic-use royalties that some publishers have refused to pay. It has quickly gained wide support and now counts more than thirty writers' organizations and ninety-five literary agencies among its endorsers. The Authors Registry began operations in February 1996. Writers unions are another powerful force taking an active role in issues related to the electronic rights of aesthetic works.

In this chapter, we will examine some of the legal issues related to electronic rights, with the help of Ivan Hoffman, an attorney who handles electronic rights and internet-related issues.

The responses to questions in this chapter are not intended as a substitute for legal advice.

A complete, searchable archive of *ASJA Contracts Watch* is available on the Web. Find it—with other valuable information and tips on freelance contracts, electronic rights and copyright—at the following Web address: www.asja.org/cwpage.htm

Voices from the industry:
Ivan Hoffman, B.A., J.D., Attorney at Law

Bio

Ivan Hoffman spent the first twenty-two years of his career practicing law, primarily in the entertainment field. Hoffman graduated from UCLA law school in 1968. He now applies his experience handling issues related to copyrights, licensing, contracts, and other forms of intellectual property matters to the new field of electronic rights and Internet law.

Q: **Has the new media changed the nature of your law practice and how?**

A: During my practice, I handled issues relating to copyrights, licensing, contracts and other forms of intellectual property matters.

By the end of 1990, I had been successful enough and, I'd like to believe wise enough, to retire from the practice at age forty-seven and a half. During the next and past five years, I wrote, taught and traveled.

When I found the Internet toward the end of 1995, I realized that I could utilize all the skills and knowledge I had previously acquired as an attorney. The legal and business issues the Internet now presents are the very issues I dealt with for those twenty-two years as an attorney. So I believe I am well positioned to provide valuable services to those in the publishing and Internet communities—so much so, in fact, that on January 1, 1996, I reactivated my law practice.

Q: **Do you spend much time on the Internet?**

I am an active participant in several e-mail-based discussion groups related to the publishing and writing communities. Additionally, I have written much about the issues of electronic rights and make the articles available on my Web site. I have also experimented with online distribution and sales of several of my books on other subjects. My most recent book *Internet Law Simplified: An Easy Guide to Making Money, Staying Out of Trouble and Protecting Your Rights.*can be found on my Web site (http://home.earthlink.net/ ~ivanlove/internet.html).

How important is the issue in electronic rights?

At the inception of any new medium, those in the already existing media are heard to cry about the imminent downfall of their cherished territory. This happened when television came in and those in the movie industry screamed about the loss of their markets. This happened when the VCR came in and those in the television industry screamed about loss of their markets. None of that which provoked the screaming has ever been true. Those with vested interests learned how to adapt to the new medium and use it for their advantage. They did so or they perished.

Today, the 'hot button' issue is electronic media and the voices of some are heard about loss of revenue and even the downfall of copyright by its advent. Instead of expending such energies crying about false wolves, writers and publishers should be figuring out how to adapt.

There are some who would hold out and not allow their creative product to be exploited "for free" as it were. It appears to me that they have missed the point entirely about the state of electronic rights at this moment in history.

The money isn't here yet, but the market is.

Failing to see that electronic rights are not about earning enough money to purchase that long-awaited villa in Spain but rather about creating an outreach far beyond one's previously wildest expectations is, to my mind, to miss the point in its entirety. To refuse to have one's work exploited in this new media even if 'for free' is to fail to adapt. And to risk perishing.

Before I got on the Net, I took a class about it and the teacher said that when any new medium comes along, there are those that are 'early adopters,' those that instantly 'get it,' see its enormous potential and jump on it. Then there are the 'later adopters,' and finally there are the 'laggards.' Those who fail to 'jump on it,' those who hold out exploiting

In the news. . .

In Europe, unlike in the US, staff writers typically retain some rights in their work. Thus, according to a report from the London Freelance Branch of the National Union of Journalists (UK), the Belgian journalists' union is suing newspaper owners over electronic re-use of members' work. The action stems from the launching of an online database service by a coalition of newspaper publishers.

—ASJA *Contracts Watch*

"Our lawyer won't allow any changes."

Best response from a writer: "Neither will mine."

—ASJA *Contracts Watch*

it because they are still working with yesterday's ideas in today's environment, run the risk of losing that 'early adopter' status.

I use the words 'for free' in quotes because free is an inappropriate word. The benefits are enormous. To see 'free' as meaning for no fee, while grammatically correct, seems to me to miss the point again. The power to reach readers throughout the world, at no cost, is hardly without benefits. The power to publish without constraints imposed by editors and publishers is hardly without benefits. In no sense of the concept is the writer or publisher giving up anything 'for free.'

The legal term used in any transaction to make it enforceable is called 'consideration.' A 'consideration' can be that which one party gains in the transaction and it is not limited to money. There is a maxim in the law business that says that 'The law will not question the adequacy of the consideration.' This means that it is up to the parties, not the law courts, to determine what the benefits are.

Having said all this, I do not suggest that one simply give away one's creativity without benefits, including monetary benefits, when the same are available. Certainly, when money is exchanged by any party to the transaction, the creator should share in that money. But the power to create the financial market can only come when the market is established in the first place. To hold back creative product at this point is to run the risk of diminishing the very market we seek to create down the road, the one that produces revenue.

If the old ideas of the wolf criers had prevailed, it is possible that the markets that later came into existence and which were in part the saving grace of those same older media might never have materialized. When some species first emerged from the oceans, what would have been the fate of us all had other species said 'Well, let's just see if it works before we try it?'

But to see the benefits in any new medium requires a bit of vision. Imagine what your childhood storytelling experiences might have been like had the little boy had vision before he cried 'Wolf!'

Who owns the copyright in a Web site?

The static world of the two dimensional text and small graphics Web site may be quickly becoming the black and white television of the Internet. As creativity and capacity catch up with each other, many of tomorrow's Web sites will be increasingly more inventive, utilizing many different media. This presents the owner of the site, the designer of the site and of course the attorney for each, with interesting new challenges in order that the rights of all parties be preserved.

In the absence of a valid written contract resolving the open issues, it is actually not quite as simple a situation as you might expect. But what is simple in the law business? These are some of the open issues:

1. We must first distinguish between the copyright in the design, the 'look' of the site and the copyright in the content. Colors, .GIFs, .JPGs, setup, hyperlinks, and other elements contributing to that design start

out being owned by the creator, in this case the web site designer. But even that is not set in stone as it were. For you undoubtedly played a hand in making the underlying creative decisions and so perhaps the copyright is owned jointly.

This is what the United States copyright statute defines as a joint work:

"A 'joint work' is a work prepared by two or more authors with the intention that their contributions be merged into inseparable or interdependent parts of a unitary whole."

But as you may see, if the respective contributions to the end product web site are distinguishable, there may be separate copyright owners of those separate elements. Not only that, but your contribution must be more than minimal in order that you qualify as a joint author. There are many conse-

""All the other writers are signing."

Oldest line in the book of Publisher-Speak, and rarely true.

—ASJA *Contracts Watch*

quences of joint authorship which are beyond the scope of this article.

2. Moreover, to the extent that the .GIFs, .JPGs and other elements were downloaded from the Net, assuming even that they themselves are free of copyright restrictions which is not always the case, neither the designer nor you can claim a copyright in that which is already in the public domain.

    On the other hand, to the extent that these graphics were created by the web site designer, it appears again that the designer initially owns the copyright therein. But if they are your creation, your logo, your photo or that of your dog, then presumptively you own the rights thereto. (Unless of course the photos were taken by someone else, in which event the photographer owns the copyrights therein and you must obtain permission to use them on your site.) I told you this was not simple.

3. Let's move on to the other substance of the site: the text. Obviously, if that has been created by you, you own the copyright therein. But it is not simply text that appears on the Net, it is also the way that the text is set up, in the form of HTML or even VRML coding. If the designer created that coding, then the coding, as distinguished from the text itself, is owned by the designer. Included in the foregoing concept of copyright in the coding is the manner in which the designer has created the hyperlinking within the site. And so you may own the text but the designer may own the way the text is set up on the site.

There may be many other elements of copyrightable material on the site. The question of copyright ownership as to each of those elements turns on who created them and under what circumstances.

Having outlined some, but certainly not all of the issues, there are two potential kinds of agreements that may be used to resolve those issues: a work for hire agreement and a copyright assignment.

In order that there be a valid work for hire agreement, several criteria must be satisfied:

1. If the designer is a valid employee of your company, then everything that the designer creates during the course and scope of his or her employment belongs to you. You own the copyright.

2. On the other hand, if you have hired an independent contractor to design the site, then there must be a valid, written agreement, signed by the parties. But note that it must be both valid and written. In this regard, to be a valid work for hire agreement you must have "specially ordered or commissioned" the work (presumably you did) and the written agreement must state that it is a work for hire agreement and this must be executed before the designer begins the work. You cannot acquire rights to the site by an after-the-fact attempt at a work for hire agreement. There is no such thing.

The Web site design work must belong to one of the statutory categories in order to qualify as a work for hire. I am assuming for the sake of this discussion that hiring the designer is a "contribution to a collective work," one of the statutory categories of permissible work for hire agreements. In this regard, it is a collective work, I am assuming, because you have created certain of the elements, the text for example, and the designer is contributing the design elements. There may be other circumstances in which the work does not fall into either this category nor any other of the statutory categories of permissible work for hire agreements, in which event you cannot rely on the work for hire contract and you must turn to the copyright assignment to transfer the rights.

And so let's assume that there is no writing between the parties that satisfies the work for hire requirements. You may perhaps acquire all the rights of the designer in the site by having the designer execute a written assignment of copyright that transfers all those rights from the

"Databases like Lexis-Nexis are just another way of distributing our magazine. You wouldn't expect more money if we signed up 1,000 more newsstands, would you?"

A database is NOT simply another means of distributing a magazine, because a database doesn't distribute magazines at all; it distributes individual articles. Online services collect a per-article fee from database users and pass a piece back to the publisher. It's as if a reader could go to a newsstand, slice your article out of a magazine and pay for the clipping alone. It is, in effect, an electronic delivery system for a reprint service.

—ASJA *Contracts Watch*

designer to you. Note however, that to the extent the designer did not create the material (as in the form of the .GIFs etc.), you do not acquire any rights therein.

You would want to acquire all rights in the site, not merely the rights to use it as your site. As a result, if you have no written, valid agreement conveying to you all these rights, you may then end up merely with a license to use your own site. This license may be exclusive rights for site only purposes or it may be non-exclusive, entitling the designer to use the very same elements created for you elsewhere.

There may be other forms of licenses conveying other rights. None of these are particularly satisfying since you may be losing valuable rights. This is, after all, your expression of you. You should be free to use your expression of your heart freely.

You must remain constantly aware that this area of electronic issues is constantly evolving and what appears to be a web site today can be a video game or a feature length motion picture tomorrow.

There may be other issues involved beyond the basic copyright ones. These may be whether the designer can put his or her logo on the site or whether the designer can use a copy of the site as part of his or her portfolio. These are more contract questions than copyright questions, although they may flow from the answers to the copyright questions.

So you can see that there are no simple answers in this new area. And it is the wisest advice to enter into a written agreement dealing with these as well as other issues that may arise.

What about using protected material?

When developing a multimedia presentation, whether for a CD-ROM, on the Internet, or a hybrid CD which has a link to the Internet, the producer or Web site owner who uses material from other media must be careful about obtaining clearances for the same. And the thicket of rights through which the user must traverse is daunting.

As a preliminary note, you should have your concept firmly in mind so that when approaching the rights owners, you know exactly what rights you need and what are unnecessary. You should pay for only those you now need or reasonably contemplate needing during the expected life of the project. It is unlikely you will obtain blanket rights, 'throughout the world, in perpetuity.'

Although you have the choice to create original content if appropriate licenses cannot be obtained, this answer deals only with using previously created content. Numerous other issues present themselves when creating original material including but certainly not limited to the acquisition of rights through valid contracts and dealing with unions and guilds, which issues are beyond the scope of this discussion.

Photographs

You must obtain clearances from the owner of the photograph. This is most often the photographer. When you see a photograph in a magazine or book, it is unlikely that magazine or book owns the copyright in the photo. What is more likely is that the magazine is merely a licensee for some limited use and that all other rights remain with the photographer. You may obtain clearances, if at all, only by negotiating with the photographer, the photographer's agent, or perhaps a clearance house.

You must also obtain permission of the persons depicted in the photograph to use their likeness. The courts of the United States and

"The exposure will be good for you. It'll get your name around. It'll sell books."

By that reasoning, you shouldn't charge for print publication either, and you should give away first serial rights to your books. Even if it seems that an online appearance can help a new book with extra exposure, will it make sense in a couple of years, when the book is out of print? The chapter excerpted in a magazine may continue to earn royalties for the magazine publisher while doing nothing for you.

—ASJA *Contracts Watch*

some other jurisdictions have recognized a 'right of publicity," a right that derives from the "right of privacy.' These rights apply to all living persons and, under certain circumstances, those dead. Our likenesses and even our names may not be used for commercial purposes without our consent, which consent, if it is given at all, usually comes at a price. If the images used are of 'ordinary' people, non-celebrities, at the very least you must obtain or have the photographer represent that he or she has obtained releases in writing from each of those whose images are distinguishable in the photograph. If these are celebrities, the fees go up, even assuming they are willing to allow their images to be so used.

Another interesting note is that also under certain circumstances, buildings may be the subject of copyright. You may need permission to either take a photograph of such a work or obtain a separate clearance from the copyright owner of the actual building in addition to the copyright owner of the photograph you use. Architectural works cre-

ated on or after December 1, 1990, and any architectural works that were not then constructed and embodied in unpublished plans or drawings on that date are eligible for protection. (There are some qualifications on this protection so you should consult with an attorney about the same.)

And even photographs of now public domain works of art, perhaps called 'classic art' such as the Mona Lisa or the like, may also be protected by copyright. While the underlying art may be free to use, a particular photographic depiction of that free artwork may be separately copyrighted and so a clearance must be obtained for using that photographic reproduction of the artwork.

Needless to say, if the underlying artwork is still covered by its own copyright, then permission to use it must also be obtained. These rights usually reside with the artist or the artist's estate.

When clearing certain works of art, an additional right must be obtained. Under the copyright law of many countries, including the United States, an artist that produces a limited number of copies of a visual art has what is known as a 'moral right.' This right protects the artist from changes made to the art and that the artist's name is properly used to identify the work.

Text

This category covers text of all sorts such as from books, magazines or the like, which are protected under the copyright law.

You must obtain a clearance to use the copyrighted material from the owner thereof, usually the publisher if it is a book, or the author or whoever now owns the same. If the book is currently in print, it is usually not difficult to find out who owns it. But if the book is no longer in print but is still copyrighted, then searching out the author or the author's estate can be somewhat difficult. But the difficulty does not eliminate the requirement.

If, as part of a multimedia project, an off-camera voice is going to read the text, then you must obtain additional rights from the text owner to do so. You may also need to obtain rights from the actor who is doing the reading.

If you intend to translate the text, separate rights are involved.

Trademarks

The use of trademarks must also be cleared. What is or is not a trademark is a tricky question if the mark has not been registered. If you see a superscripted 'R' in a circle ®, then the mark enjoys federal trademark protection. But if it is merely a superscripted 'TM' or 'SM' then the mark has not been registered. And if you see nothing next to some brand or name, it still may enjoy trademark protection! A search is necessary in order to determine whether a given mark or name must be cleared and indeed who owns either.

As a side note, under certain circumstances the use even of a person's name may become subject to a clearance. These circumstances have to do with whether or not the use may imply an endorsement of the product or is merely incidental. When in doubt, clear. Included in this category may be the use of trademarked characters such as from cartoons. These are very popular with developers since coming out with a title featuring a well-

"The business is new. Let it shake down a few years, then renegotiate."

Ever try to push the toothpaste back into the tube? Some publishers are trying to establish an industry standard in which all e-rights—and, while they're at it, other subsidiary rights—would come with first publication right. Fortunately, others see things differently. We need to convert the holdouts now, not do it their way and hope for a better deal next year.

—ASJA *Contracts Watch*

known character offers higher visibility in a crowded marketplace.

Film, Television and Radio

Initially you should be prepared to pay what in legal jargon is referred to as a 'bundle' for these rights. Obviously so, since the media from which you are seeking rights is well marketed and your desire to use the same underscores their value.

You must obtain clearances from the owner of the clip, whether from television, film or radio. This is usually the film studio, television producer or radio show producer, but may not be. It requires some checking to see who owns what.

You must obtain clearances from each actor who has appeared in the clip, even those who are now deceased, the latter because of the right of publicity issue and/or union requirements that I mentioned above. Additionally, you must clear rights from writers and directors.

To amplify a bit on the union and guild requirements, these organizations play an important part in the area of film, television and radio. Because of this, when licensing a

clip, you will most likely be required by the terms of the license to pay and be responsible for all fees due the unions and guilds for the use of the material. These are referred to as 're-use' fees. You must check with Screen Actors Guild, Writers Guild, American Federation of Musicians, American Federation of Television and Radio Artists and perhaps other guilds representing other talent.

No matter what other media you seek, you will need to include in the discussion and ultimate license issues such as:

- **The nature of the usage.**

  These issues include whether for CD-ROM, the Internet, or both, and exactly what platforms you intend to develop the material for (Windows, DOS, the Mac, DVD etc.).

- **Marketing and promotion.**

  Whether you need the right to use the material for marketing and promotional campaigns.

- **Languages and territories.**

  What languages and territories you need, which also entails perhaps additional clearances since not all owners own all rights for all languages and territories.

- **Amount of time needed.**

  How much time you need to adequately exploit the material.

And perhaps a host of other issues depending upon the exact nature of your intended use. Having said all this, other issues present themselves. For example:

If the owner of the Web site has hired an independent contractor Web site designer to develop, create and post the site, someone has to be responsible for not only obtaining these clearances but for representing and warranting that those clearances were obtained. This has to be covered in the agreement between the Web site designer and the owner.

There are of course many other issues that are involved in obtaining these licenses and clearances. They may deal with term of use, scope of use, ancillary rights and so on. These may be situation-specific and should be handled by an attorney with experience in the field.

There are many sub-issues that arise, issues involving defamation, invasion of privacy, unfair competition and e-THICS™ to name a few. I have not tried to be exhaustive of all the issues in this article and each of those issues and more must be considered in any use of material, whether licensed or created by you. It is best to work closely with an attorney who can perhaps help negotiate both the terrain and the licenses.

Music

There are several rights that are initially owned by the creator of the music and the recording embodying that music. It is important to note that separate rights exist in the music and the recording of that music in a particular version. These separate rights are themselves separated into separate rights and each must be cleared or licensed in order that they be permissibly used on a Web site.

In the news. . .

If *Cosmopolitan* and other Hearst magazines' freelancers have been told once, they've been told a hundred times: The company can't delete the e-rights clause from contracts because it can't drop individual articles from electronic databases. Not really. A writer who did three pieces for *Cosmo* "special sections" found her work in an online database. She pointed out to the advertorial producer who had contracted for the articles that their arrangement was for plain First North American serial rights. After some tugging and shoving, *Cosmo* apologized for the "inconvenience" and the articles disappeared from the database. The same happened a while ago with a book excerpt in *Cosmo*: The author persuaded his book publisher to make the magazine live up to an agreement that didn't include e-rights.

—ASJA *Contracts Watch*

The first right that may be applicable is that of mechanical reproduction of the underlying song. This is the right that allows a user to reproduce a musical composition on a copy.

This is the definition of copies under the United States Copyright law:

'Copies' are material objects, other than phonorecords, in which a work is fixed by any method now known or later developed, and from which the work can be perceived, reproduced, or otherwise communicated, either directly or with the aid of a machine or device. The term 'copies'

includes the material object, other than a phonorecord, in which the work is first fixed.

Your first response might be that putting a musical composition on a Web site is not making a 'copy' since the Web site is not a 'material object.' But of course in order to get the composition on the site, you do have to make a copy of the same using some form of reproduction software and accompanying hardware.

As a side note, this right came into the 1909 Copyright law in relationship to piano rolls. It was designed to prevent copyright owners of a

Ivan Hoffman appeared on the Canadian Internet radio show, NetTalk to promote his book, *Internet Law Simplified: An Easy Guide to Making Money, Staying Out of Trouble and Protecting Your Rights.*

Unfortunately, the producers of NetTalk eventually cancelled the show due to a lack of support from paid advertisers.

http://www.nettalk.com

song from having a monopoly on the composition since the right, then and now, is subject to what is known as a compulsory license. It is the same right that allows singers to sing someone else's song on a phonograph record, now CD. My, my how far we have come.

The second right that needs to be obtained is a right to publicly perform the composition. Whenever a musical composition is performed in public, this right must be licensed and these are usually handled by ASCAP or BMI. Since whenever a viewer logs onto the Web site containing a copyrighted composition it is a 'public performance,' clearances must be obtained.

Finally, if the music is used in timed synchronization with images, i.e. as a soundtrack to an accompanying video or even as background to a still photograph, then another right comes into play, called a synchronization right. An appropriate 'synch' license must therefor be obtained.

Separate from the rights in the song are the rights to use a particular version of the song, perhaps off of a CD by a particular artist. These rights may be owned or controlled by separate copyright owners and therefor separate licenses must be obtained.

Most often, the recording company that manufactures and distributes the recording owns the recording right while a publishing company owns the rights in the song. The license that is required is known as a 'master use' license for it is a deal in which the owner of the recording, the master, gives the right to someone else to use that recording.

As part of the license agreement, the user of the master may have to pay fees to the American Federation of Musicians, American Federation of Television and Radio Artists or others for the right to re-use the performances contained on the recording. Note, however, that if the user of the composition elects to record the composition without resort to someone else's recording, no master use license is required, nor any re-use fees. But this would not eliminate the need for the licenses regarding the song.

In the news. . .

Other magazines continue to ask for free e-use but make other arrangements when writers say no. Told by a freelancer that all-media reuse for free was not acceptable, *Historic Traveler* (Cowles) offered to delete the request or add payment of "at least 10 percent of the original fee" to the clause.

—ASJA *Contracts Watch*

61 How can writers protect their rights in cyberspace?

The issues covered in this chapter are complex. Many forms of agreements may be required in order that the owner of protected materials and the user of those materials may be protected. The negotiation of those agreements and their preparation are also complex.

infringing upon another person's rights is so very easy. Whereas in the 'real' world, it takes equipment, distribution, and so on to effectively steal some else's creativity, on the Net all it takes is a couple of clicks of a mouse. Cut, paste and you're done!

As a result of this ease, those of us on the Net must pay even more attention to protecting the other person's rights. We are all, at the same moment, both creators and users of protected materials. If we want our own rights to be taken care of, we must be very careful to protect the rights of others.

Just as we can easily infringe upon someone else's rights, they can do the same to ours. In a very real sense then, we take care of ourselves by taking care of others. 🐾

These articles and the responses to questions in this chapter are not intended to be substitutes for legal advice. The specific facts that apply to your matter may make the outcome different than would be anticipated by you. You should consult with an attorney familiar with the issues and the laws.

http://home.earthlink.net/~ivanlove/internet.html

CHAPTER TEN

Your Future as a Cyberscribe

Online journalism is where many journalism graduates are heading. It's the journalist's place to be. So how do you get a job in journalism on the Web? Head for the concept of publishing supported by advertising on the Web. It's a key theme in online journalism career development. Recently, thirteen new journals are being released on the subject of electronic journalism job development and online journalism (as trade journals).

Commercial spin-offs of the Web and commercial Web lists are growing dramatically. As the digital revolution in journalism heads toward maturity, more doors will open for writers who are prepared to take advantage of the opportunity.

New products require new writers to repackage the product and write tutorials as well as the news about the tutorials and products. They're coming from new companies designing for online publishing today what *PageMaker* and *Ventura Publisher* did for desktop publishing in the eighties. Book publishers are becoming software publishers, software publishers are becoming media companies, and writers are becoming producers.

There are many opportunities in the new media for a traditional writer from the publishing world where daily newspapers are merging and contracting. Newspapers now hire online journalists to work both at home and on staff in the office. It's a new way of communicating that is changing the way we learn and the way business is conducted.

In this final chapter, we will hear from writers who have made a name for themselves in the new media. Listen and learn. There's room for you.

The Web is energy and it's up to you to create a better tomorrow by using your writing to balance the newest media—imagery with technology, and metaphor with ingenuity.

Voices from the industry:
Heidi Swanson, Digital Editor, The Net Magazine

Bio

Heidi Swanson, 23, is a graduate of the University of California at San Diego with a degree in media and visual arts.

After graduation, Heidi moved to Idaho for three months to play with HTML and Web graphics. Using her personal Web site as her portfolio, Heidi landed her first job as Web Master and Associate Editor for *The Net* magazine.

>Date: Mon, 16 Sep 1996 23:01:09-0700

>To: anne hart <scribes@ellipsys.com>

>From: heidi@thenet-usa.com (Heidi Swanson)

>

>hey anne, Cyberscribes sounds interesting.

>I, for one, have a vision of the Internet as more than a wallowing digital strip mall avec 24-hour food court. As an editor on one of the major Internet publications, I now have the opportunity to shape and encourage the direction the Internet is headed through the magazine and individual participation on the Web. I see the Internet as part of our legacy and the legacy I would like to see is much bigger than a quick newsstand sale. It is a reflection of who we are as a global society and a celebration of the ideals we find important.

>There is definitely a place here for commerce, I just don't want to see all the skilled contributors dive head first into the crowded wading pool of Hollywood shocked sites and digi-malls just so they can pay their rent. The Web must reflect a balance of human culture, relationships, and community. It is critical that we empower, celebrate and nurture an Internet that we will be proud of in the future. We have the opportunity to give people a new type of intelligent and healthy role model, unique voices pipelined direct from someone's basement. They will have an actual accessible pulse tangible through e-mail and chat. . . not the passive, watered down, filtered, and out-of-touch content that is beamed in one direction through a television monitor.

>Check out the article in this month's Rolling Stone (with the REM cover) which kind of demystifies the idea that the Web scene is a cool place to work. Basically, wages are really low, twitch management runs rampant, and an isolated group of people are actually making money by exploiting kids straight out of college. . . .

>heidi

>*-
>http://www.cyborganic.net/people/solanna

Voices from the industry:
Daniel Schorr, Broadcast Journalist

Q: **What impact will technology have on journalism?**

A: One possible new direction has been outlined by my friend, Ellen Hume, in a study for the Annenberg Washington Program of Northwestern University on the impact of technology on journalism. She finds that "the apparently endless flow of scandals and feeding frenzies has damaged rather than enhanced journalism's credibility." The objective now, she says, must be to use new technologies to create "a trustworthy product." Addressing a "public" rather than an "audience."

Q: **What is the "new journalism" ?**

A: The smart new journalism will be both interactive and proactive, opening the door for citizen engagement. In the new news marketplace, there will be an obsession with scoops and deadlines.

I may be too old to grasp what lies ahead in a new interactive journalism geared to a new technological age. I can only surmise that anything that helps to restore public confidence in the disseminators of information will help to restore public support for the constitutional guarantee of the freedom of the press.

The men who crafted that guarantee to shield the writers of political polemics from retaliation by Congress could not have dreamed what a vast industry their brief amendment would end up shielding. But it is still, perhaps more than ever, worth fighting to protect.

Bio:

Daniel Schorr, 81, is a veteran reporter-commentator and the last of Edward R. Murrow's legendary CBS team. Still fully active in journalism, he currently interprets national and international events as a senior news analyst for National Public Radio.

Voices from the industry:
Joseph Bernt, Associate Professor of Journalism

Bio

Joseph Bernt is an Associate Professor at the E.W.Scripps School of Journalism.

His areas of interest include consumer, trade and business magazines, journalism history, media coverage of minorities and specialized audiences, public relations, and marketing communication.

Q: **How reliable is the 'Net as a source of information?**

A: While I have always been a heavy user of database reference systems for research in journalism, history, and literary studies, I am particularly unimpressed by the 'Net as a source of journalism or information.

I am not such a fossil as not to recognize that the Web has great potential to deliver information. But I also recognize that any yutz can carelessly attach partial, incorrect, unorganized, and ugly information to the Web. Searching through the junk makes using a print-driven library reference room a distinct pleasure.

The 'Net resides dead last on my search strategy—employed only after CD-ROM, library catalog, print reference materials, and discussions with experts have come up dry. I have spent too many four-hour sessions browsing to no avail to make myself a slave to the idiocy of my fellow human beings. The problem with the Web is that it is dependent on the information development skills of geeks with little training—enamored by their newfound ability to celebrate themselves and their interests.

What does that leave of value? Information produced by government, library, and some nonprofit institutions and by careful researchers. It's in this context that I think the Internet has potential for journalists and communication scholars.

If the quality of reputable print sources can be delivered via Web sites, the Internet will perform a major service, save bunches of money, and provide the educated professional class with a new tool to rule the poor and undereducated throughout the world.

If the Internet is to become truly a new 'mass' media technology, journalism programs will need training in editing and design, in traditional, and high-tech library skills. Wedding subject specialists to training in library search strategies and technologies and training in writing, editing, and design would make for a valuable undergraduate/masters-level curriculum.

Voices from the industry:
Randy Befumo, The Motley Fool

>From: MFTemplar@aol.com
>Date: Fri, 10 Jan 1997 01:22:21 -0500 (EST)
>To: scribes@ellipsys.com
>Subject: digital journalism
>
>Anne,
>
>To answer your question about how I use the Net:
>
>Basically I generate two columns a day on what is happening in the market with Internet resources as my main source of information--beyond the tons of e-mail sent by very smart readers correcting and amplifying my own comments.
>
>The Digital World opens up a plethora of immediate information that is at the disposal of the writer for an extremely low cost of access. From the America Online platform, I can get forward estimates, current press releases, company descriptions, and access to federal filings out at EDGAR.
>
>With a few keystrokes and a few hours of reading, I can familiarize myself with the current status and operating history of almost any public company, a process that would have taken hours of research at a public library.
>
>Conventional journalism published in the newspaper the day after the events happen—with only the thinnest veil of information behind it—is already dead. It just hasn't noticed yet.
>
>Randy Befumo (MF Templar), a Fool
>http://fool.web.aol.com

Bio

Randy Befumo is a principle creative voice behind *The Motley Fool,* providing investors with timely information on equity investing from a long-term perspective.

Randy's liberal arts background allows the Fool to write entertainingly about "what is one of the most boring subjects on the planet—business." He is convinced that most business journalists don't know what they are talking about—otherwise, they would make three times as much on the Street.

Randy graduated from the College of William and Mary in Williamsburg, Virginia with a Bachelor of Arts in Interdisciplinary Studies, including Religion, History and Philosophy.

Voices from the industry:
Tom Durkin, Freelance Writer

Bio

Tom Durkin has thirty years professional, award-winning experience as staff and freelance writer, journalist, editor, political advisor, ghostwriter, screenwriter, video producer, photographer, advertising and public relations consultant.

Durkin graduated cum laude, Phi Beta Kappa from UCLA with a BA in Psychology and an MFA in Theater Arts (TV/Film).

Most writers and journalists I know, both young and old, are adverse to learning how to use the power tools of their trade. Reality bites: Like it or not, being a "good" writer is not enough. You have to know how to research, write and transmit your work in cyberspace—or have enough money to pay somebody to do it for you.

Mark Twain did not complain about having to learn how to type when the typewriter was invented. He was one of the first professional writers of his era to purchase one.

I dare say if he were alive today, he'd be cruising the Net at speed at a state-of-the-art workstation— or on his wireless laptop.

And I think he would still remind us: "The difference between the right word and almost the right word is the difference between lightning and the lightning bug."

The bottom line is this: You must learn how to be a lightning writer first and foremost—but you can't be a successful writer unless you learn how to use the tools of your trade.

Welcome to life on the vertical learning curve.

When I worked downtown, commuted two hours a day and made decent money to do work that I could do faster, better and cheaper at home, I had a sign tacked to the padded wall of my little cubicle. It read: "My other office has a window." Not only does my other office have a window, it has a view.

Furthermore, it has better equipment, superior ergonomics, and it's close to home. Getting laid off has been a financial disaster, but the quality of my work life has never been better. I'm in the unusual position of frequently reporting on the technological evolution of my own profession, and my own best research indicates that, in the long run, writers—not to mention other precision professionals—will better off as independent contractors (freelancers) than employees. Of course, freelancing is still an incredibly hard way to make a living as a writer. It's worth it, if you can do it.

For writers just starting out in their careers, I think you need the experience of high-pressure, "production writing" for an employer—journalism, advertising, technical writing, whatever grunt writing job you can get—in order to gain the skills, discipline and money (the power tools of professional writing are expensive) to go it on your own.

The good news is that is it becoming increasingly possible for writers to get jobs as telecommuters. In fact, the ability to work from your own home office is beginning to become a part of the job requirement—from both the employees' and employers' perspectives.

I was a guerrilla telecommuter before the term was invented. As a working writer, I've naturally gravitated toward the power tools of my profession. Under a deadline, I learned I could just start writing anywhere, and when I stumbled across my lead, I could just cut-and-paste it at the top of my story. Writing has transformed from a tedious drafting process on typewriters to a stream-of-consciousness sculpting process on computers.

Under a deadline, I can research a fact in minutes on the Internet without leaving my chair. To get that same information could takes hours if I have to drive to a library.

Under deadline, I can push the limit up to the last seconds, even if my editor is on the other side of the country. In the bad old days, I had to mail my story two or three days in advance to make the deadline.

I learned to type on manual typewriters. I learned to write on electric typewriters. I learned to make a living as a writer on computers and the Internet.

As a writer in today's—and tomorrow's—market, it doesn't matter if you like the technical more than the business side of writing. The reality is, you've got to be literate in writing, computing and business. Nobody said this was easy.

Writers are perhaps the best examples of knowledge workers who work with their brains, not their bodies. Thus, it's almost entirely unnecessary for them to move their bodies to a traditional workplace when they can use their brains to get the information they need via phone, fax, and e-mail. I can think of few occupations that are more location-independent than writing, and today's technologies open up even more possibilities than have existed for years. 〰️

Voices from the industry:
Eigil Evert, Freelance Writer, Denmark

Bio

Eigil Evert writes for *Boersens Nyhedsmagasinm* a Danish business bi-weekly.

A journalist since 1967, Evert, 48, writes about Danish and international business, computing and the Internet.

Q: How has the Internet changed your life as a journalist?

A: The Net for me is still a wonderful undiscovered new tool for research and communication. Denmark is among the countries with the highest density of PC and modems, but still the Net seems to be in the Kindergarten Age.

Only a few on the staff of the business magazine I work for (something like *Fortune* in Danish) have converted to researching on the Net, but I have seen the light. I'm addicted and can't live without it.

I start all of my primary research on almost all issues here instead of going to the editorial library. I want to find new stuff to start with and new people to talk (or e-mail) to.

Recently I heard a lecture by Paul Saffo of the Institute of the Future talking about sensors and nanotechnology, In a few minutes on the Net, I found not only a Danish research cen-

ter but also.a list of Danish companies working on the same issues. I had my story. On the day it was published, I got e-mail from people I did not know—even though my e-mail address was not published in the magazine. Amazing.

Q: How do you see technology changing the journalist's profession?

A: I am not afraid of what the Net will do to journalism. In fact, I find that journalism will improve. Instead of just telling what happened yesterday (and who is to blame for it) the best of us will turn to analyzing the news. Anybody can write the news of the future, but it takes special skills to analyze it, and I see us turning in to be Symbolic Analysts—explaining what the late arrival of Alvin Toffler's *Future Shock* means to us all.

I am very, very optimistic about the future for the Net. It will be as common as a telephone, and will have impact on every issue of our life. I'm liberal and I'm ready. . .

Voices from the industry:
Roy S. Carson, VHeadline/VENews, Venezuela

>Date: Sun, 26 Jan 1997 17:35:04 -0500

>To: Anne Hart <scribes@ellipsys.com>

>From: Roy S. Carson <Editor@VHeadline.com.ve>

>

>Anne:

>

>VHeadline/VENews relates what's happening in Venezuela in English. Stories are written in what might be described as Fleet Street "witness reporting" style, which has already created some confusion among people used to USA "keep a God-defined impossible "objectivity") style. Readers don't want Government-mandated press releases. . . they want to know the nitty gritty just as a brother, sister, uncle or aunt were writing a letter from a far off place! Some Venezuelans don't like the fact that the news is presented in this way (especially in English), but it's already been proven in a wealth of very positive e-mails from satisfied readers as well as a few e-mail bombings when I've stepped on some sensitive toes!

>

>I believe the country will certainly move towards becoming a better place to live and invest once the "powers that be" realize that the Internet has changed their perception of the world. If they make a stupid mistake, they'll find it embarrassingly spread to the four corners of the wind and if they do something good, their praises will be sung just as far afield. Now try to get all that into USA-style journalism. . . you simply can't stay objective. . . I'm admittedly SUBJECTIVE as hell about the country in which I live and from where I report, but I'm not going to sell myself to either the government or commercial interests out of a false sense of "adoptive patriotism." The truth is that "feelings" are what count on the Internet. . .something that's been long-lost in US print journalism since the pioneering days of the early last century!

>

>best regards,

>

>Roy S. Carson

>http://www.vheadline.com.ve

Bio:

Roy S. Carson was born Belfast, Northern Ireland in 1945. He was a freelance journalist in London until 1970, when he became a foreign correspondent in Sweden covering Scandinavia for worldwide print and radio. In 1987, he was hired as Network News Editor for Independent Radio News (IRN) / London Broadcasting (LBC) and went to Venezuela the following year to cover the presidential elections. Fell in love with the country and stayed on. He is now foreign correspondent for numerous international newspapers, magazines, and radio/TV plus VHeadline/VENews which he launched as an e-mail edition on January 1, 1996 and later as a Web site on December 1, 1996.

Voices from the industry:
Tom Watson, Columnist, New York Times

Bio:

After a ten-year career in newspapers, Tom Watson founded *@NY—The New York Internet Newsletter* in 1995 with Jason Chervokas. They also write the weekly "Digital Metropolis" column for *The New York Times*.

Watson is an active freelance writer who contributes regularly to *Yahoo! Internet Life*.

>Date: Wed, 21 Aug 1996 12:29:15 -0700
>To: Anne Hart <scribes@ellipsys.com>
>From: Tom Watson <tom@news-ny.com>
>
>Okay Anne, here goes:
>
>I was a 10-year journalism veteran when I discovered the Internet and I knew immediately that I now owned the printing press. I had always wanted to be a publisher and the Net made it possible almost instantly. A year after founding @NY--The New York Internet Newsletter with my colleague Jason Chervokas, it has become a must-read for the New York new media community and opened up possibilities that weren't there before.
>
>But even for journalists who don't want to be publishers, new media is a must. First, there are many new jobs opening up in new media publishing that make it a growth sector for writers, even as newspapers continue to shrink. Second, it's just a great place to do research, quickly and easily.
>
>Journalists have the kinds of skills that are--and will increasingly be-- extremely marketable in the new media world. As the infrastructure improves, the emphasis on content--providing the "there" there--will increase and editorial types will be called into the vacuum. That's why all working journalists should get a handle on the medium. There's no room for fear of technology, just as there's no room for fear of asking the tough question. It's simply a must.
>
>Tom Watson

Voices from the industry:
Karen Kaplan, Los Angeles Times

>Date: Wed, 21 Aug 1996 12:29:15 -0700
>To: anne hart <scribes@ellipsys.com>
>From: Karen Kaplan <Karen.Kaplan@latimes.com>
>
>Hi Anne.
>
>I started writing the Tech Careers column when the Times launched the redesigned Cutting Edge technology section, which dominates Monday's Business section. The idea was to cover careers in the broadly defined technology industry, and to cover issues about technology in careers in general.
>
>I write about multimedia frequently because it is turning out to be a very important industry in Southern California. It requires the combination of skills found in the highly technical aerospace industry and the creative aspects of the entertainment business.
>
>What has surprised me about the column is the response I get from readers-- nearly half from women. When I write about multimedia, the amount of e-mail is particularly high. I hear from people who would like to get their first multimedia-related job and from people who have been designing Web pages for many months but want to know something very specific about the industry
>.
> At first I assumed it would be a male-dominated field, like computer science or the Internet. My guess is that multimedia attracts more women in part because it is a very creative field and in part because today's twenty-somethings (who make up a large chunk of multimedia employees) grew up with computers and video games.
>
>Sincerely,
>
>Karen Kaplan
>Business Desk -- Los Angeles Times

Bio:

Karen Kaplan has covered business and technology for the *Los Angeles Times* since January 1995 where she writes the weekly column, "Tech Careers" in addition to daily news and features.

She has also worked at the *Miami Herald*, *San Francisco Chronicle* and *Arizona Republic*.

Kaplan majored in economics and political science at MIT, and received a Masters in Journalism from Columbia University in New York.

Voices from the industry:
Mike McKean, Associate Professor of Journalism

Bio:

Mike McKean is a professor of broadcast news and online media at the Missouri School of Journalism. He has taught at Missouri since 1986 and recently chaired the committee that designed a new, multimedia-intensive curriculum for the school. As his home page attests, McKean is also an avid Star Trek fan!

>Date: Thu, 12 Sep 96 10:01:14 CST
>To: anne hart <scribes@ellipsys.com>
>From: Mike McKean, Assoc. Professor, Broadcast News Department
>Missouri School of Journalism
>
>Anne,
>
>I'm one of three faculty members who teach the bulk of our
New Media/Internet courses and, thus, have a good handle on the
job opportunities available to our graduates.
>
>For the next several years, there will be numerous career opportunities
 for journalists interested in new media.
>
>Both traditional media companies and new information Web sites
 (like C/Net) are looking for content providers (reporters, photographers)
and content packagers (producers, editors and graphic artists).
>
>We have graduates going straight out of j-school into new media jobs
with Microsoft, NBC, CNN, the New York Times, the Chicago Tribune and
a variety of local newspapers and television stations.
>
>Though the Internet gives the audience for news and information much
more control, most people still want someone to determine what's
important or interesting and what's not. Smart agents can't replace trained
journalists.
>
.>Mike McKean, Assoc. Professor
>
>Broadcast News Department
>Missouri School of Journalism
>
>http://www.missouri.edu/~journlm

Voices from the industry:
Tristan Louis, Internet World Magazine

Q: How did you become the Executive Director of Development for a major magazine right out of J-school?

A: I was lucky enough to discover the Internet before most anyone else. When I graduated from journalism school, few people knew or cared about the Internet which made it very difficult to look for a job in this industry. I spent a lot of time online, getting involved at the grassroot level and ended up maintaining the FAQ for the alt.internet.media-coverage newsgroup and running my own online newsletter.

Q: What was your first position at the magazine?

A: Andrew Kantor, senior editor of *Internet World*, asked me to apply for a position as a reporter at his magazine. I did and was soon hired. My job was to run the magazine's CompuServe forum. However, I soon became bored and started rede-signing the *Internet World* Web pages. Soon enough, Alan Meckler noticed that this was enough to increase traffic and thrust me to the position I'm now enjoying.

Bio:

Tristan Louis joined Mecklermedia Corporation in 1995 as Online Liaison for *Internet World* magazine where he maintained its CompuServe forum.

In July of that year, he was promoted to the position of Online Editor for *Internet World,* producing *IW Friday*, a weekly Web-based newsletter.

In September of that year, he was named Publisher of *iWORLD*, which was launched as a daily electronic newspaper.

By June of 1996, Tristan was promoted from Publisher of *iWORLD* to Executive Director of Development.

Voices from the industry:
Bonnie Burton, Web Editor, @Home Network

Bio

Bonnie Burton is a
Web Editor for @Home
Network. She has written
for *Wired*, *The Net* and
Yahoo! Internet Life.,
and lives on the Web at
http://www.grrl.com,
Grrl Enterprises.

>Date: Fri, 13 Sep 1996 10:44:25 -0700
>To: anne hart <scribes@ellipsys.com>
>From: bonnie burton
>
Subject: SURE THING ANNE.
>
>Here's what I think of the new medium as a whole:
>
>I'm a Web editor for @Home Network in Mountain View in California where
I spend all day publishing pages pointing to the weird, fun stuff online.
I freelance for Wired, The Net and Yahoo! Internet Life, but I find my most
rewarding work comes from publishing my own online zine, GRRL Zine
(http://www.grrl.com/zine.html). Here i can write about fashion, comics,
UFOs and anything else my little heart desires. I do a fan page for both
"The Real World" show on MTV and "Bettie Page the Pin-Up Model."
Publishing online gives me a creative outlet I can't find at work, and I get
to communicate with millions of people already online. I've gotten freelance
jobs from editors who just stumbled across my Web site from somewhere
else. Without the Web, I'd be lost and very, very bored.
>
>The Web and other Net-related media has shrunk networking down to a
simple e-mail. Magazine freelance writers can now send out multiple article
queries with a simple e-mail message as opposed to letter after letter via
snail mail.
>
>You can e-mail the editors of the New York Times, Wall Street Journal
and Washington Post your ideas without having to go through any phone
call daisychain of command. Young journalists striving to publish articles
in major magazines can easily get their foot in the door by writing articles
for computer magazines such as Wired, The Net and Yahoo! Internet Life.
Journalists may even skip traditional media all together and move on

to multimedia publishing such as CD-ROM magazines and online
publications where they will be free to incorporate sounds, video,
animation and even VRML.

>

>I think journalism graduates are taking the time to learn HTML and
Web design so they can showcase their writing to editors online as
opposed to the standard clippings. This way an editor can look at a
person's work with only knowing the URL address. The Web has also
shown young writers that if a major magazine or newspaper doesn't
print their work, they can always publish it themselves online for the
mass Internet community to read without any middleman roadblocks such
as advertising, censorship and editorial control.

>

>Journalists can also use the Web to interview a girl in Iraq about U.S.
war policy without having to actually GO there. We can get information
quicker and check our facts against government databases. We can
track hurricanes, follow political scandals and chat with celebrities all with
right e-mail and URL addresses. The Web has become an interactive
library/detective agency where anyone, anywhere, can access valuable
information.

>

>The Web is another transformation of Gutenberg's printing press
and journalists see that as an empowering image. The more you wander
online, the more self-published magazines and journals you'll read,
created by some kid in junior high school or a senior citizen down the
street. With discovering of the Web, it seems that everyone is a
journalist and information is truly becoming free.

>

>Sincerely,

>

>Bonnie Burton, Web Editor, @Home Network
>http://www.grrl.com

>_____

>"Tap dancing on everyone's last nerve . . ." 🐾

Voices from the industry:
Jon Phillips, Features Editor, The Net Magazine

Bio

Jon Phillips is the features editor of *The Net*, a magazine, CD-ROM and Web site that tells Internet surfers where to go and how to get there.

Prior to working for *The Net*, Phillips was editor in chief of *Blaster*, a "digital lifestyle" magazine for twenty-somethings. Phillips is thirty years old and lives in San Francisco.

Q: **Are there many job opportunities available writing for Internet-related magazines?**

A: There are only so many print Internet magazines to go around. Jobs are incredibly tough to come by. When we published an ad for a managing editor, we received about 150 responses. Everyone thinks he or she is qualified to work in new media publishing, but most so-called journalists are novices with unrealistic concepts of self. Webzines, however, are exploding everywhere, and tend to have lower standards. Some Webzines are paying by-the-word fees commensurate to print publishing models.

Q: **How did you find your job?**

A: I answered an ad in the newspaper. I also knew someone who already worked on the magazine—he gave me a good reference. During the interview, I made it very clear that I had traditional publishing experience. There's no substitute for this kind of background: New media is simply an extension of old media. During an interview, one needs to come on like gangbusters. You need to be able to prove that you have a never-ending cache of ideas; that you're meticulous, that you're professional, that you can generate content and ultimately revenue for your prospective employer. You need to speak the "language" of publishing.

I went to San Francisco State University where I majored in journalism. There's also no substitute for a formal journalism education. Journalism programs address the vicissitudes that one needs to know in order to become a "complete" magazine person. Pure freelancers lack these intangibles and it shows during job interviews. I'll always assign a higher pedigree to someone who's been through the rigors of a college journalism program, or who has worked under a seasoned professional.

Q: **What advice do you have for those entering the field?**

A: Truly fine writing and investigative skills are rare. As an editor, I put a premium on technical knowledge, so I'm willing to work with a technical expert, and craft poor grammar into a well-written story. The expert, however, must accept the fact that the story might be completely rewritten. Pride must be left at the door.

If you have strong writing and investigative skills and specialize in a certain area of new media technology, you'll be recognized and eventually rewarded. I never let a good freelancer go.

An incredible amount of money is being thrust into new media content, so entry-level jobs will continue to grow. You'll be asked to work incredibly long hours, and compensation ranges from slave wages to absurdly high levels. You have to walk in, tell your employer what you want and then negotiate until you're happy. Start-up ventures come and go every month, so be prepared to lose your job in the blink of an eye.

The Internet has also lowered the level of journalistic standards. Start-up Webzines are hiring people for a number of reasons: Sometimes an applicant's HTML skills are more important than his journalism skills. This person lands a job and becomes a "journalist" despite the fact he lacks skills previously considered requisite. Of course, many Webzines push pure fluff, so hard journalism skills become irrelevant.

I simply implore freelancers to become experts in both journalism and the technology on which they intend to report. Commit yourself to accuracy. Always think about that penetrating follow-up question and how your story can offer direct benefits to the reader. Read grammar and style books until you know these rules by heart—I'll keep a rather tech-deficient writer if he consistently submits clean copy. I can direct an investigation, but I can't write the story for the writer.

How can I reposition myself for the new media?

You may have years of experience as a professional writer, but lack a technical background. How can you begin to catch up?

What if you were recently laid-off but have years of experience writing operations documentation or public relations, advertising and marketing copy? You may be able to carry on by telecommuting to firms who need your focused business writing skills.

New media applications are spreading rapidly. However, only about 1.8% of the fastest-growing companies are high-tech themselves, leaving 98.2% to the applications of high-tech. That's why the instructional and infotainment multimedia markets require so much how-to writing. There are opportunities in multimedia for writers of fiction too, as the medium requires original stories with multiple choices of branching narratives and a variety of endings for different age and interest groups.

Here are some suggestions on how to break into this growing business.

1. **Go to work for a small multi-media company.**

   Find a new, small multimedia company and ask to be their writer. Put your writing on CD-ROM used for instructional purposes or infotainment. Join all the multimedia societies and associations to find prospective employers, and advertise in the multimedia magazines that you're in the market looking for writing work.

2. **Become an expert speaking on the subject.**

   Attend multimedia conventions and volunteer to be on the panel of speakers on the subject of writing for the multimedia markets. Or help out on the panel of speakers on multimedia writing by selecting speakers. Best of all, teach a course in multimedia writing at the local extended studies program in any college, so people will recognize you as an expert. Call the college and ask for the course development programming director. Then submit a proposal on teaching a one or two day course on how to write for the new media markets.

3. Hold a conference or seminar.

If there are no multimedia conferences or panels in your area, rent a room in a college and ask four to eight speakers to volunteer to talk about multimedia in an all-day conference. Offer them a chance to present before a captive audience and to sell their products and services or at least demonstrate them. Invite executives, entrepreneurs, students, as well as the public at large to take a free or low-cost course on multimedia and the future, writing for the new media, etc.

Don't charge more than $20 a person on your first outing— if you have self-published writing guides to sell or are seeking a publisher yourself, hold a free presentation in a local bookstore.

4. Follow the trends.

Watch the trends and follow the baby boomers as they pass through the python in locating markets for multimedia writing. Transport your skills because your skills or ability is your only job security in the electronic writing market. Contact online news publishers and offer a continuing column on what makes people tick at work, particularly in the new media industries.

5. Read industry news.

Many employers subscribe to online news and trade journal services for their employees. So articles on behavior and trends or new products pertaining to the workplace are consumed. To read up on the evolution of trends in multimedia, subscribe to research firms' studies on "hot industries" within multimedia that are developing or will develop in the near future. And make sure to always look into the application of technology as well as the production of technology.

63 What jobs will I find?

Multicast writers are needed to build the backbone (or fishbone) of the Internet. Much of the video backbone of the Internet is still tucked away and referred to as MBone by insiders who specialize in digital video production.

The new journalists who move along the fishbone to scriptwriting—adding skills and hands-on experience—are screened by their knowledge and creativity. The changing nature of journalists' skills require writers to learn intermedia scriptwriting techniques and Web development tools. In this melting pot, the more skills a writer has, the better chance of finding work in the Web-based media.

The Web has a driving need for content and journalists must move closer to entertainment writers in their skill banks to meet the demand in these emerging fields. Much of the demand will be for information about Internet-related products. Internet publishing is direct response writing where hits count, and the audience is captured and catapulted.

Here are only a few job categories that are open to writers and editors in the new interactive media:

Editorial Producer

As Editorial Producer, you'll manage programs for vertical markets, determine editorial look, design and content selection. You'll develop and implement program business requirements, including product alliance identification, competitor awareness, and brand content acquisition. To get your writer's talent in the door here, you'll need a B.A./B.S. in journalism, communications, educational technology, English, online writing, or technical writing. A general liberal arts degree in English with emphasis in creative writing works well to get you in the door.

Online Editor

Online editors summarize and maintain Web sites for a living. The job will keep you busy writing headlines and summaries or abstracts of licensed content features such as articles, tables, and illustrations. You'll do quite a bit of re-writing and editing to meet design confines. An editor in the new media codes and categorizes content pages. You'll identify key words for referencing and summarize Web sites for inclusion in the original content section. This job description requires a B.A. in English or Journalism or related areas. A knowledge of HTML and two years editorial experience will probably get you in the door.

Content Operations Manager

You'll manage the operations of acquiring, formatting, distributing, and archiving electronic content. Content includes text, graphics, audio and video together on the Web. You'll develop contingency plans and manage indexing and categorization. To get this job you'll need at least three years experience in content operations or any other digital (computer) operations experience inside any division of the electronic publishing industry.

In addition, you'll need extensive UNIX experience and familiarity with online services and the Internet. If you have great project management skills, understand HTML, Perl, and Web server environments, and a B.S. or B.A. in any subject, you're in the door.

Applications Developer

Like creating solutions for business requirements? This job will let you recommend new technologies that will ensure the timely development of a Web site. You'll recommend and coordinate vendors and write technical documents. Your goal would be to ensure the competitiveness of a Web site. Writing skills would include technical writing for outsourced work. The creative service level documents you'll write would have to verify site performance.

To get this job, have two years of experience developing network, Internet, and online applications. Besides being a technical writer, you'll have to know how to program computers in Visual Basic, C++, OLE, HTML, Java, Java Script, PERL, and CGI. Also, you'll have to be familiar with database development, and know Oracle and dBase spreadsheets.

If you're a writer who doesn't have time to acquire all these skills just to find a writing or editing job in the new media, consider being a:

Customer Service Manager

You'll provide information regarding whatever software product your corporation is offering on the Web. That could be offering the customer navigation help, advertising and content information. You'll assist with advertising production processes and ads meet specifications. You'll need five year's experience as a customer service manager supporting sales and marketing functions with strong management skills. If you can stay focused on customers and keep your creativity, you'll also need excellent communication and interpersonal skills and the ability to juggle multiple assignments, multitasking, and ad copywriting all at the same time.

To get a foot in the door as a new media writer, you might try entering as a Customer Service Representative in electronic publishing. There, you'll only have to respond to company requests for information and repackaged information. The skills you'll need would be strong customer problem-solving skills, service with a smile, basic computer skills, and a year of working on the phone to help clients learn more about the product.

Documentation Manager

Write about and maintain the system Information Services Manager or Manager of Documentation where to get in and work your way into writing you'll have to specialize in data communications and write about data communications, telecommunications, telecommuting, network and system activities, LAN systems, disaster recovery plans for the corporation, and lots of content writing of support for PC users who have Webphones and desktop video or video-conferencing equipment used with desktop publishing.

You'll need to be able to use Microsoft NT, MS office software, and Windows, have a UNIX background, and like to work with e-mail and voice mail. If you're into setting up and maintaining e-mail and voice mail, you have extra job skills that electronic publishing companies in the new media want, and the new media telecommunications businesses demand.

Where can you find these kinds of jobs? In the new companies that emphasize interactive media and telecommunications joined with electronic publishing, like Pacific Bell Interactive Media, and other large companies or small that are expanding the new media universe of talent banks. ᘔᔉᖇ

How can I learn this new way of thinking?

The hallmark of new media writing is to help reality measure up to authenticity, illustrate the paradoxical, and use oxymorons to demonstrate the theme of your content. The new media journalist must be able to do the following:

1. Think with imagery. It must feel natural to think with imagery.

2. Capture the imagination of the reader by the text and writing style alone, before visuals are inserted. If you can take away the picture and still find art in words, it has been captured.

3. Unveil and disclose moods and emotional responses.

4. Have an interest in everything going on around you.

5. Use your talent for communicating simultaneously in text, visuals, and sound.

6. Report and re-phrase events.

7. Illuminate, tantalize, and make what you write appear important, worthy, valuable, and cherished.

8. Use branching narratives in interactive books, articles, or reports and scripts to inspire. Scan the environment as you would a photo.

9. Use global, metaphoric words where there are pictures.

10. Use the new media to make three-dimensional enthusiasm come alive through robust interactive hypermedia.

Is it ever too late to start a new career?

We all give up something for the magic of freelancing full-time, but it's the possibilities-seeking personality who won't leave one corner of the Web unsurfed to find glamour-charged contingency work, free-lance assignments, distance train-ing jobs, staff telecommuting oppor-tunities, or more creative jobs in emerging technology.

If you manage information as a freelancer or are looking for a staff position, the Web is the first and best place to begin your search for employment. "Managing the Devel-opment of Technical Information" is the job category (or umbrella term) most in demand of workers, includ-ing freelancers and telecommuters, on the Web. This includes either writing or training online, and dis-tance teaching from your home to students at their computers any-where. It encompasses Web design, tracking, advertising, marketing, sales, and artistic work from digital photography to talent management.

Jobhunting Web sites promise emerging careers such as software talent manager, content writer, doc-

umentation writer or analyst, hyper-text online journalist, digital photographer's agent, virtual reality interior designer, or telecommuting pilot (setting up telecommuting sta-tions in employees' homes for gov-ernment and corporate employers).

Nowhere else but on the Web will you find people who can shape your world if you show them how. Tre-mendous freelance opportunities are available for persons who can put up multilingual Web pages. The potential for finding international clients is unlimited.

Book indexers and editors will find jobs cited in mailing lists for freelance editors. Technical editors, writers, book indexers, and other publishing specialists can post requests to news groups specializ-ing in the field. English and art teachers can write scripts for Web-based animation. If you're a comic, write comic relief for the Web. If you're a technical writer, develop your niche training people to use products. If you're a freelancer, become a new media broadcaster by giving your audience download-able streaming audio clips of your narrated writing. The newest medium is your choice.

If you're a freelance writer like me—looking for enough work to keep you busy full-time—there are thousands of writing opportunities, book contracts, and assignments if you know where to look. Sources indicate there are 60,000 new jobs each week on the Internet encompassing a variety of job categories—from computer, medical, and sales to new positions as virtual world set designer, and Web mistress or master.

Journalists, technical writers, and writers of nonfiction how-to books will find the Web to be a launching pad to writing assignments. To query a publisher or editor directly, click on any of the Web sites feedback buttons or cut and paste the editor's e-mail address and send an inquiry letter asking if they are seeking freelance writers.

Consider my personal experience finding more than twenty-five freelance writing opportunities per week on the Internet compared to before I had Internet connectivity—

when I was lucky to find one book contract a year. My income more than quadrupled when I started looking for work on the Web. I now write six magazine columns and have landed several contracts for books—compared to the pre-Internet days, when only rarely would a publisher contact me. Recently, the president of a major New York publishing company contacted me by e-mail to inquire whether I would like to write a book for that company. Only on the Net can you bypass the gatekeeper and deal directly with the decision maker—or in this case, have the decision maker contact you directly.

As a former screenwriter, teacher of creative writing and journalism, and a full-time writer for thirty-two years, I have found a tremendous increase in freelance assignments by clicking on Web sites and leaving messages of availability and experience in the e-mail boxes of publishers who are looking for writers and proposals.

I'm more productive now—in my mid-fifties—and at my visual and verbal creativity peak. Writers on the Web are judged by what they write.

Career Timeline

Journalism School Grad, 1963

Enrolled at NYU in 1959 and graduated after •

Four years with a major in English education •

With an emphasis on writing. Also studied anthropology, •

Psychology, sociology, creative writing, copyediting, •

Essay writing, teaching, and public relations. •

Job Search Begins

Applied to the Washington Post but rejected •

Because "my husband might not approve" of my working nights. •

Found a day job as a temporary typist and •

Freelanced for the Washington Evening Star •

Covering embassy row. •

A Few Odd Jobs

Hired by Copley News Service to type manuscripts •

For male journalists but asked for a promotion and got fired. •

Hired as a proofreader/editor at Computer Science Corp. through •

A contact at Mensa (of which I am a member with an IQ of 147). •

Worked as a temporary typist for over 200 firms while •

Writing 300 articles and 51 books as a freelancer. •

Continued to look for a full-time journalism job, but was told I had no experience. •

Settling Back

Gave up the struggle and started writing about journalists who do have jobs. •

Now I stay home, surf the Internet, and compete with 25-year old •

J-school graduates for freelance assignments. •

Journalism School Grad, 1997

- You graduate with a degree in digital communications.
  - You are an experienced Web master with an extensive knowledge of
    - HTML, JAVA, CGI, ActiveX, PERL, SGML, and VRML
      - And are proficient in all manner of push-in-your-face broadcasting technology.
        - You live on the Internet.

Job Search Begins

- You are hired as a new media publisher journalist at $60k.
- Then, offered a $100k job as publisher of an Internet-related magazine.
- You continue to compete with other j-school graduates,
- But salary offerings level out as thousands of new graduates flood the market.
- Technology changes and you fall behind.

A Few Odd Jobs

- The company is sold and you are forced out of the job.
  - You are over-qualified and the competition is now 25 years younger.
    - Your salary history puts you out of the running for entry level positions.
      - So, you sign up for vocational training to learn the newest technology
        - Between job interviews and freelance assignments.

Settling Back

- Technology continues to push journalists to learn more difficult skills
- That require mastering a sophisticated vehicle of the imagination.
- The highest salaries are offered to those who possess the newest skills.
- Creative writers compete with journalists for the few expressive writing jobs
- Available for only the most creative writers who can tweak your psyche.
- You take what's left of your golden parachute and buy a farm.

SPELL FOR BEING TRANSFORMED
INTO ANY SHAPE ONE MAY WISH TO TAKE

I HAVE PASSED BY THE PALACE,
AND IT WAS AN ABYT-BIRD WHICH
BROUGHT YOU TO ME.

HAIL TO YOU, YOU WHO FLEW UP TO THE SKY,
THE WHITE AND SHINING BIRD
WHICH GUARDS THE WHITE CROWN.

I SHALL BE WITH YOU
AND I SHALL JOIN THE GREAT GOD;
MAKE A WAY FOR ME THAT I MAY PASS ON IT.

— THE ANCIENT EGYPTIAN BOOK OF THE DEAD

APPENDIX A

Cyberscribes Career Classifier

This classifier consists of twenty-eight questions that are designed to measure your preferred style of writing and relationships at work. Each question presents two possible answers: 'a' and 'b'. There are no right or wrong answers—only differences in style and preference measured in shades of gray.

Use your score to match your personality type with the preferences of potential employers or teammates. Fit your type to a tee with the group of your choice.

Instructions

1. Read each possible answer and place a check mark in the corresponding box to mark your preferred response. Leave the other box blank.

2. Count the number of check marks in columns '1' and '2' for each page and write your score for each column at the bottom of each page.

3. After you have answered all the questions, transfer your page totals to the score sheet.

   Have fun!

ei...

eLLIPSYS INTERNATIONAL PUBLICATIONS, INC.

4679 Vista Street
San Diego, California
92116

■ ■ ■

Tele: (619) 280-8711
Sales: (800) 944-5551
Fax: (619) 280-8713
Email: info@ellipsys.com

Web: http://www.ellipsys.com

		1	**2**

1. You would rather promote your latest book, *Tracking Trends in Journalism* by:

   a. An author tour with book signing events and interviews held in city after city. ☐ (2)

   b. Sending your avatar on a virtual author tour with online chats staged on the Web. ☐ (1)

2. You are writing an educational interactive book. Where will your research begin?

   a. By conducting interviews out in the field with children, librarians, and teachers. ☐ (2)

   b. With your inner hunch about the trends in children's literature and entertainment. ☐ (1)

3. Most of your ideas for articles reflect:

   a. Your internal thoughts, feelings, and talents. ☐ (1)

   b. Timely topics about issues affecting real people. ☐ (2)

4. What kind of relationship do you prefer to maintain with your publisher?

   a. Direct contact and visibility in as many ways as possible. ☐ (2)

   b. Indirect contact, preferably through e-mail or snail mail. ☐ (1)

5. How do you feel after conducting an interview?

   a. Energized and ready to find more contacts and open more doors. ☐ (2)

   b. Exhausted and need to find time to re-charge and reflect. ☐ (1)

6. For which article would you rather conduct research?

   a. A two-page Q&A interview with one CEO. ☐ (1)

   b. A collection of one-line quotes from ten CEOs. ☐ (2)

7. Which work style do you prefer?

   a. To collaborate as part of a team. ☐ (2)

   b. To work alone on an in-depth project. ☐ (1)

Part I Totals ___ ___

cyberscribes.1: The New Journalists

		1	**2**

8. You have been given the assignment to report King Tut's murder. Which set of clues exposes the killer?

    a. The dates on letters Tut's widow wrote to the Hititle King asking to send a prince as a new husband and the engravings in her wedding ring sealing her unwilling marriage to Tut's male nanny, Aye.   ☐ (col 2)

    b. Your hunch that Tut's male nanny bashed his head with a hammer and later killed the Hititle prince to marry Tut's widow and assume the throne. ☐ (col 1)

9. Would you rather write:

    a. Practical how-to books that appeal to a broad audience? ☐ (col 1)

    b. Books about trend forecasting, creativity, theory, and imaginative fiction? ☐ (col 2)

10. Which company would you rather work for?

    a. A traditional fact-checking publishing house. ☐ (col 1)

    b. A socially-bold venture capitalist who pushes the limits of innovation. ☐ (col 2)

11. Which sounds like a better career opportunity?

    a. To write for a trendcasting e-zine published by a market research think tank. ☐ (col 2)

    b. To be a stripper in the production department of a four-color glossy industrial trade rag. ☐ (col 1)

12. When writing for the Web, you would rather:

    a. Keep literal sentences under ten words with bulleted lists of hyperlinks? ☐ (col 1)

    b. Use metaphor, irony, simile, and big-picture mind-mapping visuals to convey the trend? ☐ (col 2)

13. You most often write about the:

    a. Process. ☐ (col 1)

    b. Result. ☐ (col 2)

14. Which would you rather review?

    a. A handbook of Internet protocols. ☐ (col 1)

    b. An interactive novel. ☐ (col 2)

Part II Totals   ___   ___

15. How do you make most decisions?

   a. Based on logic and reason. ☐

   b. Based on what feels right. ☐

16. Which subject would you rather write about?

   a. Electronic entertainment law. ☐

   b. Digital storytelling. ☐

17. Which article would be more likely to have your byline?

   a. "Amazing E-Mail Confessions" ☐

   b. "Hackers, Crackers and Snackers" ☐

18. Would you rather write for a publisher who:

   a. Has a clear-cut strategy to outsmart the competition? ☐

   b. Cultivates a team-like relationship based on creative expression? ☐

19. Which would you rather write about?

   a. The heuristics of artificial intelligence. ☐

   b. The emotional impact of virtual reality therapy on people who fear heights. ☐

20. You've been given an assignment to write about the Web. Which topic sounds more interesting?

   a. The 3-D world of avatar romance. ☐

   b. Net robots and smart agents. ☐

21. Your editor returns your completed manuscript with many changes to be made. How do you feel?

   a. You appreciate the feedback because it will help you improve your writing. ☐

   b. You're disappointed and hurt by the criticism. ☐

Part III Totals ____ ____

	1	**2**

22. Visitors to your Web site will find:

    a. Well-organized outlines of sourcebook-style material. ☐

    b. Spontaneous surprises.   ☐

23. Which is a better description of your favorite editor?

    a. Makes a furious flurry of changes up to the last minute and comes in late and over budget.   ☐

    b. Plans manuscript revisions well in advance. ☐

24. How do you manage your time when writing?

    a. You try to prioritize your time in equally measured cycles of work and rest. ☐

    b. You prefer to work when inspired and sometimes produce your best work under pressure.   ☐

25. You are writing a hot new book. How will you promote it?

    a. Serialize the book for magazines or pamphlets. ☐.

    b. Sell to the highest bidder in a silent auction on the Internet.   ☐

26. Which job will you accept?

    a. The regular freelance position that allows you to keep your own hours.   ☐

    b. A staff position with pension and benefits. ☐

27. Which project is yours?

    a. An interactive workshop for creative writers.   ☐

    b. A tutorial guaranteed to improve your creative writing in the first lesson. ☐

28. For which company would you rather work?

    a. An old-money corporation steeped in time-honored tradition. ☐

    b. A small entrepreneurial publisher who changes on the fly with each new project.   ☐

Part IV Totals   ___   ___

Cyberscribes Career Classifier   285

Score Sheet

1. Transfer your totals from the bottom of each page to the appropriate section in the table below.

Description	Column 1	Column 2
Part I: This score indicates whether you are more introverted or extroverted by nature.	☐ **I** Introvert	☐ **E** Extrovert
Part II: This score determines whether you prefer to absorb concrete information through your five senses or take in abstract and theoretical information based on ideas, rather than facts. Sensors are firmly grounded in the present, and Intuitives look to the future.	☐ **S** Sensor	☐ **N** Intuitive
Part III: This score shows whether your judgement is based on thinking or feeling. Feelers make decisions based on personal likes and dislikes, and Thinkers decide according to the pros and cons of logic and reason.	☐ **T** Thinker	☐ **F** Feeler
Part IV: This score reveals your tolerance for ambiguity and change. Judgers are well organized and methodical and will seek quick closure. Perceivers are spontaneous and prefer to wait as long as possible for as much timely information to develop.	☐ **J** Judger	☐ **P** Perceiver

2. Circle the letter under your highest score in each category. Then write the circles letter in the corresponding blank spaces below to reveal your personality type.

3. Congratulations! You're an _____ _____ _____ _____
                                                 I   II   III   IV

To learn more about your personality type and temperament, read Chapter Two, *Understanding Your Writing Style*. There are also several good books on the subject listed in Appendix B.

APPENDIX B

Recommended Reading

- *Ancient Egyptian Book of the Dead, The,* R. O. Faulkner, University of Texas Press with British Museum Press, Austin TX, 1993.

- *Being Digital,* Nicholas Negroponte, Vintage, New York, NY 1996.

- *Bricolage*
  Web: http://bel.avonibp.co.uk/bricolage/

- *Character of Organizations, The: Using Jungian Type in Organizational Development,* William Bridges, Consulting Psychologists Press, Inc., Palo Alto CA 1992.

- *CHAT,* Nan McCarthy, Peachpit Press, San Francisco CA,1996.

- *Clicking,* Faith Popcorn and Lys Marigold, Harper Collins Publishers, 1996.

- *CONNECT,* Nan McCarthy, Rainwater Press, Grayslake IL CA,1996.

- *Finding Your Voice, Your Style, Your Way,* John K. Di Tiberio and George H. Jensen, Davies-Black Publishing.

- *Inklings*
  To subscribe:
  majordomo@samurai.com
  subscribe inklings

- *Internet Law Simplified: An Easy Guide to Making Money, Staying Out of Trouble and Protecting Your Rights,* Ivan Hoffman, B.A. J.D. 1996.

- *Jung's Typology In Perspective,* Angelo Spoto, Sigo Press, 25 New Chardon St., Boston,MA.

- *Life on the Screen: Identity in the Age of the Internet,* Sherry Turkle, Simon and Schuster, 1995.

- *LifeTypes,* Sandra Hirsh & Jean Kummerow, Warner Books, Inc. New York, NY, 1989.

- *Minutes of the Lead Pencil Club,* Bill Henderson, Pushcart Press, Wainscott, NY.

- Meyers Briggs FAQ—
A Summary of Personality
Typing, Web: http://
sunsite.unc.edu/personality/
faq-mbti.html

- Personality Types: Jung's
Model of Typology, Daryl Sharp,
Inner City Books, 1987.

- Personality Types Using the
Enneagram for Self Discovery,
Don Richard Riso, Houghton-
Mifflin, Co. Boston, 1990.

- Personality Self Portrait (Why
You Think, Work, Love, and Act
the way You Do), John M.
Oldham, M.D. and Lois B.
Morris.

- Please Understand Me, Dr.
David Keirsey and Marilyn
Bates Prometheus Nemesis
Book Co., Del Mar, CA 1984.

- Salon Magazine
Web: www.salon1999.com

- Screenwriter's Workbook, The,
Syd Field, Dell Publishing
Company, 1984.

- Suck
Web: www.suck.com

- Type Talk At Work,
Otto Kroeger, Delacorte Press,
NY, 1992.

- Gifts Differing, Isabel Briggs
Myers, Consulting
Psychologists Press, Inc.,
Palo Alto, CA, 1990.

- Personal Computer Security,
Ed Tiley, IDG Books, 1996.

- Web Developer's Guide to
Multicasting , Nels Johnson.
Coriolis Group, 1997.

- wired_women: Gender & New
Realities in Cyberspace, Lynn
Cherny and Elizabeth Reba
Weise, Seal Press, Seattle,
WA, 1996.

- Writing and Personality,
John K. DiTiberio and George
H. Jenson, Center for the
Application of Psychological
Type.

- You Just Don't Understand,
Deborah Tannen, Ph.D.
Thuesen, Dell Publishing,
NY 1988.

- Website Sound,
Patrick Seaman and Jim Cline,
New Riders Publishing, 1997

- Winning Resumes for
Computer Personnel,
Anne Hart, Barron's Educational
Series, NY 1997.

- Writing.net:
Every Writer's Essential Guide
to Online Resources and
Opportunities, Gary Gach,
Prima Publishing, 1997.

APPENDIX C

Professional Organizations

JOURNALISM ASSOCIATIONS

Australia

- Australian Centre for
  Independent Journalism
  University of Technology, Sydney
  PO Box 123
  SW 2007 Australia

  Tele: 61-0-2-9514-2488
  Fax: 61-0-2-9281-2976
  Email: acij@uts.edu.au
  Web: http://acij.uts.edu.au

- Media and Entertainment Arts
  Alliance
  245 Chalmers Street
  Redfern 2016 Australia

  Tele: 61-2-333-0999
  Fax: 61-2-333-0933
  Email:
  MEAA@Alliance.AUST.COM

Balkans

- Balkans Coordinating Center for
  Independent Media
  Vosnjakova 5
  1000 Ljubljana, Slovenia

  Tele/Fax: 386-61-1339635
  Email: ifj.fiej@K2.net.si

Belgium

- Int'l Federation of Journalists
  rue Royale, 266
  B-1210 Brussels, Belgium

  Tele: 32-2-233-2265
  Fax: 32-2-219-2976
  Email: ifj@gn.apc.org

Canada

- Canadian Assoc. of Journalists
  St. Patrick's Bldg.
  1125 Colonel By Drive
  Ottawa, Ontario K1S-5B6
  Canada

  Tele: (613) 233-2801
  Web: www.eagle.ca/caj/

- Freelance Professionals™
  Email: pmcmaster@f-pro.ca
  Web: www.mbnet.mb.ca/f-pro

- Internet Press Guild
  Email:
  membership@netpress.org
  Web: www.netpress.org

- Periodical Writers Association of
  Canada
  54 Wolseley St., 2nd Floor
  Toronto, Ontario M5T 1A5

  Tele: (416) 504-1645
  Fax: (416) 703-0059
  Web: www.cycor.ca/pwac/

China

- Hong Kong Journalist Assoc.
  Flat A, 15/F
  Henfa Commercial Bldg.
  348-350 Lockhart Road
  Wanchai HK

  Tele: 852-2591-0692
  Fax: 852-2572-7329

France

- French Assoc. of IT Journalists
  Press en Ligne
  13-15 Rue St. Symphorien
  84510 Caumont
  France

  Tele/Fax: 33-9023-05 80

Italy

- Women Journalists of the
  Meditteranean Network
  Reseau des Femmes
  Journalistes de la Méditerranée
  105, Via Calermo, Catania
  Italia

  Tele/Fax: 0039-9536-12 56
  Email: Mim@CasaNet.Net.Ma
  Web: www.serve.com/OFEC01/
  index.html

Japan

- Center for Global
  Communications
  International University of
  Japan
  Yamato-machi
  Minami Uonuma-gun
  Niigata 949-72, JAPAN

  Tele: 81 (257) 79-1111

Fax: 81 (257) 79-4441
Email: info@glocom.ac.jp
Web: www.glocom.ac.jp

Mexico

- Periodistas de Investigacion

  Web:
  http://investigacion.org.mx
  Email: lise@investigacion.org.mx

Netherlands

- European Journalism Centre
  Borchstraat 60
  NL-6211 AX Maastricht
  The Netherlands

  Tele: 31-43-325-4030
  Fax: 31-43-321-2626
  Email: secr@ejc.nl
  Web: www.regioweb.nl/ejc/
  index.htm

Saudi Arabia

- Saudi Research
  and Marketing Group
  Arab Press House
  184 High Holborn
  London WC1V 7AP England

  Tele: 0171-831-8181
  Email:
  aaa.editorial.hhsaudi.co.uk
  Web: www.arab.net

Sweden

- Investigative Reporters & Editors
  Grävande Journalister
  Box 27861
  115 93 Stockholm

  Tele: 08-164425
  Fax: 08-6623227

Email: investigative@jmk.su.se
Web:
www.jmk.su.se/dig/index-e.html

United Kingdom

- British Press Association
  PA News Centre
  292 Vauxhall Bridge Road
  London SW1V 1AE England
  Contact: Lynn Palmer

  Tele: 0171-963-7530
  Fax: 0171-963-7594
  Email:
  lpalmer@panews.press.net
  Web: www.pa.press.net

- Media Development Assoc.
  c/o Medini Fordham
  MDA
  14a Ship Street
  Brighton BN1 1AD England

  Tele: 0127-372-3331

  Email: medianet@pavilion.co.uk
  Web: www.pavilion.co.uk

United States

- American Business Press
  675 3rd Ave., Ste. 400
  New York NY 10017

  Tele: (212) 661-6360
  Email: abp2@aol.com

- American Medical Writers
  Association
  9650 Rockville Pike
  Bethesda MD 20814

  Tele: (301) 493-0003
  Email: amwa@amwa.org

- American Society of Business
  Press Editors
  4445 Cilmer Lane
  Cleveland OH 44143

  Tele: (617) 641-4616

- American Society of
  Journalists and Authors
  1501 Broadway, Ste. 302
  New York NY 10036

  Tele: (212) 997-0947
  e-mail: asja@compuserve.com
  Web: http://www.asja.org

- Association of Professional
  Communication Consultants
  3924 S. Troost
  Tulsa OK 74105

  Tele: (918) 743-4793
  Email: Attn: Sherry Scott
  71233.1664@compuserve.com

- Computer Press Association
  631 Henmar Drive
  Landing NJ 07850

  Tele: (201) 398-7300
  Email:
  102751.1445@compuserve.com
  Web: www.computerpress.org

- Electronic Publishing Assoc.
  One Rodney Square, 10th Floor
  Tenth and King Streets
  Wilmington DE 19801

  Fax: (302) 658-6548

  Web: www.epaonline.com

- Freedom Forum
  1101 Wilson Blvd.
  Arlington VA 22209

  Tele: (703) 284-2860

Fax: (703) 284-3529
Web: www.freedomforum.org

- HTML Writers Guild

  Email: spurlock@hwg.org
  Web: www.hwg.org

- Investigative Reporters &
  Editors
  138 Neff Annex
  Missouri School of Journalism
  Columbia, MO 65211

  Tele: (573) 882-2042
  Fax: (573) 882-5431
  Web: www.ire.org
  Email: bruce@ire.org

- JFORUM–CompuServe
  The Online Press Club

  Web: www.jforum.org
  Email:
  76701.13@compuserve.com

- National Institute for
  Computer-Assisted Reporting
  NICAR 100 Neff Hall
  Missouri School of Journalism
  Columbia MO 65211

  Tele: (573) 882-0684
  Email: info@nicar.org
  Web: http://nicar.org

- National Association of
  Science Writers
  P.O. Box 294
  Greenlawn NY 11740

  Tele: (516) 757-5664
  Web: www.nasw.org

- National Writer's Association
  1450 S. Havana, Ste. 620
  Aurora CO 80012

  Tele: (303) 751-7844

- National Writers Union
  Tech Writers Job Hotline

  Tele: (510) 839-6092
  Email: nwu3@well.com

- Newspaper Assoc. of America
  11600 Sunrise Valley Dr.
  Reston VA 20191

  Tele: (703) 648-1140
  Email: MDonatello@aol.com
         donam@naa.org
  Web: http://www.naa.org

- Poynter Institute
  for Media Studies
  801 Third Street South
  St. Petersburg FL 33701

  Tele: (813) 821-9494
  Fax: (813) 821-0583
  Email: info@poynter.org
  Web: www.poynter.org

- Reporters Committee for
  Freedom of the Press
  1101 Wilson Blvd., Ste. 1910
  Arlington VA 22209

  Tele: (703) 807-2100
  Legal Defense Hotline
  (emergencies only):
  (800) 336-4243
  Email: rcfp@rcfp.org
  Web: www.rcfp.org

- Society for Technical
  Communication
  901 N. Stuart St., Ste. 904
  Arlington VA 22203

  Tele: (703) 522-4114
  Email: stc@stc-ba.org
  Web: www.stc-ba.org

- Society of American Business
  Editors and Writers
  P.O. Box 838

University of Missouri
Columbus MO 65205

- Society of Professional
  Journalists
  P.O. Box 77
  16 South Jackson Street
  Greencastle IN 46135-0077

  Tele: (317) 653-3333
  Email: spj@link2000.net
  Web: www.spj.org

- Women In Scholarly Publishing
  Rutgers University Press
  107 Church St.
  New Brunswick NJ 08901

  Tele: (908) 932-7396

Venezuela

- Int'l Federation of Journalists
  Avenida Santos Erminy
  Edificio Beatriz
  Piso 7, Oficina 74
  Sabana Grande
  Caraças, Venezuela

  Tele /Fax: 58-2-713-778
          or 58-2-711-971
  Email: fip@eldish.net

TRADE ORGANIZATIONS

Computer Industry

- Association for
  Interactive Media
  1019 19th St., NW, Ste. 1000
  Washington, DC 20036

  Tele: (202) 408-0008
  Fax: (202)408-0111
  Web: www.interactivehq.org

- Association for
  Women in Computing
  PO Box 1503
  Grand Central Station
  New York NY 10163

  Tele: (212) 762-1598
  Event Hotline: (212) 533-6972
  (Dial "REL" and then "AWC")
  E-mail: awcnyc@dorsai.org
  Web: www.womweb.com/
  awc.htm

- Digital Multimedia Association
  Email:
  teresa_rodriguez@msn.com
  http://www.dmasd.org

- Electronic Artists Group
  P.O. Box 580783
  Memphis MN 55458

  Tele: (612) 331-4289

- Interactive Multimedia Assoc.
  48 Maryland Ave, Ste 202
  Annapolis MD 21401

  Tele: (410) 626-1380
  Email: info@ima.org
  Web: www.ima.org

- Multimedia Development
  Group
  2601 Mariposa St.
  San Francisco CA 94110

  Tele: (415) 553-2300
  Email: edgoffice@aol.com
  Web: www.ddg.orm

- National Computer
  Graphics Association
  2722 Merrilee Dr. Ste. 200
  Fairfax VA 22031

  Tele: (703) 698-9600
        (800) 225-6242

- Software Publishers
  Association
  1730 M St. N.W., Ste. 700
  Washington DC 20036

  Tele: (202) 452-1600
  Web: www.spa.org

Market Research

- National Infomercial
  Marketing Association (NIMA)
  1225 New York Ave. N.W.
  Ste. 1200
  Washington DC 20005

  Tele: (202) 962-8342

- Technical Marketing
  Society of America
  4383 Via Majorca
  Cypress CA 90680

  Tele: (714) 821-8672

Telecommunications

- Communications
  Industry Association
  1019 19th St. NW Ste. 1100
  Washington DC 20036

  Tele: (202) 467-4770

- International Teleconferencing
  Association
  1150 Connecticut Ave. NW
   Ste. 1050
  Washington DC 20036

  Tele: (202) 833- 2549

- North American
  Telecommunicators Association
  2000 M St. NW., Ste. 550

Washington DC 20036

Tele: (202) 296-9800

- Satellite Broadcasting and
  Communications Association
  225 Reinekers Ln., Ste. 600
  Alexandria VA 22314

  Tele: (703) 549-6990

- Wireless Cable Association
  2000 L St. NW Ste. 702
  Washington DC 20036

  Tele: (202) 452-7823

Training

- American Society for
  Training and Development
  P.O. Box 1443
  1640 King St.
  Alexandria VA 22313

  Tele: (703) 683-8100
  Web: www.astd.org

- ICIA Infocom
  Educating Computing Council
  3150 Spring St.
  Fairfax VA 22031

  Tele: (703) 273-7200

- Society for Applied Learning
  Technology
  50 Culpepper St.
  Warrenton VA 22186

  Tele: (703) 347-0055

Webcasting

- International Webcasting
  Association

  Web: www.webcasters.org

APPENDIX D

Product Locator

BROWSERS

- **Internet Explorer**
  Microsoft Corporation
  One Microsoft Way
  Redmond WA
  98052-6399

  Tele: (206) 882-8080
  Web: www.microsoft.com

- **Netscape Navigator**
  Netscape Communications Corp.
  501 E. Middlefield Rd.
  Mountain View CA 94043

  Tele: (415) 254-1900
  Web: www.netscape.com

3D BROWSERS

- **Cosmo**
  Silicon Graphics, Inc.
  2011 N. Shoreline Blvd.
  Mountain View CA 94043

  Tele: (800) 800-7441
  Web: www.sgi.com

- **WorldView**
  Intervista Software Inc.
  181 Fremont, Suite 200
  San Francisco CA 94105

  Tele: (415) 543-8765
  Web: www.intervista.com

ELECTRONIC DOCUMENT PUBLISHING

- **Acrobat**
  Adobe Systems Incorporated
  345 Park Avenue
  San Jose CA 95110-2704

  Tele: 408-536-6000
  Web: www.adobe.com

FLOW CHARTING

- **StoryVision**
  StoryVision
  171 Pier Avenue, Suite 204
  Santa Monica CA 90405

  Tele: (310) 392-5090
  Email: StoryVision@aolcom

GRAPHICS/ANIMATION/VIDEO

- **After Effects**
  Adobe Systems Incorporated
  345 Park Avenue
  San Jose CA 95110-2704

  Tele: 408-536-6000
  Web: www.adobe.com

- **Dabbler** and **Painter**
  Fractal Design Corporation
  P.O. Box 66959
  Scotts Valley CA 95067-6959

  Tele: (408) 430-4000
  Web: www.fractal.com

- **Flash** (FutureSplash)
  Macromedia, Incorporated
  600 Townsend Street
  San Francisco CA 94103

  Tele: (415) 252-2000
  Web: www.macromedia.com

- **GIF Construction Set**
  Alchemy Mindworks, Inc.
  PO Box 500
  Beeton ONT
  CANADA LOG 1AO

  Tele: (905) 936-9501
  Web: www.mindworkshop.com

- **Quicktime**
  Apple Computer, Inc.
  1 Infinite Loop
  Cupertino CA 95014

  Tele: (408) 996-1010
  Web: www.apple.com

3-D GRAPHICS

- **trueSpace**
  Caligari Corporation
  1959 Landings Drive
  Mountain View CA 94043

  Tele: 415-390-9600
  Web: www.caligari.com

GRAPHICS TABLETS

- **Wacom Tablet**
  WACOM Technology Corp.
  501 S.E. Columbia Shores Blvd.,
  Ste. 300 Vancouver WA 98661

  Tele: (360) 750-8882
  Web: www.wacom.com

HTML AUTHORING

- **Backstage**
  Macromedia, Incorporated
  600 Townsend Street
  San Francisco CA 94103

  Tele: (415) 252-2000
  Web: www.macromedia.com

- **FrontPage**
  Microsoft Corporation
  One Microsoft Way
  Redmond WA
  98052-6399

  Tele: (206) 882-8080
  Web: www.microsoft.com

- **HotDog**
  Sausage Software
  Suite 1, 660 Doncaster Road
  Doncaster VIC 3108 Australia

  Fax: (613) 9 855-9800
  Web: www.sausage.com

- **PageMill**
  Adobe Systems Incorporated
  345 Park Avenue
  San Jose CA 95110-2704

  Tele: 408-536-6000
  Web: www.adobe.com

HYPERMEDIA AUTHORING

- **Director**
  Macromedia, Incorporated
  600 Townsend Street
  San Francisco CA 94103

  Tele: (415) 252-2000
  Web: www.macromedia.com

- **HyperStudio**
  Roger Wagner Publishing, Inc.
  1050 Pioneer Way, Suite P
  El Cajon CA 92020

  Tele: (619) 442-0522
  Web:
  www.hyperstudio.wspout.com

HIGH-SPEED ACCESS

- **RoadRunner**
  Time Inc. New Media
  1271 Avenue of the Americas
  New York NY 10020-1393

  Tele: (212) 522-9761
  Web: www.pathfinder.com

- **@Home Network**
  385 Ravendale Drive
  Mountain View CA 94043

  Tele: (415) 3944-7200
  Fax: (415) 944-8500
  Email: jobs@home.net
  Web: www.home.net

STREAMING MEDIA

- **RealAudio Player/Server**
  RealMedia Player/Server
  Progressive Networks
  1111 Third Avenue, #2900
  Seattle WA 98101

  Tele: (206) 674-2700
  Fax: (206) 674-2696
  Web: www.realaudio.com

INTERNET APPLICANCES

- **Phillips Magnavox**
  One Philips Drive
  Knoxville TN 37914

  Tele: (423) 5214316
  Web: www.philips.com

- **Sony Electronics**
  One Sony Drive
  Park Ridge NJ 07656-8003

  Tele: (201) 930-1000
  Web: www.sony.com

- **WebTV**
  WebTV Networks
  305 Lytton Avenue
  Palo Alto CA 94301

  Tele: (415) 326-3240
  Web: www.webtv.net

MUSIC AND SOUND EFFECTS

- **Presentation Audio**
  Network Music, Inc.
  15150 Avenue of Science
  San Diego CA 92128

  Tele: (619) 451-0883
  Fax: (619) 451-6409
  Web: www.networkmusic.com

NETCAST DISTRIBUTION

- **AudioNet**
  2929 Elm Street
  Dallas TX 75226

  Tele: (214) 748-6660
  Fax: (214) 748-6657
  Web: www.audionet.com

- **ENEN**
  5961 Kearny Villa Road
  San Diego CA 92123

  Tele: (619) 627-4146
  Fax: (619) 627-4163
  Web: www.enen.com

NETCASTING SOFTWARE

- **Astound WebCast**
  Astound, Inc.
  PO Box 59
  Santa Clara CA 95052

  Tele: (415) 845-6200
  Web: www.astound.com

- **BackWeb**
  BackWeb Technologies
  2077 Gateway Place, # 500
  San Jose CA 95110 USA

  Tele: (408) 437-0200
  Web: www.backweb.com

- **Intermind Communicator**
  Intermind Corporation
  217 Pine Street
  Seattle WA 98101-1500

  Tele: (206) 812-6000
  Fax: (206) 812-6001
  Email: custserv@intermind.com
  Web: www.intermind.com

cyberscribes.2
The Storytellers

CYBERSCRIBES SERIES™

Anne Hart

Brainstorm hypermedia's newest leap forward into the virtual
worlds of interactive storytelling and cyberfiction. Learn from
industry insiders how to publish and sell your work online.

ISBN: 1-880663-67-8   Price: $24.95 U.S.
Publication Date: Coming Soon!

cyberscribes.1
The New Journalists

CYBERSCRIBES SERIES™

Anne Hart

Here's how to write yourself a career in online journalism, content
authoring, and scriptwriting in the interactive, visionary communications industries—electronic publishing and netcasting.

ISBN: 1-880663-65-1   Price: $24.95 U.S.
Publication Date: April, 1997

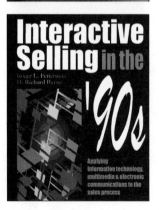

Interactive Selling in the '90s:
Applying information technology, multimedia & electronic
communications to the sales process

Roger Fetterman & H. Richard Byrne

This book proposes a vision for the successful implementation
of interactive selling systems—based on extensive research of
existing technology, knowledge of the sales and buying processes,
and interviews with industry professionals who use interactive
selling to their competitive advantage.

Languages: English, Japanese

ISBN: I-880663-00-7   Price: $24.95 U.S.
Publication Date: October, 1995

Ellipsys International Publications, Inc.
4679 Vista Street
San Diego, California 92116 USA

Tele: (800) 944-5551 or (619) 280-8711   Email: info@ellipsys.com
Fax: (619) 280-8713   Web: http://www.ellipsys.com

Distributed by Peer-to-Peer and International Thomson

Index

B

C

J

Java **5, 22, 48, 152**
    Dumb Bimbo's Guide **132**
jingles **227**
job **21, 24, 109, 268**
    entry-level **269**
    interview skills **269**
    search **276–279**
Jobs, Steve **14**
Johnson, Nels **53**
joint ventures **18**
joint work **245**
journalism **18, 23, 269**
    forum **75**
    graduate **278**
    schools **23**
journalistic standards **24, 269**
journalists **20, 26, 113, 132**
joystick **189**
.JPG file type **167**
judging personality type **110**
Jung, Carl **109, 112, 114**
junk e-mail **213**

K

Kantor, Andrew **265**
Kaplan, Karen **263**
Keirsey, Dr. David **109, 111**
Kelley, Jeff **61**
Kellner, Douglas **186**
Keyes, Edward J. **62**
kiosk **174, 182, 213**
    Internet direct response **213**
    WebTV Internet appliance **217**
Knight-Ridder, Inc. **5**
knowledge workers **259**
Kodak PhotoCD **196**
Kubie, Lawrence **102**

L

laid off **258, 270**
largest market **121**
lateral thinking **118**
laughingstock **244**

law practice **238**
Lawrence, Bob **58**
lawyer **78, 238, 240**
lectures **69**
left-hemisphere of brain **90, 197**
legal advice **78**
letter of permission **77**
Letters from Beyond the Sambatyon **177**
Levins, Hoag **48**
Lexus/Nexus **244, 257**
liberal arts education **23**
Liberty Science Center **200**
library catalog **256**
licensing fees **170**
light **64, 193**
line art **167**
linear writing **87**
    branching **180**
    documents **157**
    instructional sequencing **179**
    time **103**
links **75, 157**
literary agencies **237**
Live3D **165**
Loeffler, Carl **189**
logic **112**
look and feel **176**
Los Angeles Times **5, 75–76 263**
Louis, Tristan **265**
lust **245**
lyrics **227**

M

M's, the three **13**
Mac **152**
Macromedia **87, 164, 171, 296**
magazines **225**
magic-cookies **202**
Magnavox, Philips **56, 297**
major events **94**
male-dominated field **263**
Mann, Ron **185**
manufacturing industry **125**
market **200**
    changes **62**
    driven **123**
    research **57, 212, 292**

marketable **77**
Mars **204, 209–210**
mass medium **11**
master screenplay template **182**
Mattel Inc. **5**
Maxima New Media **177, 183**
McKean, Mike **264**
Meckler, Alan **265**
Mecklermedia **265**
media **61, 176, 253**
media-news-information culture **19**
medical product designers **190**
medieval world **125**
Mensa **278**
metaphor **90, 166, 171**
Mettke, Karl **155**
Microsoft **18, 46, 49, 114, 130, 295**
Microsoft Network **165**
Mifflin, Lawrie **19**
mind mapping **71, 207**
Missouri School of Journalism **264**
modem speed **50, 156**
    digital **14**
monetary benefits **240**
monitor resolution **156**
montage **70**
moral right **247**
Morris, Lois B. **109**
Morrison, Deborah **214**
movie
    Director **171**
    FutureSplash **169**
    interactive **154**
    QuickTime **186, 171–172**
    studios **18**
MSN **165**
    News **23**
    Cable **19**
MSNBC Interactive **18**
MTV **266**
multicasting **53**
multi-dimensional **64**
multilevel publishing **155**
multilingual **276**
multimedia **27, 291**
    objects, embedded **193**
multiple paths **63**
multi-user domain **197**

Murrow, Edward R. **255**
museum **200**
    virtual **189**
music **233**
Myer, Isabel **109**
Myers-Briggs Type Indicator **109**

N

@NY—*The New York Internet Newsletter* **262**
N&I Online **216**
narration **233**
narrator **101**
narrowcasting **58**
NASA **190, 204**
National Infomercial Marketing Assoc. (NIMA) **235**
National Supercomputing Center **208**
natural talent **136**
nature **64**
navigation tools **176**
NBC News **18, 20, 264**
Negroponte, Nicholas **14, 287**
Nelson, Theodore Holm **155**
Net, The **254, 268**
netcast **45, 66, 223**
NetScape **14, 49, 202**
    Navigator **165, 295**
NetTalk **250**
networking **266**
Networld+Interop **215**
new career **276**
new media **7, 23, 27**
New York Times 6, **18–20, 22, 266**
news **45, 58, 66**
newsgroups **109**
NewsHound **16**
newspapers **23, 253, 264**
newsroom **18, 20**
Nexis **237**
niche **124**
Nielsen **11**
nodes **193**
nonlinear script **85, 102**
Northwestern University, Annenberg Washington Program, **255**
NPR **51**
numbers, using in script **100**
Nynex Corporation **7**

product **226, 232–233**
products, cultural **6**
production writing **259**
professional **268**
    associations **23**
    organizations **289**
program production **235**
programmer **132**
Progressive Networks **52, 297**
project design **126**
promoter **111**
propaganda **26**
proposals **277**
protagonist **97**
protected material **245**
psychology **88, 109**
Psychological Type, Assoc. for **128**
public domain **242**
public confidence **255**
publisher **124**
publishing business **219, 268**
push/pull technology **45, 55, 234**

Q

qualifications **268**
Que **134**
queries, online **266**
QuickTime **171–172, 185**
    QuickTime VR **195, 200, 297**
quotes **74**

R

radio **23, 51, 248**
reading
    audience **121**
    recommended **287**
RealAudio **52, 297**
real-time **45, 211**
reductive speech **129**
reference materials **256**
relationships **112, 213**
renegotiate contract **248**
reporters **264**
reposition career **270**

research **17, 71, 190, 222, 256, 262**
right hemisphere of brain **88, 90, 197, 201**
right of
    privacy **250**
    license **237**
rights to a story **77**
Rizzoli's book store 185
RoadRunner **47, 296**
robotic control **190**
rocket packs **223**
Roger Wagner Publishing, Inc. **171, 296**
Rolling Stone **254**
routine **111**
royalty **243**
runtime **170**
Rupert Murdoch **60**

S

Saffo, Paul **260**
salary **23, 279**
sales **276**
    presentation **174**
    script formats **226**
San Francisco State University **9, 268**
satellite broadcasting **60, 190**
scandals **255**
scanner **167**
schools **184**
Schorr, Daniel **26, 255**
score **171**
Screen Actors Guild **248**
screen rights **133**
screenwriter **113, 277**
script **88**
    format, infomercial **226**
    two-column **27**
scripted interview **70**
scripting language **170**
scriptwriters **113**
    virtual reality **197**
scriptwriting **86**
search engine **8, 27, 213, 255**
seclusion **127**
security **111**

V

vector-based graphics **168**
video **294–295**
    disk players **154**
    games **263**
    how to digitize **53**
    magazine format **67**
    production **58**
VHF stations **58**
viewers **18**
virscriptor **197**
virtual
    author tour **217**
    art museum **189**
    classroom **190**
    sex **203, 206**
    theater **71, 135**
    trade shows **215**
    worlds **64**
Virtual Film Festival **223**
Virtual Places **215**
virtual reality **152, 172, 187–188**
    modeling language **192**
    visionary future **130**
visual images **70, 177, 234**
visually-oriented learners **122**
vocational training **279**
voice-over **233**
Voyager **185**
VRML **192–193**
    authoring software **297**
    ownership of **242**
Vulcan Ventures Inc. **56**

W

Wacom **296**
wages **269**
Wagner, David A. **200**
walk-throughs **188**
Wall Street **257**
Wall Street Journal **266**
wallpaper, graphics as **167**
Washington Square Films **224**
Watson, Tom **262**

Web **257, 276**
    networks **45**
    publishing **207**
    sites **202**
    story structure **104**
WebTV Internet appliance
    56, 61, 152, 297
WebTV Networks, Inc. **47, 56, 165, 297**
Westheimer, Mary **219–222**
wholesalers **220**
Windows 95 **55, 202**
wire service **22**
Wired **15, 266**
Wired News **46**
wireless communications **294**
work environment **114**
work for hire agreement **243**
workplace style **18–19, 112–113**
world file (.WRL) **192**
worlds, virtual **188**
WorldView, Intervista **165, 295**
WOW! **75**
writers **121**
Writers Guild **248**
writer's
    personalities **122**
    organizations **237**
writing **7, 109, 114**
    assignments **277**
    strategies **63, 166**
.WRL file type **192**

Y

Yahoo! Internet Life **262, 266**
Yankelovich Partners, Inc. **57, 212**
young writers **267**

Z

Ziff, Jan **51**

Colophon

CYBERSCRIBES.1: THE NEW JOURNALISTS

Designed, illustrated, and composed by Claire Condra Arias.

This book was composed with FrameMaker 4 on an NEC Pentium 100. Body text is set in 11-point Adobe PostScript Univers 47 Condensed Light. Chapter titles are set in 24-point BitStream Onyx, with question numbers at 36 points, question heads at 18 points, and footers at 14 points. The drop caps at the beginning of each chapter are set in 54-point Aladdin by Softkey. The spells from the *Egyptian Book of the Dead* are set in 11-point Bitstream Copperplate Gothic and Copperplate Gothic Heavy.

The cover was designed using Corel 4, Fractal Design's Painter 3, and Caligari's trueSpace2. The title was set in Onyx and rendered in trueSpace as a 3-D object with a marbled surface and lighting. The subtitle is set in Copperplate Gothic and the author's name in Aladdin.

The author photograph was taken in the foyer of Ellipsys International Publications, Inc. with a 35mm camera—then scanned and imported as a .TIF file.

The hieroglyph of the walking fish used as a bullet at the end of each section was drawn in Painter 3 on a Wacom tablet. An animated GIF version of the fish can be found on the publisher's Web site.

The cartouche shown above and on page xiv of the Foreword was rendered as a 3-D metallic object in trueSpace2. The cartouche represents the hieroglyphic characters for the personality type 'ENFP'. The two flags represent the letter 'E' and signify extroversion and adventure. The water symbol represents the letter 'N' for intuition. The horned snake represents the letter 'F' for feeling. Finally, the couch, pillow, and rug are the symbol for a woman and also the letter 'P'—which stands for perception.